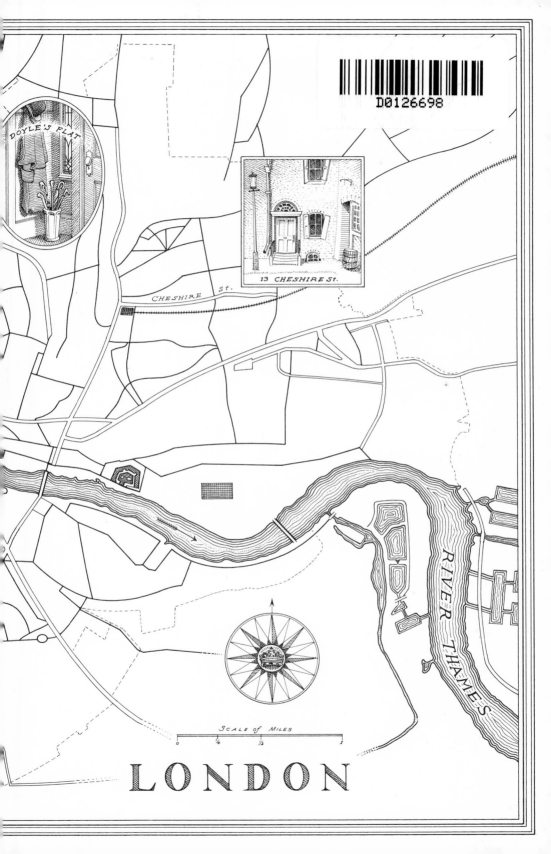

DOYLE'S FLAT

13 CHESHIRE St.

CHESHIRE St.

RIVER THAMES

SCALE of MILES
0   ¼   ½   1

LONDON

D0126698

THE LIST OF

The List of

A Novel

Mark Frost

William Morrow and Company, Inc.
New York

For Jody

This book owes its life to Ed Victor, who lit the fire.

Many thanks to Howard Kaminsky, for taking a chance; to my editors, Mark Gompertz and Paul Bresnick; and to the rest of the team at Morrow.

Many thanks as well to Rosalie Swedlin, Adam Krentzman, Rand Holston, Alan Wertheimer, Lori Mitchell, and John Ondre.

Special thanks to Bill Herbst, for climbing the next hill and telling the truth about what lies ahead.

It is the policy of William Morrow and Company, Inc., and its imprints and affiliates, recognizing the importance of preserving what has been written, to print the books we publish on acid-free paper, and we exert our best efforts to that end.

Library of Congress Cataloging-in-Publication Data

Frost, Mark.
    The list of 7 / Mark Frost.—1st ed.
        p.   cm.
    ISBN 0–688–12245–0 (acid-free paper)
    1. Doyle, Arthur Conan, Sir, 1859–1930—Fiction.   2. Detectives—England—Fiction.   3. Authors, English—Fiction.   I. Title.
PS3556.R599L57   1993
813′.54—dc20   93–12305
                                                                   CIP

Printed in the United States of America

First Edition

1   2   3   4   5   6   7   8   9   10

BOOK DESIGN BY BRIAN MOLLOY / CIRCA 86

*All the Devil requires is acquiescence . . . not struggle,
not conflict.*

Acquiescence.

THE LIST OF

CHAPTER 1

An Envelope

THE ENVELOPE WAS vellum, cream. Fine striations, crisp, no watermarks. Expensive. Scuffed at the corners, it had attracted grime as it was slid under the door, silently. The Doctor did not hear it, and his ears were keen, sharp as a crone's knees, like all his senses.

He was in the front room, had been throughout the evening, feeding the fire, absorbed in an obscure text. Forty-five minutes earlier, he had glanced up as the Petrovitch woman ascended the stairs, the scrabbly scuttle of her dachshund's claws dragging her back to an evening of heart-heavy sighs amid the torpid musk of stewed red cabbage. The Doctor watched their spidery shadows flit by, dancing off the glazed floorboards under the door. There had been no envelope.

He vaguely remembered wishing there were an easier way to examine his timepiece than extracting it from his waistcoat and cracking it open. That was why, when he spent an evening in, he set it open, on his reading table. Time, or rather the elimination of its senseless squandering, obsessed him. And he had looked at his watch when the rat dog and its scrawny, melancholic Russian mistress shuffled by: quarter past nine.

The text drew him back. *Isis Unveiled.* Surely this Blavatsky woman was mad: another Russian, like poor Petrovitch with her plum wine. When you uprooted these Czarists and tried to replant them in English soil, was lunacy some inevitable consequence? Coincidence, he reasoned; one heartsick spinster and a megalomaniacal, cigar-chomping Transcendentalist did not constitute a trend.

He turned to study the photograph of Helena Petrovna Blavatsky in the frontispiece: the preternatural stillness, that clear, penetrating gaze. Most faces instinctively shrank from the insectoid jumble of the camera. She reached out and swallowed it whole. What was he to make of this curious tome? *Isis Unveiled.* Eight volumes to date, more threatened, all in excess of five hundred pages—and this only one-quarter of the woman's oeuvre—a work purporting to assimilate and eclipse, with a ringing absence of irony, every known spiritual, philosophic, and scientific system of thought: in other words, a revisionist theory of all creation.

Although, according to the biographical passage under her picture, HPB had spent the better part of her fifty-odd years trotting the globe communing with this or that occultist ashram, she coyly attributed the book's genesis to divine inspiration, courtesy of a steady roster of Ascended Masters materializing before her like Hamlet's Ghost, claiming that occasionally one of these Holy of Holies stepped inside her head and assumed the reins: *automatic writing,* she called it. True, the book possessed two distinctly different styles—he hesitated to term them "voices"—but as to content, the thing was a flea market of mumbo jumbo: lost continents, cosmic rays, root races, evil cabals of black magicians. To be fair, he had in fact employed similar notions in his own writing, but that was fiction, for God's sake, and she was offering this as theology.

With that debate agitating his mind, he looked up and spied the envelope. Had it just been set there? Had some faint beneath-conscious perception registered as it slipped over the jamb and pulled his eyes to it? He remembered hearing nothing—no approach, no crack of bended knee, no glove on wood or paper, no one receding—and those timeworn stairs announced a visitor as reliably as a brass fanfare. Had immersion in Blavatsky so narrowed his senses? Not likely. Even in the surgeon's theater, with the dying, strapped down, spurting fluids, shrieking in his face, he picked up sounds around him like a restive cat.

Nevertheless, the envelope was there. Could have been there for . . . ten o'clock now . . . a good forty-five minutes. Or perhaps its courier had only just arrived and remained still standing just outside his door.

The Doctor listened for signs of life, aware of his heart accelerating

An Envelope

and the acrid, irrational taste of fear. He was no stranger to it. He silently drew from the umbrella stand his stoutest walking stick, flipped it deftly in his hand, and with its gnarled, blackened knob poised, opened the door.

What he saw, or didn't see, in the corridor's flickering gaslight would be a subject of internal contention for some time to come: Accompanied by a sharp suck of air as the door swung inward, an enveloping shadow fell away from that hall with the speed of a magician's black silk handkerchief snatched off an ivory tablecloth. Or so in that moment it seemed.

The corridor was empty. He registered no sensory impression of any person having just been present. Nearby he heard the whine of an ill-tuned violin; more distantly, an infant's colicky howl, hooves on cobblestone.

Blavatsky must be having her way with me, he thought; that's what one gets for reading her after dark. "I am suggestible," he muttered, as he withdrew to his rooms, locked the door, replaced the shillelagh, and turned his attention to the matter in hand.

The envelope was square. No writing on it. He held it to the light; the bond was thick, unyielding any silhouette. It looked perfectly ordinary.

Reaching into his Gladstone, he retrieved a sharp lancet and, with the surgical exactness that was his custom in all routine procedures, pierced and slit the crown. A single sheet of vellum, thinner stock than the envelope but matched, slipped smoothly into his hand. No mark or monogram adorned it, but this was clearly a gentleman's— or gentlewoman's—correspondence. Folded once, a clean crease, he opened it and read:

> SIR:
>
> *Your presence is required in a matter of utmost urgency pertaining to the fraudulent public practice of the spiritualist arts. I am told of your sympathy to the victims of just such adventurers as these. Your aid is indispensable to one who may not be named here. As a man of God and science, I beseech your timely response. An innocent's life hangs in the balance. Tomorrow night. 8:00. 13 Cheshire Street.*
>
> GODSPEED

First of all, the writing: block-printed, clean, and precise, an educated hand. Words embossed deeply in the hearty parchment, the pen

11

gripped tightly, the hand pressed firmly; although not scripted in haste, the urgency was genuine. Written within the hour.

This was not the first such entreaty he had received. The Doctor's campaign to expose fraudulent mediums and their loathsome ilk was well known to certain grateful members of London society. He was not a public man and sought no public recognition, taking measures to avoid such exposure entirely, but word of his work occasionally found its way to those in need. Not the first such appeal, no, but certainly the most dire.

The paper carried no scent or perfume. No identifiable flourishes. The hand was as studiously sexless as the stationery. Anonymity this complete was practiced.

A woman, he concluded: monied, learned, vulnerable to scandal. Married or related to someone of note or station. A dabbler in the shallows of the "spiritual arts." That often described those who have recently suffered, or fear they are on the verge of suffering, a profound loss.

An innocent. A spouse or child. Hers.

The address given was in the East End, near Bethnal Green. A mean spot: no place for a highborn woman to venture alone. For a man largely unfettered by doubt amid even the worst uncertainty, there would be none regarding his response.

Before delving back into Blavatsky, Dr. Arthur Conan Doyle made a mental note to clean and load his revolver.

It was Christmas Day, 1884.

❖   ❖   ❖

The flat where Doyle lived and worked occupied the second floor of an aging building in a working-class neighborhood of London. These were humble quarters, a sitting room and a cramped sleeping chamber, inhabited by a modest man of limited means and a steady, confident manner. By nature, and now in practice, a healer, Master of Surgery these three years, a young man approaching his twenty-sixth year and the cusp of entry into that unspoken fraternity whose members quietly carry on despite conscious awareness of their own mortality.

His physician's faith in the infallibility of science was ingrained but brittle and laced with a spiderwork of faults. Although he had fallen from the Catholic Church a decade before, there persisted in Doyle a hunger for belief; as he saw it, it now remained the exclusive province of science to empirically establish the existence of the human soul. He fully expected science would eventually lead him to the higher reaches of spiritual discovery, and yet coexisting with this rock-ribbed certainty was a wild, weightless yearning for abandon, a ripping away of reality's masking complaisance to incite a merging with the mystic, a death in life leading to greater life. This longing prowled his mind like a wraith. He had never spoken of it, not once, to anyone.

To appease that desire for surrender, he read Blavatsky and Emanuel Swedenborg and a host of other long-winded mystics, scouring obscure bookshops in search of rational proof he could quantify, confirmation he could hold in his hands. He attended meetings of the London Spiritualist Alliance. He sought out mediums and seers and psychics, conducted his own parlor séances, visited houses where the dead reportedly did not rest. In every instance, Doyle brought to bear his three cardinal principles—observation, precision, and deduction; these were the cornerstones upon which he had constructed his sense of self—and he recorded his findings clinically, privately, without conclusions, preamble to some larger work whose shape would reveal itself to him only in time.

As his studies deepened, the wrestling within him between science and spirit, these two irreconcilable polarities, grew increasingly clangorous and divisive. He pressed on nonetheless. He knew too well what could happen to men who surrendered that fight: To one side stood the self-appointed pillars of morality, manning the ramparts of Church and State, sworn enemies of change, dead inside but lacking the good sense to lie down; at the other extreme lay a host of wretches chained to asylum walls, wearing their own filth, eyes burning with ecstasy as they communed with an illusory perfection. He drew no judgmental distinction between these extremes: He knew that the path of human perfectibility—the path he aspired to walk—lay exactly on the midpoint between them. It remained his hope that if science was unable to lead him down that middle path, perhaps he could help science find its footing there.

This determination generated two unexpected results: First, when in this spirit of investigation he chanced upon some fraud or advantage taken of the weak of mind or heart by scoundrels for deceitful gain, he would without hesitation unmask the perpetrators. Low and foul characters, these swindlers generally sprang from the criminal class and understood only the idiom of violence: hard words, tables overturned, physical threats promised and delivered. At the urging of a Scotland Yard confidant, Doyle had recently begun to carry the revolver after the exposure of a counterfeit Gypsy provoked a dagger attack that nearly provided him with firsthand experience of the Great Beyond.

The second: Living with these contradictory impulses—the desire for faith; the need to prove faith genuine before embracing it—left Doyle with the simple human need to compose his unresolved reactions. He found the ideal forum in writing works of fiction, reducing his shapeless experience of this murky netherworld into straightforward narrative lines: stories of mythic planes, dread and eldritch deeds committed by plotters of evil intent, contested by men from the world of light and knowledge—not unlike himself—who ventured knowingly and for the most part recklessly into the darkness.

In service to that vision, during the previous years Doyle produced four manuscripts. His first three efforts had been dutifully submitted to a succession of publishers, where they were uniformly rejected and returned, then consigned to the depths of a wicker footlocker he'd brought back from the South Seas. He was still awaiting responses to his most recent composition—a rousing adventure story entitled "The Dark Brotherhood"—which he considered his most accomplished work for a number of reasons, not the least of which being his fervent desire to lift himself out of shabby-genteel poverty.

As to his physical appearance, suffice it to say that Doyle was man enough for the tasks he set himself, sturdy, athletic, without vanity but not above a conditioned twinge of shame if he encountered social betters while wearing cuff or collar frayed by his financial limits.

He had seen enough of vice to be sympathetic to the captives of its hooks and snares without ever having been entangled there himself. He was not boastful and by inclination held greater stock in listening than speaking. Of human nature, he hoped for basic decencies, and met its inevitable disappointments without rancor or surprise.

The fairer sex aroused in him a natural and healthy interest but also on occasion tapped a vein of vulnerability, a pocket of frailty and indecision in an otherwise solid granite facing. This tendency had never offered more of a predicament than the standard vexations and anxieties posed to any younger man in the pursuit of love. As he was about to discover, it would soon present far graver consequences.

CHAPTER 2

13 Cheshire Street

Thirteen Cheshire Street stood packed in the center of a residential shanty row as flimsy as playing cards. Four steps led to a doorway with a pronounced starboard lean. The building could not yet be fairly considered a hovel, but that day was not far off. It appeared to possess no inherently sinister qualities. It appeared to possess no quality whatsoever.

Doyle looked on from across the street. He had arrived an hour earlier than requested by the letter. Light was in scarce supply, foot and street traffic scant. He kept to the shadows and waited, certain his presence had not been detected, watching the house through a small optic magnifier.

A pale aurora of gaslight limned the curtains of the forward parlor. Twice during his first quarter-hour, shadows pressed between the light and lace. Once the lace moved, a hand appeared, a dark male face dimly seen studied the street below, then withdrew.

At 7:20 a squat figure covered in an accretion of dark, tattered shawls ambled down the street, climbed the stairs, and methodically knocked three times, paused, then rapped a fourth. Five feet tall, well over fourteen stone, head and face obscured against the cold. High-button shoes. A woman. Doyle raised the magnifier to his eye; the shoes were new. The door opened, and the figure entered. Doyle saw neither the interior hall nor the figure's admitter.

Five minutes later, a young boy sprinted into view, straight to the door, where he repeated the same knock. Shabbily dressed, an urchin, carrying a bulky, irregular bundle wrapped in newspaper, bound by twine. Before Doyle could focus the glass clearly on the bundle, the boy entered.

Between 7:40 and 7:50, two couples arrived, the first on foot, working class, the woman sallow, heavily with child, the man thick, built for manual labor, uncomfortable in what Doyle reasoned was his best set of clothes. They also employed the signal knock. Through the glass, he watched the man hectoring the woman as they waited, her eyes downcast, defeated, a habitual state. He couldn't quite make out what the man was saying; an attempt to read his lips yielded the words *Dennis* and *blagglord*. Blagglord? They entered; the door closed.

The second couple came by carriage. Not a hansom, a private vehicle, dark leathers, steel-span wheels, the horse a handsome chestnut. Judging from the gelding's heavy lather, they had traveled at high speed from somewhere forty-five minutes to an hour away. Heading west, that placed them in Kensington, with Regent's Park the northern extreme.

The coachman dismounted and opened the door. His dress and deferential manner did not contradict what he appeared to be, a career servant, fifty, muscled, and dour. A young man alighted first, slender and pallid, bearing the tremulous conceit of a privileged university student—as broad cultural types went, not an inordinate favorite of Doyle's. Wearing an elaborate cravat, dickey, and beaver hat, he'd either come straight from a social function or considerably overestimated the formality of his destination. Curtly brushing the coachman aside, he lent a hand to the coach's second passenger as she descended.

She was in black, as tall as the young man, willowy and supple, swaying in emotional currents that seemed considerable. Bonnet and shawl framed a pale oval face; a familial resemblance to the younger man—his sister, Doyle chanced, two or three years his senior—but the glimpse of her features was brief as the young man took her arm and ushered her quickly to the door. He knocked straightforwardly, the signal apparently unknown to them. As they waited, the young man attempted to press her on some persistent point—perhaps imprecations against their rough surroundings; it appeared he had accompanied her under protest—but despite her apparent frailty, a steadiness in the set of her eyes indicated her will was the stronger.

13 Cheshire Street

The woman glanced anxiously about the street. This is the author of the note, and she is looking for me, Doyle realized. He was on the verge of starting across to them when the door opened, and the house swallowed them up.

Shadows played against the parlor curtains. Employing the glass, Doyle saw the woman greeted by the man whose dark face he had spied earlier at the window, accompanied by the pregnant woman; she took the brother's hat, the woman's shawl. The dark man gestured modestly, indicating they should adjourn to an inner room, and with the woman leading the way, they moved from sight.

She is not acting out of bereavement, concluded Doyle. Grief collapses inwardly. What's propelling this woman forward is fear. And if 13 Cheshire was a snare, she had walked eagerly into its jaws.

Pocketing the glass and reassuringly fingering his revolver, Doyle abandoned his post and crossed the street toward the coachman, who was leaning diffidently against his cab, lighting a pipe.

"Pardon me, friend," said Doyle, putting on an affable, half-pixilated smile. "This wouldn't be where they're having on that spiritualist thing-amajig, now would it? I was told Thirteen Cheshire."

"Wouldn't know about that, sir." Flat, nothing. Most likely the truth.

"But wasn't that Lady . . . Lady Whatzis and her brother . . . well, of course, you're their driver, aren't you? Sid, isn't it?"

"Tim, sir."

"Tim, right. You fetched my wife and me from the station when we visited out to the country that weekend."

The man peered uncomfortably askance at Doyle, feeling a social obligation to harmonize. "Out to Topping, then."

"That's right, out to Topping, when they had everyone out for . . . "

"For the opera."

"Right-o, the opera . . . Last summer, wasn't it? Now be honest, Tim, you don't remember me, do you?"

"Summers Lady Nicholson's got people out all the time," Tim offered as apology. "'Specially that opera crowd."

"Now I'm trying to recall: Was her brother there that weekend, or was he off at Oxford?"

"Cambridge. No, he was there, I think, sir."

"Of course, it's coming back now—I've only been out to Topping just the one time." That's enough, thought Doyle, I'm pressing my luck as it is. "Fond of the opera, are you, Tim?"

"Me, sir? Not my cuppa. The track, more like."

"Good man." A glance at the watch. "Look, it's nearly eight, I'd best get inside. Cheers. Keep warm."

"Thank you, sir," said Tim, grateful for the consideration or perhaps more so for Doyle's departure.

Doyle took the steps. Lady Caroline Nicholson—the full name leapt immediately to mind. Husband's father in government. Hereditary peerage, Topping their ancestral manse, somewhere in Sussex.

Which knock to use? The covert: three raps, a pause, then a fourth. Get someone to the door, then sort it out. He raised the cudgel end of his walking stick, but before he made contact, the door swung open. He couldn't recall hearing the latch disengage. Probably not closed properly; the cant of the doorframe, a gust of wind.

He entered. The center hall was dark, bereft, bare boards underfoot that never knew a rug. Closed doors to the left, right, and straight ahead. Stairs straining upward like bad teeth. The boards protested underfoot with every cautious step. After three such steps, the open door behind him swung shut. This time he distinctly heard the latch engage. Doyle reassured himself by recalling a gust of wind that preceded the closing of the door, of sufficient force to initiate the securing of the latch.

Except that the single candle on the table, its sallow flame now alone between Doyle and total darkness, had not flinched or faltered in its ovoid capsule. Doyle passed his hand over the flame; it danced agreeably, then he noticed that beside the candlestick on the table was a glass bowl, ensnaring stark ebon highlights from the flickering flame.

The bowl's mouth spanned the breadth of both his hands. The glass was dense, smoky, richly textured with a pattern. This filigree depicts a scene, Doyle realized as he traced a pair of conical horns sprouting from an upright animal's head. His eye drifted to a dark mass of something wet and charry in the bowl; flaked and blackened, it gave off a disagreeably ripe tang. Fighting an instinctive wave of revulsion, he was about to insert an exploratory finger into the fluid when with a moist *glug* something shifted beneath its surface, something not inert. The bowl began to vibrate, its edges rimming the table, giving off a high glassine hum. Right, well, we can come back to this, he thought, backing away.

Low voices from behind the door directly ahead of him, soft, rhythmic, almost musical, consonant with the vibration, perhaps responsible for it. Not a song: more like a chant, the words indecipherable—

The door to the right opened. The boy he'd seen before stood there, looking up at him without surprise.

"I'm here for the séance," Doyle said.

13 Cheshire Street

The boy's brow furrowed, scrutinizing, enigmatic. Older than originally estimated, small for his age. Quite a bit older. Grime smudging his face, a mobcap pulled low over the ears, but dirt and cap not entirely obscuring wrinkles at the brows and corners. Quite a mass of wrinkles. And there was nothing of the child in those unnerving eyes.

"Lady Nicholson is expecting me," Doyle added authoritatively.

Calculation occurred behind the boy's look, and his eyes suddenly went alarmingly vacant, as in *vacated*. Doyle waited a long ten seconds, half expecting the boy to keel over—a petit mal seizure perhaps—about to reach out to him when his presence snapped crisply back into place. He opened the door and bowed stiffly, waving Doyle through. An epileptic, clearly much abused, growth stunted by malnutrition, perhaps a mute. East End streets play host to legions of these lost ones, Doyle allowed himself unsentimentally. Bought and sold for less than the coins in my pocket.

Doyle moved past the boy into the parlor, the chanting voices closer now, issuing from behind closed sliding doors directly ahead. The door snicked shut behind him, the boy gone. Doyle treaded softly to the doors, and as he listened, the voices within went silent, leaving only the sibilant hiss of the gas jets.

The doors slid open. The boy stood on the other side now, waving him forward. Behind him, across a surprisingly commodious room, the séance was already in progress.

❖ ❖ ❖

The modern Spiritualist Movement began with an act of fraud. On March 31, 1848, mysterious rapping sounds were heard in the home of the Foxes, an ordinary Hydesville, New York, family. The sounds continued to manifest for months whenever their two adolescent daughters gathered in the same room. In the following years, the Fox sisters capitalized the resultant national hysteria into a thriving cottage industry: books, public séances, lecture tours, hobnobbing with celebrated faces of the day. It wasn't until the end of her life that Margaret Fox confessed the enterprise had been nothing more than an increasingly sophisticated series of parlor tricks, by which time it was far too late to still a *vox populi* starved for authentic experience of the supernormal: Science's assertion of primacy over the rusting tenets of Christian worship had created a seedbed that Spiritualism took root in like wild nightshade.

The Movement's stated objective: Confirm the existence of realms of being beyond the physical, by direct communication with the spirit

19

world through mediums—also known as *sensitives*—individuals attuned to the higher frequencies of noncorporeal life. Having discovered and developed this ability, the medium invariably struck up a "relationship" with a spirit guide, who served as interlocutor of a cosmic lost and found: Since most of the medium's supplicants were survivors of some recent death, they aspired to little more than reassurance that their dearly departed had arrived intact on the far side of the Styx. It was the spirit guide's task to authenticate the contact by retrieving proof from Aunt Minnie or Brother Bill, usually in the form of some hermetically private anecdote shared exclusively by both bereaved and lamented.

In response to these simple inquiries, information flowed from the spirit through rapping, a series of knocks on tables. More accomplished mediums entered a trance during which the spirit guide "borrowed" the host's vocal cords, assuming the voice of the loved one with startling accuracy. A few manifested an infinitely rarer talent: producing large volumes of milky, malleable vapor from their skin, mouth, or nose, a substance with all the appearance but none of the properties of smoke: It did not disperse or react to atmospheric conditions, behaving rather as a three-dimensional tabula rasa able to assume the shape of any idea or entity. It was one thing to hear Aunt Minnie knock on the table, quite another to see her take shape before one's eyes in a cloud of clotted, autonomous fog. This strange stuff was called *ectoplasm*. It was photographed on countless occasions. No adequate debunking for it emerged.

Beyond the hordes of the grieving and confused, two other, smaller subsets consistently sought out the services of the mediumistically inclined. Motivated by similar impulses—albeit with diametrically opposed ends in mind—they divided along an obvious line of demarcation; seekers of light and worshipers of darkness. Doyle, for example, was driven by a conviction that if one could pierce the appropriate sphere of knowledge, the eternal mysteries of health and disease would fall within our reach. He researched the exhaustively documented case of one Andrew Jackson Davis, an illiterate American born in 1826, who while still an adolescent discovered an ability to diagnose illness through the use of his *spirit eyes*, perceiving the human body as transparent and the now visible organs as centers of light and color, the hues and gradations of which corresponded to their well-being or lack thereof. In this talent, thought Doyle, one could glimpse the once and future genius of medicine.

Worshipers of darkness, on the other hand, were striving to unlock the secrets of the ages for their own exclusive benefit, as in: Imagine the pioneers of electromagnetism deciding to keep that discovery to themselves. Regrettably, as Doyle was about to discover, this group was considerably more unified than their opposite number, and they had traveled a good deal closer to achieving their objective.

❖   ❖   ❖

On this same night, at that same moment, less than a mile from the events about to unfold at 13 Cheshire, a poor and wretched street-walker stumbled out of a pub in Mitre Square. Boxing Day had been a bust; what few coins she'd collected for services rendered had been quickly spent attempting to quench her unquenchable thirst.

Her livelihood depended on the urgency induced by cheapjack gin in unfortunates like herself for the meager dollop of human comfort afforded by three minutes of intercourse in alleyways redolent of rubbish and raw sewage. Her looks were long gone. She was indistinguishable from the countless others in her trade teeming through London's lowlife.

Her life began in some rural Arcadia where she was once her parents' joy, the prettiest girl in the village. Did her eyes sparkle, her skin aglow with health, when she opened her legs to the passing swain who planted the glamour of the city in her head? Had she arrived with hope intact? Did her sweet dreams of happiness die slowly as the liquor devoured her cells, or did a single catastrophic heartbreak snap her will like a clay pipe?

Cold bit through her decomposing coat. She thought dimly of families glimpsed through frosted windows eating Christmas dinner. It could have been an actual memory or a woodcut on a half-forgotten greeting card. The image fell away, replaced by thoughts of the squalid room across the river that she shared with three other women. The idea of sleep and the paltry comforts of that room animated her; her legs lurched numbly forward, and in that diminished state she decided that once across the river she would use the shortcut to Aldgate that crossed the abandoned lot near Commercial Street.

CHAPTER 3

A True Face

LADY NICHOLSON SPOTTED Doyle first, framed in the open doorway. He saw recognition, a rapidly rising blush of relief, instantly dampened to ward off discovery. A nimble mind, he concluded, slightly preceded by the thought, Here is the most beautiful face I have ever seen.

The table was round, covered in pale linen, in the center of the shadowy room. Light pooled from two candelabras flanking the table east and west, walls falling away into darkness. The cloying musk of patchouli hung heavily in the air, along with a dry crack of static electricity. As his pupils dilated, against a backdrop of dense brocaded tapestries suspended in the air, Doyle could make out six figures seated at the table, holding hands; to Lady Nicholson's right was her brother, the pregnant serving girl to his right hand, then the man Doyle identified as her husband, to his right the dark man from the window, and finally the medium, whose right hand held Lady Nicholson's left. Mediums borrowed most of their theatrics direct from the standard liturgical repertoire: smoke, gloom, and grave, incomprehensible gibberish. This assembly had produced the chanting he'd heard, an incantation of call and response initiated by the medium, ritualistic prologue to create the proper atmosphere of dread and ceremony.

A True Face

The medium's eyes were closed, her head inclined back to the ceiling, exposing the fleshy wattles of her throat: the short, round woman in the new shoes, her accumulation of shawls discarded. Over the years, Doyle had catalogued the city's many practitioners, genuine article and charlatan alike: This one was unknown to him. She wore black, a wool weave, neither cheap nor extravagant, with a white bib collar, sleeves bulging with flesh buttoned to her wrists. Her face was bloodless and as studded with moles as cloves in an Easter ham. The woman's solar plexus palpitated in a violent cycle of respiration. She was on the threshold of entering, or effectively simulating, trance.

Lady Nicholson's color was high, her knuckles white, caught up in the performance, flinching in response to the progressive stranglehold applied by the medium's hand. Her brother's frequent, solicitous looks to her prevented his wholesale purchase of the game, as did, Doyle suspected, his habitually sardonic disposition. The way the pregnant woman's head postured upward signaled the traditional abandon of the blindly devout. Seen in profile, his jaw muscles working furiously, her husband's narrowed gaze fixed on the medium—agitation or anger?

The Dark Man saw Doyle next. His eyes pierced the air between them. Obsidian black, set like jeweled stones in deep round holes. Sallow cheeks the color of polished teak, pitted with pocks down to a sleek jaw and chin. Lips like razors. The expression in the eyes was fervent but unreadable. He released the hand of the man to his left and extended it toward Doyle, fingers paddled together, thumb extended.

"Join us." The Dark Man appeared to whisper, but the voice carried.

The man's gaze fell from Doyle to the boy, who turned to meet it obediently. A command passed between them. The boy reached up and grasped Doyle's hand: The fingers felt raspy and unpleasant. As Doyle let the boy draw him forward into the room, a discordant current spiked through the back of his neck and prompted the phrase *You're someplace else now.*

The boy led him to an empty chair between the two men. Lady Nicholson's brother looked up at him with slack puzzlement, as if his appearance represented one too many elements to process cogently.

As he accepted the Dark Man's offered hand with his right and settled into the waiting chair, the man to his left seized Doyle's free hand and clenched tight. When Doyle turned to Lady Nicholson, seated directly across from him, he encountered the ardent gaze of a woman who had just had a lifetime's polite, social dissembling torn away by the chamber's tonic of wonder and terror, awakening to find herself brazenly alive. That vitality illuminated her extraordinary beauty. Her aquamarine eyes danced kaleidoscopically, and high color brushed her pale cheeks. Doyle summoned just enough wherewithal through his bedazzlement to notice she was wearing makeup. She mouthed the words *Thank you*. Doyle felt an involuntary thump and a skip in his chest: My heart, he observed with interest.

The intrusive jolt of an alien voice broke the connection.

"We have strangers here tonight."

It was a man's voice, deep-chested, round, and burnished as rocks in the bed of a cold stream, veined with a seductive, graveled tremolo.

"All are welcome."

Doyle turned to the medium. The woman's eyes were open, and the voice was issuing from her throat. Since the last time he'd glanced at her, it appeared to Doyle that the woman's facial structure had perceptibly changed shape, from pie-shaped to a cast more ruddy, skeletal, and square. Eyes gleaming with a reptilian glint, her mouth slithered into the salacious grin of a sensualist.

Remarkable: In his studies, Doyle could recall only two accounts of this phenomenon observed in mediums while in trance—*physio-logical transmogrification*—and had never before encountered it *in situ*.

The medium's lidded gaze wandered leisurely around the table, avoiding Doyle, precipitating tremors he could feel coursing through the hand of the man to his left. The medium engaged the brother until he was constrained to turn away like a shamed dog. Then the eyes settled on his sister.

"You . . . seek my guidance."

Lady Nicholson's lips trembled. Doyle was uncertain she'd be able to summon a reply, when the Dark Man beside him spoke first.

"We all, humbly, seek your guidance and wish to extend our gratitude for this evening's visitation." His voice had a hiss in it, damage to a vocal cord. The accent was foreign—Mediterranean perhaps—Doyle couldn't yet pinpoint it precisely.

So this man was amanuensis, the medium's liaison to the paying customer, usually the brains behind the operation. He had clearly cultivated the fervid conviction of the true believer that served as his own best advertising. Fraud began here; an opportunistic salesman exploiting what in many instances were mediums with some measurable facility and a childish incomprehension of the workaday world's mercantile realities. As a man in Gloucester had put it to him, describing the sensitive abilities of his own otherwise dim-witted son, "When they give you a window into another world, I warrant you forfeit a few bricks."

A True Face

This was the team: medium, handler, all-purpose urchin, serving woman with child for emotional credibility, burly husband providing muscle, others unseen perhaps standing by. Clearly, Lady Nicholson was their target. Not an altogether unwitting one—she had sent Doyle the precautionary note—but one whose distress was sufficiently compelling to outweigh her misgivings. It remained to be seen how they would react to Doyle's unexpected arrival—but then, so far, *unexpected* didn't seem to particularly apply.

"We are all beings of light and spirit, both on this side and on your physical plane. Life is life, life is all one, life is all creation. We honor the life and light in you as you would do in us. We are all one on this side, and we wish you on your side harmony, blessing, and peace everlasting." This came from the medium in a burst, with the feel of a standard, practiced preamble, before she turned to the Dark Man and nodded politely, his cue to formally begin the proceedings.

"Spirit welcomes you. Spirit is aware of your distress and wishes to help in any way it can. You may address Spirit directly," the Dark Man said to Lady Nicholson.

Wrestling with a sudden, profound uncertainty, Lady Nicholson did not answer, as if to voice the first question were an admission that effectively laid waste to a lifetime's accumulation of inherited beliefs.

"We can go, we could go," her brother leaned in to offer.

"Begin with your son," said the medium.

She looked up, startled and instantly focused.

"You've come to ask me of your son."

Tears pooled quickly in her eyes. "Oh my God."

"What would you ask of Spirit?" The medium went through the motions of smiling, but the effect appeared simulated.

"How did you know?" Tears ran down her cheeks.

"Has your son crossed over?" The smile persisted.

She shook her head, uncomprehending.

"Has there been a death?" asked the Dark Man.

"I'm not sure. That is, we don't know...." She faltered again.

"The thing is, he's disappeared. Four days now. He's only three years old," the brother offered.

"His name is William," the medium said without hesitation. It would have been the Dark Man's job to find that out.

"Willie." Her voice brimmed with emotion; she was taking the hook.

Doyle throughout glanced surreptitiously around the room, at the ceiling, behind the tapestries, searching for suspended wires, projection devices. Nothing so far.

"You see, we've already been to the police. It's no good—"

"We don't know if he's dead or alive!" Her pent-up grief exploded. "For God's sake, if you know so much, then you know why I'm here." For a brief moment, her eyes found Doyle's and felt his sympathy. "Please. Please, tell me. I shall go mad."

The medium's smile lapsed. She nodded gravely. "One moment," she said. Her eyes closed; her head angled back again. The circle of hands remained unbroken. The silence that followed was thick and urgent.

A gasp broke from the pregnant girl. She was staring at a spot some six feet above the table where a perfect sphere of white mist was materializing, spinning like a globe on a central pivot. Expanding, fleecy extensions spun out from its core, breaking the circle down into a flat, square plane. By varying their density, the shards spread out and began purposefully assuming the dimensions of a random topography, foot-hills, rifts, peninsulas, all within the invisible confines of borders as rigid as a gilded frame.

A map? The shifting slowed, and the features crystallized, until with a rush of condensation the true nature of the vision appeared: a work of shadow and light, bleached of color, less precise than a photograph but more animated, suggestive of motion and distantly of sound, as if this scene were being viewed at great remove through some crude, impersonal lens.

In it, a young boy lay curled up at the base of a tree. He wore short pants, a loose tunic, stockings, no shoes. His hands and feet were tightly bound with rope. The first glance suggested sleep, but closer examination showed the chest heaving, coughing, or sobbing—it was difficult to determine, until the ghostly and unmistakable sound of a child's pathetic, heartsick cries filtered into the chamber.

"God in heaven, it's him, it's him," Lady Nicholson moaned. The sight leveled her, not into despondency but a rapt, febrile alertness.

More details of the unearthly daguerreotype emerged: A small stream ran through the forest bed a few feet from where the boy was lying on a frost-tinged carpet of leaves. The rope that held the boy's wrists extended to a low-lying branch of the adjacent tree. The woods thickened behind him, clustering, evergreens. An object lay on the ground near the boy's feet: small, square, man-made: a can, bearing the letters ... C U I ...

"Willie!" she cried.

"Where is he? Where is he?" the brother demanded, his attempt to generate outrage mitigated by dumbstruck astonishment.

Lost inwardly, the medium offered no response.

"Tell us!" the brother demanded, and he meant to speak further, but the air in the room was rent by a shattering, discordant blast of trumpets, an insane trilling, bound by no discernible harmony or rhythm. Doyle felt stunned, assaulted, pinned down by the oppressive weight of the vibrations.

"The horn of Gabriel!" shrieked the man to Doyle's left.

Now something black and odious crept into the edge of the image suspended above them: A shadow felt more than seen, oiled, foul and malignant, gathering mass without seeming to coalesce, the presence insinuated itself into the vision, seeping through the spectral wood, advancing toward the helpless child.

An inescapable conviction that he had witnessed this entity the night before in the hall outside his door left Doyle groping vainly for some rational causation. His mind shouted at him: *This means not Death but Annihilation.*

The cacophonous nightmare grew deafening. A long brass horn appeared in the air, opposite the picture, bobbing erratically. *Now that's their first mistake*—Doyle seized purchase on the thought. Could he detect a telltale flash of filament at the trumpet's bell?

Drawing itself into a hungry spiral around the boy, the phantom sucked the last bit of light from the vision, swallowing the sound of his cries, on the verge of consuming him whole. Lady Nicholson screamed.

Doyle sprang to his feet and yanked his hands free. He picked up his chair and hurled it at the image; it shattered like liquid glass, dispersing and sputtering into emptiness. Its suspending cables severed; the brass trumpet clattered noisily onto the table.

Rolling to avoid the blow he knew was coming, Doyle felt the fist of the man to his left connect sharply below his shoulder blade. In one swift move, Doyle snatched the trumpet from the table and swung it viciously up and around, catching the man square on the side of the face. Blood spurted from a gash as he stumbled and fell to his knees.

"Villains!" Doyle shouted, galvanized. He reached into his pocket for the revolver when a heavy blow landed on the right side of his neck, paralyzing his searching hand and arm. He turned to see the Dark Man lift a leaded truncheon to strike again and raised his left arm to fend it off.

"Fool!" The voice issued from the medium. Grinning maliciously, eyes blazing, she swiftly rose straight up into the air above the table. Distracted, the Dark Man turned to face her, truncheon still raised. Doyle felt the hands of the wounded man grab him roughly from behind.

"You fancy yourself a seeker of *truth*?" the medium mocked him.

She held out her palms, the skin roiled and rippled with hideous subcutaneous congestion. When she opened her mouth, a flowing volume of gray aqueous vapor billowed forth from both mouth and hands. Suspended in the air, the vapor traced the outline and then filled in the image of a full-length frame mirror. As the surface of the mirror refined itself, the medium's reflection appeared in the spectral glass.

"Then behold my true face."

Out of the void behind her likeness in the mirror floated another form, dim and indistinct, which settled on and then imposed itself over the medium's reflection, pouring into it like water saturating sand, until all that remained was an entirely new visage: a skull-like creature with red runny, abscessed sockets for eyes, skin gray and in many places gnawed down to the bone, writhing pockets of black stringy hair sprouting from more than the usual places. Independent of the medium, who remained still, merely smiling, the creature looked down at Doyle and opened the spoiled cavity that served as its mouth. Its voice was the one they had been hearing all along, but it now came exclusively from the fiend in the mirror.

"You imagine that you do *good.* See what your good has wrought."

Two hooded figures moved out from behind the tapestry, moving so swiftly that Doyle had no time to react. One clouted Lady Nicholson's brother across the head with a dimly glimpsed weapon; the wound spouted crimson as he fell away. The other grabbed Lady Nicholson and drew a long, thin blade smoothly across her throat, severing the vessels, arterial blood pumping furiously. The cry in Lady Nicholson's throat died in a drowning rattle as she slumped out of sight behind the table.

"God! No!" Doyle screamed.

A demented cackle from the monster filled the air before the ectoplasmic mirror exploded in a loud report of light.

One of the murderers now drew his sights on Doyle and nimbly jumped up onto the table, poised to leap down and strike at him with the mallet that had splintered the forehead of Lady Nicholson's brother, when Doyle heard something whoosh by his ear: a shape, a black handle bloomed at the throat of the assassin. He stopped on top of the table, dropped his weapon, and groped blindly at his chin; a dagger had pierced the span of his neck, pinning the material of the hood, drawing it down over the eyes. The man staggered, then toppled over.

With a grunt, the accomplice holding Doyle fell backward and away; he was free.

An unfamiliar man's voice spoke urgently in his ear. "Your pistol, Doyle."

Doyle looked up to see the Dark Man turning toward him with the truncheon raised. Doyle pulled the pistol from his pocket and fired. His left knee shattered, the Dark Man bellowed and fell to the floor.

The shape was moving behind Doyle now, kicking the candelabra, extinguishing half the room's light. Doyle just had time to note that the medium had vanished when his attention snapped back to a blur of gray; the advancing rush of the second assassin. Still unseen, Doyle's benefactor overturned the heavy table, throwing the murderer back. Hands pulled Doyle to his feet.

"Follow me," the voice instructed.

"Lady Nicholson—"

"Too late."

Doyle followed the voice into the darkness. They passed through a door, down a corridor. Doyle felt disoriented—this was not the way he had entered. The door at corridor's end fell as Doyle's confederate kicked it open, oozing a crepuscular light into the space. They were still interior. Doyle could make out a tall, rangy profile, see the man's breath vaporize in the cooling air, nothing more.

"This way," the man instructed.

He was about to lead them through another door when a shape leapt from the dark with a feral growl and ripped into the man's forward leg. He staggered, crying out in shock. Doyle fired a shot at the dim shape of the attacking animal. It yelped and fell back, howling in pain. Doyle fired again, stilling its cries.

The man shouldered through the door. In the shaft of light that fell back through the doorway, Doyle saw the still body of the street urchin, crimson flowing from its wounds, jaws pulled back in a death grimace, exposing blood and meat in its sharp, canine teeth.

"Almost there," the man said, and they left the terrible house.

CHAPTER 4

Flight

His deliverer took the lead in a headlong dash down the dark alley outside. Unable for the moment to see the wisdom of any alternate course, as he followed, Doyle strained to keep the man's flowing cloak in sight. They turned once, twice, and turned again. Seems to know where he's going, Doyle thought wanly, his bearings yielding to the rattrap rookery of shacks and shanties through which the man's path threaded them.

Breaking out of an alley onto a paved street, the man stopped short; Doyle's momentum carried him halfway into the street before the man yanked him back into the sheltering darkness. His grip was tremendously strong. Doyle meant to speak, but the man silenced him with a sharp gesture and pointed at the corner of an intersecting alley across the way.

Stepping around that corner into view was the surviving gray-hooded killer: crouched over, moving steadily, deliberately, eyes to the ground, a coiled predator tracking its quarry. What possible signs could it be searching for in the hard pavement? Doyle asked himself—and then, more alarmingly: How did it get here so quickly?

Flight

Doyle heard a whisper of steel on steel as his companion, face still obscured by shadows, sharp profile etched against the wall, drew from the walking stick he carried the base of a hidden blade. Doyle instinctively reached for his revolver. His friend's hand lay frozen on the butt of his rapier, as still as stone.

A carriage approached from the left. Four immense black stallions roared into view, clattering noisily to a stop on the cobblestones. The six-seat coach stood huge and black as pitch. No driver was visible. The man in the gray hood moved to the side of the coach. A window slid open, but no light issued from within. The man nodded, but it was difficult to know if words were exchanged; nothing cut through the night but the labored sputtering of the horses.

The gray hood turned from the cab and looked directly into the alley where Doyle and friend were sheltered; both shrank back against the brick. The hood stepped toward them, stopped, and cocked its head like a hound tracing frequencies beyond human range. It stood like that for some time, the chilling blankness of the man finding perfect expression in the lifeless countenance of the mask. Doyle's breath died in his chest—Something's not right, he thought—and then he realized there were no holes for the eyes.

The door to the black carriage swung open. A short, strident, high-pitched trilling filled the air, halfway between a whistle and some less human vocalization. The gray hood instantly turned and leapt inside, the door slammed shut, and the steeds hammered the heavy carriage away, fog swirling greasily around the hole it carved in the mist.

As the clip of the hooves faded, Doyle's companion eased his weapon back into place.

"What the devil—" Doyle began, his breath bursting out in a rush.

"We're not safe yet," the man stilled him, voice low.

"All very well and good, but I think it's time we had a brief chat—"

"Couldn't agree more."

With that, the man was off again. Doyle had no choice but to follow. Keeping to the shadows, they stopped twice when the shrill whistling sounded again, each time at a greater remove, leaving Doyle to consider the disagreeable possibility that more than one of these hoods were on their trail. Doyle was about to break the silence when they turned a corner and came upon a waiting hansom cab, a compact cabbie atop the driver's perch. The man signaled, and the hack driver turned, offering a view of the ragged scar running obliquely down the right side of his face. He gave a brusque nod, turned to his horses, and cracked the whip, as the man opened the door of the moving vehicle and jumped aboard.

"Come on, then, Doyle," the man said.

Doyle followed up onto the stair, turning when he heard a dull thump to his right; a long, wicked blade had just penetrated the cab door, its quivering razor tip mere inches from Doyle's chest. A shrill, insistent variation of the vile whistling filled the nearby air. Doyle looked back: The gray hood was twenty yards back, drawing another, identically vicious dagger from its belt as it sprinted toward him at improbable speed. With a prodigious leap, the hood jumped onto the running board of the accelerating coach, clutching for purchase in the open doorway. Hands pulled Doyle back into the cab; he scuttled to the far corner, digging for his pistol, trying to remember which pocket he'd left it in, when he heard the opposite door open. He looked up to see a flash of flapping coattail; his friend had fled, leaving him trapped in the cab with their relentless pursuer—where was his pistol?

As the hooded figure captured its balance in the doorframe and raised the weapon, Doyle heard the scuff of weight shifting on the roof, then through the open window saw his friend swing down into view and drive both feet into the open door, slamming it shut and rocketing the point of the embedded dagger completely through their attacker's chest. With a hideously muted mewling cry, the hood kicked and clawed ferociously at the invading blade, mauling its hands indiscriminately, then went suddenly and entirely limp, pinned to the door like a bug.

Doyle struggled to his knees in the jostling sway of the carriage and moved to the hooded man. Rough clothes. Hobnailed boots, almost new. Feeling for a pulse and finding none, Doyle was about to remark on the curious absence of blood when his defender reached in through the window, pulled off the gray hood, and tossed it away.

"Good Christ!"

A hatch pattern of symmetrical scars crisscrossed the stark white face. The man's eyes and lips had been crudely knitted up with a coarse, waxy blue thread.

Holding on from the roof, Doyle's companion reopened the door, and the body swung out with it: Suspended outside the rapidly moving cab, the corpse exhibited violent spastic movements as the coach bounced and jolted along. With a strong pull, the man drew the long knife back through the door, releasing the body from its attachment, and it fell away into obscurity.

In one deft move, the man pivoted into the cab, pulled the door

Flight

shut behind him, and took a seat across from the stunned Doyle. He took two deep breaths and then . . .

"Care for a drink?"

"What's that?"

"Cognac. Medicinal purposes," said the man, offering a silver flask.

Doyle accepted it and drank—it *was* cognac; exceedingly good cognac—as the man watched. Doyle saw him clearly for the first time in the pale amber light of the cabin lantern—his face was narrow; streaks of color painted his sharp cheeks; long, jet-black hair curled behind his ears. High forehead. Aquiline nose. Strong jaw. The eyes were remarkable, light and sharp, colored by a habitual amusement that Doyle felt, to say the least, was currently inappropriate.

"We could have that little chat now," the man said.

"Right. Have a go."

"Where to begin?"

"You knew my name."

"Doyle, isn't it?"

"And you're . . . "

"Sacker. Armond Sacker. Pleasure."

"The pleasure I should say, Mr. Sacker, is distinctly mine."

"Have another."

"Cheers." Doyle drank again and passed back the flask.

The man unfastened his cloak. He wore black, head to toe. Lifting a leg of his trousers, he exposed the bloodied bite on his calf given by the feral boy.

"Nasty, that," said Doyle. "Shall I have a look?"

"No bother." The man took a handkerchief from his pocket and soaked it with cognac. "The puncture itself's not the worry, it's the damn tearing action when they prattle their heads about."

"Know a bit about medicine, then."

Sacker smiled and without flinching compressed the handkerchief tightly to the wound. Closing his eyes was the only concession to what Doyle knew must be extraordinary pain; when they reopened, no trace of it remained.

"Right. So, Doyle, tell me how you came to be in that house tonight."

Doyle recounted the arrival of the letter and his decision to attend.

"Right," said Sacker. "Not that you necessarily need me to tell you this, but you're in a bit of a fix."

"Am I?"

"Oh, I'd say so, yes."

"How, exactly?"

"Mm. Long story, that," the man said, more warning than excuse.

"Have we time for it?"

"Believe we're well clear for the moment," he said, parting the curtains for a brief look outside.

"I'll ask some questions, then."

"Better you didn't, really—"

"No, better I do," said Doyle, pulling the pistol from his pocket and resting it on his knee.

Sacker's smile broadened. "Right. Fire away."

"Who are you?"

"Professor. Cambridge. Antiquities."

"Could I see some form of identification to that effect?"

Sacker produced a calling card verifying the assertion. Looks authentic, thought Doyle. Not that that counted for much.

"I'll keep this," said Doyle, pocketing the card.

"Not at all."

"Is this your carriage, Professor Sacker?"

"It is."

"Where are we going?"

"Where would you like to go?"

"Someplace safe."

"Difficult."

"Because you don't know, or because you don't wish to tell me?"

"Because, as of this moment, there aren't all that many places you can truly consider safe: Doyle . . . safe. Not much overlap there, I'm sorry to say." He smiled again.

"You find that amusing."

"To the contrary. Your situation is obviously quite grave."

"*My* situation?"

"Rather than worry, however, in the face of adversity it's always my inclination to take action. That's what one should do in any event. General principle. Take action."

"Is that what we're doing now, Professor?"

"Oh my, yes." Sacker grinned again.

"I yield the floor," said Doyle darkly, his frustration with this cheerful enigma mitigated only by the man having twice within the hour saved his life.

"Another drink first?" he asked, offering the flask again. Doyle shook his head. "I really would recommend it."

Doyle took another drink. "Let's have it, then."

"You've attempted to publish a work of fiction recently."

"What's that got to do with any of this?"

"I'm endeavoring to tell you." He smiled again.

Flight

"The answer is yes."

"Hmm. Rough business, the publishing game. Fairly discouraging, I imagine, but then you don't strike me as the easily discouraged sort. Perseverance, that's the ticket."

Doyle bit his tongue and waited while Sacker took another nip.

"You recently circulated a manuscript of yours for publication entitled—have I got this right?—'The Dark Brotherhood'?"

"Correct."

"Without any notable success, I'm afraid—"

"You don't need to rub salt in the wound."

"Establishing the facts, old boy. Haven't read it myself. I'm given to understand your story deals at some length, as fiction, with what one might characterize as a . . . thaumaturgical conspiracy."

"In part." How could he know that? thought Doyle.

"A sort of sorcerers' cabal."

"You're not far off—the villains of the piece, anyway."

"A coven of evil masterminds colluding with some, shall we say, delinquent spirits."

"It's an adventure story, isn't it?" said Doyle defensively.

"With a supernatural bent."

"Fair enough."

"Good versus evil, that sort of thing."

"The eternal struggle."

"In other words, a potboiler."

"I'd hoped my sights were set a bit higher," Doyle complained.

"Don't listen to me, friend, I'm no critic. Are you published anywhere?"

"A few stories," Doyle replied, with only modest exaggeration. "I'm a frequent contributor to a monthly periodical."

"What would that be?"

"It's for children, I'm sure you wouldn't know it."

"Come on, what's it called?"

"*The Boy's Own Paper*," said Doyle.

"Right, never heard of it. Tell you what I think, though; nothing wrong with a bit of entertainment, is there? That's what people want in the end, after all, a little diversion, a ripping good tale, leave behind their troubles and woe."

"Stimulate a little thought while you're at it," Doyle offered sheepishly.

"And why not? Noble aspirations yield greater achievements."

"I appreciate the fine sensibilities—now would you please tell me what my book's got to do with what's happened tonight?"

35

The man paused, then leaned forward confidentially. "The manuscript was circulated."

"By whom?"

"Someone with *connections.*"

"Circulated where?"

"Into the wrong sorts of hands."

Doyle paused and leaned in to meet Sacker halfway. "I'm afraid you're going to have to be a bit more specific," Doyle said.

Sacker held Doyle's his eyes mesmerically and lowered his voice.

"Picture if you will a group of extraordinary individuals. Ruthless, intelligent, even brilliant persons. Well placed, enormously rewarded by the world for their skills and achievements. All distinctly lacking what you and I would call ... basic morality. United by one common pursuit: acquisition of power without limits. Hungering for more. Obsessively secret—exactly who they are is impossible to say. Rest assured they are real. Does this sound at all familiar to you?"

Doyle could barely speak. "My book."

"Yes, Doyle. Your book. You've written a manuscript of fiction, but by some elusive process you have drawn down into your work an uncanny approximation of the depraved plottings of a malignant sect of black magicians, seeking an end not at all unlike that pursued by your characters. Which was to—"

"To elicit the help of evil spirits in annihilating the membrane that separates the physical and etheric plane."

"In order to—"

"Gain dominion over the material world and those who inhabit it."

"Right. And if tonight's séance was any indication, my friend, they have breached the battlements and set foot across the threshold."

"It's not possible."

"Do you believe what your eyes saw in that room?"

Doyle found he was unwilling to hear his answer.

"It is possible," Sacker maintained.

Doyle felt a jolt of dislocation, as if he were in a dream. His mind struggled to stay above the flood tide of shock and dismay. The fact was, he had borrowed not only the title of his book but his villains' motives from the woolliest works of Madame Blavatsky. Who would have thought his petty larceny would come so hideously home to roost?

"If my book has fallen into their hands ... "

"Put yourself in their shoes: What purpose does life hold for these diseased monsters without the threatening presence—real or imagined—of formidable enemies, whose very existence serves only to heighten their demented self-aggrandizement?"

Flight

"They think I've somehow stumbled onto their plan...."

"If they mean to kill you outright they probably wouldn't have gone to all this trouble, which leads me to believe they want you alive, if that's any comfort to you."

"But surely they must know . . . I mean, they can't think . . . for God's sake, it's only a book."

"Yes. Pity, that."

Doyle stared at him. "What's all this got to do with you?"

"Oh, I've been onto these rogues a good sight longer than you have."

"But I haven't been onto them at all; until this moment I never even knew they existed."

"Yes, well, I wouldn't care to try telling them that, would you?"

Doyle was speechless.

"Fortunately, my tracking them put me close at hand this evening. Unfortunately, I'm something of a marked man now as well."

Sacker rapped sharply on the roof. The carriage came to a sudden halt.

"Rest assured: We've put a real spoke in their wheel tonight. Keep your wits about you, and don't waste a moment's time. And I wouldn't bother going to the police with all this, because they *will* think you mad, and word will only filter up to someone who could do you even greater harm."

"Greater than murder?"

All trace of a smile vanished. "There are worse things," he said, then opened the door. "Best of luck, Doyle. We'll be in touch."

Sacker extended a hand. Doyle shook it. In his dazed, bewildered state, the next thing he knew, he was standing on the street outside his front door, watching the scar-faced cabbie tip his hat, turn, and whip the carriage hurriedly into the night.

Doyle looked down at the hand Sacker had shaken. He was holding a small, exquisitely crafted silver insignia in the form of a human eye.

CHAPTER 5

Leboux

A MAELSTROM WHIRLED INSIDE Doyle's mind. He looked at his watch: 9:52. An ironmonger's cart rattled by. Doyle shivered with nostalgic longing as the prosaic, quotidian world in which he'd spent all but the last two hours of his life receded from him like dying sunlight. In the time it takes to bake bread, he had seen his life, if not his entire conception of the universe, turned on its head.

In the stillness left by the passing of the cart, forms and faces swam out of the dark; every shadow seemed to pulse with hidden, unspeakable danger. Doyle hustled to the presumed safety of his doorstep.

A face looked down at him from a high window. His neighbor, the Russian woman, Petrovitch. Wait—had there been a second face behind hers? Another look: both faces gone, curtains swaying.

Did his staircase, always a trigger for the pleasant prospect of home and its attendant comforts, now exude an aura of dread menace? No longer certain he could trust his instincts, Doyle took revolver in hand, trusting its filled chambers to contend with whatever might await, and slowly ascended the twenty-one steps. The door to his rooms came into view. It stood open.

The wood where the doorknob used to reside was splintered like so many matchsticks. The debris lay here, on the floor outside—the knob torn off, not kicked in. Doyle leaned back against the wall and listened. Certain that nothing stirred inside, with a light touch he eased the door open and gasped at what lay before him.

Every square inch of the front room looked to have been drooled or saturated with a clear, viscous fluid. Streaked and textured, as if a gigantic brush had been maniacally stroked from floor to ceiling. A smell like scorched mattress ticking permeated the air. Lazy smoke curled up from where the substance lay thickest. Stepping inside, he felt the ooze suck at the soles of his shoes, but no residue clung to them when he lifted his foot. It moved to the touch, it had body, but its crust remained integral, intact. Doyle could discern the tessellated pattern of his Persian carpet suspended inside the stuff, like a scarab frozen in amber. He examined his chair and davenport. Side table, oil lamp, ottoman. Candlesticks. Inkwell. Teacup. The surface of every object in the room had been partially liquefied, then cooled and hardened.

If this was a warning—an inescapable conclusion—what exactly was its messenger trying to communicate? Perhaps to incite the question, What kind of damage could they perpetrate on a human body? Doyle picked up one of his books from the desk. It seemed to weigh about the same, but it wobbled in his hand, spineless as an overcooked vegetable. He could still turn the thickened pages, could almost make out the blurred, distorted text, but the thing lying limply in his hand no longer remotely resembled his enduring idea of what constituted a book.

Moving as quickly as the slippery flooring would allow, Doyle made his way to the bedroom. As he opened the door it drooped in on itself, the top corner folding over like a dog-eared page. Doyle saw that the strange liquefaction had penetrated a few inches into the next room and then abruptly stopped: His bedroom had escaped the same debasement.

"Thank God," Doyle muttered.

Pulling his Gladstone bag from the closet, he dropped into it the invertebrate book, a change of clothes, his shaving kit, and the box of ammunition he kept hidden in the upper reaches of the armoire.

Back through the vulcanized room, Doyle stopped at the door—someone outside, the scuff of a shoe. He bent down to peer through the extruded keyhole and saw Petrovitch leaning against the balustrade, hands clutched to her scrawny bosom.

"Mrs. Petrovitch, what's happened here?" he asked, exiting to the hall.

"Doctor," she said, grasping his offered hand fearfully.

"Did you see anything? Did you hear something down here?"

Nodding vigorously. He couldn't recall the extent of her English, but it seemed at the moment particularly lean.

"Big. Big," she said. "Train."

"A sound like a train?"

Nodding again, she tried to supply the sound, accompanied by a series of generalized, extravagant gestures. She's been into the wine again, Doyle realized. Not without provocation. Glancing past her, he noticed another woman hanging back at the foot of the descending stairs. The second face he'd seen in the window: a short, stout woman, round face, penetrating eyes. Something familiar about her.

"Dear Mrs. Petrovitch, did . . . you . . . *see* . . . anything?"

Her eyes grew round and large, and she traced the outline of a huge shape with her hands.

"Big? *Very* big?" Doyle offered encouragingly. "A man, was it?"

She shook her head. "Black," she said simply. "Black."

"Mrs. Petrovitch. Go to your rooms. Stay there. Do not come down here again until morning. Do you understand?"

She nodded, then as he turned to go tugged on his sleeve and pointed to the woman behind her.

"My friend is—"

"I'll meet your friend another time. Do as I've told you, Mrs. Petrovitch, please," he said, gently removing her hand. "Now I really must go."

"No, Doctor . . . no, she—"

"Get some rest now. Have a nice glass of wine. There's a good Petrovitch. Good night now. Good night." The delivery of which carried him down the stairs and out of her sight.

✿   ✿   ✿

He kept to the busiest streets and to each street's busiest side, seeking the light, walking always toward the thick of the crowd. No one approached or accosted him. He met no one's gaze and still felt the burn of a thousand malevolent eyes.

Doyle spent what remained of the night at St. Bartholomew's Hospital, where he was known, only an hour of it sleeping on one of the cots set aside for working physicians, in a room surrounded by a dozen others, none of which afforded him the security of sanctuary. Displaying his bedrock rectitude, and perhaps more revealingly his fear of ridicule, he spoke to no one, not even his closest colleagues, of his trouble.

The light of day brought few sparse grains of salt to the previous night's adventures. There must be clear physical explanations for everything that occurred at the séance, Doyle told himself—I just haven't hit on them as yet—no, stop; even this is a deception I'm imposing on myself. The mind depends on equilibrium and will seek it at any cost. This doesn't mean I accept all of what Sacker told me as gospel, but the unvarnished truth is, I have passed through a doorway that has vanished behind me; therefore I cannot go back. Therefore I must go forward.

As he walked out into the cool morning air, he found his terror and disorientation receding, and what quickly came to the fore was fury at the brutal slaying of Lady Nicholson and her brother. Her face would not leave his mind; her beseeching eyes, the cry as she fell. She sought my help, and I failed her in life; I will not do so now, he vowed.

Despite Sacker's admonition, his first stop upon leaving the hospital that morning was Scotland Yard.

❋   ❋   ❋

An hour later, Doyle was standing outside 13 Cheshire Street with Inspector Claude Leboux. The thin, grimy sunlight brought no rehabilitative cheer to the place but only accentuated its glum neutrality.

"You say they went in here, then?" Leboux asked.

Doyle nodded. He had spared the details from his friend to this point. The word *murder* had been employed, judiciously but effectively. He had produced Lady Nicholson's note. No mention yet of spirits or gray hoods and blue thread. Or Professor Armond Sacker.

Leboux led the way up the steps and knocked. He was a solid Midlands ox of a man. A florid red handlebar mustache was the only decorative flourish he allowed himself, but its immaculately groomed and radiant plumage rendered any other such signatory moot.

Doyle had spent a year as ship's physician with Leboux onboard a navy cutter, sailing to Morocco and ports south, during which their unlikely friendship had gradually germinated. Leboux was Royal Navy, fifteen years older, rudimentarily educated, a man of sufficient reticence to have his intelligence routinely questioned by the sharpies on board. But as Doyle discovered over the course of many card games and desultory conversations in the bow's netting as they languished in tropical doldrums, Leboux's diffidence shielded a sensitive heart and a character of unwavering morality. His mind seldom strayed from the parallel tracks of fact and truth—he prided himself on his lack of imagination. Those tracks took him straight from the navy to the London police and up the ranks in short order to his present position of inspector.

A small, fair Irishwoman Doyle had not seen before opened the door.

" 'Elp you?"

"Scotland Yard, Miss. We'd like to have a look around."

"Wot's this about?"

Towering over her, Leboux leaned in and intoned, "Trouble, Miss."

"I don't live here, you know, I'm just visiting me Mum," she said, backing away as they entered. "She's upstairs, sick as a dog she is, ain't left the bed in weeks. This ain't to do with her, is it?"

"She's a tenant, your Mum?" Leboux asked.

"That's right—"

"Who lives down here, then?" Leboux asked, stopping at the right-hand door the weird boy had opened for Doyle the night before.

"Don't know. Some foreign bloke, I think. Not here much. Neither am I, to be fair, only since Mum took ill."

Doyle nodded to Leboux. "Foreign" was a fair enough description of the Dark Man, and Doyle had mentioned him to Leboux. Leboux knocked on the door.

"Know the name of this man, Miss?" he asked.

"No, sir, I surely don't."

"Were you here last night then?"

"No, sir. I was home. Down Cheapside."

The queer glass bowl was gone from the table, Doyle noted. The pattern of splattered wax indicated someone had taken that candle and moved quickly. Leboux opened the door, and they entered the parlor.

"This as it was, Arthur?" Leboux asked.

"Yes," Doyle replied. "The séance was through here."

Doyle opened the sliding doors. The room as revealed appeared entirely different from the one in which he'd spent those dreadful minutes. Cramped with dusty, fussy furniture. No round table or hanging tapestries. Even the ceiling seemed lower.

"This isn't right," Doyle said, as he moved deeper into the room.

"Somethin' happen to the fella who lives here, then?"

"You go on up and visit your Mum now. We'll call if we need you," Leboux said, closing the doors in the young woman's face.

"They've replaced the furniture. The room was nearly empty."

"Where was the violence done, Arthur?"

Doyle moved to the spot where the table had been sitting. A plump love seat now occupied the space where Lady Nicholson had fallen.

"Here," he said, kneeling down. "There was no rug; the floor was bare."

As he moved it aside, Doyle noticed the imprint of the love seat's leg in the rug was deep and encrusted with dust. Leboux lent him a hand lifting the love seat away, then together they rolled back the carpet. The underlying floorboards were unstained and shiny with wear.

"It's been cleaned, you see. The whole room, top to bottom. They've removed every trace," Doyle said, a bit frantic.

Leboux stood above him, stoic, noncommittal. Doyle bent to examine the floor more closely. He took a pipe-cleaning tool from his pocket and scraped at the joist between the slats: His efforts yielded a small portion of a dried dark matter. Doyle brushed the crumbs into an envelope and handed it to Leboux.

"I think you will find this substance is human blood. Lady Caroline Nicholson and her brother were murdered in this room last night. I recommend an immediate effort be made to alert their family."

Leboux pocketed the envelope, took out a pad and paper, and dutifully wrote down the names. They proceeded to conduct a more detailed examination of the room. Nothing discovered led them to further understanding of the crimes committed or the identity of owner or occupant. Following the path through the nest of corridors that had led Doyle and Sacker to the alley proved equally fruitless.

As they stood in the alley looking back at the house, Doyle sketched in the details of the murderous engagement. He made no mention of Sacker, or his use of the pistol Leboux himself had given him months before. Leboux crossed his arms, stock-still, betraying no sentiment suggesting the relative credulity of what he heard. A good while passed before he responded. Doyle was accustomed to waiting out his friend's epic silences: One could almost hear the tumblers of his mind clicking like slow hands on an abacus.

"You say this attack on the woman involved the use of a blade," was Leboux's first comment.

"Yes. A wicked-looking affair."

Leboux nodded, and then with some new sense of purpose in his eyes, said, "You'd better come with me then."

❋ ❋ ❋

They walked three blocks to the vacant lot at the corner of Commercial and Aldgate. Police had sequestered the area. Bobbies manned the corners, directing away passersby. Leboux led Doyle through the cordon to the center of the lot where, that previous night, just as Doyle was arriving back at his rooms, the short, sorry life of the streetwalker known as Fairy Fay had come to a brutal and malicious end.

The rough canvas serving as her shroud was lifted. She was unclothed. The body had been eviscerated and the organs removed. Some were missing; the rest were neatly arranged outside of the body, in a pattern the significance of which was impossible to divine. The job had been quick, precise, and, as Doyle surmised from the absence of ripping at the entry points and edges of the wounds, executed with furiously honed instruments.

Doyle nodded. The canvas fluttered back over the corpse. Leboux trudged a few paces away. Doyle followed. Another Lebouxian silence ensued.

"Would that be Lady Nicholson then, Arthur?" he finally asked.

"No."

"Was this woman at the séance last night?"

"No. I've never seen her before."

With shock, Doyle realized that Leboux was probing for some weakness in his story. A policeman first and foremost, Doyle reminded himself, and the mood among the officers was grim and tight. Few, if any, had ever been exposed to the fruits of an act this savage and willful, certainly never in the routine of London police work.

"No one's come forward?" he asked.

Leboux shook his head. "Prostitute most like. Now. Those blades you described, could they have done this work?"

"Yes. Very possibly."

Leboux blinked myopically. "Could you describe the assailants?"

"They wore hoods," Doyle said, neglecting to mention that both killers had themselves been dispatched. Given that unholy facial stitching and the lack of blood from the mortal wounds they'd received, he didn't feel Leboux was of a mind to consider the question, How do you kill something if it's already dead?

Leboux of course sensed that Doyle was withholding key parts of his story, but was mindful enough of their friendship, and sufficiently convinced that Doyle had been through an authentically dire experience, to allow him to part company at this point. Watching Doyle walk away, Leboux felt daunted by the number of complications left to sort out. But after all, as he invariably said whenever confronted with a task of such complexity, that's what time was for.

Upon first viewing the woman's loathsomely mutilated corpse, one of the troubling thoughts he was still contending with had been, This is the work of a doctor.

CHAPTER 6

Cambridge

THE FIRST PREREQUISITE of elaborate mental exercise was a full
stomach. Doyle hadn't eaten since his ordeal began the night before.
He walked into the first crowded tavern he happened across, sat by
the fire, and ordered a large breakfast, thankful that what little
money he'd left in his rooms hadn't fallen victim to the gelatinous
infestation.

Afterward he pushed back his plate, lit a pipe, put his feet up, and
felt the onset of that relaxed but heightened state of awareness wherein
his mind hummed at maximum efficiency.

If, as Sacker had suggested, there was a conspiracy behind these
events, it reasonably involved only a few individuals. Conspiracy requires secrecy. The greater number of people involved, human nature
being what it was, the less likely secrecy became. The extent to which
13 Cheshire had been sanitized in those few short hours surely supported conspiracy. How to keep the requisite subordinates in line?
Fear. Their ability to inspire it seemed beyond reproach. Black magicians? He was not personally acquainted with any, but that was no
guarantee their numbers weren't legion.

As to the manuscript . . . true, he'd contrived the villains' identities himself—and a fair piece of invention it was, too, if he did say so—but as to their actual objectives, means, motives, and so forth, the damnable truth was he'd more or less cribbed the "Dark Brotherhood" from Blavatsky. Which begged the question, if they were after him because of his book, how close to the truth of what they were up to had that lunatic Russian wandered? And if she had that much right, what credence did that lend to the rest of her harebrained works?

The séance. More problematic. Perhaps. The levitation: wires and pulleys. The mirror could have been done with, well, with mirrors. The head of the beast a puppet of some kind, perhaps concealed in the bundle he'd seen that boy carry into the building. Conclusion: There could be logical explanations for the effects he'd witnessed, albeit of a more ingenious and sophisticated order than he'd encountered before. . . .

Wait just a moment—here he was perambulating around this garden of unearthly delights like a vicar on holiday. The fact remained there were bloodless blind men with Oriental daggers stalking about London trying to carve him like a Christmas goose. He had seen these things: fat women floating on air, heart-stopping black shadows, red-eyed creatures in phantom looking glasses, that poor wretch lying back there in the weeds. The brother as he fell, already lifeless. Lady Nicholson's little boy, alone in that dark wood. The look on her face as the blade was drawn across. . . .

He shuddered, drew his coat more closely around his shoulders, and glanced around the room. No one was looking his way.

Yes, all right, I was already half in love with her, he admitted. Maybe they are after me, but what they've done to that poor woman and her family in springing the trap makes my blood boil, thought Doyle. They think they have me routed, on the run, well, revenge is a dish the Irish have been serving cold for countless generations. And whoever these godless devils might be, they are about to discover how severely they have underestimated this particular Irishman.

Sacker. The encounter in the cab, all the attendant shocks, there had hardly been time to summon a coherent question. Doyle took out Sacker's calling card. He needed to confront the man while he had his wits about him. Cambridge was less than two hours by train. Tim, their driver, told him Lady Nicholson's brother had been at university there, a possible connection. At last, an occasion to be grateful for his lack of success as a physician; there were no critically ill patients for whom his sudden absence would prove a hardship. He'd make for Liverpool Street Station, straightaway.

As he replaced the card in his bag, his eye caught the cover of the altered book. *Isis Unveiled.* He'd been in such a state he hadn't even noticed. He lifted it, shielding its deformity from the rest of the room. Blavatsky: an appropriate companion for the journey he had embarked upon. Her photograph was still discernible through the rippling layer of...

Good Christ. No, it couldn't be. He looked closer. Yes.

The woman he'd seen with Petrovitch on the stairs of his building last night. It was her: Helena Petrovna Blavatsky!

✲   ✲   ✲

The cab pulled up outside. He ran into the building.

"Mrs. Petrovitch!"

Dashing by his apartment, Doyle was told by a quick glance inside that nothing had changed since last night. He took the stairs three at a time to Petrovitch's floor and knocked vigorously on her door.

"It's Dr. Doyle, Mrs. Petrovitch!"

He noticed smoke seeping out from under the jamb.

"Mrs. Petrovitch!"

He threw a shoulder to the door, once, twice, stepped back, and with a heavy thrust kicked the door open.

Petrovitch lay on the floor, in the center of the room, unconscious. Smoke grew thick, but the room was not yet involved in flame; heavy brocaded curtains smoldered, lace curtains had already combusted.

Doyle ripped down the curtains, furiously beating back the fire so he could reach the fallen woman. He touched her and instantly knew she was dead. Redoubling his effort with the curtains, some anxious moments later he had the blaze dampened. Doyle closed the woman's eyes and sat down to try to reconstruct what had happened.

Petrovitch's dachshund wiggled out from under a sofa and nuzzled pathetically at its mistress's ear.

Doyle studied the room: An open decanter of wine stood on a table, the stopper beside it, next to an open tin of digitalis pills and some drops of candle wax. A small crystal goblet lay on the floor near the body; trailing away from it, in the rug, a crimson stain. The table from where the candle had fallen lay between her and the window. The window was open.

She'd lit a candle. Felt a chest pain—she had heart trouble; that much he knew. She poured a glass of wine, opened the pill tin. The pain grew stronger, alarmingly so. Feeling claustrophobic, she opened the window to let in some air, and in doing so toppled the candle.

Cambridge

When the curtains caught fire, she panicked. Her heart gave out. She fell.

Two objections. First, there was a fresh watermark on the table. The wineglass had been set down—it should have fallen toward the curtains, along with the candlestick. Second, there were a number of pills on the floor near the body. Even now, the little rat dog was gobbling one up off the rug. Perhaps she had dropped the tin and was in the process of replacing them when . . . no, there were no pills in her hand.

He examined the tin. Lint and other detritus were mixed in with the pellets themselves. So the pills had been spilled and then replaced—

At the sound of a whine and a cough, he turned in time to see Petrovitch's dog keel over, spasm, and then lie still. Dead—better off, in a way, thought Doyle: It wasn't a dog anyone else was likely to love—foam bubbling at the corner of its mouth. Poisoned.

So someone had poisoned Petrovitch and perhaps not surreptitiously. Doyle lifted her slightly; there were pills under the body as well. Livid bruises on either side of her jaw. She had struggled, knocking the tin away, scattering the pills. Her assailant forced the poison on her, then quickly tried to replace the pills in the tin before fleeing out the open window. Yes: There was a scuff mark on the windowsill. The candlestick knocked over during the struggle or perhaps more deliberately by the killer to obscure the deed. The body was still warm. The killer had left this room within the last ten minutes.

Another death to lay at his crowded doorstep. Poor Petrovitch. Impossible to imagine the woman could have herself inspired an enmity that would result in murder.

Careful not to touch the pills themselves, Doyle closed the tin and placed it in his bag and was at the door when he noticed a spot of white peeking out from behind a small mirror on the wall.

He pulled out a piece of paper and read:

> DOCTOR DOYLE,
> *Urgent we speak. I am off to Cambridge. Petrovitch*
> *will tell you where to meet me. Trust no one. Nothing*
> *is as it seems.*
>
> HPB

Dated that morning. Blavatsky in Cambridge. The killer had stilled Petrovitch but missed this note. He left Petrovitch to heaven, with no doubt now as to his own destination.

49

THE LIST OF 7

*   *   *

Doyle detected no one following him to the station, nor was he aware of anyone watching him purchase his ticket or board the train. After he took a corner seat with an unobstructed view of the door, no one entered the car who took even passing notice of him.

As the train chugged away, Doyle scanned a stack of discarded tabloids, searching vainly for mention of Lady Nicholson's disappearance. The engine's tail of exhaust folded indistinguishably into the city's morning mantle of soot and smoke. As he watched the street life flit by outside his window, Doyle's envy for the plain uneventfulness of those ordinary lives gave way to an edgy excitement. However fraught with danger, a mission beckoned, and mission signified purpose, the lodestone of his internal compass. In spite of fatigue, his senses felt sharply attuned: the sweet pungency of the sandwich he'd bought for the journey, the agreeably warm froth of the bottled beer, the ripe mundungus of Moorish tobacco in the air.

A bulky Indian woman took the seat opposite Doyle, her brown face obscured by a veil that revealed only her almond eyes and a daub of decorative scarlet on the forehead between them. An external representation of the mystical third eye, recalled Doyle from his Hindi dabbling, the window to the soul and the unfolding of the thousand-petaled lotus. He caught himself staring at her when the rustle as she rearranged the armful of parcels she carried brought him back to himself. He doffed his hat and smiled agreeably. The woman's response was inscrutable. High caste, he decided, assessing her clothes and comportment. He wondered idly why she wasn't traveling first-class, accompanied by family or chaperon.

The rhythmic rattle and roll of the tracks abetted the postprandial drowsiness of the alcohol, and as the train left the London environs, Doyle drifted toward sleep. He awoke sporadically, for moments at a time, and dimly remembered seeing his subcontinental traveling companion hunched over a small book, running her finger along lines of the page. Sleep finally overtook him. His dreams were hot and swift, a phantasmagoric amalgam of flight, pursuit, dark faces, and white light.

With the jolt of the car coming to a sudden stop, he awoke to full consciousness, aware of some commotion. Along with the rest of the car's occupants, the Indian woman was looking out the window to Doyle's left.

They were in farming country. A rough road ran alongside the tracks, bisecting a vast tract of fallow land, planted with a failing crop of winter corn. A large hay trailer pulled by two huge drays had over-turned in the ditch beside the road. One of the horses, an immense chestnut still tethered to the rig, bucked wildly, kicking at the air. The other, a dappled gray, lay on its back in a gully, struggling and braying, mortally injured. A young lad, the coach's driver, tried to approach the wounded animal but was restrained by two adult farm laborers. Looking farther down the road, Doyle saw what had perhaps been the cause of the accident.

Was it a scarecrow? No, although it bore the same basic silhouette, this was larger, much larger, than the conventional field figure, approaching nearly ten feet. Not made from straw—more molded and contoured. Wicker, perhaps. The figure mounted what appeared to be a cross—were those spikes—railroad spikes—pinning the arms to the wood? Yes, no mistaking, rising above the faltering corn rows just off the road, facing the tracks. It was a crucifix. And on its head was no crown of thorns. These were unmistakably horns, conical, sharp, and twisting. Doyle's mind flashed to the beast he had seen engraved on the glass bowl in the hallway of 13 Cheshire Street. This was, as near as he could remember, almost certainly the same image.

As awareness of the figure spread through the car, there was a rising sentiment among the passengers to put the torch to this blaspheming display, but before any reaction organized itself, the whistle sounded, and the brutish vision receded as the train pulled away. The last sight Doyle registered was one of the farmhands, over the protests of the boy, approaching the fallen horse with a shotgun.

The Indian woman, after a long look at Doyle, which she averted the moment his eyes met hers, resumed her reading. The remainder of the two-hour trip passed without incident.

❀   ❀   ❀

There was the poster—photograph included, if there were any fur-ther doubts—plastered to a pillar just outside the Cambridge rail station.

LECTURE TONIGHT. THEOSOPHICAL SOCIETY. H. P. BLAVATSKY. Eight P.M., the Guildhall near Market Place. Her whereabouts determined to the minute and location with four hours to spare, Doyle set out for King's College and the offices of Professor Armond Sacker.

The afternoon's sallow light was just beginning to fail. Doyle followed the road alongside the fens hard by the River Cam and down King's Parade into the old town center, raising his muffler against the brisk wind blowing down across the broad, open byway. Charles Darwin walked these paths as a student. Newton as well. Byron, Milton, Tennyson, and Coleridge. The hallowed colleges reminded him of his youthful disappointment when his family's modest circumstances required his attending the less financially rigorous University of Edinburgh. The deleterious effects produced by coming of age in the class system still resonated ripples of discomfort in his proud heart.

Across the commons from St. Mary's Church stood the great classical facade of King's College. Doyle passed through its gingerbread gatehouse and screen and found the court within entirely deserted with darkness quickly coming on.

Entering the only building to display a light, he heard a scuffling sound, and a wheezy snort that drew him to the entrance of a long library. A wizened clerk shuffled piles of books in a seemingly aimless pattern between the stacks and a mammoth wheeled cart. His face was mean, red and puckered, while his vulpine black robes and ill-fitting wig threatened to engulf the shrunken man entirely.

"Pardon me, I'm wondering if you could direct me to Professor Sacker."

The Clerk snorted again, taking no notice of him.

"Professor Armond Sacker. Antiquities," said Doyle, raising his voice considerably. "Mostly Egyptian. Some Greek—"

"Lord God, man!" The Clerk caught sight of him from the corner of his eye and lurched back against the cart, clutching his chest in fright.

"Terribly sorry. Didn't mean to startle you—"

"There's a bell!" the Clerk yelled. "You're supposed to ring the bell!" He attempted to regain his footing by leaning back against the cart, but his insubstantial mass was enough to motivate the wheels ever so slightly backward. Consequently, man and cart began crabbing slowly away from Doyle down the lengthy library corridor.

"I'm sorry, but I didn't see a bell," Doyle said.

"That's what's wrong with you boys today! Used to be students had respect for authority!"

Mortal fear of corporal punishment will do that to a body, Doyle was tempted to reply. Nudging the cart feebly ahead, the Clerk continued to retreat, not quite able to gain leverage to right himself, while Doyle kept pace equidistant behind.

"Perhaps if you displayed the bell in a more obviously visible location," Doyle offered pleasantly.

Cambridge

"There's a smart answer," the Clerk spat viciously. "When school's in session, I'll have you vetted to the Proctor's Office."

"You have it wrong there, you see, I am not a student."

"And so you admit you have no legitimate business here!"

The Clerk raised a long, bony finger in misguided triumph. From his squinting, Doyle realized the unpleasant little man was nearly as blind as he was deaf. And unless he was very much mistaken, this venomous old bookworm was a retired proctor himself; in his day Doyle had suffered plenty at the gleefully sadistic hands of the man's ilk.

"I am looking for the office of Professor Armond Sacker," Doyle said, producing Sacker's calling card—they had by now traveled twenty yards down the hall, and Doyle felt no impulse whatsoever to assist the toadish misanthrope back to his feet—holding it just out of the sweeping arc of the man's reach, "and I can assure you, sir, my business with him is exceptionally legitimate."

"What sort of *business*?"

"Business I am not prepared to discuss with you, sir. Business of a more than passing urgency. And I daresay that if you are not prepared to assist me straight off, it will put me in a very foul humor indeed," Doyle said, pointing his walking stick at the man and smiling intently.

"Term's over. He's not here," the Clerk admitted, fear or exhaustion tilting him toward the cooperative.

"Now we're getting somewhere. So there is, in fact, a Professor Armond Sacker."

"You're the one who wants to see him!"

"And having established that the good Professor walks among us, if we could now turn our attention to where the Professor might be—"

"I'm sure I don't know—"

"Take careful note, if you would, my choice of words, sir: 'might be,' not 'is,' employing the speculative, as in speculation, sir: Where *might he be*?"

With a jolt, the cart collided with the wall at the corridor's end. The Clerk slid down to the floor, legs splayed, back against the cart, his pinched visage as pink as a well-scrubbed pig. He pointed up and to the right at a nearby door.

"Ah," said Doyle. "The Professor's office?"

The Clerk nodded.

"You've been most helpful. If I should happen to speak with your superiors during my visit here, I shall not fail to mention your timely and generous assistance."

"Pleasure, sir. Pleasure indeed." The Clerk's treacly smile revealed a badly matched set of false choppers.

Doyle tipped his hat and entered Sacker's door, closing it after him. The room was high, square, and lined with dark-wooded bookshelves, serviced by a ladder resting against one wall. Crowding the central desk were stacks of haphazardly open volumes, maps, compasses, calipers, and other cartographic tools.

The smoldering dregs of a bowl of tobacco sent up weak mist from an ashtray. The pipe, an elaborately carved meerschaum, was warm to the touch—the office's occupant had vacated the room, at most, five minutes before, a departure hastened by Doyle's voice in the hall? This Sacker was nothing if not an odd fellow, but would he purposefully avoid Doyle after what they'd been through together? If so, for what conceivable reason?

Surveying the desk, Doyle cataloged two standard texts on ancient Greece, a volume of Euripides, a monograph on Sappho, and a well-worn *Iliad.* Maps of the central Turkish coast, dotted and lined with calculations. Doyle hazarded a guess that the object of this quest was the legendary city of Troy.

An overcoat and hat hung on a rack by the far door. A walking stick leaned against the wall; a bit short for the lanky Sacker, Doyle thought. He opened the far door, which led to a small antechamber—no doubt where students sweated out their tutorials—and then passed through another door, leading into a vast hallway.

Perched on the newel posts on either side of a grand ascending staircase, large winged gargoyles stood sentry, scowling at one another: one a griffin, long of tooth and talon, the other a reptilian basilisk, scabrous and scaled. The day's last light through the leaded-glass windows imparted a ghostly glow to the marble walls and floors. Total darkness was only minutes away and, saving a penny during the holiday, none of the gas jets were alight. Doyle listened but heard no footfalls.

"Professor Sacker! . . . Professor Sacker!"

No reply. A chill ran through him. He turned around. The gargoyles glared down at him from their posts in the stairwell. Doyle set off to find a privy—had those statues been facing his way when he entered? A memory of their having faced each other persisted—perhaps Sacker had gone to answer nature's call.

He found every door along the hallway locked. Turning repeatedly as the corridor meandered, by the time Doyle realized he could no longer see his hand before him, he was not at all sure where he was.

Cambridge

The air felt as frigid and heavy as the blackness was dense. He wiped the sweat from his hands. Fear of the dark was not something he commonly fell prey to, but after the last two days all such presumptions were forfeit. Attempting to retrace his steps—there had been lights burning in Sacker's office, a place that now seemed a haven of warmth and security—he kept one hand on the cool marble wall and took each step cautiously.

An intersection. *Did I turn right or left here?* His answer was not confident. Right then.

Fear of the dark is a primitive, instinctual leftover, he reminded himself: Our remote forebears spent the better part of their lives groping blindly in the dark—and since there could be huge, carnivorous predators lying in ambush around every turn, it seemed altogether a very sensible response—but that by no measure meant the same dangers still existed in the modern civilized— What was that?

Doyle stopped. A sound, some distance away. What was it? Stay calm. It could be help, a neutral or friendly presence. Even Sacker himself. *Perhaps we'll hear it again. Perhaps it would be a fine idea if we didn't move from this spot until we do. Err on the side of caution, and not only because we're plunged into absolute darkness in an unfathomable maze and there are pitiless, unspeakable horrors tracking us from who knows which side of the etheric membrane—*

Wait . . . there it was again.

Try to identify. Not a footstep, was it? No. No smack of heel, no shuffling skid or impact on marble whatsoever.

Go on, Doyle, you know perfectly well what you heard.

Wings. A flap of wings. Leathery, cartilaginous.

Well, perhaps a sparrow or pigeon's flown through a window and gotten lost in the halls—let's be honest, shall we? Late December, even if birds were still about, that was not the exercising of a small or even midsized wingspan, if there exists anywhere in the world a bird that could produce that sound, that could displace that much air—

It's coming this way. Those first two flaps issued from a stationary position, loosening, limbering up, almost as if the— Doyle, put your mind in order, man: Allow into your head the idea that those stone gargoyles on the stairs can fly, and in two ticks you'll find yourself chained to a pallet in Bedlam.

On the other hand, something immense is moving through the air and coming closer, so from a purely precautionary standpoint, let's move on. Don't run, Doyle, use your walking stick ahead of you, like that—quietly, please—find a door, there's a good fellow, any door will do—got one: locked. Damn. On to the next.

Rummaging for bird facts—do they see well in the dark? Depends on the bird, doesn't it? How's their sense of smell? Do they have one? They must: Their entire lives constitute an uninterrupted search for food. Terrifically reassuring. What have we squirreled away in there about the eating habits of gargoyles?

It's not possible, but the wings seem to be advancing and receding simultaneously. Unless there are two of them; one on either side of the stairs for a grand total of—enough!

A door, Doyle, and please hurry, because one of them just rounded the corner we recently turned, which puts it fifty feet behind us and closing rapidly—

There: Grip the handle and turn and push and enter and close the door behind you. Can you lock the door? No bolt. Can you recall any avian facts that would support the possibility of a bird turning a doorknob? Be serious. Is there a window in this door? Solid oak. Blessed old, thick old door, God save the English craftsman—

You heard that, didn't you? A settling of weight, a soft scratching on the marble floor. What goes with wings? Talons. And if talons were raked across this good old solid oak door, they would undoubtedly produce something remarkably similar to the sound we're hearing now.

Time to see what kind of room we're in, and more essentially, what other exits it offers. Reach in the pocket, find the matches, move away from the door, and strike a— Good Christ!

Doyle dropped the match and recoiled to ward off a blow that never arrived. This surprised him, because what he'd seen in the split second as the match ignited, bearing down on him at an imposing angle, was the face of a ghoul, hideously denuded of skin, yellowed teeth bared in a militant grimace. He waited. Surely, he'd be feeling its foul breath on his face. Hands shaking, he lit another match.

A mummy. Upright, in its sarcophagus. Beside it, on display, a coiled staff of Ra. Maneuvering the match to reveal more of his surroundings, Doyle realized he'd stumbled into a room of Egyptologiana. Amphora, jewelry, preserved cats, gold-inlaid daggers, hieroglyphed slate: Egypt and its detritus were all the rage these days, no world tour complete without an excursion to the Pyramids at—

Boom! Banging on the door. *Boom!* The hinges groaned painfully. Thanks to his panicked exclamation, whatever was out there knew he was inside—

Cambridge

The match burned his finger. He dropped it and lit another, looking for a—please God—yes, there, a window. He moved to it as quickly as keeping the match alive would allow, fixed the position of the latch lock, discarded the match, grabbed the latch, turned—the pounding on the door insistent, massive bulk heaving itself against splintering wood—and the window flew open. Doyle looked down at an uncertain drop, no time to hesitate, tossed out his bag and stick and followed them, absorbing the shock of the fall with his knees, tucking and rolling, scooping up bag and stick and sprinting away from the Tomb of Antiquities.

✿   ✿   ✿

He stopped to catch his breath under the vaulted exterior arch of St. Mary's Church. He waited ten minutes in the shadows for the dreadful flapping to emerge from the darkness, for some vile avenging shadow to blot out the stars and streak down at him out of the sky. As his breathing steadied, the sweat that had soaked his shirt cooled, leaving him cold and shivery. Lights burned invitingly in the nave. He moved inside.

What had he escaped from? In the warm, sane light of the church, the question turned on him; had his imagination transformed perfectly ordinary circumstances—say, an overzealous night watchman whose corduroy pants produced an insistent hissing—into a wallow of self-generated terror? He had studied how the strain of combat could induce in soldiers all manner of hallucinatory mental phenomena. Was he not now laboring under an even more insidious strain, in that his antagonists were unknown to him and could be, as Sacker had suggested, any passing stranger in the street? Perhaps this was their preferred method of assault, driving their victims mad with a constant, noncorporeal menace more sensed than seen. Show a man a target he can strike back against, and you lend him a footing. Attack him with inexplicable night sounds, will-o'-the wisps, macabre scarecrows by the sides of train tracks, incite the stuff of his own nightmares, and the suggestive vagueness of it alone could send him reeling into lunacy.

Standing at one of the transept chapels, Doyle entertained an impulse to light a candle in appeal to some conventional higher power of good, for guidance or aid. GOD IS LIGHT AND IN HIM IS NO DARKNESS AT ALL, read the inscription.

There was a lit taper in his hand; he'd caught himself nearly in the act. *Curious: I'm standing square in the fulcrum of man's eternal*

57

dialectic between faith and fear; are we beings of light, gods waiting to be born, or pawns in a struggle of higher forces vying for control of a world beneath their separate, unseen realms? Unable to commit himself to either side of that argument, Doyle extinguished the taper without lighting a candle.

With returning to see if Sacker had returned to his office an option of exceptionally limited appeal, the prospect of food and drink presented the preferred alternative; feed the body, quiet the mind. Then a visit to an individual uniquely qualified to lead him out of this metaphysical mire was in order: HPB.

CHAPTER 7

HPB

ONE FULL STOMACH and two hours later, Doyle was sitting amid a modest gathering of Transcendentalists at the local Grange Hall listening to H. P. Blavatsky hold forth from center stage. No lectern, no notes, she spoke extemporaneously, and even if the essential content and continuity of the lecture proved elusive in retrospect, the effect was undeniably mesmerizing.

"—there has never been a religious leader of any stature or importance who *invented* a new religion. New forms, new interpretations, yes, these they have given us, but the truths upon which these revelations were based are older than mankind. These prophets, by their own admission, were never originators. The word they preferred was *transmitters*. They never, any of them, from Confucius to Zoroaster, Jesus to Mohammed, they never said, These things I have created. What they said was, invariably, These things I receive and pass on. And so it is today."

As her passion mounted, her eyes flashed liked sapphires. Blavatsky's round, diminutive figure assumed protean dimensions, while her heavily accented English, broken and tentative to start with, flowed in a grammatically impeccable silver stream.

THE LIST OF 7

"There exists in the world today sacred wisdom which dwarfs our puny notions of history; I am speaking of books of ancient origin, vast depositories of them, hidden for centuries from the Western eye; the Northern Buddhists of Tibet alone possess three hundred and twenty-five volumes, fifty to sixty times the amount of information contained in the so-called Bible, recounting two hundred thousand years of human history. Let me repeat that: two hundred thousand years of recorded human history. 'But that's pre-Christian! What an assertion! She must be insane! She must be silenced!' I can hear the venerable Archbishop crying out all the way from Canterbury."

She cocked a hand to her ear, the comic effect of which did not elude her audience. Doyle glanced around the room and noticed that the Indian woman who had ridden up with him on the train was sitting one row over, smiling at HPB and nodding approvingly.

"What was the most devastating act the Christians took against their precedents? How did they begin their fanatical and systematic erad- ication of the Ancient Knowledge? Answer? The Gregorian calendar. So simple: Year One. Time *begins* with the birth of the Nazarene prophet—oh there were some mildly significant events before this, but the years run backward, you see, away from this Supreme Moment, into the void of insignificance. We men of the True Church, we'll decide when time begins. And so with one stroke prove definitively that the writing implement *is* mightier than the saber.

"Do you see how damaging, how trivializing this decision is to all the history that preceded it? How this one act, born not of the tra- ditional Christian pieties, but from the *fear* of unwelcome truths— that is, truths contradictory to the best interests of those currently in power—cuts human progress off from the most powerful spiritual resources it has or will ever have available to it."

Bold talk in a Christian country. Doyle had to admire the woman's verve and evident common sense. This was no fuzzy-headed mystic with her head in cloud-cuckoo-land.

"You have to grant them this. These early Christians. They were tenacious. Did their work well. They scoured the world for these Ancient Doctrines, and they obliterated them, almost entirely, in the Western world. The library at Alexandria, the last great archive whose contents straddled the pre- and post-Christian worlds, burned to the ground. Do you suppose this act of willful spiritual vandalism was an accident?

"This is why our travels, our work as Theosophists, must always take us to the East. That is where the knowledge is. From where it has always emanated forth. Fortunately, the Adepts of the East had the sound historical sense to conceal their sources from these Western marauders, Holy Crusaders intent on their own parochial destiny, oblivious to the true concern of man: human spiritual evolution. And so you ask yourself, why has this knowledge of the Secret Science remained hidden from the Western masses? Would it not be in the best interests of these alleged Enlightened Ones to share their secrets with the emerging civilizations? Let me ask you this: Would you give a candle to a child in a roomful of gunpowder? These truths have been passed down by spiritual leaders, from generation to generation, since time began. They remain secret because contained within are the keys to understanding the essential mysteries of life. Because they are Power! And woe betide us all if they should ever fall into the wrong hands."

Her eyes rested on Doyle for the first time, then moved on.

"So this is our lot; even as we labor endlessly to bring these truths, in their reduced, acceptable form, before the court of public opinion, we should not delude ourselves that our efforts will be welcomed in our lifetimes. Quite the contrary. We must expect to be rejected, attacked, ridiculed. No scholar or scientist will be permitted to regard our efforts with any degree of seriousness. It is simply our job to open the door, if only this much." She held up two slightly parted fingers. "It will fall to each generation of fellow explorers who succeed us to open that door a little wider."

Now she seemed to turn her attention directly to Doyle. He felt the force of her eyes as she held him benignly in her gaze.

"How is this to be done? you ask. Imagine you are a tourist, and you are traveling in a country that is very well known to you, a country in which you have spent your entire existence. You are familiar intimately with its roads, rivers, cities, people, and customs. It represents the sum of all you know, and so you therefore, quite naturally, assume it represents the sum of all that is. Imagine then that while upon your travels, you have quite unexpectedly arrived at the border of another land. A land not identified anywhere on your most impressive collections of maps. This country is ringed, on every side, by insurmountable mountain ranges, so you are unable to see down into this strange land from your position. But you are determined to go there. You are enthusiastic. You have courage. You have, for lack of a better word, a certain faith. What must you do?"

Scale the mountain, Doyle thought. Blavatsky nodded.

"And remember," she said, "when the path appears impassable, when your prospects are ruined, when even death seems imminent, you will have no other choice but to destroy the mountain. In this way, and this way only, will you enter the New Country."

With this perplexity, her presentation was at an end. Applause was brief and polite. Blavatsky bowed slightly, a slight smile not without irony on her lips, which seemed to Doyle to say, You are not applauding me, because these are not truly my words, but I acknowledge the divinity and comedy of our collective spiritual-physical paradoxical condition and commend you for your recognition of it.

Most of the crowd drifted out, satisfied with their evening, some smugly dismissive, others self-congratulatory on the subject of their own open-mindedness, a few stimulated to greater thought that would result in soul-searching to last the better part of the evening, or even, for one or two, into the next day, before the blanket of routine muffled that restless stirring back down to the parade of days.

Knowing he must speak with the woman, Doyle lingered on the edge of the circle of acolytes who pressed in around her, hungry for more direct experience of the truths she was peddling. An assistant— Doyle presumed he was an assistant by his habitually clerical nature— male, early twenties, set up a table of HPB's books nearby, offering the volumes Doyle was already familiar with at extremely reasonable prices.

The questions she fielded were earnest, if predictable, and she answered with wit and a brevity that bordered on the discourteous. She was clearly not one of these charismatics Doyle had occasionally come across, whose express objective was to inspire a dependency, emotional and inevitably financial, among their faithful. She was, if anything, impatient with her standing as a figure of social curiosity and emphatically disinterested in the glamorous, self-aggrandizing aspects of the teacher-student dynamic. This is her gift, Doyle thought. She stirs the pot. What the individual does with the information from there was not her responsibility. Sensible and pragmatic and not a little appealing.

"What do you have to say about the various religions?"

"Nothing. There is no religion higher than truth."

"Why do you think elders in other religions are afraid of what you are saying?"

"Bigotry and materialism."

"Are you saying Jesus was not the Son of God?"

"No. We are all sons and daughters of God."

"But are you saying he wasn't divine?"

"Quite the contrary. Next question."

HPB

"What about the Freemasons?"

"Whenever anyone asks about the Freemasons, I must say good night. Read my books, and to the greatest extent that you can manage, remain awake. Thank you."

With that, she withdrew through a door at the side of the stage, and the remainder of the crowd dispersed. A short, nattily dressed woman with a monocle and walking stick appeared at Doyle's side.

"Dr. Doyle?"

"Yes."

"My name is Dion Fortune. HPB would like to speak with you. Would you come this way please?"

Doyle nodded and followed. The woman's name was familiar; she was a founding member of the London branch of the Theosophical Society and an author of some note in the esoteric world. Doyle noticed the Indian woman lingering at the book table as Fortune led him through the door.

❊ ❊ ❊

Her handshake was firm and cool. She looked him right in the eye with concern and warm support.

"I am most pleased to meet you, Dr. Doyle."

Having vouchsafed the initial introductions, Dion Fortune took a seat by the door. They were in a cramped dressing room next to a rumbling furnace. A spacious, well-traveled satchel stood open on a table—HPB's only luggage; her possessions and appointments were as utilitarian and utterly lacking in ostentation as her wardrobe.

Doyle returned the salutation, knowing he would feel remiss without telling her immediately of the events in London.

"Petrovitch is dead," he said.

Her features hardened. She asked immediately for exhaustive, specific details. He recounted the tale exactingly, as well as his conclusions, finally producing the tin of poison tablets from his bag. Blavatsky examined them, sniffed them, nodded.

"Would you like to drink with me?" she asked. "I recommend something stiff."

She pulled a bottle from her bag. Fortune produced some glasses.

"Vodka," she said, offering him the first glass.

"I thought spiritual teaching argued against the use of hard liquor," Doyle said lightly.

"Most spiritual teaching is hogwash. We must still move through the world as the personality into which we were born. I am a Russian peasant woman, and vodka has a most agreeable effect upon me. *Na zdorovia.*"

She downed the drink and poured another. Doyle sipped. Fortune abstained. Blavatsky dropped into a chair, slung a leg over one of the arms, and lit a cigar.

"There is more you would like to tell me, yes?"

Doyle nodded. He was grateful for the vodka, as it seemed to elicit a smoother recitation of his story. She stopped him only once, to ask for a more detailed description of the wounds and external arrangement of the organs of the fallen prostitute.

"Would you be kind enough to sketch them for me as close to memory as possible?"

Fortune handed him pen and paper, and Doyle complied, handing Blavatsky the result. She studied the drawing, grunted once, then folded the paper and dropped it in her bag.

"Please continue," she said.

He guided her through the trip to Cambridge, his near encounter with God-knows-what in the Antiquities Building, and then showed her the altered book from his rooms.

"What could have caused such a thing?" he asked.

"Ectoplasmic detonation. An entity breaking through from the other side. This is what Petrovitch summoned me to see. Very bad. Of course, at the time I assumed they were after Petrovitch—perhaps they were, secondarily. Be thankful you weren't home at the time. Go on, Doctor."

Doyle's mind spun. "Madame Blavatsky, what can you tell me about the Dark Brotherhood?"

The question prompted a veiled exchange of looks between HPB and Fortune that he was unable to interpret.

"Evil beings. Materialists. Enemies of holy spirit. You should read my work on the subject—"

"I *have* read your work on the subject, Madame." Only too well, thought Doyle. "I need to know if you believe these beings are real."

She knocked on the table. "Is table real? Is glass real?"

"It appears that they are, yes."

"You have your answer then."

"But are these beings people—I mean, are they in human form, or do they just swim indiscriminately around in the ether?"

"They are spirits who desire human form. They *hunger,* hovering around it, seeking entry."

"For which, as you write, they require the cooperation of the living."

"Cooperation and sacrifice, yes. They must be invited onto this plane through the enactment of rituals and so forth," she said, somewhat disinterestedly. "Describe for me if you would this Professor Armond Sacker."

"Tall, rangy. Midthirties. Prominent nose, high, intelligent brow, light eyes. Long fingers. Athletic."

This prompted another look between his hosts.

"Is something wrong?" Doyle asked.

"As it happens, I'm to have supper with Professor Sacker this very evening," she replied.

"But you know him then," Doyle replied excitedly.

"For many years."

"You know him well."

"Very well indeed. That will be his step arriving outside our door even now."

There were in fact footsteps outside the door, two sets, and then a knock. Fortune opened the door, revealing the young book clerk.

"Professor Sacker to see you, Madame," said the clerk.

"Show him in," she replied.

Doyle rose. The clerk moved away from the door, and Professor Sacker entered. HPB greeted him warmly with a kiss to either cheek.

"How good to see you again," she said.

"And you, my dear, and you," Sacker replied loudly.

Fortune welcomed Sacker familiarly as well and then presented him to Doyle, and Doyle shook the infirm hand of the stooped, diminutive, white-haired eighty-two-year-old man before him.

"Sorry, what was the name again?" asked Sacker.

"Doyle."

"Boyle?" He was nearly shouting.

"Doyle, sir. Arthur Doyle."

"Fine. Will you be joining us for supper then, Oyle?"

"I don't honestly—I don't know, sir!"

"Professor, please go ahead to the restaurant with Mrs. Fortune. I will be along to join you momentarily," Blavatsky said, making herself understood by the old man without raising her voice. She signaled Fortune, who smoothly guided Sacker out of the room.

Blavatsky turned back to Doyle, reading the shock on his face.

"Listen carefully, Doctor," she said. "I am leaving early in the morning for Liverpool and from there in two days' time sailing to America. You must try to remember everything I tell you, which as you have ably demonstrated will not be difficult for you."

"I'll try. If I could ask—"

She held up a hand to silence him. "Please do not ask questions. They will only serve to irritate me. There is a great urgency in you, and I do not doubt what you have told me, but this is a most dangerous time for many initiates in many places, and my presence is promised elsewhere. I do not expect you to understand. Please accept that what I have to tell you will be of some use to you and move forward."

"If I have no other choice."

"Good. Optimism is good. Common sense is good." She put out her cigar. "As mystics are to the occult, there are individuals known as sorcerers to *Magick*. *Magick* is the Left-Handed Path to Knowledge; it is the shortest way to the Enlightenment we all seek. It has a higher cost. It seems to me that what the man who presented himself to you as Professor Sacker has told you was correct in many details: You *have* been made a target by a group traveling the Left-Handed Path."

"Who are they?"

"This is unknown—"

"The Dark Brotherhood?"

"There are many names for that loose confederation of souls. Their hand is visible behind the sinister actions of countless factions around the world; do not mistake them for some benevolent protective order of lodge brothers. They are our counterparts in exploring what lies beyond, but their sole ambition is material power. They are exceedingly malicious and more than capable of ending your life, as they have done to my dear friend Petrovitch, who was, by the way, a highly advanced Adept who had been watching your progress with interest for some time—"

"My progress?"

She stilled him again and fixed him with her hypnotic gaze, which flared again with the persuasive power she had evidenced earlier onstage.

"You must not waver in your determination. It is your strongest asset. You must not fear, for that will let them in. Regarding all of these phenomena you have described, some of which I must admit are new to me—the blue thread, the strange state of your rooms, and so on—you must remember this: All of these manifestations they create mean absolutely nothing."

"Is that true?"

"Not really, but I strongly advise you to adopt this attitude at once, or things will not go well for you. By the way, may I have this copy of my book? I should like to study it. They appear to have penetrated the skin and altered its molecular structure. If this is true, it is not good."

He handed her the book, gulping back the impulse to ask her *why?*

She studied the book for a moment before placing it in her satchel and turning to him for another long look.

"When things appear darkest, you have friends unknown or unseen—"

"Professor Sacker—"

"The Professor Sacker you have met tonight is a scholar of ancient Mystery Cults. He is a sympathetic colleague of ours, an academic with no direct knowledge of your lamentable situation. The fact that the man who contacted you used his name is of great significance, which I encourage you to investigate."

"What should I do?"

"What should you do? That is a most excellent question," she said seriously. "What do you think you should do?"

Doyle thought for a moment.

"I think I should visit Lady Nicholson's estate. Topping."

"A sound idea. You are in the grip of a most interesting dilemma, Doctor. I sincerely hope our paths may cross again someday. Do you have copies of all my books?"

"As a matter of fact, they were lost in the—"

"Please see the boy outside. He will provide you with new editions at absolutely no cost. I trust they may prove useful to you."

She turned away and began packing her satchel. Doyle suddenly remembered the talisman sitting in his pocket.

"Excuse me, Madame . . . but what do you make of this?" and he showed her the metallic eye Sacker's impostor had given him. She took it from him, looked it over, tried to bend it, then bit down on it. It bore no marks, which drew a nod of approval.

"This is very good. If I were you, I would wear it around my neck."

She handed it back and closed up her satchel.

"But what does it mean?"

"It is a symbol."

"A symbol of what?" he asked, somewhat exasperated.

"It would take too long to explain. I must go now. I would invite you to supper, but I don't wish to unduly alarm the Professor. His health is frail, and we need him to finish his work before he passes on, as he is scheduled to do so later in the year."

"Scheduled?"

"Come, come, Doctor. There is more on heaven and earth and so on. Shakespeare was an extremely advanced Adept. I trust you've read him extensively."

"Yes."

"Ah, the English educational system. Give us a kiss. A blessing on your head, Doctor Doyle. *Do svidan'ya.*"

A swirl of her cloak and she was out the door. Doyle's head swam. He spotted a large book on the floor beside her satchel, picked it up, and followed her.

She was nowhere to be seen. Nor was the young clerk. A short stack of her other works had been left behind on the table in the empty Grange Hall. He looked at the cover of the larger book in his hand.

Psychic Self-Defense, by H. P. Blavatsky.

CHAPTER 8

Jack Sparks

Now I'M REALLY on the griddle, Doyle thought: Blavatsky confirms that assassins are indeed on my trail—cold comfort there—and no practical help forthcoming from her, since she's clearly more interested in pursuing her own mysteriously imperative agenda. Who would have thought that after all this danger, one would place so low in her hierarchy of spiritual distress?

But then what did I expect, really, that she'd drop everything and rally to my defense? And if she had, what help could she actually have given? A middle-aged gunnysack of a woman with common personal habits and a cadre of effete, intellectual bookworms? I don't envy the poor buggers she's bustling off to rescue in my stead, I can tell you that. A stern talking-to and a bottle of vodka aren't what's in order here, no sir: What I need's a heavily armed squadron of steely dragoons standing picket, sabers at the ready, ready to lay down their lives.

He was walking again through the commons toward King's Parade.

My flat ruined, Petrovitch murdered—what will Leboux make of that when the body turns up?—prostitutes carved up in the street like a dog's breakfast, a child kidnapped, his mother killed before my eyes as sorcerers lure me into ambush, rescued by impostors, misdirected into a wild-goose chase where I'm nearly meat for some stone Gothic basilisk. I never did like Cambridge, breeding ground for ruling-class contempt, perpetuating the whole rotten system—easy, Doyle: Let's not drag in the whole litany of a lifetime's social complaints. One calamity at a time, old man.

First things first: lodging for the night. Not much money left. No one to contact for help: Blavatsky had been his best hope in that department. Her damned books felt like an anchor in his bag. The vanity of the woman; ask for help, she weighs you down with her collected works and flees the country.

He had a plan, after all: Topping. Now what does one say to the husband? "Delighted to meet you Lord Nicholson— Yes, most unusual weather for this time of year, your forsythia are thriving beyond all reasonable expectation. By the way, were you aware that your wife, Caroline, and her brother had their throats cut and brains bashed out in a squalid London tenement just the other day? No? Yes, sorry to say; I happened to be in the room at the time—"

All right, there was time enough to consider what his approach should be before he got there. The task at hand was getting through the night ahead of him alive.

An inn. Good. That's a start.

❉   ❉   ❉

Doyle decided not to leave his bag in the room, although he felt secure enough to leave his coat on the bed. He took a seat by the fire in the public room and kept the bag in contact with his leg at all times. A half-dozen other patrons occupied the cozy snuggery: two elderly, donnish-looking men, a young married couple, and two solitary travelers, neither of whom in mien or aspect appeared to pose any threat.

Doyle nursed a hot buttered rum and studied the metallic eye. He considered Blavatsky's advice—perhaps I should make an amulet, what harm could come from it? Something caught his eye: the Indian woman again, ascending the stairs. Staying the night, apparently. Came up for the lecture. Probably returning to London tomorrow.

The false Sacker came back into his mind. He had presented himself as friend and rescuer but if that was truly the case, why give a false name? Why that particular one? Couldn't he just as easily be in league with the villains, insinuating himself into Doyle's confidence for some more sinister purpose? For all Doyle knew, during their carriage ride he might have been cheek by jowl with the Grand Master of the Brotherhood.

Jack Sparks

The wind came up and rattled branches against the window. A gust kicked up the fire, shaking Doyle out of his reverie. The mug was empty in his hand. He heard horses nickering uneasily outside. He discovered with some surprise he was alone in the room. How much time had passed? Eleven-thirty. He'd been sitting there for nearly an hour.

With a howl of wind, the front door flew open, gaslight guttered in the rush of air, the room darkened, and in strode a towering figure in black, face obscured by a high-collared cloak and tricornered hat. The man banged impatiently on the desk and looked around. Doyle obeyed an impulse to pull back behind the chair and avoid the intruder's eye, although it denied him a view of the man's face. Doyle chanced another look in time to see the proprietor scurry out from a back room: The smile instantly vanished from the innkeeper's face. Although Doyle could not discern what the stranger was saying, the fulminating, gut-tural intent of his tone was unmistakably menacing.

Picking up his bag, Doyle discreetly made his way to the back stair, making certain the man at the desk did not see him. As he ascended, the only distinct words he heard were the intruder's specific request to view the register, and he knew intuitively that the man was looking for him.

"Right. Retrieve my coat from the room, and I'll be on my way," he murmured to himself as he moved down the hallway and fumbled the key into the lock. Take some small comfort, Doyle; if they've come for you again, at least this time it's in recognizably human form.

He entered and saw that the window on the far wall was flapping open, the rain that was just starting to fall splashing in over the sill. He moved to close it, and as he reached outside for the latch, the sight on the street below sent a chill crackling to the base of his spine.

Standing at the inn's entrance was the same pitch-black carriage they'd seen on the night of the séance. A figure in a black-cowled cape held the reins of the four black stallions. Doyle pulled the window in toward him, the figure looked up at the movement, the cowl fell away, and Doyle saw the gray hood covering the figure's face. It pointed at him and emitted its deafening high-pitched wail.

Doyle slammed the window shut and reached into his bag for the pistol and hustled to the door. Moving down the hall, he heard cries of pain from below; they were tormenting the poor innkeeper—bas-tards, I'll fill them with holes—and he was fixed to hurtle downstairs to confront them when he heard a rush of footsteps on their way up. And another sound . . .

"Psst." Where was that coming from?

THE LIST OF 7

"Psst." At the end of the hallway, the Indian woman stood in a half-open doorway beckoning to Doyle with a crooked finger. Doyle hesitated.

"Hurry, for God's sake, Doyle," the woman said. In a man's voice.

Doyle ran for the door and entered as behind him the attackers reached the floor he was on and headed toward his room at the far end of the hall. The room's other occupant was removing the long veil, and Doyle for the first time saw this person's face.

"You . . ."

"Help me out of these clothes," said the man he'd known as Professor Armond Sacker.

Doyle gaped at him. The sounds of heavy blows and splintering wood ran down the corridor.

"Don't be a silly pudding, Doyle, they just discovered you're not in your room."

Doyle assisted as the man stripped off the padded sari, revealing the same black outfit he'd worn the night they'd met, and quickly toweled off the brown makeup on his face.

"You've been following me," was all Doyle could manage.

"They've found you much faster than I anticipated, my fault entirely," the man said, tossing the towel aside. "Is your pistol loaded?"

Doyle checked the chambers. "No, I'd completely forgotten."

The sound of banging on doors, and the startled cries of the floor's other occupants, was moving toward them down the hall.

"I suggest you hurry, old man," the man said coolly, kicking the sandals off his feet and pulling on a pair of soft leather boots. "We'll have to take the roof."

Rummaging through his bag for the box of ammunition, Doyle heard a creak and looked up to see one of the gray hoods opening the window above the bed. Grabbing the first solid object he could find, he reared back and hurled it at the creature, hitting it dead square in the center of the hood, knocking it away from the window. They heard a clatter of roof shingles, then a heavy impact below.

The man picked up the projectile from beneath the window.

"Good old Blavatsky," he said, with a brief admiring glance, handing the edition of *Psychic Self-Defense* back to Doyle. "Off we go then."

Pocketing the veil he'd worn earlier, the false Sacker climbed through the window. Doyle finished loading the pistol, hoisted out his bag, accepted the man's offered hand, and joined him on the roof.

"You have a great deal of explaining to do," Doyle said to him.

"Right with you, Doyle," he said. "What say we first put some distance between ourselves and these bloodless fiends, fair enough?"

Jack Sparks

Doyle nodded. The man started away, straddling the roof's spine, Doyle following closely, each step on the rain-soaked shingles perilously slick. The storm howled around them.

"What do I call you?" Doyle asked.

"Sorry? Frightfully hard to hear out here."

"I said, what's your name?"

"Call me Jack."

They made their way to the rear edge of the roof. The street twenty feet below was empty. Jack put two fingers into his mouth and whistled loudly enough to pierce the wind.

"I say, Jack . . ."

"Yes, Doyle."

"Your whistling like that, is that such a good idea?"

"Yes."

"But I mean, their hearing seems awfully acute by my reckoning."

"Acute doesn't quite cover it."

They waited. Jack unfolded the veil from his pocket, which Doyle noticed was nearly ten feet long and heavily weighted at either end. Doyle heard movement behind them; another gray hood appeared, loping down toward them over the crown of the roof.

"Shoot that one, will you?" Jack asked.

"I'll wait till it's a bit closer, if you don't mind," Doyle said, raising the pistol and drawing a bead on the figure.

"I wouldn't wait too long."

"I'd be happy to let you try—"

"No, no—"

"Because if you think you can do better—"

"I'm brimming with confidence in you, old boy—"

The hood was no more than ten feet away. Doyle fired. The creature, incredibly, dodged the bullet and continued to slowly advance.

"Not trying to be critical, you understand. It's just," Jack said, beginning to twirl the scarf above his head in a tight circle, "they're a good deal quicker than they first appear. Better to lay down a dense field of fire and hope they dodge into it."

Doyle fired again; the creature slipped left, the bullet ripped through its shoulder, it staggered, righted itself, and still came on. Wiping the rain from his eyes, Doyle aimed down the sight of the gun.

"These things," Doyle said, "they're not quite alive, are they? In the traditional sense."

"Something like that," Jack said, and let fly the scarf. It whistled through the air and caught the creature at the throat. Both weighted ends whirled out and stemmed around the neck, gaining speed until

73

the weights thwacked its skull with the sound of a melon being crushed by a wagon wheel.

"Now, Doyle!"

Doyle fired point-blank into the face of the hood. The thing toppled over, skidded down the slates, and fell from sight.

"Damn," Jack said.

"Thought it went rather well."

"I was going to use that scarf to get us off the roof."

"Handy little item."

"South American, actually, although they've been using a variation in the Punjab for centuries."

"If you don't mind my asking, how *will* we get down, Jack?"

Doyle thought he heard a carriage approaching below.

"We'll have to jump, won't we?"

Jack was looking intently down at the street and a now-visible approaching carriage.

"Really? We won't get far on a pair of broken legs—"

Before Doyle could further organize his objections, Jack grabbed him by the belt and jumped off the building. They hit the roof of the moving carriage and ripped right through the fabric, landing in a heap on the cushions of the cab.

"Good Christ!"

"Are you in one piece?"

Doyle quickly took inventory; save some discomfort in the ribs and a slightly turned ankle finding himself surprisingly intact.

"I think I'm all right."

"Well done."

As they rushed past the coach outside the inn, Doyle dimly made out dark figures scrambling after them in the downpour. Jack rapped on what was left of the roof and the driver, the same small scar-faced man who'd driven them before, appeared in the gap above.

"Evasive tactics, Barry," Jack said. Barry nodded and turned back to his work. Doyle heard the crack of the whip, and the cab quickly accelerated.

Jack settled back into the seat across from Doyle, holding up a hand to the water cascading down onto them through the roof.

"Sorry about the rain."

"Quite all right. We'll have another chat then, as we go?"

"Not just yet. We'll be getting out in a moment."

"Getting out?"

The carriage clattered across a short bridge and came to a sudden halt. Jack leapt from the cab and held open the door.

Jack Sparks

"Come on, Doyle, we haven't got all night," he said.

Doyle followed him back into the deluge. Jack waved to Barry, and the cab sped off again into the darkness.

"This way," Jack said, leading them down a steep embankment under the bridge they'd just traversed. "In here."

Jack pulled Doyle in under the relative dryness of the span of the bridge. Gripping his bag with one hand, Doyle used the other to haul himself onto a support strut, a precarious perch a scant few feet above the rising torrent of the stream below.

"Are you secure?" Jack had to yell to make himself heard.

"I believe so," Doyle replied, but the remark was obliterated by the deafening thunder of a carriage and four hurtling across the bridge a foot above their heads. The sound moved away, quickly swallowed up by the storm.

"Was that them?" Doyle finally asked.

"Barry'll have them running circles around Trafalgar Square before they realize we're not on board."

Doyle nodded, reluctantly admiring the man's resourcefulness. Some time went by. Doyle stared at Jack, who smiled amiably.

"What do you suggest we do?"

"I suggest that we sit here until the rain lets up," Jack said.

More time passed. Jack seemed quite content to wait it out in silence. The same could not be said for Doyle.

"Look here, Jack, or whatever your name is, before we go any farther, I'd very much like to know exactly who you are," said Doyle, realizing his patience was at an end.

"You'll have to forgive the subterfuge, Doyle, but there's a certain logic to all this, which you'll soon come to appreciate," he said, and smiled again, reaching into his jacket and retrieving his silver flask.

"So who are you then?"

"John Sparks, Jack to my friends, special agent to Her Majesty the Queen. Happy to make your acquaintance," he said, offering the flask. "A little brandy to keep the chill off, Doctor?"

CHAPTER 9

By Land and Sea

Clinging to the bridge's underbelly, fearful of plunging into the icy cataract below, Doyle did not, during the remainder of the night, enjoy a moment's rest. Sparks, on the other hand, seemed to float in and out of a serene meditative slumber, upright, his arms nonchalantly wrapped around a sturdy timber.

The rain abated as the first light of dawn warmed the eastern sky. No clouds obscured the western horizon. Sparks's eyes sprang open, fresh and alert as a thoroughbred on Derby Day.

"The morning has promise," announced Sparks, after vaulting out of their hidey-hole onto the bridge like a Hungarian gymnast.

Stiff as a corpse, wet, famished, and bruised, Doyle dragged himself out onto the road, stifling with considerable effort his irritation at the man's enthusiasm as Sparks flew through an exotic routine of improbable Yogic postures, accompanied by vocalizations that suggested the nocturnal braying of ill-bred cats. Slack-jawed and glassy-eyed, Doyle found his thoughts diminished to visualizing cream-drenched kettledrums of hot buttered oatmeal or elaborately protracted ways for Sparks to die, one of which featured a strikingly original use of the oatmeal.

By Land and Sea

With a profound exhale and a salute to the rising sun, Sparks finished his exercises and for the first time acknowledged Doyle's presence.

"We should be on the march," Sparks said.

He smiled and walked briskly away down the road. It wasn't until Sparks had nearly disappeared around the next corner that the urgency of sticking close to the man cut through the foggy lowlands of Doyle's brain. He took off after Sparks, breaking into a run, his sodden boots squishing with every step. Even after catching him, Doyle had to maintain a trot to keep pace with Sparks's invigorated stride.

"Where are you going?" Doyle asked.

"A moving target presupposes motion, Doyle," Sparks replied, between deep, naturalist breaths. "Unpredictability, that's the key."

Lord, the man's insouciance was aggravating. "So where are you going then?"

"Where are *you* going?"

"I'm quite sure I don't know."

"Look at you; you're going *somewhere*."

"I'm left with the impression that I was going with you."

Sparks nodded. There was another long pause.

"So where are we going?" Doyle asked.

"We should get off this road soon enough, I can tell you that."

The narrow lane was bounded on either side by dense forest. "You think it unsafe?"

"At present that's a fair description of just about anywhere." Sparks halted suddenly. His head moved back and forth like a bird, registering exactly what sort of sensory information it was difficult to ascertain.

"This way," he said, and quickly ran off into the woods.

Doyle followed, alarmed. Sparks led them so deep in that the road was no longer visible. Stalking through a gully of second-growth ferns on the forest floor, he slowed his step, came to a halt, and gently drew aside a column of brambles, revealing a spotty gooseberry bush.

"Let's eat," said Sparks.

They denuded the bush, harvesting a handful of berries apiece. They were malformed and bitter, but Doyle savored each one like napoleon creams.

"You like your food, do you, Doyle?" Sparks asked, watching him eat. "You look like a proper trencherman."

"I wouldn't turn down a proper meal, no."

"Nourishment. There's a subject. There'll be a lot to say about that before too long. The general health."

"Jack, if you don't mind, I'd rather not talk about the general health just now."

"Not at all."

"I'd just as soon talk about my health in particular; my health *vis à vis* these determined attempts upon my life. My health as in, I'd prefer to go on having it, thank you very much."

"I understand completely."

"Good, Jack. I'm glad that you understand."

"I don't need to walk a mile in your shoes to see how bleak things look from where you're sitting," Sparks said, rising to his feet, stretching, ready to press on.

"I wish I could say that were some small comfort to me."

"Comfort's a luxury we're a bit short on at the moment—"

"Jack: Where . . . are . . . we . . . going?" Doyle said, refusing to budge.

"Where do you want to go?"

"I'd prefer to hear your answer first."

"Not as easy as all that, Doyle—"

"That's fine, but to be honest with you, Jack, I was counting on—depending on, actually—your advice and counsel in this matter."

"Here it is, then: Where I want to go at this particular moment in time is not to the point. Not at all."

"Not to the point."

"No. The point is, where do . . . *you* want to go?"

Doyle considered shooting him, but the consumed berries, despite their aesthetic inadequacy, had planed the rougher edges off his temper. "I had entertained some vague plan of going to Topping. The home of the late Lady Nicholson. That was my most recent intention."

"Good. Let's be off," Sparks said, and he started walking away.

"Just like that?"

"It's you who wants to go there, isn't it?"

"So you endorse the idea, then," said Doyle.

"Sounds serviceable. Do you know where it is?"

"Haven't a clue."

"How were you planning to get there?"

"My plan hadn't evolved quite that far."

"East Sussex. Near the town of Rye. Come on, Doyle, we've a long walk ahead of us," said Sparks, setting off through the copse of woods.

"I do have more questions for you," Doyle said, rising to follow him.

"Fit discussion for the open road, are they?"

"I should think so."

By Land and Sea

"Not this road, mind you. Our route will by necessity be somewhat discursive."

"So I might have suspected."

The sun continued its morning climb, chasing the chill from their bones, blotting up the first layer of damp from their clothes. They kept to the main thoroughfare for no more than a mile before reaching an almost invisible intersection with an overgrown cart path. After some private deliberation, Sparks guided them to the left, down the forgotten byway. From that point forward, he demonstrated the presence of a formidable internal compass, never hesitating over a change of direction, even when the sketchy track they were following entirely disappeared for extended stretches at a time.

Such as it was, the path fell away from the forest, down into a rolling valley of lush farmland. In the brilliant sunlight, the rich loam of the fields engaged and delighted the senses. A choir of songbirds kept faith with the day's emerging gentility. Doyle found it difficult to hold his worries squarely in mind and once caught himself starting to whistle. Sparks grabbed a handful of dry grass, thoughtfully examining and then chewing the stalks, one after another.

At Sparks's request, Doyle recounted his experiences since they had parted in London, remembering, as Sparks had importuned him to avoid the police altogether, to leave out his visit with Leboux of Scotland Yard. And quite cleverly, too, Doyle congratulated himself.

"So after leading the inspector to Thirteen Cheshire Street, you returned to your flat and discovered the body of Mrs. Petrovitch," Sparks said.

Buffeted, Doyle tried to bluff his way through.

"Allow me to unburden you, Doyle: Don't bother lying to me—"

"How did you know?"

"What does it matter? The damage is done."

"But you must tell me, by what manner of reasoning did you—"

"I was following you."

"Even then? Before the Indian getup?"

"Throughout, more or less."

"For the purpose of protection, or in the hope that I'd draw trouble?"

"Those ends are not working at cross-purposes—"

"Likewise for your presence in Cambridge."

"I had additional objectives there as well—"

"Such as?" asked Doyle, pressing what he now felt sure was the interrogatory advantage.

"Lady Nicholson's brother was an undergraduate at Gonville and Caius. I made some inquiries at the Bursar's Office."

"While I was off looking for 'Professor Sacker.' "

"That was the most opportune time, yes."

"I suppose that was your reason for giving the false name," Doyle concluded. "If I went to Cambridge to seek you out, you could keep one eye on me while you tracked down the brother—"

"Well considered, Doyle."

"As it happened, your best-laid plan nearly had me for birdseed."

"Most unfortunate."

"I don't suppose you have an explanation for what-the-devil was chasing me in the halls of the Antiquities Building."

"No. Sorry," said Sparks, without a hint of misgiving, then, sprightly, "Not without interest, though, is it?"

"A moment hardly goes by without my thinking of it. So what did you discover about the brother?"

"Last name, Rathborne; Lady Nicholson's maiden name. First name, George. He left school three days before the vacation on what he told the proctor was urgent family business. Hasn't been seen or heard from since."

"Nor will he be, poor devil. What about Madame Blavatsky?"

"Fascinating woman."

"Agreed. What has she to do with any of this?"

"I would say she's an interested and sympathetic observer."

"You're saying she's not involved?"

"You're the one who's spoken to her, what do you think?"

"Don't you know her?" Doyle asked, exasperation mounting again.

"Never met the woman. Effective speaker, though. Intriguing blend of crusading pilgrim and patent-medicine salesman. You'd almost swear she was American."

"And forgive me, Jack, but I must ask, what is this tommyrot about you working for the Queen?"

Sparks stopped and looked at him with unimpeachable sincerity.

"You must assure me that you will never breathe a word to another soul of that association. It cannot be spoken of safely even here, alone in a remote glade. Lives far more precious to the preservation of the Empire than our own depend upon your discretion. I confided in you, with the utmost reluctance, only to impress upon you the gravity of the matter in which you are now regrettably involved. How I wish that it were otherwise."

By Land and Sea

Sparks's heartfelt invocation of the Crown brought Doyle's royalist sympathies to the fore, crippling his ability to find further objection with Sparks's veil of secrecy.

"Do I interpret you correctly to assume that this involves a threat to the lives of certain . . . highborn individuals?" asked Doyle carefully.

"Indeed it does."

"Can I . . . be of any assistance to you in this matter?"

"You have already. You're a most capable chap."

A threat to the Queen: Doyle could barely contain himself.

"Since you find my abilities not entirely without merit, I should like to place myself at your continued disposal."

Sparks studied him with equal parts compassion and cold assessment.

"I shall take you at your word," replied Sparks. "Do you have the insignia I gave you the other night?"

"Right here." Doyle retrieved the engraved eye from his pocket.

"Hold it in your left hand, please."

"Madame Blavatsky suggested I make an amulet of it."

"I see no harm in that, so long as you wear it away from casual glance," Sparks said, drawing an identical insignia, in the form of an amulet, out from under his collar. "Now raise your right hand and repeat after me."

"Is it some sort of Masonic ritual?"

"We haven't got all day, Doyle."

"Right. Carry on."

Sparks composed himself and closed his eyes; just before Doyle began to feel discomfited by the silence that ensued, Sparks broke it.

"From the point of Light within the Mind of God, let Light stream forth into the minds of men. Let Light descend on Earth."

Doyle repeated the words, trying to breathe life into them even as he labored to decipher their meaning. Mind of God. Light. Light in the form of knowledge: Wisdom.

"From the center where the Will of God is known," Sparks continued, "let purpose guide the little wills of men—the purpose which the Masters know and serve."

More problematic. Unchristian, not that that was especially troubling. The Masters. Blavatsky had written of them: mythological elder beings, gazing dispassionately down at the follies of man. Every civilization developed its own version: Olympus, Valhalla, Shambhala, heaven . . .

"From the center which we call the race of men, let the Plan of Love and Light work out, and may it seal the door where Evil dwells."

81

Now they were getting somewhere: the door where Evil dwells; Doyle felt qualified to say that, if he couldn't pinpoint its exact location, he had definitely heard something knocking.

"Let Light and Love and Power restore the Plan on Earth."

The Plan. Whose Plan? he wondered, and exactly how did they, whoever *they* were—now that he, presumably was one of them— intend to go about restoring it?

"What do we do now? Is there a secret handshake, something to seal the bargain?" asked Doyle.

"No. That's it," said Sparks, stuffing his amulet back under his collar.

"What does it mean exactly, Jack?"

"What did it mean to you?"

"Do good. Fight evil." Doyle shrugged.

"That'll do for a start," Sparks said, and he began to walk again.

"Not very dogmatic. For that sort of thing."

"Refreshing isn't it?"

"I was expecting, you know, a pledge of fealty to Queen and country, something along chivalric or Arthurian lines. This was pantheistic and positively nondenominational."

"Glad it meets with your approval."

"And what does the eye represent?"

"I've told you as much as I'm able for the moment, Doyle," Sparks replied wearily. "Anything more would not be in your self-interest."

They walked on. The fields ran uninterrupted in every direction. From the arc of the rising sun, Doyle figured they were traveling due east.

Hunger presently raised its insistent voice, darkening Doyle's mood. Yes, Sparks had pulled his fat out of the fire on more than one occasion. Nothing in his actions suggested he was anything other than what he represented himself to be, but he remained impenetrable, and the cloaking of royal secrecy around his true purpose rang discordantly. Doyle was in no position to reject the man's assistance, no more than he was of a mind to forfeit his surprisingly welcome company, but common sense prevented the full conferring of his trust. It was as if he were traveling with an exotic jungle cat, its defensive abilities beyond reproach but whose very nature demanded of its keeper a tireless, wary scrutiny.

Perhaps if he questioned Sparks more cleverly, he'd inadvertently yield up details from which the astute observer could assemble a more telling portrait of the man. A number of Doyle's speculative inferences were on the verge of congealing into conclusions. It remained for him to find the right moment to confront Sparks with them and, whether by the shock of recognition or the false vehemence of denial, determine their acuity.

Along the cart path there appeared every so often hedges and occasional embankments and at one point the crumbling remains of stone brickwork, underfoot or along the shoulder. Doyle had noticed the remains from time to time without more than passing curiosity, but as they traversed a more extensive patch of the ruins, his examination of them drew comment from Sparks.

"This is an old Roman road. A trade route running to the sea."

"Is that where we're going, the sea?" *Well played, Doyle, devilishly clever the way you slipped that in.*

"Of course, paths like this one were in use long before the Romans crossed the channel," Sparks continued, completely ignoring his question. "The early Celts used this path, and Neolithic man before them. Strange, isn't it? The same path used by so many different cultures, down through the ages."

"Convenience, I should imagine," Doyle said. He hadn't thought about it, in truth. "A new lot comes along, the old path is there, remnants of it anyway, why bother cutting a new one?"

"Why not, indeed? Make things easier; there's the history of mankind in a thimble, eh, Doyle?"

"In a roundabout sort of way."

"How do you suppose our prehistoric forebears chose this particular path to begin with?"

"Shortest distance between two points."

"Could be these were the same paths the animals they were hunting used before them," said Sparks.

"That has the ring of truth."

"And why do you think the animals blazed this particular path?" Sparks had slipped into the tone of a Sophist leading the ignorant step by step to the sacred land of truth.

"Something to do with the availability of water or food."

"Necessity, then."

"Their lives are ordered by it, aren't they?"

"Are you familiar with the Chinese philosophy of *feng shui*?"

"Never heard of it."

"The Chinese believe the earth itself is a living, breathing organism, and just as the human body has veins, nerves, and vital energies running through it, regulating maintenance and behavior, so too does the earth."

"I know their system of medicine is based on such an assumption," Doyle added, wondering what this had even remotely to do with Roman roads in Essex.

"Exactly so. *Feng shui* assumes the presence of these lines of force and attempts to bring human existence into harmony with them. Practitioners of *feng shui* are trained and initiated as rigorously as members of any priesthood, increasing their sensitivity to these powers and their ability to accurately interpret them. The building of homes, roads, churches, the entire five-thousand-year-old Chinese Empire—the most enduring civilization our world has produced—was constructed in strictest alignment with these principles."

"You don't say."

"Aside from his obvious ignorance, filth, and lack of sophistication, what quality could most recommend to us prehistoric man?"

"He was quite handy with his hands," Doyle said, struggling to keep up with the man's mental vaults.

"He was in harmony with the earth," said Sparks, paying no attention to Doyle's answer. "At one with nature: part *of* it, not apart from it."

"The noble savage. Rousseau and all that."

"Precisely. And as a consequence, ancient man possessed an exquisite sensitivity to the ground he walked, the woods he hunted, the streams from which he drank. He didn't need to practice *feng shui;* he was born with it, innately, as were the animals he depended on for survival."

"So the paths they traveled fell along the lines of some vibratory pattern in the earth."

"Crisscrossing the countryside seemingly at random, these paths may constitute nothing less than the electromagnetic nervous system of the planetary being itself."

"On the other hand, they might just be roads," Doyle countered.

"Might be. But what if I were to tell you that at the intersections of these lines of force, where the—whatever you might wish to call it; the Chinese call it the 'breath of the dragon'—where this pulsating energy is at its zenith, early man erected his temples and holy places, on many of which now stand the Christian churches we make use of today?"

"I'd say the whole thing bears further examination—"

"Stonehenge is such a place. Likewise the ancient abbey at Glastonbury. And Westminster Abbey, which was built on the site of the Romans' Temple of Diana, sits squarely atop the most vigorous nexus of these lines of force in all of England. What does that suggest to you?"

By Land and Sea

"There's a good deal more in heaven and earth and so on."

"Yes, Horatio. Even more intriguing when you consider that the Greek deity Hermes—the ancient Greeks were aware of these forces, don't you doubt it—was the god not only of fertility, as was Diana, but also of *roads*. And what did our Celtic ancestors do to honor Hermes? They erected columns of stone at significant crossroads. Mere signposts? Or primitive conductors of this earthbound energy?"

"But the Celts didn't worship a Greek god," Doyle contended, growing more confused.

"No, the Celts called him Theutates. But when the Romans completed their conquest of Britain, Caesar himself remarked on how easily the natives had been persuaded to worship Mercury, the Roman version of Hermes. Theutates is depicted as carrying a large staff entwined with a serpent, as are both Hermes and Mercury with the caduceus—"

"Two snakes on the caduceus, actually."

"And what does the caduceus symbolize, Doyle?"

"Healing. The power of healing."

"Precisely. Suggesting that if one taps into the power of the serpent, i.e., 'the dragon'—the lines of force in the earth: the *natural* force—they gain the power to heal. What if all this talk about 'dragons' in Celtic legend wasn't about literal monsters at all? Do you recall what old Saint George was suddenly able to do after 'slaying the dragon'?"

"Uh—"

"Heal the sick! Brave knight ventures out, sticks his lance into—not an actual dragon, in our revised scenario, but the 'coiled serpent' of natural power. Like dropping a conducting wire into a vast reservoir of energy, thereby taming the 'beast.' George then goes straight on to become patron saint of England, it's graven in our English schoolboy minds! Power, Doyle, the elemental power of the planet, running under, around, and through us even now, and we're too blinded and distracted by life's pettifogging natterings to see it!"

Each new idea made Doyle's brain ache. Perhaps there was a vitality-affecting undercurrent beneath these bricks, and it was draining him dry.

"And what was the first use civilizations tried to make of this force once they'd acquired it? What did we use those ancient temples for? Come on, Doyle, think!"

Doyle hazarded a guess. "Animal sacrifice?"

"Healing! Heal the sick; raise the dead. We appealed to the gods to make us whole; the medical and theological professions were one and the same then. Not unlike two serpents entwined around a straight line of force, come to think of it," said Sparks, surprising himself with the discovery. "Do you remember who the eldest son of Hermes was?"

"Forgive me, it's slipped my mind," said Doyle, feeling slightly dizzy.

"The great god Pan, father of paganism and earth worship, the one the Christians decided to eradicate by calling him the Devil, because poor old, fun-loving Pan also represented that most unchristian of human attributes: unbridled male sexuality."

"Pity."

"Granted Pan has his mischievous side; he particularly liked to lie in wait for travelers in desolate areas, jump out of the weeds, and spook the living wits out of them, inducing a feeling in the victim called Pan-ic."

"I really need something to eat," Doyle said. The surrounding countryside, in spite of its bucolic, sun-drenched beauty, was beginning to look increasingly threatening.

"Isn't the mind extraordinary? One loose brick on the road leads us from *feng shui* all the way to Pan. By God, maybe there is something to the energy of this old road: I feel marvelously invigorated!"

Doyle wiped his brow with a handkerchief as Sparks looked out over the fields, reviewing the crop of his recent thinking like a proud farmer.

"If this lines-of-force business is true, if this road truly is sacred, how do you account for the fact that it's fallen into such utter disrepair?" asked Doyle, self-satisfied with the sharpness of his rebuttal.

"In that single observation, Doyle, you express with epigrammatic precision the fundamental tragedy of modern man. We have fallen from grace, our ancient, instinctual link to the natural world forgotten. We're guests who no longer respect the house they inhabit, but rather treat it as a rough clay to be molded to our basest use. Think of the charnel-house factories of London, the befouled air, the mines, child labor; the countless devalued lives broken and discarded by the infernal machinery of the age. The eloquent ruins of this simple country path inscribe the eventual downfall of our vaunted civilization."

Doyle felt a tingling rush through his body, whether moved by the surprisingly tender outrage of his companion or some combination of starvation and sunstroke, he was quite unsure. It was near midday by now and unseasonably warm. Undulations of heat massaged the horizon line.

"What's that?" Doyle asked, and he pointed to the road behind them.

They had climbed and descended a sequence of gentle hills as the path moved down through the valley. A dark miragelike heat devil was

By Land and Sea

fluttering toward them along the line of the road. Its rhythmic, fluid movements suggested the beating wings of a gigantic crow.

"Perhaps we'd better clear off the road," Doyle said.

"No."

"Do you think that's, um, wise, Jack?"

"We're in no danger," said Sparks, standing his ground.

Before too long, they could hear beating hooves: a single horse, at a sustained gallop. The shape metamorphosed through the distortion of the heat and revealed itself to be a solitary rider, a long black cloak flowing in its wake. Slowing as it approached, the rider appeared to a startled Doyle as a welcomely familiar face.

"Why, it's Barry. It's Barry, isn't it?" said Doyle, unexpectedly cheered by the prospect.

"No. It's not Barry," Sparks said.

He moved away to greet whoever it was as the horse covered the last few paces, and the man, who by every test of scrutiny Doyle could apply appeared to be none other than Barry, their erstwhile driver, dismounted and shook hands with Sparks.

"Good man, Larry, no trouble then," said Sparks.

"Kept a sharp butchers. N'trouble a'tall, sir," said Larry, who Doyle still insisted was Barry, not Larry.

"Larry is referring to the scattering of berries and wheat I've left along the way," Sparks explained to Doyle, as they moved to him. "There's not another tracker in all of England who could follow so scant a trail."

"None that is save y'self, sir," Larry added modestly. He was an East Ender, wiry and compact, as Barry had been, with the same curly brown hair and lively blue eyes that Barry had; that Barry has, Doyle meant to say, still convinced this could be none other than the man himself.

"Larry and Barry are brothers," Sparks said, seeing Doyle's evident confusion. "Identical twins."

"We were, anyway; Barry's a one's wot got the scar, sir, which you'll notice is distinctly lacking on my physiognomy," said Larry, helpfully offering up his right, decidedly unscarred cheek to Doyle as testimony.

"Right," said Doyle. "No scar at all." As if he'd noticed from the start.

"Larry and Barry are something of a legend in certain London circles," Sparks said. "The sharpest pair of crack men you'd ever hope to meet."

"Crack men?"

"Burglars, sir," said Larry, smiling politely as if discussing tea-party etiquette with a maiden aunt. "Bit a' the old slash and grab, practitioners of the wedge, jemmy, and center bit, if you get my meanin'."

"I understand your meaning quite distinctly," Doyle said, affronted by the man's casual criminality.

"A perfect partnership," explained Sparks. "No one knew they were twins. On sheer technique alone they were ten leagues ahead of anyone else in the field."

"We ain't educated, but we 'ad an education, if you get my meaning," elaborated Larry.

"You'll appreciate the elegance of their methodology, Doyle. One of them goes out on the town and holds forth in a pub, cadging drinks, carousing, generally making a spectacle of himself."

"And that part's not the lark you might assume it to be, sir," said Larry, gravely. "A form of entertainment, that's how we seen it—emphasis on *performance*. Barry, now 'e's a singer, see, wit' a vast repertoire to draw from, whilst I favored epic recitation of the ribald lim'rick."

"So while the one's publicly and visibly engaged, the other brother goes about the fieldwork."

"That being the targeted burgle, in and out wit' the grab bag clean as a nun's wimple," added Larry.

"Both of them as quick as mice and able to work their way into places you wouldn't believe humanly possible," Sparks went on—enjoying himself just a little too much with this story, thought Doyle.

"Barry, see, 'e can dislocate 'is shoulders in a tight spot and collapse 'imself down like an umbrella—"

"They're never seen together in public, so even if the brother on the job is pinched red-handed, forty eyewitnesses in the pub are ready to swear they spent the evening in the accused's flamboyant company. Absolutely foolproof."

"And Bob's your uncle it was, too, sir," Larry continued. "That is, till one dark day Barry buys hisself a bit a hard cheese. Always after the ladies, Barry was: a tragic flaw. On this one particular night, he's flouncing a fishmonger's daughter. He's laid a mighty siege to the citadel of this dolly's virtue: The more defense she musters, the more engines of war Barry marshals onto the field of honor. Four in the morning, right there in the shop among the sardines. He's broken through her battlements, overrun the palace guard, and is about to breach her *sanctum sanctorum* when her old dad barrels in, unexpected like wit' a catch a' North Sea haddock, and before Barry can half pull his knickers on, the man whacks a cleaver 'cross his chops, cuts him right to the bone—"

By Land and Sea

"We can safely leave out the medical details, Larry," said Sparks.

"Right. Sorry, sir," Larry said earnestly, searching Doyle's face for any wounded sensibility.

"There's a place for the likes of you and your brother," replied Doyle. "It's called prison."

"No question about it, sir. And no doubt that's where we'd both be languishin' to this day, deservedly so, if it weren't for the good graces of Mr. Sparks 'ere."

"A long story we shan't belabor the good doctor with at the moment," Sparks said authoritatively. "Did you spy anyone else on the road?"

"I can say wit' some confidence that your avenue of escape remains undetected, sir."

"Welcome news. Now, my friend, what have you brought for us?"

"Beggin' your pardon, gents, 'ere I am gabbin', and you must be as parched as a medieval monk's manuscript."

It turned out Larry had brought in his saddlebags a great many things that, if he hadn't been in such poor humor to start, would have gone a long way toward substantially revising Doyle's judgment of the wayward brothers. Sandwiches to start, numbers of them, in abundant variety: deviled ham, rare roast beef and sharp cheddar, turkey and mayonnaise, mutton slathered in horseradish sauce. And with them packages of nuts and sweets and water and cool beer. And perhaps most welcome of all, a change of dry clothes for them both.

They supped off the road, the horse grazing nearby in the tall alfalfa. Larry brought them up to date on his recent movements. Stationed for the last day and a half at the Cambridge railway office, upon receiving a coded wire from Barry in London—he'd led the pursuers a merry chase halfway back to town before eluding them entirely— Larry had taken to his horse and tracked down Sparks and Doyle off the beaten path. Although Doyle assumed it fell along the lines of employment, he found the exact nature of Barry and Larry's relationship to Sparks difficult to pin down and felt more than a little uneasy in asking. The proximity of such a clearly criminal personality, however putatively reformed, aroused in Doyle an Old Testament stoniness that the sandwiches and beer did little to dissolve, despite Larry's sunny attempts to ingratiate himself.

Freshly fortified, and wearing dry shoes again, Doyle and Sparks set off once more down the old Roman road. Larry mounted and rode off ahead of them to perform some undisclosed advance-guard action. The sight of his flapping cloak disappearing over the next hill brought back the memory of a recent and more sinister visitation.

"Who's after me, Jack? Who's that man in black I saw last night?"

A seriousness of aspect clouded his disposition. "I'm not certain."

"But you have some idea."

"He's a man I've been looking for. Last night was the closest I've come to him in many years. He's the reason I was at the séance the other night."

"Is he some part of this evil confederacy you've alluded to?"

"I believe this man you saw is their field general."

"It's someone you know, isn't it?" asked Doyle, with a flash of intuitive certainty.

Sparks looked at him sharply. To Doyle's amazement, there was in Sparks's cool eyes a flicker of fear. Shocking and unexpected.

"Perhaps." Then Sparks raised a roguish eyebrow with customary confidence, his more familiar self again. This unearthing of genuine fright, its mere presence, humanized the man, bringing him closer to the common ground of Doyle's understanding.

"Does it occur to you how little reason there is for me to believe anything of what you've told me?" said Doyle ungrudgingly.

"Certainly."

"I have the experience of my senses to rely on, but these tales you spin . . . why couldn't there just as easily be a thousand other equally, if not considerably more, plausible explanations?"

Sparks nodded in rueful consensus. "What else are our lives finally but a story we tell ourselves to find some sense in the pain of living?"

"We have to believe life has meaning."

"Perhaps it can only be as meaningful as our own ability to make it so."

What a variety of feeling his friend had exhibited in so short a span of time. Doyle found himself amazed again at the violent elasticity of emotion, more mutable than summer weather. And he saw his opening.

"I completely agree," said Doyle. "For instance, I know next to nothing about you, Jack, factually speaking, and yet I'm still able to construct an idea of you—a story of you, if you will—that may or may not bear any relation to who you actually are."

"Such as?" said Sparks, suddenly keen.

"You're a man of about thirty-five years, born on your family's estate in Yorkshire. You are an only child. You suffered a severe illness as a boy. You have a lifelong love of reading. Your family traveled extensively in Europe during your youth, spending a considerable amount of time in Germany. Upon your return, you were enrolled in public school and upon graduation attended college at Cambridge. More than one college, I think. You studied, among other things, medicine and science. You play some sort of stringed musical instrument, probably the violin, and you do so with no little virtuosity—"

"This is astounding!"

"You briefly entertained the idea of a career as an actor and may in fact have spent some time on the stage. Military service was an option you also considered, and it's possible you journeyed to India in 1878 during the Afghan Campaign. While in the East, you spent time studying religions, among them Buddhism and Confucianism. I believe you have also traveled in the United States."

"Bravo, Doyle. You do amaze me."

"That was my intention. Shall I tell you how I came to these things?"

"My accent, what trace of it remains, gave away Yorkshire. By my manner and apparent means, you correctly assume I spring from family holdings sufficient to support myself in some comfort, without pursuing a life in commerce."

"Correct. Your vivid imagination leads me to believe you were invalided in childhood—perhaps the cholera epidemic of the early sixties—during which you entertained yourself by reading voraciously, a habit you maintain to this day."

"True. And my family did travel regularly through Europe, particularly Germany, but I can't for the life of me surmise how you arrived at that."

"An educated guess: Germany is the preferred destination for upper-class families of your parents' generation attempting to instill in their children some systematic appreciation of literature and culture. I suspect the Germanic lineage of our last few sets of royals has had much if not everything to do with that tendency among the landed gentry."

"Well reasoned," Sparks conceded. "One misstep: I do have an older brother."

"Frankly, I'm surprised. You bear the natural confidence and ambition of an eldest and only child."

"My brother is considerably older. He never traveled with us and spent the better part of my early life away at school. I hardly knew him."

"That explains it then."

"I did attend Cambridge—Caius and Magdalene—studying medicine and the natural sciences, which you arrived at through my familiarity with the town itself and the apparent ease with which I retrieved the information regarding young Nicholson."

"Right again."

"I also briefly attended Christ Church at Oxford."

"Theology?"

"Yes. And, I'm embarrassed to say, amateur theatricals."

"Your knowledge of makeup and disguise led me to it. The effectiveness of your Indian ruse led me to believe you'd been to the Orient."

"I never entered the military, sorry, but I have traveled to the Far East and did indeed spend many hours in the comparative study of religions."

"And the United States?"

"You did not fail to notice my occasional use of the American vernacular."

Doyle nodded.

"I spent eight months tramping the Eastern Seaboard as an actor on tour with the Sasanoff Shakespearean Company," said Sparks with the tone of a penitent in the confessional.

"I knew it!"

"I thought Mercutio my finest hour on the stage, although in Boston they seemed to favor my Hotspur," he said, mocking his own vanity. "Now I follow your line of thinking on every one of these deductions save one: How on earth did you know I play the violin?"

"I once treated a violinist of the London orchestra for a badly sprained wrist sustained in a bicycling accident. He had a distinctive pattern of small calluses, from fingering the strings, on the pads of the fingertips of his left hand. You possess that same pattern; I assume you play the instrument as devotedly, if not as expertly, as my patient."

"Marvelous. I do congratulate you on your powers of observation."

"Thank you. I pride myself on them."

"Most people drift through life in a perpetual haze of self-conscious introspection that entirely prevents their seeing the world as it is. Your diagnostic training has granted you the priceless habit of paying attention to detail, and you have clearly labored to develop that skill to a profound level. It suggests that you have also worked with equal diligence to develop an advanced philosophy of living."

"I guess I've always felt the less said about such things, the better," said Doyle modestly.

" 'Let actions define the man for the world, while the music of his soul plays for an audience of one.' "

"Shakespeare?"

"No, Sparks," Sparks said with a grin. "Shall I have a go at you then?"

"What? You mean, what have appearances told you about me?"

By Land and Sea

"The prospect that I've met my match in the exercise of observational deduction brings my competitive tendencies racing to the fore."

"How will I know these are legitimate inferences and not facts you've gathered by some covert means?"

"You won't," said Sparks, flashing his grin again. "You were born in Edinburgh, to Catholic parents of Irish descent and modest means. You fished and hunted extensively in youth. You were educated in Jesuit parochial schools. Your lifelong passions have been literature and medicine. You attended medical school at the University of Edinburgh, where you studied under an inspirational professor who encouraged you to develop your powers of observation and deduction beyond the scope of their diagnostic application. Despite your medical training, you have never relinquished your dream of one day making your living exclusively as a man of letters. Despite your indoctrination in the Church of Rome, you renounced your family's faith after attending séances and encountering experiences too difficult to reconcile with an adherence to any religious dogma. You now consider yourself a confirmed, albeit open-minded, agnostic. You are very handy with a revolver. . . . "

And so they passed the remainder of the afternoon, this meeting of the minds a great refresher for men so accustomed to the solitary exercise of their more acute faculties. Although occasional farms and one or two more developed settlements appeared in the distance, they stayed to their primeval path, quieting hunger and thirst as they arose from the stores that Larry had left them. They passed through meadows and birch woods and blasted, fallow flatlands, until sundown found them at path's end on the banks of the River Colne, a wide and lazy waterway meandering through the fields and retiring farming villages of the Essex countryside. After a quiet evening meal under a sheltering oak, as darkness fell, Larry appeared again, putting in to shore near their camp at the helm of a twenty-foot sloop, seaworthy and strong, a lantern hanging off the bow. They boarded her while Larry held the gunnels. A worn canvas lean-to and a pallet of blankets offered shelter amidships. Under a clear night sky and the light of a three-quarter moon, they pushed off and drifted silently downstream with the current, passing unnoticed through a sleepy riverside town. At Sparks's insistence, Doyle took the first turn in the bunk, and before the boat had traveled another half-mile downriver, the gentle rolling of the water carried the weary doctor down into the dreamless arms of grateful sleep.

THE LIST OF 7

❀   ❀   ❀

The river conveyed them uneventfully through the night, past Halstead and Rose Green, Wakes Colne and Eight Ash, wending through the knotty sprawl of ancient Colchester near dawn and then down past Wivenhoe, where the river widened out, preparing to meet the sea. Although they passed a number of barges and other small ships at anchor during the night, here they began to encounter for the first time larger vessels under steam. Larry hoisted the mainsail to aid their progress against the incoming tide and a following southeasterly bellowed the canvas, skating them around the cumbersome, cargo-laden traffic that snarled the channel.

Two brief, vertical catnaps were all Sparks had allowed himself during the journey and seemed to be all he required. Doyle slept through the night, waking refreshed and more than a little startled to find them passing landfall and approaching the open sea. With the wind full at their backs, they came about and made for the south. Sparks took the rudder as they rolled into the heavier swells, Larry took his turn on the blankets, and Doyle joined Sparks aft. Although conditions were favorable, Doyle could see by his touch on the helm and his feel for the wind that Sparks was an expert sailor. They soon left all sight of the river behind, keeping the barren reaches between Sales and Holliwell Point visible to starboard.

The restless touch of the waves and the air's salt tang brought back to Doyle a cornucopia of long-forgotten memories of days at sea. The pleasure they imparted must have crept into his features, for Sparks soon offered him the rudder. He gladly accepted. Sparks settled himself comfortably down into a coil of rope, pulled a packet of tobacco from his boot, and filled a pipe. With only the crisp crack of the sail and the screech of the seabirds to distract him, Doyle greedily drank in the riches of the unobstructed seascape. Whatever manner of ordeal they had embarked upon seemed infinitely more manageable out here, in an open boat, dwarfed by the ocean's immensity, a sight Doyle had oftentimes found comforting in far rougher waters than these.

It suddenly occurred to him: Why not complete the fugitive act and make for the Continent? As a seafaring man, Doyle knew there were a thousand distant, exotic ports of call into which a man could vanish and re-create himself, places his nameless, faceless persecutors would never hope to find. As he considered this possibility, it occurred to him how remarkably little bound him to his current life—family, friends, a few patients—but no wife, no child, no onerous financial

obligations. Remove the sentiment of love and discover how dangerously fragile are rendered one's ties to the familiar world. How seductive the possibility of utter change. It was all Doyle could do to
resist ruddering hard to port and setting course for the unknown.
Perhaps that was the genuine siren's song of legend, the temptation
to jettison the ballast of the past and rush weightless and unencum-
bered down a dark tunnel of rebirth. Perhaps that was the soul's destiny
regardless.

But as he stood at the brink of that decision, into the vacuum created
by that shimmering lure of escape returned his primal conviction that
when confronted by authentic evil—and he felt certain this is what
pursued him—to move off one's ground without a fight was an equal
if not greater evil. An evil of failure and cowardice. One might pass
a lifetime, or an endless string of lifetimes, without ever facing such
an unequivocal assault as this against the covenant of what a man holds
true about himself. Better to lose your life in defense of its sanctity
than to turn tail and live out what remained of one's allotted days as
a beaten dog. It was a hollow refuge that gave no shelter from self-
loathing.

So he did not steer their boat to the east. No matter if his enemies
were more numerous or powerful, they could flay the skin from his
muscles and boil the bones before receiving the satisfaction of surrender. He felt fierce and cold-minded and righteous. And if they had
harnessed some unholy power, so much the better: They were still
flesh, and all flesh could be made to bleed.

"I don't suppose you remember the name of that last publisher you
submitted your book to?" Sparks asked, gazing lazily over the side.

"Could have been any one of several. My account book was lost in
the shambles of my room."

"How unfortunate."

"How did they do it, Jack? I can manufacture an explanation for
nearly everything else that's happened—the séance and even beyond—
but I can't for the life of me see that one clear."

Sparks nodded thoughtfully, chewing on his pipe. "From your description, it appears the parties responsible have happened upon some
method to effect a change in the molecular structure of physical
objects."

"But that would imply they're actually in possession of some dreadful
arcane power."

"Yes, I suppose it would," Sparks said dryly.

"I find that unacceptable."

"If that is in fact what they've done, our opinions on it won't provide much of a deterrent, old boy. And while we're on the subject of inadequate explanations, there's also the matter of the gray hoods."

"You said that you didn't think those men were . . . *exactly* alive."

"You're the doctor."

"For an informed opinion, I'd need to examine one of them."

"Given their persistence, I'd say there's a better than fair chance you'll have that opportunity."

Their conversation had roused Larry from his rest. He crawled out from under the lean-to, rubbing the sleep from his eyes.

"Larry's seen one of them up close, haven't you, Larry?" asked Sparks.

"Wot's 'at, sir?" he asked, rummaging in his saddlebag for a sandwich.

"The gray hoods. Tell Dr. Doyle."

"Right. This was a few months back, sir," he said, tearing carnivorously into his Westphalian ham and cheese. "I'm on the job of tailin' a certain gent'l'man wot we've had before our attention for some time—"

"A material suspect in my investigation," added Sparks.

"Right. Now every Tuesday night this gent made a reg'lar habit of leavin' his fine Mayfair home by way of patronizin' a notorious, if not celebrated, house of joy in the nearby neighborhood of Soho, where his tastes tended to run in a somewhat unconventional direction—"

"That's not our concern at the moment, Larry," Sparks corrected.

"I read you correctly, sir. So after establishin' this pattern of the gent'l'man's migratory tendencies over a period of time, on this one occasion, 'stead of following him to his weekly assignation, I speculate upon myself to remain behind, enter the man's house in his absence, and have a butchers about the premises to see wot's wot," he continued with his mouth full, pausing for a generous tug of beer to wash down the last few Promethean bites.

"Old habits die hard," said Doyle dryly.

"Not to feather my own nest, sir, no sir, I'm right sworn off it, me and Barry both, God's truth," he said, crossing himself. "No, I cased his 'omestead in the strictest eventuality the gent might by chance've left some telling trifle lyin' about wot would lead us direct to a fuller understandin' of him and his compatriots' devious intentions."

"A list or communiqué of some sort," added Sparks.

"Just so. Even if such a thing had been left for instance inside a safe secreted away behind a map of the Hyperborean wilderness or a fancy oil portrait of his cows and kisses—that is, his missus—fussied up somewhat, idealized like, a bit shorter in the tooth and slimmer amidships than she might naturally be if truth were known, that's the artist's prerogative after all, idn't it, and I'm sure the bloke was paid handsomely for his trouble; these artistic types, he don't need a map to know which side his bread's buttered on—sorry, I digress. Whatever the case may be, I was nonetheless bound and determined and in full possession of the required talents to secure such an item, wherever it might be found." He finished the sandwich, drained his beer, belched explosively, and tossed the bottle overboard.

"So I opened the safe. Unfortunately, I discovered within its confines nothing much more interestin' than a fat stack of stock certificates— worth a queen bee's honey, they were, too; right difficult to move on the street, mind you, you'd raise a lotta eyebrows luggin' that lot 'round, although the old Larry and Barry wouldn't'a half minded havin' a bash, not for a minute—along with a few French postcards of recent vintage that in no way contradicted, in fact tended to confirm wot I 'ad already ascertained regarding the man's unorthodox intimate preferences, and finally a last will and testament leavin' lock, stock, and barrel of his considerable estate to none other than the fat woman so generously depicted in the paintin'.'"

"So in other words you found nothing," Doyle said impatiently, annoyed by the man's incorrigible loquacity.

"Not what I'd hoped for, no sir. However, after tossing the rest of the joint with no less disappointing returns, as I made my way back through the basement to the casement window wherein I had gained my entrance, I spied a door standing ajar. A mudroom or root cellar, which had escaped my attention on the way in. But wit' me eyes now more accustomed to the darkness, I noticed a shoe inside that door. A boot, to be exact, standing motionless. I could see a pants leg as well, to which said boot was clearly attached. I stood there, still as Nelson's statue, and studied this tableau for a full ten minutes. It was a hobnailed boot, steel around the toe, clean as a baby's bonnet. A very serious boot this was. A boot not to be trifled with. One swift kick to the midsection and your insides are as completely rearranged as a newlywed's furniture. During those ten minutes, that boot never moved. I tossed a penny into that room that in the stillness of that basement sounded like a naval gun salute. Not a twitch. This embold- ened me no end. I took the initiative. I opened the door."

"One of the gray hoods," said Doyle.

"That it was, sir. Seated on a stool, in the dark, face covered, hands on its knees thusly—"

"It didn't react?"

"To the extent, sir, that my thought at this point was I had stumbled upon the spoils of some mysterious theft from Madame Tussaud's Chamber of Horrors. This figure before me did absolutely nothing to suggest to my senses that I was sharing this small room with a living human being."

"What did you do?"

"I lit a candle from me pocket in order to carry out a more thorough examination. I cautiously reached out and touched the man's hand. A quick jab, like that. Nothing. I dripped hot candle wax on him. When that failed to win a response, I took out my pigsticker and gave him a nick. Never moved a muscle. But even though that skin was gray and cold as fish on a plate, something in my little brain kept telling me the man was not dead, not in the way of my understanding. Caught a chill, I did. The hair on the back of me neck stood up and said 'ello, and I've been in the presence of the recently departed more than a few times without so much as a never-you-mind. This lay entirely outside of my experience."

"Did you feel for a pulse or heartbeat?"

"I confess the thought of touching that squiff again was a bit too rich for my blood. I did what I thought the next best thing. I took off the hood."

"The blue thread—"

"Yes, sir, he did have a line of the blue thread, here, binding the lips, a rough job it was, too, and recent by the look of it—"

"And the eyes?"

"The eyes were closed, but the lids were not sewn shut—"

"Was he breathing?"

"Let him finish, Doyle," said Sparks.

"I don't know, sir, I didn't really have the luxury to check out that aspect of the situation, you see, 'cause when I got my first good peep at his airs and graces, I realized I knew this fella—"

"You *knew* him?"

"Yes, sir. Lansdown Dilks, a strong-armer from Wapping, a past master, he was, we all knew him in the life, a very bad character, too. That is until they pinched him cold, breakin' the neck of a shopkeeper in Brixton—"

"He was imprisoned?"

"Imprisoned, convicted of murder most foul, and packed off to prison three years ago. So you can imagine my surprise to find the old boy in a Mayfair root cellar with his lips upholstered like a windup soldier waitin' for a twist on the key in its back—"

"What did you do?"

By Land and Sea

"I heard the front door open upstairs. And at the sound of it, Lansdown's eyes opened."

"His eyes opened?"

"You heard me correct, sir."

"Did he . . . recognize you?"

"That's difficult to say, sir, 'cause I blew out that candle and was out the door, through that window, and halfway down the alley outside before the room got dark. And if I had it to do over, I'd do the same again. Lansdown Dilks was unpleasant enough in his previous incarnation to warrant the strict avoidance of his company; I figure the odds were hard against this new state havin' effected any positive turn in his disposition."

Doyle couldn't articulate a response. The wind shifted. Clouds were gathering off to the west. It seemed suddenly ten degrees colder. The ship's timbers groaned as they crested a wave.

"Whose house was this?" Doyle finally asked.

Sparks and Larry exchanged a guarded look that Doyle intercepted and to which he took immediate exception.

"Good Christ, man!" he said preemptively. "If I'm the one they're after, I've a right to know. In for a penny, in for a pound—"

"It's for your own protection, Doyle—" protested Sparks.

"A bloody lot of good that's done me! I'm a witness to murder, two murders—three, including Petrovitch—I can't return to my own home, my whole life's undone! And I have the pleasure of looking confidently forward to a life of abject terror until they butcher me like market beef!"

"Easy on, Doctor—"

"I'm either with you, Jack, on the inside of what you know from this moment on, or to hell with you and this whole business—you can put in to shore right now, drop me off, and I'll take my chances!"

Despite his inbred horror of making a scene, Doyle secretly enjoyed the cleansing effect of his outburst. It seemed to unlock a door inside Sparks, although it still remained for the door to be opened. Doyle took out his revolver and pointed it at the ship's hull.

"You've got ten seconds to make up your mind before I blow a hole in this damn boat, and you'll be lucky if any of us make it to shore," he said coolly, cocking back the hammer. "I'm quite serious."

Larry made a casual reach into his pocket.

"No, Larry," said Sparks, without looking at him.

Larry removed his hand. They waited.

"Time's up, Jack," Doyle said, raising the gun, ready to fire.

"The house belongs to Brigadier General Marcus McCauley Drummond. Royal Fusiliers, retired. Put the gun away, Doctor."

"I'm not familiar with the name," said Doyle, easing his finger off the trigger but not relaxing the hammer.

"General Drummond's service record was distinguished primarily by its lack of distinction," said Sparks, in a clipped tone free of asperity. "His officer's commission was purchased with family money, whereby his inexplicable rise to top rank comes clear: The Drummonds are one of the nation's most prominent munitions manufacturers, our foremost suppliers of bullet and mortar shot. They own plants in Blackpool and Manchester as well as three German companies producing heavy artillery. General Drummond was not a particularly avid consumer of his own inventory; during his twenty years of service no troop under his command ever fired a shot in anger.

"Upon the death of his father six years ago, the General cashiered out and assumed control of the family concern. The aggressiveness that was in such scant supply during his years in service to the Crown found its voice in commerce: Sales and profits have tripled. Last year Drummond married his eldest daughter into the Krupp family of Munich, his most formidable competitor on the Continent. The result is a potential monopoly. The General is now poised to dominate the international as well as domestic market. He is currently negotiating to purchase the company that manufactures the very service revolver you are holding in your hand. Is there anything else you wish to know?"

Doyle released the hammer and lowered the gun.

"What drew your attention to Drummond in the first place?"

"Orders," said Sparks, managing in a single word to invoke eight hundred years of monarchy, thereby rendering further inquiry in that direction tantamount to sedition.

Doyle was not immune to the potency of such a suggestion. He replaced his gun in the bag and sat down. International munitions manufacturers. Orders from the Queen. His mind reeled.

"My father always said a man's most useful virtue is to recognize when he's in over his head," he said wearily.

"Have a sandwich, guv," said Larry kindly, offering the basket.

Doyle took one. Eating always made him feel better. At least he could still rely on that.

"I don't suppose you could prosecute Drummond for harboring a fugitive."

"There was no trace of Mr. Dilks or any other gray hood on Larry's subsequent visits to the General's house," Sparks explained. "Even so, the case presents more insurmountable difficulties."

By Land and Sea

"How's that?"

"According to the records of the Central Criminal Court, the prisoner Lansdown Dilks died in the hangman's noose last February. Authorities were kind enough to post us a photograph of his headstone."

The sandwich sagged in Doyle's hand. His jaw was agape.

"The other point I should like to illuminate for you, Doyle, is that, generally speaking, conventional prosecution of whatever adversaries I might in the execution of my duties pursue is not necessarily, by any means, my primary objective," Sparks said quietly. "I am not, in other words, at all times necessarily bound to discharge my responsibilities within the strictest confines of the law."

"No?"

"Not strictly, no. This frees me to rely on the talents of men under my command who would otherwise find the prerequisites for employment within the established law-enforcement system . . . unduly rigorous."

Doyle turned to Larry, who smiled, cracked open a bottle of stout with the gap in his teeth, and offered it to him.

"I see," Doyle said, and took the beer.

"Now, Doctor, I have confided in you the true nature of my business," Sparks said, leaning back and relighting his pipe. "Are you still of a mind to cast your lot with me, or shall I instruct Larry to put in at the next negotiable beach?"

Sparks seemed perfectly content to wait him out indefinitely. For a moment, South America leapt irrationally into Doyle's mind as a third, immensely attractive alternative. He drank his beer and tried to brake the wheel of fortune spinning in his head.

"I'm with you," said Doyle.

"Good man. And glad we are to have you," said Sparks, energetically pumping his hand.

"Welcome aboard, sir," added Larry, beaming.

Doyle thanked them, smiling wanly, secretly yearning for even the smallest confidence in the wisdom of his choice. The question of his enlistment settled, they busied themselves with trimming of lines and sails to fit the changing conditions of the sea. As the sun reached its ascendant, land appeared on the southern horizon.

"The Isle of Sheppey," Sparks said, pointing south. "If the wind holds, we should make land at Faversham by sundown. It's a full night's ride from there to Topping. If you don't mind, I think it advisable we push straight on through."

Doyle said he didn't mind.

"The late Lady Nicholson's husband is a man by the name of Charles Stewart Nicholson, son of Richard Sidney Nicholson, the earl of Oswald, who over the years has quietly become one of the wealthiest men in England," said Sparks, with a note of contempt. "I'm most eager to meet Charles Stewart Nicholson. Would you like to know why?"

"Yes," answered Doyle neutrally, content now to let Sparks dictate his own rate of revelation.

"Lord Nicholson, the younger, came to my attention last year when he sold a large tract of family land in Yorkshire to a blind trust. Surrounding this seemingly commonplace transaction was a legal miasma that proved tremendously difficult to penetrate: Someone had gone to considerable lengths to conceal the identity of the buyer from the public view."

Sparks paused, watching Doyle's confusion with amused interest.

"Would it surprise you to learn that the man who purchased Nicholson's land was Brigadier General Marcus McCauley Drummond?"

"Yes, Jack. Yes, it would."

"Yes. It did me, too."

CHAPTER 10

Topping

THEY DID INDEED reach Faversham by nightfall. Negotiating the outer reaches of the Isle of Sheppey, they sailed up the generous arm of the sea known locally as the Swale, took a narrowing channel upstream, and put in at the edge of the oyster beds in shallow waters outlying the old town.

Larry leapt off the bow, pulled them ashore, grabbed their bags, and scampered up an embankment, disappearing from view. Doyle and Sparks gathered the remainder of their possessions and followed his path up the hill. Waiting for them on the ridge above was a brougham with a brace of fresh horses, and helping Larry load in was none other than brother Barry. Doyle found it nigh onto impossible to discern one from the other until he moved close enough to spy Barry's disfigurement. Larry took evident pleasure in properly reintroducing Barry to his valued friend, the esteemed Dr. Doyle. Barry was not nearly so talkative as his brother, quite the contrary, but between the two of them Larry's generous endowment of gab amounted to an equitable disbursement of verbal capital. Doyle found his chilly opinion of the twins beginning to thaw with prolonged exposure to Larry's homely warmth. The only dissonance he experienced came while attempting to reconcile Barry's sour mien and retiring disposition with Larry's characterization of him as a rampant, indefatigable womanizer.

Once the carriage was packed and travel-ready, Larry bid Doyle a friendly farewell—he was leaving on some undisclosed assignment— and walked blithely off into the night. Barry assumed the driver's seat, Doyle joined Sparks in the enclosed cab, and they drove away.

"Where's Larry off to?" Doyle asked, looking back through the curtains at Larry's receding figure, already missing him a little.

"Cover our tracks and make his way to London. There's work to do," said Sparks. A dark mood had crept over him with the night. He was remote and avoided eye contact, mulling over something tough and disagreeable. With no invitation to engage, Doyle did not press for conversation and eventually drifted off to sleep.

He awoke to weight shifting overhead. The carriage was still moving. Sparks was no longer in his seat. Doyle fumbled for his watch: half past midnight.

The door opened, and a small steamer trunk appeared in the opening.

"Don't sit there, Doyle, give us a hand," he heard Sparks say.

Doyle helped wrestle the trunk onto the seat opposite as Sparks pushed it through, reentered, and shut the door behind him. His color was high again, his spirits burnished to their former brightness.

"How is your weekend etiquette?" asked Sparks.

"My what?"

"Houseguest skills, billiards, table talk, all that rubbish."

"What's that got to do with—"

"We're visiting a gentleman's country house for New Year's Eve weekend, Doyle. I'm trying to ascertain your aptitude for the upper crust."

"I know which fork to use, if that's what you mean," said Doyle, his ears burning with pride.

"Don't take offense, old boy, I need to determine which part you're going to play. The less suspicion we arouse among Lord Nicholson and his posh crowd, the better."

"What are my choices?"

"Master or manservant," said Sparks, throwing open the trunk to reveal its two halves packed with wardrobe appropriate to either role.

"Why don't we just tell them I'm a doctor?" Doyle asked, hoping he wouldn't have to shed his comfortable middle-class skin for a vertical move in either direction.

Topping

"That's boxing clever. There's every reason to suspect your enemies may be waiting for us there. Why don't you have cards printed and solicit for patients while we're at it?"

"I see," said Doyle. "You're suggesting we arrive incognito."

"Baron Everett Gascoyne-Pouge, and valet, R.S.V.P.," Sparks said, producing an invitation to the year's end party, addressed to same.

"How did you come by this?"

"It's a facsimile."

"But what if the real Gascoyne-Pouge should decide to come?"

"There is no such person," said Sparks, barely concealing his displeasure at Doyle's puny leaps of imagination.

"Ah. Printed yourself. I'm with you now."

"I was starting to wonder."

"Sorry, I'm always a bit thick just after sleep," Doyle explained, yawning. "Takes a moment to stir the soup again."

"Quite all right," Sparks said, handing him the working-class clothes. "And I'm sure you'll find the servants' quarters at Topping will be more than adequate."

"But, Jack, don't you think they'll see right through this charade?" Doyle stuttered, staring down at the valet's vestments. "I mean I suppose I can muddle through playing the part well enough—"

"No one ever looks at the servants, Doyle. You'll blend in like a black cat in a coal bin."

"But I mean, what if they *should* notice me, Jack? They may not have a clear idea of your appearance, but they certainly know what I look like."

Sparks stared at him hard. "Right," he said. He rummaged around in the trunk and pulled out a razor. "We'll have Barry pull over so you don't endanger your sense of smell."

Doyle's fingers flew protectively to his mustache.

✿   ✿   ✿

Gray dawn of New Year's Eve found them entering an arched gate and making the approach to Topping Manor down a straight and narrow lane lined with stately oaks, their sere branches reaching out to form a craggy canopy. Dressed in the unfamiliar garb of his new profession, Doyle had managed only a few minutes' more rough sleep, troubled by dreams of hopelessly incompetent servitude, followed with unmasking and capture by unknown figures. Queen Victoria had figured prominently; he remembered serving tea only to have her discover a dead mouse floating in the pot. That distressed

105

him far more than the hard treatment he suffered at the hands of his shadowy captors, and he woke with a start, bathed in a sheen of cold sweat.

He realized his waking had been precipitated by the carriage braking to a stop. Doyle heard the door open and close before his eyes could properly inform him that Sparks was leaving the coach. Fumbling for the door, Doyle dragged himself outside.

The rows of oaks ended abruptly where Barry had brought them to a halt. The majestic trees had at one time apparently marched on ahead, accompanying the road for an additional hundred yards; now not only the oaks but every tree from that point forward had been felled, stumps scorched and blasted, and all ground cover burned. Rising abruptly out of the torched flatland before them was a solid wall thirty feet high, makeshift, unbalanced, constructed from the untrimmed bodies of the downed trees, coarsely mortared with rocks, bricks, straw, dead grass, and wattles. Early light reflected off chunks of broken glass set in the binding caulk and all along the rampart. The wall ran off for a considerable distance in both directions and then doubled back, appearing to entirely enclose the manor house and grounds inside. The highest parapets and crenellations of Topping Manor itself, a late Gothic masterpiece, were visible above and beyond the mysterious fortification. No smoke rose from any of her chimneys. No gates or entrances interrupted the unbroken face of the wall. Viewed from their perspective, this crude eruption of a barrier spoke of nothing but terror, haste, and madness.

"Good Christ . . ."

"It would appear the fate of our party is in some jeopardy," said Sparks.

"What's happened here?"

"Barry, take the carriage round, see if they've left a way in. The doctor and I will investigate on foot," Sparks instructed.

Barry tipped his cap and drove off to circumnavigate the fortress as Sparks and Doyle picked their way forward through the devastated field.

"What do you see, Doyle? What does this tell you?"

"The fire was set recently, I'd say within the week. Probably the last step in the disfigurement. Discoloration around the stumps is similar; suggests they were all cut down within a short period of time."

"A great number of men, working together," said Sparks.

"How close is the nearest town?"

"At least five miles. The wall isn't the work of craftsmen, Doyle. The servants of the manor must have done the work."

"Without supervision or any evident design."

"No joints or mortises. No thought to quality or longevity."

"Someone wanted a barricade put up quickly."

"Why, Doyle?"

Doyle stopped and looked at the wall, ten feet away, trying to feel the panic and urgency of its builders. "No time. Something coming. Something that needed keeping out."

"They started building before Lady Nicholson and her brother were killed. How long did she say her son had been missing?"

"Three days before the séance."

"Before he was kidnapped as well; that could've been the reason. Fear of abduction. Protect your young—the oldest instinct in the human heart."

"A child can be moved, sent away," countered Doyle. "It's almost too rational a reason. This feels like the work of someone who's gone utterly mad."

"Or been driven there."

Sparks stared grimly up at the wall's vast reach. Two sharp blasts from a cabbie's whistle pulled their attention away to the right.

"Barry," said Sparks, taking off at a sprint, shouting back over his shoulder at his less agile companion. "Come along, Doyle, don't dawdle."

Doyle ran after him, rounded the corner, and turned left. Barry waved to them, standing beside the brougham, a quarter-mile away, half the visible length of the wall. Doyle labored to keep pace with Sparks and was completely breathless by the time he reached them.

Barry had summoned them to a rough passage hacked through the barrier, a head taller than a man and twice as wide. Wood chips covered the ground, mostly outside the entrance. A weathered ax lay on the ground nearby. Gazing through the opening, they could see stables and the house beyond. There was no sight or sound of activity inside.

"Complete your survey of the wall, please, Barry," ordered Sparks. "I predict we'll find this provides us with our only access."

Barry jumped aboard the cab and headed off down the wall.

"Someone was cutting their way in, not out," said Doyle, examining the edge of the gap.

"And after its completion."

Doyle nodded in agreement. "Who cut through? Friend or enemy?"

"Keeping something out favors the latter, doesn't it?"

Nothing stirred within, but they stayed where they were, as if some invisible obstruction as solid as the logs remained between them and the grounds of Topping Manor, until Barry returned from his survey to confirm that this portal was indeed the only entrance.

"Shall we have a look, then?" Sparks said casually.

"After you, Jack," said Doyle.

Sparks instructed Barry to remain with the horses, slid his rapier from his walking stick, and ventured through the hollow. Doyle drew his revolver and joined him. They began by patrolling the wall's interior perimeter, hugging the redoubt as they worked their way around. It was evident that most of the wall's labor had been completed from inside. Ladders and stacks of unused logs were abundant. Bales of hay and other binding materials lay near pits packed with congealed clay. The wall ran a consistent fifty yards from the front of the building proper, but in the rear, where the architecture of the manor was more irregular, the wall moved considerably closer, in spots no more than ten feet away.

The grounds, once clearly immaculate and groomed, were a ruin. Hedges crushed, statuary toppled, grass trampled and slashed. One stretch of wall barreled through the remains of a topiary garden; odd bits of the animals' spiny bodies extruded from the base as if severed by a train. A child's playground had been equally mangled, smashed toys scattered about. A weathered hobbyhorse lay where it had fallen in a pile of sand, its painted exertions a parody of rictus.

Ground-floor windows had been barricaded from inside the house, curtains drawn around planks, tables, unhinged doors that had been randomly employed. Some windows were broken, glass fallen to the inside. Every door they tried was locked and immovable.

"Let's try the stables," said Sparks.

They crossed to and entered the freestanding stable on the far side of the graveled drive. No like effort had been made to secure it; the door stood open. Saddles and gear lined the shelves and pegs of the tack room. The grooms' quarters were neat and tidy: beds made, personal effects filling the drawers and bed stands. A half-eaten kidney pie sat on a plate on the table in the common room, beside it a teapot and cup of cold tea. The orderliness of the place in the shadow of such monstrous chaos felt deeply unsettling. Sparks eased open a creaking door that led directly to the stables proper. The barn appeared empty.

"Listen, Doyle," Sparks said quietly. "What do you hear?"

After a moment. "Nothing."

Sparks nodded. "In a stable."

"No flies," said Doyle, realizing what was missing.

"Nor birds outside, either."

They moved down the center, opening the stall doors one after the other. All were empty, but in some the ripe memory of horses lingered.

"They set most of them free early on," said Sparks.

"Must've used some to pull in the wood, don't you think?"

"The drays, yes. They let them go once they had the logs they needed. But there have been horses boarded in at least three of these stalls since the wall was finished."

The last door wouldn't budge. Sparks silently indicated his intentions. Doyle nodded, took the rapier from him, and raised his pistol. Sparks took two steps back, whirled, and kicked the door full force. It flew open with a loud crack. Inside the stall a body lay on its stomach in the straw, its left leg jutting out from the knee at an impossible angle.

"Easy, Doyle, he's well past causing us harm."

"Must've had his foot against the door," said Doyle, lowering the gun.

They stepped cautiously in toward the body. It wore high boots, breeches, a shirt and waistcoat, the working costume of a footman.

"What's this then?" asked Sparks, pointing to the floor.

Straw throughout the stall was clotted with thick trails of a dried, murky secretion: shiny, almost phosphorescent, laid down in a rambling, crazy-quilt pattern. From the body, the trails separated and led up and over the walls. It emitted no odor, but something about the silvery hue and oleaginous composition of the substance prompted one's gorge to tumble.

"No smell from the body, either," said Doyle. "It hasn't decomposed."

Sparks looked at him with comprehending curiosity. They knelt beside the corpse. Its clothes shone, polished and glossy, coated with the same strange residue. They put their hands under it and turned the body over; it was shockingly weightless, almost entirely devoid of mass, and then they saw why: The face was mummified, only the barest netting of flesh covering the bones. The eye sockets were empty, shrunken, the hands as delicately skeletal as a dried flower buried in the pages of a family Bible.

"Ever seen the like?" asked Sparks.

"Not in a body that's been dead less than twenty years," Doyle replied, examining it more closely. "As if it's been preserved. Mummified."

"Had the life sucked right from his bones."

Sparks squeezed one of its clutched fists in his hand; it collapsed into a thousand dusty fragments, like a broken filigree of frozen lace.

"What could have done this?" Doyle said quietly.

A form moved behind them outside the stall.

"What is it, Barry?" Sparks said, without turning around.

"Some'fin' you ought have a look at out here."

They left the stall and followed Barry outside. He pointed to the rooftop of the manor. A thin ribbon of smoke issued from the tallest chimney.

"Started 'bout five minutes ago," Barry said.

"Someone's alive in there," said Doyle.

"Good. Let's ring the bell and announce ourselves."

"Do you think that's wise, Jack?"

"We've come all this way. Don't want to disappoint our host."

"But we don't know who's in there, do we?"

"Only one way to find out," answered Sparks, striding purposefully toward the house.

"But the doors and windows are all obstructed."

"That won't prove much of an obstacle to Barry."

Sparks snapped his fingers. With a tip of the hat, Barry ran ahead and without skipping a beat leapt onto the front of the house, grabbed purchase for hand and foot in the margins between bricks, and scampered up to the second floor with the ease of a spider on a web. Pulling a jemmy stick from his coat, within seconds he persuaded a window to yield, pushed it open, and poured himself through to the interior.

Doyle was fraught with anxiety at what horror might be lying in wait for the little man. Sparks calmly pulled a cheroot from his jacket, struck a match with his thumbnail, and lit the smoke, all the while keeping a cool eye on the entrance.

"Just be a moment now," Sparks said.

They heard movement on the other side of the door, the ragged scratch of heavy weight being dragged across a tiled floor, then a lock disengaging. A moment later, Barry opened the front door, and they entered Topping.

Tables and chairs had been stacked and jumbled against the door, which Barry now had the good sense to lock again behind them. Loose paper and rubbish littered the great hall. A decorative suit of armor lay defeated and broken on the black-and-white tile. With no daylight penetrating the occluded windows, the air was close with a heavy and oppressive gloom. Glimpses into vast public rooms opening out on either side of the entry revealed no substantial abuses, only disarray and neglect.

Topping

"Yes, I'd say the party is definitely off," said Sparks, casually flicking away an ash.

"There's a gent upstairs in 'a hall," Barry said unobtrusively, pointing to the grand staircase before them.

"What was he doing?" asked Doyle.

"Looked like 'e was polishing the silver."

Sparks and Doyle looked at each other.

"Why don't you have a look around down here, Barry," Sparks said as he started up the stairs two at a time.

Barry nodded and moved off into an adjoining room. Doyle found himself standing alone at the bottom of the stairs.

"What about me?" Doyle asked.

"Wouldn't fancy walking these halls by myself," answered Sparks, as he reached the top. "No telling what one might bump into."

Sparks waited as Doyle ran up to join him. They moved into an intersection with a rambling hall that zigzagged off in both directions. Closed pairs of opposite doors lined the walls. There was no less light, but the air of menace was palpably thicker. Moving to the left, they turned the first corner and came across a thick white line of some granular substance poured across the width of the hall; Sparks knelt down and wet a finger, dabbed, sniffed, and then tasted it.

"Salt," he said.

"Salt?"

Sparks nodded. They stepped over the salt and continued down the hall. Mirrors and canvases hung in the spaces between doors; every one had been turned to face the wall. They stepped over a second line of salt and rounded another turn. Here the hallway stretched away into the murk as far as the eye could see. At the far end, there was both movement and light; a candle was burning. As they moved closer, eyes adjusting to the dark, they saw the person Barry had described.

He sat on a three-legged stool, a pear-shaped, balding hulk of a man, middle-aged, pasty, and hollow-eyed. He wore butler's livery, stained and grimy, buttons missing or fastened askew. Swallowed in folds of excess flesh, his features were doughy, ill defined. His buttery neck spilled over a collar gray with sweat. Laid out before him was a silver service, full settings for forty, set in precisely measured rows. In his pudgy hands, he held a tattered rag and a gravy boat, rubbing and buffing one with the other obsessively, polish and a basin of water on the floor at his feet. He muttered darkly as he worked, his voice a raspy whisper with plummy undertones.

"The forequarter of lamb requires three hours . . . two hours for the oyster pudding—must find the whetstone; carving knifes aren't sharp enough—rosettes and a pastry bag for the charlotte *à la Parisienne* ... for the ptarmigan a Madeira sauce ..."

He took no notice of Sparks and Doyle as they approached and stopped at the edge of the silver display.

"Croquettes of leveret ... a fricandeau of veal ... boned snipe stuffed with forcemeat ..."

"Hello," said Sparks.

The man froze without looking up, as if he had imagined the sound of another voice, then, dismissing the possibility as unimaginable, returned to his handiwork.

"Shells for the quail and pigeon pies ... yeast dumplings with truffles and *foie gras* ..."

"Here's a bright specimen," Sparks whispered to Doyle, then: "I say; hello there!"

The man stopped again, then slowly turned and looked up at them. His eyes seemed to have trouble focusing; he blinked and squinted repeatedly, as if the sight of them was too much to hold within a single field of vision.

"Yes, hello," said Sparks congenially and, now that he had the man's attention, more quietly.

Tears sprang from the man's eyes, and great lachrymose heaves erupted from deep inside him, rippling the fabrics encasing his slack, corpulent belly. His eyes disappeared into the mountainous recesses of his brow as waves of moisture skied shamelessly down his wobbling cheeks.

"There now, fellow," said Sparks, with a concerned look at Doyle, "can't be as bad as all that, can it?"

The gravy boat danced in his dangling hands as thunderous sobs racked his body. If his center of gravity had not been so low and prodigious, he would surely have plopped off his stool.

"Now, now, what seems to be the trouble here?" asked Doyle, slipping into his best bedside manner.

A succession of wheezes, gasps, and explosive eructations followed, as the man attempted to navigate the hot torrent overwhelming his emotional creek bed. His wet pink mouth convulsed like a trout beached in the mud.

"I'm ... I'm ... I'm ... I'm ..." A lame stutter was all the man could manage between palpitating spasms.

"It's quite all right. Take your time," said Doyle indulgently, as if cajoling a widow to discuss her neuralgia over a glass of elderberry wine.

Topping

"I'm ... I'm ..." The man inhaled mightily, captured and held the air at its apex, struggling as it vibrated hotly inside him, until he grabbed hold of his breath by the scruff of the neck—one could almost see him do it—and expelled it explosively out of his throat: "... not the cook!"

The man seemed shocked by the sound of his own voice, his lips stuck in a quizzical O.

"You're not the cook," Sparks repeated back to him, to clarify.

The man shook his head violently to confirm, then fearing he'd been misunderstood, nodded vigorously in agreement, accompanied by a swelling orchestration of bovine snorts, braps, snurrs, and gleeps, as he was clearly not yet equal to another assault on the peaks of articulation.

"Has someone ... mistaken you for the cook?" asked Doyle, perplexed.

The man moaned most unhappily and shook his head again, his jowls whipping around him like an aspic.

"Let me make absolutely certain we all share in the same common understanding," said Sparks, with a complicit look to Doyle, "that you, sir, are most assuredly ... not the cook."

The rationality of Sparks's reply appeared to hammer a plug into the punctured keg of the man's misery. The waterworks subsided. His shuddering flesh slowly settled. He looked down and seemed genuinely bewildered to discover the gravy boat in his ham-sized hands—then, as if there were nothing else to do when one found a gravy boat in one's hands, he began idly to polish it again.

"What's your name, my good man?" Sparks asked gently.

"Ruskin, sir," the man replied.

"I take it that you are currently in the employ of this good house, Ruskin," said Sparks.

"Butler, sir. In charge of pantry, plate, and scullery," said Ruskin, without a hint of pride. "Worked my way up from the knife and brushing room. Fourteen years old when I came to the Manor. The Master and I, we grew up together, after a fashion."

"Why are you polishing the silver, Ruskin?" asked Doyle gently.

"Got to be done, doesn't it?" Ruskin replied calmly. "No one else to do it, is there?"

"Not the cook, certainly," Sparks said, sympathetically leading him on.

"No, sir. A very wicked and a lazy man, the cook. Pa-*ree*-si-an," he intoned, as if no further explanation were necessary. "No discipline in him. Cuts corners. Never learned the value of a day's labor for a day's wage, in my opinion. Better off without him, we are. Good riddance to bad rubbish, if I may speak candidly, sir."

"So you've been left with the cooking as well," said Sparks, with a nod to Doyle, now able to trace the root of the man's despair.

"That I have, sir. Now the menu, that was settled weeks ago. Had it printed up for the table settings." He patted his pockets, smearing himself with polish. "Have a copy here somewhere."

"That's quite all right, Ruskin," said Sparks.

"Yes, sir. And a glorious dinner it is, too," said Ruskin, with a faraway light in his eye that Doyle associated with the dangerously unbalanced. Or perhaps it was the contemplation of all the food that so transported him.

"And there's a problem with the dinner, is there?" asked Sparks.

"We find ourselves a bit understaffed at the moment, and with the cook gone as he is, well, I'm afraid it's all a bit beyond my reach. . . ."

"Cooking the dinner," said Doyle helpfully.

"Exactly, sir. I plan to get on to the cooking straightaway, after discharging my other responsibilities. There's a great deal to do, and one needs time to cook the dinner properly, but I've committed the menu to memory should there be any confusion," said Ruskin, absentmindedly patting his pockets again. "Dear. Dear, dear. I've misplaced my watch."

"Quarter to nine," Doyle said.

"Quarter to nine. Quarter to nine," he repeated, as if the whole idea of time were alien to him. "The guests will be arriving—oh, are you gentlemen here for the dinner?"

"We've arrived somewhat ahead of schedule," said Sparks, trying not to alarm him.

"Then you are the first, actually—welcome, welcome—oh dear, I beg your humble pardon, gentlemen, I haven't offered to take your bags," Ruskin said, attempting to rouse his quivering mass off the stool.

"It's all right, Ruskin; our man has the situation well in hand," said Sparks.

"Are you sure? I should drive your carriage round to the barn—"

"Thank you, Ruskin, it's taken care of."

"Thank you, sir." Ruskin settled back down. He sagged visibly, and his skin turned a deeper shade of gray.

"Are you all right?" asked Doyle.

"I'm passing tired, sir. Truth is I could do with a bit of a lie down before the festivities, just a few minutes is all, but you see, there's so terribly much to do," said Ruskin, short of breath, dousing the abundant sweat from his forehead with the rag, streaking his brow with metallic black.

"Are you expecting quite a lot of guests for New Year's Eve, Ruskin?" asked Sparks.

"Yes, sir, near to fifty. Quite the gala. Quite exceeding himself this year, the Master is."

"The Master's here in the house, is he?"

"Yes, sir," said Ruskin with an exhausted sigh, a hint of moisture appearing at the corners of his eyes. "Not himself. Not himself at all. Won't leave his rooms. Shouts at me through the door. Won't take his breakfast."

"Could you show us to him, Ruskin?" asked Sparks.

"I don't think the Master wishes to be disturbed at the moment, sir, all due respect. He hasn't been well lately. Not well at all."

"I understand your concern, Ruskin. Perhaps it would set your mind at rest if Dr. Doyle here were to have a consultation with him."

"Oh, are you a doctor, sir?" Ruskin said, looking up, his face brightening, an effect not unlike a full moon rising.

"I am," said Doyle, holding up his bag by way of evidence.

"If you could direct us to the Master's chambers, we'll leave you to your work," said Sparks, and then, in response to Ruskin's second elaborate attempt to rise: "No need to announce us, Ruskin, I'm sure we can manage—are his rooms on this floor then?"

"Far end of the hall. Last door on your right. Knock first, if you would."

"Thank you, Ruskin. The silver looks splendid."

"Do you really think so, sir?" Ruskin said, eyes whelming with pathetic gratitude.

"I'm sure the dinner will be a great success," said Sparks. He gestured for Doyle to follow and started back down the hallway. Doyle hung back.

"What's the wall for, Ruskin?" Doyle asked.

Ruskin looked at him, screwing his face into a puzzle. "What wall, sir?"

"The wall outside."

"I'm sure I don't know what you mean, sir," said Ruskin, with blank but attentive concern.

Sparks signaled Doyle to discourage pursuing the point. Doyle nodded, then stepped carefully forward through the field of silver. As he moved closer to Ruskin, Doyle could see that the man's lips were parched and blistered, his eyes as red as embers. He put a hand to Ruskin's pale forehead; it was burning with fever. Ruskin stared up at him with the blind adoration of a beloved and dying dog.

"You're not feeling very well, are you, Ruskin?" Doyle said softly.

"No, sir. Not very well, sir," he said weakly.

Doyle took out his handkerchief, dipped it in the water basin, and tenderly wiped the grime off Ruskin's forehead. Beads of moisture ran down his broad face; Ruskin dabbed at them hungrily with his tongue.

"I think it would be a very good idea," said Doyle, "for you to go to your room now and rest for a while."

"But the preparations, sir—"

"You needn't worry, I'll speak to the Master. And I'm sure he'd agree that the dinner will proceed much more smoothly if you're properly refreshed."

"I am so very tired, sir," he said, pathetically grateful for the kindness, his mouth drooping, his chin trembling with the approach of more tears.

"Give me your hand now, Ruskin. Let's help you up . . . here we go."

With all his strength, Doyle was able to leverage the fevered wretch to his feet. Ruskin wobbled like a tenpin struck with a glancing blow. Doyle wondered just how long the man had been sitting there. He retrieved a vial from his vest pocket, asked Ruskin to hold out his hand, and tapped into his pillowy mitt four pills from the vial.

"Take these with water, Ruskin. They'll help you to rest. Promise me you'll do as I ask."

"I promise," Ruskin said, with the grave docility of a child.

"Off you go then," said Doyle, handing him the candle and patting him on the shoulder; the fabric of his shirt was wet and clammy.

"Off I go," Ruskin echoed with cheerless, empty mimicry.

Ruskin's lumbering steps down the hall recalled to Doyle's mind a shopworn elephant in leg irons he'd once seen in a circus parade. After Ruskin had shambled out of sight, Doyle and Sparks moved back along the corridor the way they'd come.

"We can be sure of one thing," said Sparks. "Ruskin didn't chop that hole in the wall. He couldn't knock the skin off a rice pudding."

"I don't think he's left the house in weeks. The Master's most loyal servant."

"At this late date, the Master's only servant. This house employed a staff of thirty in its heyday. Not the most congenial atmosphere at present, wouldn't you say?"

Topping

They reached the intersection just as Barry was coming up the stairs.

"House is empty. Boarded up," Barry said—more to the point than his brother, thought Doyle—"Kitchen's a mess. Been up to a fair amount of spud-bashin' without botherin' 'bout the washin' up."

"The work of the lamentable Ruskin, no doubt," said Sparks.

"Two queer things," Barry continued. "There's salt been poured in all the hallways and across the thresholds—"

"Yes, and the other?"

"There's a false wall in the larder off the kitchen. Behind it's a door—"

"To where?"

"Couldn't get it open without me tools. Below stairs by the smell—"

"To the cellar."

"Already been to the cellar: This ain't the cellar. And there's an odd wind coming up under that door."

Sparks showed keen interest. "Bring our bags in from the carriage if you would, Barry. And then open that door."

Barry doffed his hat and headed back down the stairs.

"So if we agree Ruskin was on the inside and couldn't have managed it, who cut the hole through the wall?" asked Doyle, as they continued down the hall.

"It was our late friend from the stables, the footman. Peter Farley's his name; he'd been away on business, the transfer of four horses to Topping from family property in Scotland," Sparks said, handing Doyle a paper.

"What's this?" Doyle asked, unfolding the paper and reading.

"A bill of lading: a list of horses' names, their descriptions, analysis of their health. Signed Peter Farley. I found that in the pocket of the footman's coat, hanging on a peg in the groom's bedroom. Sometime during the last few days—follow my thinking—Farley returns with the horses. The wall has gone up in his absence; clearly some madness has overwhelmed his home. He's four prized horses to tend and feed after a hard ride and perhaps a wife or family working inside—he must find a way in."

"That's why he cut through instead of scaling the wall."

"There's broken glass set on its edges to discourage such access. And remember the dimensions of the hole."

"Just high and wide enough for a horse to pass."

"He worked fast for the better part of a day. He had to get those horses in quickly; there are a great number of deep hoofprints in the ground around the entrance."

"Something was spooking them. Something approaching."

"Unfortunately for our brave stablehand, the door he carved to save those horses proved his undoing."

"I don't follow."

"Reason it out: The hole is finished, he leads the horses to stable, which he finds deserted but otherwise unaffected. He doesn't venture into the main house, that's not his place; he's a simple man, his world is in that barn. If the Master's gone off his kilt and built a big wall, it's no concern of his. He puts the horses up, brushes them down, feeds them. He makes himself some tea and heats up a meat pie. He hears something outside, something disturbing the horses, leaves his supper on the table and goes to the barn to investigate, where he's done in by something his doorway has allowed to follow him inside the compound."

"Poor devil. What could have done such a thing to him?"

They had negotiated their way to the end of the hall, outside of what Ruskin had described as the Master's doorway. The floor at this end of the corridor was completely covered with a layer of salt.

"What good is salt? What does it provide defense against?" pondered Sparks.

The air was shattered by a loud crash of breaking crockery and an angry holler from inside the room.

"Foppery! Fops and frippery! Ha!"

Sparks put a finger to his lips, asking for silence, and knocked on the door. No response, but the sounds inside ceased. He knocked again.

"Everything all right, sir?" asked Sparks, but what issued from him was an uncannily accurate rendering of Ruskin.

"Go . . . away! Go away and play trains!"

"Begging your pardon, sir," Sparks continued with the guise, "but some of the guests have arrived. They're asking to see you."

"Guests? The *guests* have arrived?" the voice trumpeted, with equal measures of incredulity and contempt.

"Yes, sir, and the dinner's ready. We should be sitting down; you know how you disfavor a meal when the entrées go cold," Sparks went on. Doyle could have closed his eyes and never suspected the obese unfortunate wasn't nearby.

Footsteps moved to the door inside. A series of bolts were thrown.

"If there's one thing I can't bear, you gelatinous cur," the voice said, rising in pitch and volume, "it's the squalid perpetuation of lies!" More latches unlatched and locks released. "There is no party, there are no guests, there is no dinner, and if I hear another word

118

from your wormy, liverish lips about any of this slumgullion, I shall with my own hands strangle the life from your swinish neck, boil your corpse in a pit, and render the fat for Christmas candles!"

The door was pulled open, and they were confronted by a man of average height and build whose blandly pleasant features were framed by a wild nimbus of matted blond beard and hair that had known no recent acquaintance of brush or comb. His eyebrows sprang up like untended hedges overrunning the ridges of his forehead. The eyes were bulbous, opalescent, and light as cornflowers, set wide apart on either side of a sharply beaked nose. He had attained at least forty years, but his face had an unlined schoolboy youthfulness that seemed less due to sound breeding than a petulant refusal to assimilate experience. He wore a black silk dressing gown over a loose blouse, peculiar cork-soled boots, and jodhpurs. And he was holding a double-barreled shotgun half a foot from their faces.

No one moved. "Lord Nicholson, I presume," Sparks said, as pleasant and collected as a missionary on call.

"You're not Ruskin," Nicholson said with conviction, and then, unable to resist the opportunity for another disparagement: "That postulant oaf."

"Baron Everett Gascoyne-Pouge," Sparks said, affecting the diffident accents of a jaded dandy, as he produced the New Year's Eve invitation with sardonic detachment. "I understand you've canceled the party, old boy; somehow my invite seems to have slipped through the net."

"Really? How odd. Quite all right, come in, come in! Delighted!" said Nicholson, lowering the gun, instantly the exuberant host.

"The bags, Gompertz," Sparks snapped at Doyle, who realized with a jolt he was suddenly required to perform the functions of his assigned role.

"Right away, sir," Doyle said.

Doyle brought his bag, the only bag they carried, through the door, which Nicholson quickly closed and bolted behind him. There were at least six locking devices, all of which he engaged.

"I'd given up hope, you see," said Nicholson boyishly, pumping Sparks's hand. "Wasn't expecting a soul. Put it out of my mind, really. Truly an unexpected pleasure."

If ever there is an individual more desperately in need of the company of his own class, thought Doyle, I never hope to meet him. The truculent ranting against his pitifully stalwart manservant had already disposed Doyle to an instant dislike of Lord Charles Stewart Nicholson.

THE LIST OF 7

Heavy curtains were drawn in the high-ceilinged room, broadening the somber mood set by ponderous medieval furnishings. Dust lay deep. A musk of urine and fear-sweat lathered the thick atmosphere. The floor was littered with broken cups and plates and the remains of old meals: bones, crusts of biscuit. Bladed weapons and a tarnished and dented coat of arms hung above the weak fire sputtering in the fireplace.

Nicholson crossed to the mantel, feverishly rubbing his hands together. "How about some brandy?" he asked, plucking the stopper from a cut-crystal decanter and sloppily filling two tumblers without waiting for a reply. "I'm having some." He greedily gulped down half a ration and poured a refill before conveying the second glass to Sparks. "Cheers, then."

"Thanks ever so," said Sparks disinterestedly, making himself comfortable in front of the fire.

"Shall we have your man go below stairs?" said Nicholson, lurching into a seat across from Sparks and slurping his drink. "I'm sure Ruskin could use the help, the incompetent podge."

"No," Sparks replied, with just the right tinge of listless authority. "I may need him."

"Very good," said Nicholson, eagerly deferring to the superior rank suggested by Sparks's indifference. "Tell me, how was the journey down?"

"Tiring."

Nicholson nodded like a marionette. He sat on the edge of his chair, eyes wide with empty enthusiasm, took another sloppy drink, and wiped his moist lips with his sleeve. "So it's New Year's then, is it?"

"Hmm," replied Sparks, gazing apathetically around the room.

"Do you see my boots?" He held up his dressing gown like a dance-hall coquette, raising a foot and wiggling it before them. "Cork-soled. They do not conduct electricity. Three pairs of socks. No, sir. No e-lec-tro-cu-tion for me. Even if it will make the trains run faster. Ha!"

Sparks demonstrated the wherewithal to recognize this as a remark to which there was no proper response. Nicholson collapsed back in his chair as if every other idea had been drained from his head. Then, furiously animated by an impulse of abject courtesy, Nicholson sprang from his seat, grabbed from the mantel a red Oriental lacquered box, ran to Sparks grinning like a deranged monkey, and with a flourish snapped it open. "Smoke, Baron?"

Topping

Sparks sniffed sourly, picked out a cigar as if it were a foul kipper, and held it poised in front of his face. Nicholson's hands flew wildly through his gown until he found a match, casually struck it against the box, and held it for Sparks. Sparks puffed and rolled the cigar delicately around in his mouth, evening out its ignition.

"From Trinidad," said Nicholson, lighting one for himself as he sat back down. "Father has a plantation down there. Wanted me to run the bleeding place for him. Can you imagine? Ha!"

"Bloody hot," Sparks offered, with token empathy.

"*Bloody* hot," he amplified. "Bloody hot, and the niggers steal you blind besides. Bloody backward sods with their native smells and their chanting at night and their black faces sweating. But may I tell you? Beautiful women. Bee-*you*-tee-ful women."

"Really."

"Whores, every one of them, even with little tar babies hanging round their necks like macaques in the bugging zoo. They'll drop their knickers in the street for the change in your vest pocket," said Nicholson, hoarse with illicit carnality. "You could have yourself a go down there, I'm here to say. Fancy a little dark meat on your dolly mops, you could have a bit of fair sport, let me tell you, that's a bit of tropical splendor, that is. Ha!" He brushed his hand licentiously along his crotch and poured another brandy. "I could do with some sport about now; satisfy the inner man. Comes a point you don't much care what sort of package it comes by way of, either." He winked at Sparks suggestively.

The idea of Lady Nicholson as his *spouse,* that her handsome refinement had ever been subject to the vicissitudes of this baboon's degeneracy, filled Doyle with moral outrage. If some unspeakable horror was hot on the heels of this besotted wastrel, he was suddenly of a mind to pick up an andiron and finish the job himself.

"How is your father, the Earl?" asked Sparks, his tone betraying no reaction or judgment.

"Still alive!" said Nicholson, as if it were the funniest thing imaginable. "Ha! Clinging to life, the mean bastard! No title for young Charles here, living on a pittance, tied to the old man's purse strings— and you don't think that's the way he likes it? You don't think the thought of me scraping by, hardly able to sustain my house with the barest necessities, doesn't treble his heart at night when the Angel of Death hovers? Ha! Spite in his veins. Gone scatty. Spite and ice water and horse piss and why isn't he *dead yet!*" In a paroxysm of wrath,

121

Nicholson flung his tumbler into the fireplace and jumped repeatedly up and down, knees reaching to his shoulders, spinning and screaming in the grip of an infantile frenzy.

Doyle and Sparks stole a look that wondered just how hazardous a lunatic the man was. Then, just as suddenly as he'd begun raving, Nicholson snapped out of his fit and strode to the mantel for another tumbler, which he calmly filled, all the while gaily singing a chorus from the latest Gilbert and Sullivan.

"And how's your wife?" Sparks asked.

Nicholson stopped humming, his back to them.

"Lady Nicholson. How is she?"

"My wife," Nicholson said, coldly.

"That's right. I saw her recently in London."

"You saw her."

"Yes. She wasn't looking very well."

"Not well."

"Not well at all. Her color was very poor."

What is he on about? thought Doyle.

"Her color was poor," said Nicholson, his back still turned to them. He put a hand in the pocket of his gown.

"Poor to positively unhealthy, if you ask me. Perhaps she was worried about your son. How is your son?" An unmistakable antagonism was creeping into Sparks's tone.

"My son."

"I say," said Sparks, with a chuckle, "do you just parrot back the words when you're asked a polite question, or didn't your father ever teach you to answer them properly?"

Nicholson turned back to Sparks. He was holding a pistol. His lips curled in a malicious smile.

"Who are you?" Nicholson asked.

"So you won't answer—"

"*She* sent you, didn't she?"

"You're confused."

"My wife sent you—you're her lover, aren't you? The filthy whore—"

"Mind your words carefully—"

"You're fucking her, aren't you, don't try to deny it—"

"Put that gun down, you stupid boy!" shouted Sparks with ringing authority, without moving a muscle. "Put it down this instant!"

Nicholson froze like a dog hearing a whistle above the range of human hearing. The twisted smile melted off his face, revealing the bereft, self-pitying mask of an unloved child. He lowered the gun.

"Now, young man, you will answer properly when you're spoken to," Sparks said.

"I'm sorry," whimpered Nicholson.

Sparks rose quickly, snatched the gun from Nicholson's hand, and slapped him twice, hard, across the face. Nicholson crumpled to his knees and began to weep like a baby. Sparks emptied the chambers of the pistol, pocketed the shells, and tossed the gun to the floor. He grabbed Nicholson by the lapels and pulled him roughly to his feet.

"If you ever speak rudely to me again," Sparks said intently, "or speak of your wife rudely, or make any more crude remarks on any subject whatsoever while in my presence, you will be very severely punished. Do I make myself clear, boy?"

"You can't speak to me that way!" Nicholson sniveled. Sparks shoved him back into a chair, where he landed with a startled cry. His red weeping eyes were fixed on Sparks, who picked up his walking stick and advanced on him.

"You are a mean and wicked child—"

"I'm not either!"

"Hold out your hands, Charles."

"You can't make me—"

"Hold them out *this instant.*"

Whimpers bubbling from his lips, Charles offered up his trembling hands, palms raised.

"How many does our naughty boy here deserve, Gompertz?" Sparks asked Doyle, flexing the stick in his hands.

"I should give him one more chance to be cooperative, sir, before administering any reinforcement," Doyle said, not bothering to quell his revulsion at Nicholson's utter collapse.

"Right. Did you hear Gompertz, Charles? He's suggesting I be merciful. Do you think that's a very good idea?"

"Y-y-y-yes, sir."

Sparks whacked him heavily across the palms. Nicholson howled.

"Where is your wife?" Sparks asked.

"I don't know—"

Sparks hit him again.

"Ahh! London, London, I think. I haven't seen her in three months."

"Where is your son?"

"She took him," said Nicholson, sobbing, tears and snot running freely down his face.

"Have you seen your son since?"

"No, I swear!"

"Why did you build the wall, Charley?"

"Because of her."

"Because of your wife?"

"Yes."

"Did you build it after she left?"

Nicholson nodded.

Sparks raised the cane. *"Why?"*

"Because I'm afraid of her."

The cane crashed down on Nicholson's hands again. "You are a very obstinate boy: *Why* are you afraid of your wife, Charley?"

"Because . . . she worships Satan."

"You're afraid of her because she worships Satan?"

"She worships Satan, and she consorts with devils." Sparks hit him hard again across the palms. "It's true, it's true, I swear to Jesus it's true," Nicholson cried out miserably. His ability to offer continued resistance was absolutely shattered. Doyle could see that Sparks realized it; he leaned down beside Nicholson now, his voice boring into him like a drill bit.

"What does your wife do that makes you so afraid?"

"She makes the bad things come."

"What bad things are those, Charley?"

"The things that come at night."

"Is that why you built the wall, Charley? To keep the bad things out?"

"Yes."

"Is that what all the salt is for?"

"Yes, yes. It hurts them."

"What kind of things are they?"

"I don't know, I've never seen them—"

"But you've heard them, haven't you, at night?"

"Yes. Please don't hurt me anymore, I'm begging you," Nicholson groveled, trying to wrap himself around Sparks's boot.

"You sold some land of yours last year, Charley. Quite a lot of land, do you remember that?" said Sparks, kicking him away. "Answer me!"

"I don't remember—"

"Listen to me: You sold some land in the north that was deeded to

Topping

you; it belonged to your family. You sold it to a man: General Drummond."

"The General?" Nicholson looked up, stupid and grateful at the sound of something familiar.

"Do you remember, Charley? Do you remember the General?"

"The General came here. He came with my wife."

"The General is a friend of your wife's, is he?"

"Yes, yes, they're good friends. The General's a nice man. He brings me sweets and caramels. He brought me a pony once. A dappled gray. I named him Wellington," Nicholson babbled, retreating further into childhood. Whatever starch had kept his adult personality intact throughout the siege of Topping evaporated before their eyes.

"He made you sign some things, didn't he, Charley, the last time the General was here. Legal documents. Some pieces of paper."

"Yes, so many, so many papers. They said I had to sign, or he'd take away my pony," he said, beginning to cry again.

"And immediately after you signed these papers, that's when your wife left you, isn't it? She left with the General?"

"Yes, sir."

"And she took your son with her, didn't she?"

"Y-y-yes, sir."

"How long were you married?"

"Four years."

"Did she live here with you at Topping that entire time?"

"No. She came and went."

"Where did she go?"

"She never told me."

"What did your wife do before you married her?"

Nicholson shook his head, drawing an honest blank.

"Did she ever tell you anything about her family?"

"She said her family owned a . . . publishing company."

"In London?" Doyle asked involuntarily.

"Yes, in London," said Nicholson, now indiscriminately servile.

"Where in London, Charley?" said Sparks.

"I went there once. Across from the big museum—"

"Russell Street?"

Nicholson nodded. There was a loud hammering at the door.

"Out the window," shouted Barry from the hallway.

From somewhere below, they heard the sound of breaking glass. Sparks moved to the window and drew the curtain. Doyle joined him.

The figure in black from the inn at Cambridge was moving across the courtyard toward the front door, a half-dozen gray hoods fanning out across the grounds behind him.

"More of them this time," said Sparks calmly.

"Is it her?" cried Nicholson in terror. "It is, isn't it? She's come for me!"

"We're going to leave you now, Charles," said Sparks, not without some kindness. "Load your gun, lock the door after us, don't open it for anyone, and happy New Year to you."

Sparks tossed the bullets toward Nicholson and stepped rapidly to the door. Working together, Sparks and Doyle had the locks undone in moments, and they moved out to join Barry in the hall. Doyle's last glimpse before Barry pulled the door shut behind them was of Lord Nicholson keening hysterically, scrambling on his hands and knees trying to gather up the scattered bullets.

"Brought in the bags," Barry said as they ran down the hall. "Went back to feed the horses; that bleedin' growler's flyin' hell-bent down the lane."

"All the exits blocked?" Sparks said, drawing out his blade.

"Yeh. We've lost the coach. More of them hoods this go-round."

"Did you manage to open that door in the pantry?"

"I've had me hands full, haven't I?" said Barry, showing a bit of crust.

"Quickly, Barry, they won't be long getting in."

"Shouldn't we bring Lord Nicholson?" asked Doyle.

"He's done enough damage."

"But they'll kill him—"

"He's past redemption."

They ran down the stairs and through the great hall. A heavy pounding began at the door. Windows shattered all along the front wall; an arm groped through an opening, hand looking for a latch. Barry led them away, through a knotted sequence of rooms to the kitchen and into the adjacent larder.

"Watch this," said Barry.

Barry pulled a sack of flour off a shelf in the larder; the opposite wall rose up and disappeared into the ceiling like a sash-weighted window, revealing behind it the mysterious door he'd described.

"Ingenious," said Sparks. "My compliments to the architect."

"Got a lock on it you won't find in some banks," said Barry, as he unfolded a cache of his tools and went to work on the formidable padlock.

A crash from somewhere deep in the house announced the invaders had breached the outer fortifications.

Topping

"Give me a hand here, Doyle," said Sparks, pushing a table against the kitchen door. They piled the rest of the room's furniture on top of the table, readied their weapons, and waited for Barry to punch through.

"What's your diagnosis of the woeful Charley?" asked Sparks.

"Incipient madness. Probably tertiary syphilis," said Doyle.

"Dead from the neck up. More holes in his brain than a beehive."

They heard hurried, muffled footsteps on the stairs and floors above. The *thwack* of Barry driving a spike into the lock resounded in that small space like a gunshot.

"Easy on, Barry."

"I'd use a blancmange, but I don't fink it would have the same effect," said Barry, annoyed.

"Thank you, Barry," said Sparks, batting back the sarcasm.

"I wish he'd remembered the name of that publishing house," Doyle said.

"We'll find it easily enough. Provided we make it back to London alive—how's it coming, Barry?"

"Have it off in a pig's whisper."

"Even allowing for the delusions common to his illness, it appears Lady Nicholson wasn't quite the innocent we took her for," admitted Doyle.

"Women seldom are."

Barry broke through the lock and pushed open the door. The smell that greeted them on the wind that rose from below was dank, ageless, and as stale as the grave. Sparks took the lead, and they went down the first few steps. Carved right out of the earth, they were steep, slippery with moss, and crudely crafted. The light from the kitchen penetrated only a short distance beyond where they stood before the steps disappeared into Stygian blackness.

"Got a lantern here," said Barry, plucking an oil lamp off a hook on the earthen wall. He struck a match and lit the wick; its pale amber glow plowed only a small dent in the subterranean murk. Sparks took the lantern and started down.

"Mind your step. It's slick as ice," said Sparks.

"Pull that knob by the jamb, if you'd be so kind, guv," requested Barry.

Doyle gave the knob a yank; the false wall slid smoothly back down into the larder, concealing the entrance.

"The door, too, if you would," advised Barry.

Doyle shut the door and laid across it a welcomely substantial iron bar, sealing them in, committing them to their descent. The stairs seemed to go on interminably. Their footsteps echoed flatly, as the mossy dirt steps gave way to rough-hewn rock. The walls soon receded; sheer drop-offs into darkness fell away to either side. The lantern's faint illumination could only hint at the ghostly limits of a vast cavern opening up around them. Wind whistled and howled. They heard the squeak and rustle of vermin below them scurrying away from human approach.

"What is this place?" asked Doyle.

"The only hand of man in here are these steps," said Sparks. "A natural formation. Topping house was constructed over it. Maybe a sea cave."

"We're a good fifteen miles from the shore."

"Thank you, Barry. An underground river then."

"Don't hear any water," Barry said skeptically.

"That doesn't mean there couldn't have been one here once, does it?"

"No," said Barry, his tone admitting to only the faintest possibility.

"Perhaps Lady Nicholson dug this pit so she could commune with Satan during the full moon," said Sparks, with a wink at Doyle. How could the man joke about such a thing? Doyle thought. And at a time like this.

"Will they follow us?" asked Doyle.

"It'll take some doing to find that door."

"Unless Nicholson gives it away."

"The man can barely remember his name."

No sooner were those words spoken than their feet hit level ground. They paused to establish their bearings. The cavern felt as forbidding as a dark and deserted cathedral.

"A stiff wind's blowing through from somewheres," said Barry, sniffing the air.

"Then it's simple; we'll follow it to find our way out."

They moved away from the stairs into the cave proper, each step kicking up puffs of a fine black dust. Small wings fluttered in the currents above them, swooping acrobatically through the artificial night.

"Bats," said Sparks, prompting Doyle to reach for his hat. "Don't bother, Doyle. They see a good deal better down here than we do—"

With a loud clang, Sparks crashed into a solid obstruction and dropped the lantern, plunging them into a void of darkness.

"Hell!"

"You s'pose 'at's where we've wandered to?"

Despite the circumstances, Doyle was beginning to appreciate Barry's terse waggery.

"Be quiet, won't you? Help me find the lantern."

Doyle reached out and put his hands on the object with which Sparks had collided; it was rounded, cold and smooth, with machined edges, and it was massive. He knew what it was, but deprived of sight was unable to put a name to it.

"I fink you broke it."

"You think so, do you?"

"Seeing as how all I can feel wot's left is little pieces. Would you like me to light the candle I've got 'ere in me pocket?"

"Why, yes, Barry, I'd like that very much."

Just as Barry's match was struck, Doyle realized what they had found.

"Good Christ! Do you know what this is?"

They were in darkness again.

"What's wrong now, Barry?"

"Dropped the candle, 'fraid the Doctor gave me quite a start—"

"Jack, do you know what you've found?"

"I would if Barry could find his candle—"

"Got it," said Barry as he lit another match.

"It's a train!"

And so it was. A jet-black iron-forged full-gauge steam engine, with a trailing coal car bearing a full load, on steel tracks curving away ahead of them into the darkness.

"A Sterling Single," said Barry. "A real beauty."

They climbed into the engine cab and examined the mechanics by the light of Barry's candle. Gauges and pumps were intact and seemed in working order. Water tank full. A load of coal already sitting in the furnace.

"Looks as if someone was anticipating a hasty departure," ventured Doyle.

"Remember his repeated incoherent references to trains. I'd venture to say we have Lord Nicholson's indelicate condition to thank for this good fortune," said Sparks, as Barry lit an oil lamp set into the wall of the cab.

"Why didn't he use it himself?" asked Doyle.

"Chances are he forgot it was here. Know anything about piloting a train, Doyle?"

"Light the coal in the firebox, for starters," said Barry, before Doyle could answer.

"Thank you, Barry, why don't you run ahead down the tracks and see if any switches need throwing?"

"I knows about engineerin'. Our old dad was a brakeman, see. Took us out on runs all over the south of England when he weren't drinkin'—"

"That's fine, Barry, do you suppose I'm entirely ignorant to the ways of the railroad?"

Muttering, Barry leapt down with his candle and moved along the tracks. Sparks contemplated the array of gears and handles that confronted them.

"Let's light the coal as Barry suggests, Doyle, and then"—Sparks bit on a finger as he pondered—"which one of these ooja-ka-pivvies do you suppose we should pull?"

They nurtured a fire in the furnace and bellowed it to full, red-bellied life. Barry returned to report that the track looked in good condition and ran ahead uninterrupted for at least a mile. Sparks asked if there was any reason why they shouldn't proceed, gracefully allowing Barry an opportunity to scan the pressure gauge and humbly advise that they should wait until the boiler had built a full head of steam, then release the hand brake, engage the drive shaft, and shift the engine into forward gear.

"Have a go at it, Barry," said Sparks, as if having to call on his prodigious and intimate storehouse of train lore was the most tiresome task imaginable.

"Right," said Barry, with a privately amused smile.

Barry turned on the headlamp; its Cyclopean beam pierced the darkness like a ray of wisdom. Doyle and Sparks stood on the open platform at the rear of the cab, looking back anxiously from time to time at the stairs. No assault on the door above had reached their ears, but waiting was difficult nonetheless. Time seemed to stand still in the funereal vault. The rhythmic *schuss* of the steam valves echoed through the chamber like the breathing cycle of an enormous, slumbering beast. The weight of the cavern walls led them to feel they were in the belly of some monstrous, watchful dragon, patiently waiting for all human endeavor or ambition, no matter how grand and willful, to fail the test of mortality. The story of the great manor house on the rocks above, a three-hundred-year pageant of continuous human history—loves, births, schemes, marriages, victories, reversals, deaths, intrigues, betrayals, madness, melodrama; all reducible to dust—would scarcely constitute a single intake of breath in the life span of this leviathan. Kings and kingdoms might fall, but these walls would remain, self-sufficient, silently mocking. Few things are more routinely and cheaply regarded than human existence, thought Doyle, seldom less so than by those in full-blooded possession of it. An hour spent in the bowels of this frigid, aboriginal cave was a harsh reminder that nature itself radiated the same heartless indifference.

Barry threw down the hammer; the pistons spasmed twice and then caught steel on steel. Friction threw sparks into the air. With the protesting shriek and groan of rusty muscles, the wheels inched slowly forward on the tracks.

"We're movin'!" Barry shouted over the engine. He stuck his head out the side window and guided them toward the tunnel, controlling his impulse to blow the steam whistle out of sheer exuberance.

"Where will it take us?" asked Doyle, nearly sagging with relief.

"On to London if our fuel holds and the tracks don't end," said Sparks, patting the cab wall like a canny horse trader. "I've always fancied a private rail car. This little charmer could come in right handy."

The chamber closed down around the tracks at the far end. Barry had to pull his head back inside the window as they rolled slowly into a narrow tunnel cleaving naturally through the earth. The walls squeezed in until their clearance was only a scant few inches.

"Do you suppose they'll kill them, Jack?" Doyle asked soberly, his mind still on the madman and his manservant.

Sparks grew more somber. "Yes, I imagine they will. I would imagine they already have."

"Nicholson had something they wanted," said Doyle after a moment.

"Two things: his land and his son. Both of which they've now had in their possession for some months."

"The land could be for any number of purposes—"

"Agreed—too early to speculate. We need more information."

"But why the boy?"

Sparks thought for a moment. "Control. A way to control his mother."

"But it seems clear, doesn't it, that she was a confederate all along," said Doyle, much as it pained him to think poorly of the woman.

"A possibility, although we can't know what sort of coercion they brought to bear on her—precisely what the boy would have been good for."

"That seemed to be the case on the night she was killed."

"Consider the scenario that, feigned or genuine, her grief over the child's 'kidnap' was skillfully employed to lure you into their trap. Her usefulness expired, they double-crossed and murdered both the Lady and her hapless brother."

"It fits, although the brother's role is rather ill-defined."

"He's called away from school on urgent business; she's enlisted his help against coconspirators she can no longer trust. Or perhaps he was in concert all along, putting pressure on from another angle. You said he seemed to be berating her while they waited at the door."

"If I didn't know better, Jack, I'd almost think you were defending the woman." But in the dim glow of the lantern, Doyle could see dark dissatisfaction lining Sparks's face.

"Something's not right," he said.

"On the other hand," said Doyle, remembering the light in her deep blue eyes, "all we have to support the idea she was in league with them are the semicoherent ravings of a deranged and jilted husband."

Sparks didn't reply, eyes withdrawn, lost in some private ratiocination. They rode slowly through the narrow tunnel in silence.

"There's light up ahead!" Barry announced.

As best as the walls would allow, they peered out into the tunnel ahead where the beam of the headlamp was losing ground to the emerging light of day. Moments later the train broke free of the confines of the earth and spirited them into the open air for the first time since they entered the misfortunate house.

"Bravo, Barry!"

The tracks hugged the slope of a sheer ravine, a river running swiftly below. In the distance behind them, up a steep slope and above the trees, peered the machicolations of Topping's highest towers. Thick, quarrelsome pillars of black smoke spewed around them into a threatening gray sky. There might be rain, those clouds suggested. But even a deluge would not come in time to spare the venerable life of Topping Manor.

"They've put the torch to it," said Barry in dismay. "All that silver . . ."

"Maybe they didn't find the door. Maybe they think we're trapped inside," said Doyle hopefully. "If they believe we're dead, they'll slacken off the chase."

"He would see me quartered and then watch the body burn before making such an assumption," said Sparks grimly.

Doyle studied Sparks as he looked back at the burning building, sweeping the horizon for any sign of pursuit, his eyes as taut and feral as a predatory bird.

"Who is he, Jack?" Doyle asked quietly. "The man in black. You know him, don't you?"

"He's my brother," said Sparks.

CHAPTER 11

Nemesis

THE TRACKS RAN to the south and east along the ravine, parallel to the river for the next few miles, the slope descending gradually down to join the river on the flat seacoastal plain. Through their constant vigilance, the three men aboard the train were given no indication that the enemy had gained awareness of their escape. Not long after reaching level ground, they intersected a sweeping half-moon curve of rail that bowed off to the east. At Sparks's instruction, Barry brought the engine to a halt, leapt from the cab, and threw the switch that would jump them to the tracks leading away from the river. As the engine came back up to speed, Sparks and Doyle stripped to their shirts, shoveled coal from the tender to the scuttle, and shouldered the scuttle to the furnace. Despite their exposure to the frigid winds, the hard labor soon had them soaked in sweat. They banked the fire to maximum blaze, pulling as much power from the roiling steam as the boiler would yield, the throttle wide open, exacting as substantial an advantage on the race back to London as they could from their sturdy iron steed.

Nothing further was offered by Sparks about his brother. He entered another of those spells of remoteness that invited no inquiry, and they had the intensity of what soon became backbreaking work to divert them. Barry spurred the train on ferociously, taking curves at precarious speeds, never slowing for occasional stray livestock, using only the whistle and the sheer power of his will as he screamed at the animals to clear the tracks. More than one rural stationmaster ran out from his office as they roared past his post to stare dumbfounded at Barry, who responded with a wave and a roguish tip of the hat, an unscheduled juggernaut jeopardizing the methodical orderliness of the world of trains. Barry displayed an intimate knowledge of the spidery network of tracks that laced the Kent and Sussex countryside, switching them on every occasion away from primary routes onto seldom-used freight lines. At one point, when they came alongside a parallel set of tracks and began to gain on the passenger train carrying New Year's Eve travelers from Dover to London, Barry whipped his charge like a jockey in the homestretch of the Irish Sweepstakes, whooping and hollering and throwing his hat in the air as they raced past the unnerved rival engineer. Barry was a daredevil, plain and simple.

Well before dark, Barry by necessity slowed their pace when they entered the labyrinthine tangle of switches and turnarounds congesting the arteries of every approach to London, the time their breakneck sprint across the open countryside had gained them forfeited by these final miles. When they finally pulled onto a sidetrack off a private yard in Battersea, owned by some unnamed acquaintance of Sparks, night had firmly fallen. Leaving Barry to secure the engine's harbor, Sparks and Doyle walked to a nearby busy thoroughfare and hailed a hansom cab. Sparks directed the driver to an address across the river, somewhere on the Strand.

"Where do we go, Jack?" asked Doyle. "They seem more than capable of finding me anywhere."

"They've anticipated our movements, which have up until now been necessarily and painfully predictable. It's a new game. A crowd's the best refuge on earth, and London's riddled with more holes than a bloodhound could suss out in a lifetime," said Sparks, fastidiously wiping the coal dust from his face with a handkerchief. "I say, Doyle, you should get a look at yourself; you're as black as the ace of spades."

"From this point on, I would greatly appreciate being consulted about our plans and movements, Jack," said Doyle, trying largely in vain to remove the grime with his sleeve. "I daresay I'll have the occasional thought or opinion that could have some positive effect on our efforts."

Sparks looked at him with affectionate amusement, which he nipped under cover of solemnity before Doyle could take offense. "That has been established beyond dispute. The hardships of these last few days would've reduced most men to runny porridge."

"I do appreciate it. But to put it more bluntly, I should like to know exactly what you know. That is, *everything* you know."

"You're perilously close already—"

"Close will, I'm afraid, no longer be sufficient to my needs, Jack. I shall honor whatever secrets you impart to the death. I trust my actions to date give you no reason whatsoever to doubt the sense of taking me further into your confidence."

"I have no such doubts."

"Good. When should we begin?"

"After a hot bath, over oysters brochette, lobster, and caviar, accompanied by the sound of vintage corks popping," said Sparks. "It is New Year's Eve, after all. What do you say to that?"

"I would have to say," said Doyle, his mouth already watering, "that is a plan I can endorse without the slightest reservation."

✿   ✿   ✿

The cab deposited them in the center of the Strand, one of London's liveliest avenues, never busier than on this moonlit New Year's Eve, before a not particularly inviting lodging hotel. A dingy awning announced it as the Hotel Melwyn. Two steps up from a doss house, a full flight down from even the threadbare middle-class accommodations to which Doyle was accustomed, it was nonetheless one of the few places in town where two gentlemen—rather, a gentleman and his valet—blackened head to toe by a day's hard labor in a coal car, could draw nothing more from clientele and staff than a passing disinterested glance.

With a wink at the knowing clerk, Sparks signed the register as "Milo Smalley, Esquire" and paid cash for two adjoining rooms near the stairs on the second floor. Baths were requested for both men and inestimably enjoyed in a communal chamber at the far end of the hall where more than a few gentlemen were taking the waters. A cursory monitoring of the room's level of chat gave Doyle to realize that, however modest its exterior, the Melwyn seemed the way station of choice for an entire class of discriminating, and sporting, men-about-town. As he emerged from the bath, for the first time since shedding his mustache and muttonchop whiskers, Doyle caught sight of himself in a mirror. Add the cosmetic wire-rimmed glasses Sparks had lent him from his bag of tricks, plus the valet's haircut Barry had administered, trimmed to the bristle, and Doyle was greeted by a face he had to look at twice to be certain it was his own.

Heartened by the substantial changes wrought in his appearance, scrubbed, shaved, and the first to return to their rooms, Doyle was surprised to discover unfamiliar luggage near the door, fresh evening clothes laid out on the bed, and the esteemed Larry-brother-of-Barry lighting a fire in the hearth. Delighted by this unexpected reappearance, Doyle was near to the point of embracing their diminutive accomplice, who seemed as equally pleased to clap eyes once again on him. Though Doyle was unreasonably desirous of relating to Larry an account of their adventures, Larry held up a hand to silence him before he'd uttered a word.

"Beggin' your pardon, guv, but me brother's already dealt me the hand, from soup to nuts to the hail and rain—train, that is: There's the gods smilin' if ever they have—and a passing strange tale it is, too, sir—and by the way, if I might comment, I do congratulate you on the haircut; I see my brother's fine handiwork in evidence here—he was apprenticed to the service of a barber for a few misguided months many moons ago; it was the barber's daughter he wished to service, truth be known—but I must say, Doctor, that with the new trim and the removal of your side levers there you have in the totality of your being more than achieved the desired effect of deflecting one's apprehension of your own true nature; why, truth is, if I hadn't known it was you, I'd've hardly known ya."

"You've been busy, I see, Larry," said Sparks, toweling off as he reentered the room. "Will you tell us what you've discovered, or shall I?"

Larry glanced trepidatiously at Doyle.

"No confidence will be violated," said Sparks. "The Doctor has put down such roots into the secret soil of our campaign, it would take dynamite to dislodge him. You may speak freely—no, wait!" Sparks narrowed his eyes and scrutinized Larry, who smiled bashfully, well acquainted with the routine to follow.

"After your pleasure, sir," said Larry, and then with a wink to Doyle, "Fancy this, then."

"A survey of Drummond's house informed you the General has not returned since we last spied him departing for the north two days before Christmas. You have discovered the London address of Lord and Lady Nicholson, a yellow-brick two-story detached in Hampstead Heath, a house equally devoid of occupants at the time of your visit. You have within the hour rendezvoused with Barry at your favorite public house, the Elephant and Castle, where he told you of our recent enterprises while you drank two pints of bitters and ate a . . . shepherd's pie."

Larry shook his head and smiled broadly at Doyle. "See? I love it when 'e does that."

"Come now, Larry, tell me; how have I done?"

"Spot on, sir, 'cepting it wer'n't shepherd's pie, sir; it was a bit of kate and sydney for me tonight."

"Steak and kidney, of course, it's a holiday night; you splurged," said Sparks, as he began to dress himself, then to Doyle, "Crumbs on his jacket."

"And a spot of gravy on his cravat, here," said Doyle, pointing, up to the challenge. "Not to mention the clinging, persistent odor of stale hops and cheap rolling tobacco common to public houses."

"Mary and Joseph, don't tell me: Not you, too, sir?"

"Go on, Doyle; tell him how I arrived at my conclusions," said Sparks.

Doyle studied the incredulous Larry for a moment. "Determining General Drummond's whereabouts would have been your primary task upon returning to London. If he were in town, I doubt you'd have had time to even enjoy that drink with your brother, let alone find and fetch us fresh clothes. Therefore, the quick resolution of your first objective allowed you to proceed with the second; by no mean stretch of logic a search for the Nicholsons' London home. There is a fine yellow powder ground into the knees and elbows of your clothes, no streaks or tears indicate that any sudden or violent movements were undertaken, so the two-story house of yellow brick you then methodically climbed and gained entry to was also fairly obviously empty. The distinctive red clay on the edges and soles of your boots is peculiar to the hills of Hampstead Heath. By the way, the Elephant and Castle is also my favorite public house, and I have enjoyed many a fine steak and kidney pie there in my day."

"Well done, Doyle!"

"'Cor . . . 'cor blimey . . .'" Larry took off his hat and shook his head.

"If Larry's been rendered speechless, we should alert the news-papers: It's a phenomenon more rare than a full solar eclipse," said Sparks.

"And 'ere I was thinkin' me and Barry was the only twins in our immediate circle," said Larry, regaining the use of his tongue. "Two halves of the beechnut is wot we got 'ere. Romulus and Remus. Flip sides of the same shillin'. We've done more than well to have you with us, sir," he said sincerely.

Nemesis

"Thank you, Larry. I take that as high praise indeed," replied Doyle.

"Aren't you two the old sentimental sweethearts," said Sparks, finishing the loop on his bow tie. Larry and Doyle separated, somewhat abashed, Doyle to his dressing, Larry to the crumbs on his jacket. "Larry, what about our dinner?"

"Nine-thirty at the Criterion—oysters on the half shell, lobsters on the boil, gay and frisky and a bottle of whiskey—they're expectin' you."

They finished dressing for that happily anticipated appointment and presented themselves on the stroke of the half hour not far down the Strand at the revered doors of the Criterion Long Bar. Their elegant evening wear rendered them invisible among the flood tide of swells frequenting the dining room, the perfect camouflage on this most festive of London nights. Many was the time that Doyle, the beleaguered medical student, had pressed his nose to the windows outside, viewing the *haute monde* in their natural habitat with the curiosity and envy of a snubbed anthropologist, but never had he crossed over that storied threshold until this evening.

Sparks was well known to the maître d'. Chilled champagne awaited them, a platoon of attentive captains and waiters standing by to assure that their glasses never emptied. An unctuous manager extended personal felicitations of the house, and a sumptuous, gout-inviting succession of mouth-watering comestibles proceeded to rain down on them like the fortuitous bounty of a culinary god. Doyle scarcely had breath to speak between bites and gulps, throwing himself into the consumption of the feast with bacchanalian abandon. The champagne carbonated the shadow of doom that had dogged their last few days and effervesced it to oblivion. Around them the room seemed impossibly lithe and gay and filled with light, women glowing with Athenian glamour, the men fortified by some Herculean ideal. What a place! What a city, what a dynamic race of people! It wasn't until an ambrosian flambé of cherries, meringue, and vanilla ice cream had landed in front of them that the weightless balloon of Doyle's undivided pleasure begin to sink back into the range of conscious awareness. The dinner was not yet at an end and already felt like a dream, for he knew that the moment their discussion, which up through the supernatural dessert had been as carefree as a clergyman's Monday, turned back to the life that awaited them outside of this cloistered Olympus, the bill would come due in more ways than one.

The last dishes were cleared away. Sparks lit a cheroot and warmed the honeyed nectar of his brandy over a candle. "So . . . " he said, gaveling the proceedings back to order, " . . . as to my brother."

Doyle had not expected him to open with that trump card, but he was more than willing to accept candor from the man as he found it. He nodded, betraying no impatience, willing his mind to focus in again, as he meditatively rolled the Benedictine around in his snifter.

"Do you find it as troubling as I that the *corpus* of human hope is pegged so directly to the concept of our social progress?" asked Sparks. His tone was open and inviting, far from rhetorical. What this non-sequiturial tack had to do with his brother, well, Doyle had waited out far more tortuous tangents than this with far less expectation of return.

"Yes, Jack, I do," said Doyle, warming to the task. "I look around at this golden room, the pleasure it gives me, all these fine, handsome people, the meal we've just enjoyed, and I am tempted to say . . . this is the best civilization has to offer us: the human harvest of education, scientific advancement, social evolution.

"But these are transitory satisfactions. An illusion. And how infinitesimal a percentage of the people alive in our world this sample represents. As we sit here priding ourselves on our refinement, not a stone's throw from these windows there is a surfeit of human suffering and misery as terrible as any human being has ever endured. And I am forced to consider: If so many are left behind, do our achievements count for nothing? What value does our passing through this life leave behind us? What gifts, if any, will our age bequeath to the generations that follow?"

"That question's not for us to answer," replied Sparks. "Following generations make up their own minds about our contributions. And how is any age remembered? By the work of man's hand or of his mind? The Elizabethans left us poetry that speaks to us because we share a language. The Egyptians built the pyramids, but we can't know their secret thoughts. Their greatest discoveries may be beyond recovery. Perhaps it's simply a matter of what survives."

"But which is more important? Will our age be judged by our monuments, our bridges and train stations, or by our science and arts?"

"Our expanding knowledge of medicine has certainly succeeded in prolonging the physical span of human life," said Sparks.

"Yes, but the conditions imposed by our prosperity have necessitated most of those discoveries. I won't dispute that the convenience and comfort of life, for some, even many, are greatly enhanced by the objects we're now able to mass-produce. But weigh against it the cost, the by-products of industry: subhuman labor conditions, scarring of the earth, poisonous air. Without these medical advances, most of us might not long survive our 'prosperity.' And for many of the lower classes that do survive, even if their physical lives are lengthened, what value does that surplus provide if that life is stripped of joy, of kindness, or the time to enjoy the fruits of their labor?"

"The suffering of the unfortunate aside—and all men suffer, don't they, each to his measure, in his own way—doesn't it seem clear that science has us on the cusp of a new epoch? Think of the marvelous inventions they say we'll soon enjoy: electricity in every house, the motorized car. Telephone, typewriter. Enhanced communication, freedom to travel. Warmth and light in the home. Ignorance banished by education."

"You assume that surrounding ourselves with these new, arguably liberating devices will fundamentally change some persistent qualities in the human character."

"Which qualities are those?"

"The will to power. The impulse to hoard. The instinct to fend for ourselves at the expense of others."

"The instinct to survive," said Sparks, as if Doyle were taking him exactly where he wished to go. "Ensuring the survival of the strong."

"At the expense of the weak."

"Just as in nature—life as a competition, Doyle, a fight: for air, light, for strong, attractive mating partners, for space or food. Nature does not announce to its components, 'Life requires of you no aggression, for I have provided on this earth an abundance, an embarrassment of riches,' " Sparks said, vehemently tapping his fingers, rattling the glasses on the table.

"And when those same powerful impulses are expressed by the human animal, as in every other kingdom of nature—"

"Dominion. Domination. Material greed. The root of human conflict."

"We are in agreement," said Doyle.

Sparks nodded, his eyes hot with discovery. "It's inescapable. Man is compelled to obey the instinct to dominate, because of our uncon-scious imperative to survive. And this message is so persuasive and commanding it overrides every other biological impulse—compassion, sympathy, love, any of the niceties sacred to the privileged lives in this room—well after our physical safety has been secured and every serious threat to our existence completely eliminated."

"A paradox, then," said Doyle. "Does man's will to live present the single greatest danger to our survival?"

"If human nature does not soon demonstrate the ability to willfully change its course, I submit to you that it does," said Sparks, leaning forward, lowering his voice, holding Doyle taut in his gaze. "I offer in evidence the life of one Alexander Sparks. Born to wealthy parents, a beloved first child, indulged and cosseted through early childhood by every creature comfort known to man. Nurtured and protected to a fault, a world of privilege and possession opening to him as generously as the petals of an evening primrose. Quite independent of these influences, the boy soon demonstrates a remarkably headstrong native character. An insatiable curiosity. An intellect of cold and calculating genius. A will like tempered steel. By anyone's standards, an exceptional child.

"Through his first years, he remains blissfully unaware of the vagaries of fortune flesh is heir to. With his father stationed half a world away on diplomatic assignment, the boy grows up surrounded by women who want nothing more than to pamper and indulge his every waking whim. The jewel set in the center of that adoring circle is the child's mother: a celebrated beauty, a woman of style, strong moral fiber, and fierce intelligence. She dotes slavishly on her boy, devotes herself to him without limit. He comes to perceive himself as God's chosen one, an infant Sun King, with absolute power over a domain extending in every direction as far as his eye can see. A boy who wanders the woods of his estate feeling command not only of the people around him, whom he regards as his subjects, but the wind, water, and trees as well. His world is a paradise, and he its undisputed master.

"Then, one day, in his fifth summer, the adored and loving mother of the king disappears from sight, gone a second and then a third day, without explanation. Even the boy's tempestuous rages, the most potent weapons in his considerable arsenal, are not sufficient to effect her reappearance. None of his subjects offers any reasons for her absence, only winks and Gioconda smiles. Until the fourth day, when he is once again allowed access to her bedchamber, and discovers, to his astonishment and horror, that in her arms lies a hideous usurper. Helpless, wrinkled, crimson-faced, pissing and mewling like a cat. A baby. In an instant, the boy sees through the fiend's pathetically transparent, manipulative deceptions, but is stunned to discover his mother has fallen completely in thrall to this tiny demon. This monster has the temerity to lie before him on his mother's breast, mocking him, demanding and receiving her loving ministrations that in his clear understanding of the world were intended solely for him and him alone."

"You?" asked Doyle quietly.

Sparks shook his head. "A sister. It even has a name. Madelaine Rose. The Sun King is wise enough to recognize that when an enemy holds a superior position, his best course is to withdraw and marshal his forces to fight another day. He smiles and offers no protest to this hideous affront, understanding only too well the danger he is facing. He conceals his disgust that such a puny, feckless creature could wield enough influence to threaten the life of his glorious reign. How could this vile incubus have so unequivocally mesmerized the woman, who had never demonstrated anything but the greatest good sense to worship him without end or reservation? The boy leaves that room with his map of the world cracked to its foundation. He lets no one see the slightest hint of his humiliation. His instinct for survival tells him the safest strategy against this unprecedented challenge to his absolute rule lies in letting his subjects continue to believe that nothing in the kingdom, or within their king, has changed. He waits a week, two weeks, a month, to see if his mother's deranged infatuation with the pretender will break like a fever. He examines his adversary dispassionately, satisfying his curiosity as to its form and evident weaknesses, giving his mother to believe that he finds the repellent, sluglike bundle as irresistible as she does. He endures the collective enslavement of his subjects to the monster's hypnotic allure—these stupid women want nothing more than to prattle on about it incessantly with him! He lets them chatter, watches his rival bask in their affections, and all the while formulates his revenge. He insinuates himself into his mother's confidence, encouraging her to talk with him about the thing, hoping to find the key to its terrible appeal. He familiarizes himself with the demon's routine—sleeping, waking, crying, eating, shitting— all it seems capable of doing, what a dim mystery the source of its magnetism remains. The contempt that knowledge brings serves only to multiply his determination to take action: decisive, swift, and merciless.

"Not long after, late one warm summer night when the house is at rest, he creeps silently into his mother's chambers. She is in bed, sound asleep. The monster lies in a cradle, on its back, awake, smiling a toothless grin, cooing, happily kicking its arms and legs about, as if an arrogant belief in its own invulnerability renders it immune to the treachery the Sun King has come to realize lurks behind every friendly face. Illuminated in a shaft of moonlight, the thing's eyes catch his as he peers down at it, and in a moment his steely determination to act stands on a precipice—he's flooded with shame and remorse at his hatred of the little creature, he wants to take and hold the baby in his arms, feel its happiness enveloping him in a warm, beneficent, healing sphere of love and forgiveness. Feeling himself pulled inexorably into the monster's orbit where he's seen so many fall before him, at the last possible instant he tears his eyes away. Horrified to realize how close the thing has come to ensnaring him. For the first time fully comprehending the danger this evil genius presents."

"No ... " said Doyle involuntarily.

"He picks up a small satin pillow, and he puts it over the thing's face, and he holds it there hard until the creature stops kicking its arms and legs and lies still. It never makes a sound, but as it dies, the mother awakes with a scream! How pernicious was its hold on her! It's had communion with the woman even as life took leave of its tiny body. The Sun King runs from the room—his mother has seen him, he is sure she has seen him leaning over the cradle—but when she moves to its bed and finds the inert remains of his midnight work, her mind comes undone. Such a heart-stopping wail shakes the very walls of the house that if allowed to rise unimpeded into the night might shatter the gates of heaven. As the boy lies quaking in his bed, his mother's cry drives a spike deep into the frozen reaches of his heart. It is a sound he will call upon the memory of for many years to come, and it gives him more pleasure than a thousand kisses.

"His mother collapses. The house is within minutes of her discovery awash in a sea of grief. To the king's surprise, he is smothered by the sympathetic comforts of his bereaved subjects, imagining, these stupid peasants, that he must be every bit as stricken as they. The bewilderment he offers in response tends only to confirm that conviction, and they clasp him ever closer to their heaving bosoms. His mother disappears again into guarded seclusion. This time the women are only too eager to bring him constant reports of her condition; she's had a setback today, the night did not go well, she's resting comfortably, she took no food again this morning. He rejoices at the fervor with which the woman appears to embrace her just punishment for his betrayal. A week passes, and his father returns from his distant overseas post; he had never even seen the usurper. His eyes are clouded with sympathy as he greets the young king, but after spending an hour behind the closed door of mother's chamber he goes directly to his son and takes him alone into his room. He doesn't speak. He holds the boy's chin in his hand and gazes at him for the longest time. It is suspicion with which the man searches the young king's eyes—so she *did* see him in the chamber, this look tells him, but there must be some uncertainty—suspicion, not naked accusation. The king knows well enough how to conceal the entrance to the place he keeps his secret. He shows his father nothing: no remorse, weakness, or human feeling. Blank opacity, open and unreachable, the boy returns the look and sees something replace suspicion in his father's eyes. Fear. The father

Nemesis

knows. And the boy knows his father is powerless against him. The man withdraws from the room. The king knows the father will never challenge his authority again.

"They bury the thing in a lavender box, adorned with garlands of spring flowers. The boy stands quietly, watching his subjects weep with abandon, allowing them to lay their hands on his head as they pass by the grave, atonement for their transgression, paying obeisance to their one, true master. After the funeral, when his mother reappears and they meet, formally, in a public room, he sees something has irreversibly changed between them. She never again looks upon him with the loving gaze that had been her custom before the pretender came. She hardly ever dares to meet his eyes at all. He is no longer allowed entrance to her private chamber. Over the following days, he overhears many tearful, whispered conversations between mother and father, brought quickly to an end when his presence is detected, but he's confident no overt action will be taken against him. His father leaves to resume his duties overseas in Egypt. The boy spends more and more time in contented isolation, pursuing his studies, feeling his powers grow, in solitary walks of peaceful contemplation. Over time, the shroud of silence spreads from his mother to overtake all the subjects of his kingdom. There are no more pretenses of affection toward him. The currencies of exchanges with his inferiors are reduced to their basest coin: power and domination. His storehouse is filled to bursting with both commodities. He has retaken his throne."

"Good Lord . . ." said Doyle softly, wiping a tear from his eye. "Good Lord, Jack . . ."

Sparks seemed singularly unmoved by the story. He calmly took a drink and then continued: a cold, dispassionate recitation. "The next summer, the woman discovers she is once again with child. The news is kept from the boy, but as a precaution Alexander is packed up and sent away to boarding school the moment her condition becomes visibly self-evident, months before the child is expected. This proves no hardship to Alexander. He is more than ready to expand his sphere of influence beyond the confines of the garden walls. Fresh meat, he says, looking about hungrily at the new world that greets him; populated not just with adults, who he can already manage easily enough, but boys his own age, whole battalions of them, as pliant and malleable to his tools as uncut stone. And they are, none of them, parents or headmasters alike, witting enough to realize they have crowned the fox and set him up a palace in the henhouse. The next spring, hidden from his view and far from the reach of Alexander's grasp, a second son is born."

This time Doyle's question was left unspoken.

"Yes, Doyle. My entrance onto the stage."

"Did they ever let him near you?"

"Not for the longest time, for years, was he even aware of my presence, nor I of his. Alexander stayed at school through terms and all the holidays, even Christmas. Summers he was sent to stay with distant relations overseas. My parents paid a visit only once a year, every Easter week. My father, who had been serving all this time in the diplomatic corps, retired to stay close to myself and my mother. In spite of the damage done, I believe they were able to find some small measure of happiness in the home we made together. It certainly seemed that way to my unknowing senses; I was well and fairly loved. I suspected nothing of my brother's existence until I was near ready for schooling myself, when a man who worked in the stables, my confidant and favorite among the staff, let slip some reference to a boy named Alexander who'd ridden there years before. My parents had never spoken his name, but when I confronted them with my discovery of another boy riding at our stable, they admitted his existence to me. I did not interpret their reticence as having anything at all to do with their feelings toward Alexander—needless to say, no mention was ever made of my late sister—but once I learned that I had an unknown older brother, my curiosity became insatiable. After realizing my parents were not to be more forthcoming, I pumped the servants endlessly for news about this mysterious boy. They were clearly under orders to tell me nothing, and this blanket of silence surrounding Alexander only served to increase my eagerness. I ached to know him. I tried in vain to secretly gain his address so I might write to him. I prayed that God would soon acquaint me with the boy who I was convinced existed solely in order to serve as my companion, protector, and coconspirator."

"They never let you, did they?" asked Doyle, alarmed at the prospect.

"Only after two years of relentless campaigning and six months of bargaining—I was never to write to or accept letters from him; I would never be alone in his company: I eagerly accepted every one of their conditions. That year we paid our Easter visit to my brother's public school together. I was seven. Alexander was thirteen. We greeted each other formally, shaking hands. He was a striking boy: tall, sturdy, with black hair and riveting eyes. He seemed to me the soul of comradeship. Our parents were not prepared to leave us alone even for an instant, but after a few hours in which he exhibited such polite and openhearted enjoyment of both my company and theirs, their vigilance relented as we walked back from dinner through the gardens. As we turned a hedge ahead of them, Alexander pulled me from view, pressed a note into my hand, urging me to conceal it from our parents at all costs and to read it only when my absolute privacy was secured. Along with it he gave me a black polished stone, a talisman, which he assured me was his most treasured possession, and which he fervently wished me to have. I accepted the terms of his offerings gladly and, for the first time in my life, willfully concealed an event of such import from my parents. The first wedge between my life and theirs had been driven, the narrowest gap opened that had never before existed, and it was of my brother's conscious design."

"What did the letter say?"

"Predominantly innocent schoolboy chat—his daily routines recounted in prosaic detail, victories and tribulations in the classroom and on the playing fields, anecdotes about his colorful collection of classmates, what to expect of school myself, the clubby whys and wherefores of getting on with both teachers and chums—all in the confident tone of the wiser, worldlier brother advising a young charge on the eve of embarking on his own educational career. It assumed a comfortable familiarity that played as if we'd known each other all our lives. Friendly, generous, evenhanded, more than a little funny—in short, precisely the sort of letter I had dreamed about receiving from the idealized older brother I'd imagined. Nothing overt that would have upset my parents if they had ever found it, which I took every precaution to prevent. There was no self-pity, bemoaning our parents' abandonment of him. No complaints at their lack of interest. To the contrary, he wrote about them with the greatest consideration and affection, grateful for the opportunities they had given him at this wonderful school, how proud he hoped to one day make them, how he longed to repay their kindnesses to him a thousandfold. Not until the last paragraph did he conceal the hook around which he had spun the fiction. The ingenuousness, the absence of rancor toward my parents, his heartful openness toward our mutual discovery—all evidence of a clever, cunning, even exceptional personality. It wasn't until this last reference that the full extent of his malignant genius was manifest."

"What was it?"

" 'Although it seems clear that we must face all the difficult trials of our lives alone, just to know that you are alive, my brother, gives me the secret strength I have always sought to carry on.' " Sparks spoke the words quietly, with grave exactitude. "The stoic bravery, the hinted-at but unnamed difficult trials—how magnified, how operatic, they became in my imagination—and the suggestion that I could

147

in my small, seven-year-old way somehow ease the pain of this shining exemplar was irresistible to my freshly minted mind. I was far too green to resist such an appeal. It whispered that he must know my capacities better than I knew myself. That in time, in his wisdom, he would reveal them to me, leading me to the discovery of my true identity, which I of course hoped would be in partnership with him, united against the world. If he had asked me even then, in that first letter, I would have thrown myself onto a bayonet."

"How did you respond?"

"He ended with instructions on how, if I so desired, I might safely write him back. The school had strict orders from my parents to intercept and return to them all of Alexander's arriving correspondence. I was to address the letter to a classmate of his—a fiercely devoted cadre of boys had served him unswervingly since his arrival; their number increased every year—and the letter would be discreetly passed on. Of course, the clandestine nature of it only served to amplify my enthusiasm: I wrote him back at once, emptying the contents of my heart; the longing I had for just such a champion in my life came running out of me like spring water. I made a sweet, simple fool of myself."

"You were only a boy," said Doyle.

Sparks showed himself no such clemency. His eyes were reduced to black pinpricks of self-directed rage. Draining his brandy, he promptly called for another. "I've never told any of this to another soul. Not a word."

Doyle knew Jack would accept no solace from the hollow sympathies he had to offer. Sparks's drink arrived. He fortified himself before continuing.

"I sent my letter to him. He of course anticipated my letter and had seen to it that arrangements allowing an exchange to continue were already in place—his writing back to me was problematic; sending it directly was out of the question. With an embroidered account of parental cruelty, he had recruited one of his adjutant's cousins, a quiet, reliable youth who lived in the village near our home. Under his cousin's signature, the man would receive Alexander's letters—which, once the dam broke, arrived at a steady rate of at least two a week—bicycle out to our estate, and leave them in a biscuit tin I had buried near an ancient oak, a landmark on our property that I frequented, well out of sight from the main house.

"So my correspondence with my brother began. It was from the start voluminous, the contents academically vigorous and far-reaching. Alexander's interest in and ability to penetrate the deeper workings of the world, and in turn make them explicable to me, was astonishing. His command of history, philosophy, art, and science, prodigal. He was able to engage his schoolmasters on a level of discourse that far surpassed what most had experienced at university and to do so in such a charming, unassuming manner that Alexander was generally regarded as more colleague to them than student. His school had in its halcyon past produced generations of MPs and a handful of prime ministers—you can see how effortlessly this sort of thinking takes root; here was the sort of boy, they swooned, who appears once in a generation.

"Alexander had polished himself to a shine every bit as supremely dazzling in the social graces as he was natively in the academic. He realized his ultimate goals, which were at this stage of his life already remarkably articulated, would require of him an uncommon brilliance of form as well as mind: manners, voice, wardrobe. As a result, he could at the age of twelve not only pass muster but positively thrive in any class or social setting far exceeding his years. To develop the physicality he would need to meet his objectives, he followed a brutally rigorous regimen of exercise, spending the hours other boys squandered in play or with their families alone in the gymnasium. He stayed to this discipline so single-mindedly that by the time he reached thirteen Alexander was frequently mistaken for a man of twenty. The full, lustrous benefit of his effort at self-improvement—his religion, if you will: The conventional observances of Christianity he was required to endure he treated as an inconvenience, if not an outright joke—he of course passed on in his letters to me. He portrayed himself as the avatar of self-perfection, the first of a new breed: the Superior Man. In crucial but unobtrusive ways, by design untraceable to him by my parents, I embraced his guidelines for self-improvement; they became the keystone of my early life. I wholeheartedly intended to re-create myself in his image. I became his disciple."

"Not altogether to your detriment."

"By no means. The developments and skills he outlined have been in and of themselves supremely beneficial. I would without hesitation recommend their employment as the foundation of any ambitious educational system. But having once achieved them, to the pursuit of what ends these advances were to be employed my brother never went so far to say. Nor did his instructors ever bother to inquire; dedicated excellence in and of itself is so rare and bewitching a quality in the humdrum world that they were blinded by Alexander's radiance."

"What was his purpose, Jack?"

"That has only become clear with time," said Sparks. "He never divulged a hint of it during those early years to me, let alone anyone else."

"You must have had your suspicions."

"I had no inclination to question his motives—"

"But surely his nature must have revealed itself, even inadvertently."

"There were signs along the way, but they remained so cleverly obscured that any connection between them or interpretation of them would have proved impossible for even the most determined observer."

"What kind of signs, Jack?" asked Doyle, feeling a collar of dread draw close around him again.

"Accidents. Happenstances. A month before we met, one of the boys in Alexander's class died mysteriously. They raised honey bees on the campus, part of a science study course. The boy was found one night near the hives. He'd been stung to death, stung thousands of times. A clumsy boy, given to pranks; he must have stirred the insects up in some way, provoked them, the school concluded. The boy had been a close confederate of my brother's, but not in a way that would generate undue scrutiny. No one knew that they had quarreled recently. No one knew that the boy had balked at one of Alexander's imperious commands, threatening to leave his circle of intimates and expose their secrets."

"What sorts of secrets?"

"Blood oaths. Violent hazing of new schoolboys admitted to the group. Torture of small animals. All done in the manner of boys being boys, but each act consistently and progressively carried beyond the norm. That is, until this incident. No one knew the boy had been lured to the hives that night by a note from another of Alexander's lieutenants—written by Alexander himself in exact approximation of the boy's hand. Requesting a meeting. Voicing a similar desire to defect from Alexander's influence. When the boy arrived, he was knocked unconscious, the note removed, and his body hurled into the hives."

"He must have told you all this," said Doyle.

"I'll come to that. When we first met, I remember being drawn to a curious necklace Alexander was wearing: a bee, preserved in amber."

Doyle shook his head in wonder.

"There's more. In the fall of Alexander's thirteenth year, in the town near the school, a series of strange sightings were recorded. A number of young women, all from respectable homes—this was for the most part a comfortable, upper-middle-class community—reported that while walking late at night they felt they were being followed. Some thought they were being watched inside their bedrooms. They never saw a face, and only on rare occasions a dark shape, dressed all in

Nemesis

black—a man, a good-sized man, of this they were certain. He maintained distance, never approached them, never directly posed a threat, but the sense of menace the figure imparted was nonetheless considerable.

"One night, one of these girls awoke to find this shape standing over her bed: She was paralyzed with fright, unable to cry out, and the figure fled silently out an open window. This incident was sufficient to incite the local constabulary to swift, collective action. Young women were forbidden to walk at night alone. Curtains were shut, windows locked tight. Patrols organized in areas where the figure had been seen. It seemed effective; the sightings stopped abruptly, did not recur over the course of the winter, and as spring approached, the urgency of these extra measures taken months before grew tiresome: Windows were thrown open to the welcoming air, evening walks undertaken again with presumptions of safety.

"Until one night in early April when the town's comeliest young woman was assaulted near the banks of the river. Sexually assaulted. After satisfying himself upon her, the attacker flew into a rage, and she was beaten savagely. She never saw his face. He never spoke, never made a sound; she could identify him only as 'a black shape.'"

"Was Alexander suspected?"

"In the course of their investigation, town officials routinely questioned authorities at Alexander's school—although everyone felt certain a grown man was responsible, as his size and strength would indicate, most likely the same man who'd been seen the previous fall. Students themselves were sequestered on the campus after dark. And all of them accounted for, in their beds at the time of the attack."

"Easy enough to arrange that. It was your brother, of course."

Sparks nodded. "His interest in the fairer sex was asserting itself, and he had a new hunger to feed. Alexander had seldom chosen to moderate his appetites, and then only as an exercise in self-discipline. He had nothing but contempt for the fumbling chaperoned introductions school and society offered as the rituals of courtship. He stalked these girls and then struck without hesitation or remorse. Moral reservations for such an act fell completely outside the tenets of his philosophy; such considerations were, as he wrote to me, a childish refuge for the weak and indecisive. Most people lived with all the courage and conviction of Jersey cows bred for the slaughterhouse. The Superior Man took what he wanted from the world—and often the world was only too willing to award it—without any concern for the consequences."

"Unless he was caught."

"The chances of that, as he saw it, were too slight to even merit concern. He was supremely confident of his ability to outwit anyone. This attack occurred, by the way, two days before my meeting him. The polished black rock he gave me that day was taken from the riverbed where the girl was violated: his trophy of the conquest."

Doyle swallowed back a wave of disgust. "There must have been talk of the rape during your visit. Did your parents connect him to it?"

"Despite their experience with him—which you realize only resulted in a dread suspicion, never certainty—I don't believe that my parents as yet comprehended the singular wickedness of Alexander's mind."

As yet—Doyle took note of the phrasing.

"A much-ballyhooed search of the countryside for the assailant, of course, yielded nothing. It was a crime of cold calculation, not passion; he had covered his tracks expertly."

"He committed no other crimes?" asked Doyle.

"Not in that town. Not for the time being. At Alexander's request, through an arrangement made by his professors, he spent that following summer in Salzburg, studying chemistry and metallurgy at the university. For good measure, he studied the foil and épée at the renowned fencing academy, another skill of which he soon gained mastery. A boy of thirteen, remember. His routine was established: He worked to sharpen scientific abilities during the day—this pup among the graybeards, creating new compounds and alloys in the laboratory, his knowledge growing to the encyclopedic—and his stealth and footpad skills at night. Alexander trained himself to require little sleep, an hour or two at most, freeing him to spend the hours between midnight and sunrise on the prowl. His nocturnal ramblings were every bit as directed and purposeful as his scientific studies: designed specifically to test and steel his nerves."

"How so?"

"Gaining entry to people's houses. He'd sit for hours in their bedrooms. Blend into shadows and corners. These people passing within inches of him, and his heart never increased a beat. Watching them sleep, taking small tokens of his visits—trophies again, he always comes back to this—never items of any great value, trifles, trinkets that wouldn't be missed. He became able to see nearly as well in the dark as most people do at noon. He grew to prefer the darkness to the daylight, whose hours he now spent exclusively indoors, in rapt study. By the end of Alexander's Austrian summer, he could move through the night like a ghost, silent, invisible.

"The night before his scheduled return to England, he allowed himself a single indulgence of the burgeoning appetite he had kept in check these many months. There was a particular girl whose room he had happened upon initially by chance. He found the sight of this girl asleep in her bed so powerfully excited him he was compelled to visit her obsessively. A blond beauty of seventeen, the only daughter of a prosperous burgher, she was in possession of many voluptuous charms, made all the more alluring by her seeming innocence of them. His interest assumed the form of a perverse courtship; he took to following her during the day. He found it thrilling to stand beside her in a shop, to pass her in the street and return her unsuspecting smile, but even so he never dared to speak to her. I believe that somewhere in the recesses of his heart he felt for this girl an authentic stirring of romantic love. He wrote poetry for her. Once he left a single red rose in a stemmed vase by the window. Alexander grew bolder with each succeeding visit, drawing back the covers, touching her hair. As he watched his beloved sleep, he began to impart requited yearning into her every unconscious gesture. He longed to reveal himself to her, to hold and possess her. But in the cold light of day, the tremors and weakness that welled up from the summoned memory of her beauty he found intolerable: The Superior Man could not abide such gaping vulnerability to the unruly fancies of another heart.

"So on his last night in Austria, Alexander slipped into her room for the final time. He doused a handkerchief in chloroform and placed it over his beloved's mouth. He carried her from the house undetected into the surrounding woods, where he set upon her and indulged his desires upon her like a night demon. When he was sated, he carried her much deeper into the woods, quieting her with the drug whenever she began to stir, bound her hand and foot, and laid her gently down in a bower of pine branches. By the time the panicked villagers found her at the end of the following day, Alexander was on the packet sailing back to England."

"He didn't kill her," said Doyle, surprised and relieved.

"No. Nor did he brutalize her after satisfying himself, as he had the other girl. I believe his feelings for her were more complicated, more personal, than any he had experienced before. With the warring sides of his nature at a standoff, the impulse to despoil had not won out. Upon his return, Alexander wrote eagerly to tell me about his 'summer romance.' When I wrote back with what I suppose was some hint of skepticism—ignorance, really, I had no knowledge of the ways of men and women aside from what he'd told me—as proof he sent me a lock of her hair."

"Always attempting to enlist you as his accomplice."

"But as little as I knew, as I held that blond lock in my hand, I felt the first shudder of misgiving about my brother's true nature. Something unpleasant radiated from that beautiful curl, some residue of suffering. I sensed somehow it was *wrong*. I discarded it immediately, threw it into the stream near my old oak, and I didn't write to Alexander for a week. In his next letter, he never mentioned the girl, nor did he voice any displeasure that I had not responded, going on as if nothing had happened. I gratefully buried my uneasiness as an aberration. Our correspondence resumed."

Waiters were turning down the gas jets in the dining room. A small orchestra in another room began to play a Strauss waltz. Handsome couples took to the dance floor. The gay mood prevailing in the room, the dancers swirling about them, made no inroad to the core of Sparks's private burden. He stared into his drink, face drawn, his eyes haunted and febrile.

"And so we went along. The letters. Our yearly Easter visit. The only interruption to our exchanges came when travel to Europe with my family began. Even then there was always a packet of letters waiting upon my return. Alexander was absolutely faithful to me and I to him, always eager to hear of my growth and progress, never overstepping the bounds our parents so vigilantly maintained. Never exhibiting anything but loving interest in my development. Or so I assumed. I realize now he was measuring my progress against the meticulous records he had kept of his own—like a rat in a laboratory experiment—to see if his methods for the development of the Superior Man were verifiable. And not least to reassure himself that my rate of advancement lagged well behind his; by no means would the student ever be allowed to surpass his master.

"As he entered his last year of school before university, and I neared the age, and nearly the size, he'd been when we'd first met, his letters stopped, without warning. I wrote to him repeatedly, with increasing desperation. No reply. Worse yet, no explanation. I felt as if a limb had been cut from my body. I wrote again and again, pleading with him to answer; what transgression had I unknowingly committed? Why had he forsaken me?"

"His work with you was finished."

"No. His intention was to shock me, by demonstrating how swiftly his favor could be withdrawn, to plant a seed of terror in me that tightened his grip and rendered me even more dependent. Four months went by. A thousand scenarios of doom flowered in my imagination, until finally I was able to absolve myself of responsibility: It must have been my parents, I decided. They've discovered our link and taken decisive action against us; they've had Alexander moved, quarantined somewhere out of reach. Perhaps they really were as devious and vengeful as his letters over the last year had subtly begun to suggest. Their absolute steadiness of disposition with me did nothing to allay my suspicions, but only increased them. Whenever I inquired into his well-being, which I dared not do too frequently, they assured me Alexander was well and thriving. I knew it was a lie! He must be languishing, cut off from me at their command, every bit as bereft and miserable as I was. I wanted to retaliate, without giving them the satisfaction of knowing I was stung, so I began to willfully conceal my feelings from them, to put up the same stone wall of polite but distant self-sufficiency I'd seen Alexander assume in their presence. They sensed immediately that something was not right with me, but I refused their entreaties and denied any discomfort, all the while counting the days and hours until that Easter, when Alexander and I would be reunited. To my great surprise, our parents made no effort to deny us that meeting, which only served to confirm my conviction that their treachery was of a high and exalted order.

"When we finally did meet, Alexander betrayed not the slightest uneasiness or dissatisfaction with our parents, and he was as pleasant and convivial with me in their company as always. Sitting on the veranda sipping hibiscus tea, we looked the very model of the upright English family, spending most of our time discussing Alexander's entrance to university that fall. Calling on the reserves of self-control Alexander had taught me so well, I restrained every impulse to pull him aside and beg for the truth about his withdrawal. The long afternoon was nearly passed before the opportunity came, once again on the walk through the gardens after dinner, ritualized now through the years of our visits, the two brothers ten paces ahead of their parents. Our faces and gestures betrayed no urgency; his words to me were few, but they were resonant with that conspiratorial tone of affiliation that I had longed all these months to hear. 'See your way clear to Europe this summer. In July. Alone.' He suggested Salzburg, famous for its music academy. I was stunned. How shall I manage it? With what resources? It seemed entirely beyond me. He said all that was up to me, but however I should do it, this was by far the most important assignment he would ever give me. I would try, I swore to him. I would try my best. You must succeed, he said, at any cost. Our parents appeared behind us, and that was the end of our exchange."

"He wanted to meet you there," said Doyle.

"That, of course, was my assumption. Immediately upon our return home, I threw myself into what had up until that point been, at best, my desultory efforts to master the violin. What had been compulsory now became compulsive; I spent hours in practice every day. My dedication to the work was never questioned, only encouraged by my music-loving parents. To my amazement, I discovered that I possessed no small aptitude for the instrument, almost to the point of prodigality. I was able to coax from those strings the music of a private universe, as if I had discovered an entirely new language that in many ways I found more eloquent than speech. From time to time, I would bemoan the lack of instructors adequate to the rapidly advancing level of my playing. I let mention that I had heard of a musical conservatory in Austria where the great talents of our age had found nurturance for the skills that carried them on to their splendid international careers.

"When some weeks later my parents presented the idea of my enrolling at that very academy for the coming summer, I feigned astonishment and showered them with boundless gratitude for their perceptiveness and generosity. I didn't know which gave me more pride: my cunning in securing the appointment or my actual achievement with the instrument. The next day I wrote Alexander the last letter I would ever send him, one cryptic sentence: 'The job is done.' I received no reply. In the middle of June, my parents accompanied me to Brighton—along with the valet who was to be my traveling companion—where they saw me off on my first solitary European adventure. I set sail for the Continent, arrived in Austria two days later, and was straightaway enrolled in the Salzburg lyceum, where I busied myself in my studies and waited for July and word from Alexander to arrive."

The dance floor was by this time filled with revelers. The orchestra began to assay the sentimental favorites of the day, as the hour of the New Year drew near. A frantic, angular energy animated the crowd, their enjoyment of the occasion hovering uncertainly between bona fide excitement and dutiful obligation.

"Did he send word?"

Sparks looked up at Doyle, his eyes transparent and cold. Doyle saw further into Sparks's private reaches than he had ever been previously allowed.

"Not in the way I had expected. In the second week of July, I was called out of my private instruction and taken to the headmaster's office. My valet was there; the poor man was terrified, pallid and waxen. Whatever is wrong? I asked, but I knew the answer before a word was spoken."

Doyle hung on his every word. Every other eye in the room was on the large clock that loomed over the bar. As the last seconds of the dying year dwindled away, the crowd began counting down.

"Ten, nine, eight . . ."

"You will have to return to England immediately. Tonight, the headmaster told me," said Sparks, raising his voice in order to be heard over the mob. "There's been a fire."

"Seven, six, five . . ."

"Are they dead? Are my parents dead?"

"Four, three, two . . ."

"Yes, John, he said. Yes, they are."

The count ended, and the room erupted cacophonously. Streamers swirled through the air. Noisemakers ratcheted. Lovers kissed, strangers embraced. The band played on. Doyle and Sparks sat through the crescendo of the the celebration, their eyes locked, unmoving.

"Alexander," Doyle said, although he knew Sparks could not hear him. He could not even hear himself.

Sparks nodded. Without another word, he rose from his seat, threw a pack of pound notes down on the table, and sliced though the crowd toward the door. Doyle followed after, his passage more reminiscent of a rugby scrum than Sparks's surgical maneuvering, pushed through the mad clamor at the door, and squirted out onto the street. Doyle fought his way upstream to his friend, who stood under a lamppost, out of the flow of foot traffic, lighting a cheroot. They walked down a side street, away from the crowds. Soon they reached the river. Across the Thames, a fireworks display threw vibrant sparklers into the air, reflecting darkly on the black gelid water.

"Two days to get home," said Sparks after a while. "The house was simply gone. Ashes. Locals said the flames could be seen for miles. A conflagration. Started at night. Five servants lost their lives as well."

"Were the bodies . . . ?"

"My mother's was never recovered. My father . . . had somehow got out of the house. They found him near the stables. Burned beyond recognition. He hung on to life for nearly a day, asking for me, hoping for my arrival. Near the end, he summoned the strength to dictate a letter to his priest. A letter for me. The priest gave it to me soon after I arrived."

Sparks gazed out over the river. The wind blew cold. Doyle shivered in his dinner jacket, too mindful of his friend to draw attention to his own petty discomfort.

"Father wrote to tell me that I had once had a sister who lived for fifty-three days. My brother, Alexander, had murdered the girl in her cradle, my mother half witness to the deed. This was why they'd kept us apart and never told me of him all these years, and now, as he and my mother were being taken from this life, why he implored me with his last breath to forsake my brother's company forever. There had been something wrong in Alexander from the beginning. Something not human. His mind was as glittering and false as a black diamond. Against their better nature, they had always held the glimmer of some persistent hope that he had changed. They had allowed that hope to feed on the lies with which Alexander had deceived them. And now, for the second time—for which my father blamed no one but himself— they had paid the terrible price of relaxing their guard. That was where my father's letter ended."

"There must have been more."

Sparks looked back at Doyle. "The priest went out of his way to warn me that my father was in a deep state of shock when they had spoken, that he might have been, God rest his soul, even quite de- ranged in the torment of his final hours. Therefore I should not con- sequently accept everything he, my father, had said to the man as gospel. I looked into his eyes: I knew the fellow, this priest, I'd known him since I was a child. A family friend, kind, well-meaning. Weak. And I knew he was withholding something from me. I was well versed enough in sacred doctrine to threaten him straight-faced with the damnation of Judas if he lied to me about my father's last confession. That quickly melted his resolve. He handed over to me the second half of Father's letter. I read it. It became clear that what the priest had hoped were the mad ravings of a dying man, his mind ravaged by pain, was in fact the unspeakable truth."

Sparks paused, steeling himself before carrying Doyle the last few steps into the core of his nightmare.

"Theirs had never been an easy marriage, my father wanted me to know. Two strong wills, two independent spirits. They had known great passion and caused each other tremendous sorrow. During their life together, he had loved other women. He offered no apology. He expected no sympathy or understanding. Shortly before Alexander was born, their difficulties reached such an impasse that he accepted the post in Cairo as a trial separation. Stung by his withdrawal, Mother formed an unnatural attachment to the little boy, calling upon Alex- ander to fill a role in her life for which he was quite naturally ill-suited. The effects were unwholesome.

"During a brief, unsuccessful reconciliation, my sister was con- ceived. Father returned to Egypt unawares. He did not even learn of

Nemesis

the pregnancy until weeks after her birth. By the time he could free himself to return to England, the disaster had already occurred. Mother was severed; she desperately craved the comforting, unconditional love she had come to depend on from Alexander, but she was also unable to deny the horror her eyes had witnessed. Father wanted the boy sent away forever, punished, made a ward of the state. Self-divided as she was, my mother threatened to take her own life if he initiated such an action. Thus stalemated, Father took his leave once again. A year later, in a last attempt to salvage the tenuous covenant remaining between them, my father returned from overseas for good and extracted from her the compromise that resulted in Alexander's banishment, a third pregnancy, and the reorganization of their marriage around a second son. The son they would raise together. A son beloved by both parents, not one exclusively. I don't believe they were altogether unhappy during my early years. Far from it. They surrendered to the life they had forged and made their sorry peace with it."

Sparks flicked the butt of his cigar down into the turbulent current. Doyle was reeling inside. He braced himself, for he sensed the worst of all was about to come.

"On the night they died, my father retired early to his rooms. He read for a while, then fell asleep before the fire. My mother's voice woke him, crying out in pain. Going to her chamber, he discovered her bound hand and foot to the posts of the bed. He was struck from behind and fell, unconscious. When he regained his senses, he was tied securely to a chair. My mother was on the bed as before. A figure was on top of her, assaulting her intimately. A figure all in black. She was screaming as if she had lost her mind. The figure completed the loathsome act and turned and smiled, and my father was greeted by the face of his oldest son."

Doyle turned away, short of breath, gasping for air. He was afraid he might be ill.

"Alexander was in no hurry to take leave of their company. He had already killed all the servants in the house; with gruesome detail, he described how each of them had died. He held my parents prisoner in that corrupt purgatory for more than four hours. He poured kerosene onto the bed, dousing my mother. He lit one of father's cigars and sat beside her, blowing on the tip, reddening the ash. He held it on her skin and told her not to bother with her prayers: They would not be sent to hell when he killed them for their sins against him. They were already there: This was hell. And he, their tormentor, was the Devil.

"Alexander untied my father and presented him with a choice: You

159

can now either make love to your wife for the last time or fight with me. My father attacked him in a blind rage. He was still a strong and powerful man, but Alexander beat him easily, expertly and unmercifully, taking him time and again to the edge of unconsciousness, each time pulling him back only to begin again, administering more refined punishments. Things were said to my father that made him realize this nightmarish automaton they were in the grasp of was not in any recognizable way a human being. At last he slipped away into the refuge of darkness.

"Father was awakened the last time by a terrible heat. His skin was burning and the room consumed by fire, the bed and my mother's body already destroyed. My father somehow got himself out of that room, into the hall. The whole interior was ablaze. He hurled himself through a window. The fall broke his legs. He dragged himself away from the house, where my friend from the stable found him."

Sparks exhaled heavily. He slumped slightly forward, his face in the shadows. Doyle leaned over the rail and was sick into the river. He coughed and sputtered, but it was not unpleasant to void his body of the liquor and rich food. It all seemed foul in the company of what he'd just taken in. He waited for his head to clear.

"Sorry . . ." A half-whisper was all he could manage. "Sorry."

Sparks nodded imperceptibly and waited for Doyle to retrieve his dignity.

"I asked to see my father's body. Again the priest resisted, this time without conviction. My friend from the stable took me to a potting shed, the only structure on the grounds the fire had spared, where bodies recovered from the wreckage lay on rough tables under vulcanized sheets. I did not recognize my father's face. I looked at his hands. The gold of his wedding band had melted and reformed around the exposed bone of his ring finger. Then I noticed that in the palm of that hand a queer pattern was burned into the remaining flesh. I studied that pattern, drew it later from memory, and still later remembered where I had seen it before.

"Over the years, my father had brought from Egypt a great number of ancient artifacts. An entire room in our house was dedicated to his collection. I had always been fascinated by a silver insignia in the shape of the eye of Thoth. Aware of my interest, Father made a necklace of it and gave me the insignia on my seventh birthday. When we first met and Alexander gave me that black rock which he said was his most precious possession, to reciprocate I sent him my prized necklace in a letter. My father soon noticed it was missing. I told him I had lost it swimming in the river, never quite sure that he believed me.

"I knew Alexander had taken to wearing the necklace on his nightly visitations. He felt it possessed some mystic property, that its power somehow helped him remain invisible. So I knew that every word my father had spoken to the priest was true; he had ripped the insignia from Alexander's neck as they fought. He wanted to die with that necklace in his hand. So I would see it, and I would know."

Doyle had by now regained enough self-possession to speak. "But Alexander must have reclaimed it from him."

"Not before it had left its mark seared into his flesh."

"Did they find Alexander?"

Sparks shook his head. "Vanished into the air. The school never saw him again. Alexander's course had been set for years; now his two most profound goals were accomplished. He was already far beyond the pale. Three weeks after the funeral, a package arrived at our solicitor's, addressed to me. Origin of postage unknown. A letter in a neutral hand described the murder of the boy at the beehives, the attack on the woman by the river, and the assault on the girl in Germany. It explained the origin of the keepsakes Alexander had given me over the years. And he included this: the last and most repellent of his trophies."

Sparks was holding the silver insignia in his hand.

"You kept it," said Doyle, mildly surprised.

Sparks shrugged. "Nothing else was left. I needed something . . ." said Sparks, more searchingly. "I needed a way to organize my feelings."

"For revenge."

"More than that. I don't mean to suggest it happened overnight. It took many years. I needed . . . meaning. Purpose. To be twelve years old and have in that single blow your entire world destroyed, everything you believe in and cherish eradicated . . ."

"I understand, Jack."

"There is evil loose in the world. I had dwelled in its shadow. I had tasted it. I had seen its basest products. It flourished in a body and soul that entered into life through the same passage I had taken here. I had willingly placed myself in its hands, allowed myself to be consciously molded by its bearer into his own image." Sparks looked again at Doyle; he seemed youthful and open and filled by the black wind of his terror.

"What if I was like him? I had to ask that, Doyle, do you see? What if the same vile, twisted spirit that drove him to these unspeakable crimes was alive in me? I was twelve years old!"

Tears filled Doyle's eyes in sudden comprehension of the boy the man who stood beseechingly before him must have been. To face such grief, to suffer such a loss, was unimaginable. He could offer his friend no comfort, there was none to be given, other than his silent, heartfelt tears.

"I had to believe that the skills my brother instilled in me I had learned for a purpose," Sparks said, throaty with determination. "They had no innate moral property; they were tools, neutral, still useful. I had to believe that, I had to demonstrate to myself that this was true: There could be more than one sort of Superior Man. The salient point with which I aligned my compass was my choice alone; justice would be my North Star, not mendacity and deluded self-worship. I would stand for the bringing of life, not death. If it was my fate to share his blood, then it was my obligation to balance the scales his presence here disrupted; I would deliver into this world a force to counter the darkness to which my brother had succumbed. I would redeem my family name or die trying. That was my mission. To stand opposed, to set myself in his way. To become his nemesis."

His words revived the faltering pulse of hope in Doyle's chest. They stood in silence for a time and watched the river.

CHAPTER 12

Bodger Nuggins

THE NIGHT TURNED bitter cold. The walk back to the hotel was one of the longest miles in Doyle's memory. Sparks withdrew; he seemed hollowed out, emptied. Doyle felt equally flattered that Sparks entrusted him sufficiently to confide and burdened by the weight he would now to some degree have to shoulder. Never had the turning of the New Year left such a feeble impression on him. They made their way past drunks, lovers, hordes of young celebrants cheering and carousing because of this dimly conceived passing—the death of the "old," the birth of the "new," the charade of quickly forsaken resolutions to transform one's petty vices into virtues. Man's arbitrary attempts to demarcate time with this imposed significance seemed as profitless as the scratching of hens' feet in the dirt. And how could one presume that man's essential character was capable of change when a being the likes of Alexander Sparks testified prima facie to the contrary?

Entering the hotel by a discreet rear entrance, they settled into their rooms, lit a fire, and broke open a bottle of cognac. Doyle felt his defiled system balk at the infusion of new liquor, then warm to its heat and welcome the soporific soothing. Sparks stared at the fire, the dancing flames reflecting in his dark eyes.

"When were you next aware of his hand at work?" asked Doyle, breaking the long silence.

"He left England, spent time in Paris, then drifted south. From Marseilles he sailed to Morocco and then crossed Northern Africa to Egypt. He arrived in Cairo less than a year after the killings."

"He left a trail."

"Having committed the Original Crimes—patricide, matricide: Shall we call these the Original Crimes, Doyle? I think in all fairness that we may—the last obstacle to the wholesale indulgence of any wanton or dissolute impulse he might suffer was permanently removed. Having achieved absolute dominance of family and school, his original environments, his intention was now to establish himself in the world. His first task was the amassing of capital toward financial independence. The night of my parents' murders, before setting the fire, he stole from my father's collection of Egyptiana the most priceless treasures— there were a great number of them. Alexander went to Cairo to peddle them. The returns he garnered became the foundation for his soon-to-be considerable fortune."

"Other crimes were committed as well," Doyle surmised.

"There were a series of distinctive murders that year in Cairo. My father had kept a mistress there, an Englishwoman, a colleague in the foreign service. Soon after Alexander arrived, she disappeared. A week later her head was found in the *souk*, the marketplace. Beheading is customary with adulteresses in Muslim cultures, which naturally threw suspicion toward a local. Except that a red letter A had been sewn into the skin of her forehead. By the way, the woman's name was Hester."

Doyle felt his gorge rise again. He realized that to be of any value to Jack in the struggle against his brother, he would have to harden his emotional resolve. If there were no limits to what the man could do, which seemed evident, it would prove no advantage to be left reeling with horror in reaction to his every outrage.

"The following week he dispatched a prominent art dealer, an Egyptian man, along with his wife and children. My conclusion: The man extended negotiation on a piece of my father's collection beyond the limits of Alexander's patience. The item in question, a ceremonial dagger, was the murder weapon. Alexander was not above embellishing his handiwork with macabre flourishes. There had been a spate of hysteria in Cairo about the curse of the mummy's tomb, from whence this dagger and a number of other items in the dealer's possession had been plundered. The man's apartment was trampled over with bare, dusty footprints and littered with strips of decaying linen. Threads of this linen were found lodged in the necks of the wife and children, whom he had strangled, and encrusted on the handle of the knife, with which he had cut out the art dealer's heart. They discovered the missing organ beside the body in a ceremonial bowl covered with the ashes of tannis leaves, believed to be the key ingredient in the ritual formulated by priests of the pharaohs for resurrection from the mummified state. Can you detect the touch of Alexander's hand in all of this?"

"Yes," said Doyle, remembering the death of the London streetwalker.

"The next month an archaeological site in the desert was raided in similar fashion, a tomb only partly uncovered. Two guards were found inside, strangled, and many of the inventoried artifacts inside the crypt were missing, including the mummified remains of the tomb's principal inhabitant. Again the locals found it provident to attribute the killings to a vindictive corpse, risen to exact revenge for the defiling of his grave."

"Alexander was developing an interest in the occult."

"As his mastery of the physical world grew more accomplished, his interests moved naturally toward magic and the immaterial plane. Egypt has had that effect on more than a few Europeans. There's a dread power in those ancient temples. This is where Alexander received his first taste of what dedicated study of the black arts could deliver. Once that hunger was awakened in him, it became the center of his existence. And a hunger fueled by greed is never satisfied by feeding; it only increases the rapacity of the appetite."

"Where did he go from there?"

"From what I was able to reconstruct, the next few years Alexander drifted throughout the Middle East, seeking entrance to various Mystery schools: Zoroastrians, the Sufis, *hashishims*—assassins—the murderous cult of the Old Man of the Mountain—"

"But they were eradicated centuries ago."

"According to official history, yes, their fortress stormed by the Ottomans, their numbers decimated. But some highly placed Turks will tell you that small sects of devotees have survived, in Syria and Persia, secreted in remote mountain freeholds. They also say that the unsurpassed killing techniques of the *hashishims* are still evidenced in enough unsolved politically motivated murders to lend that theory considerable authenticity. If they do still exist in any form, be assured Alexander was most capable of not only seeking them out, but extracting from them their most treacherous death-dealing secrets."

"When he came after me, I'm thankful I didn't know then what I know now," said Doyle, with halfhearted levity. "I might have dropped dead at the sight of him."

Sparks's look suggested that possibility was a good deal more than a joke.

"India was Alexander's next destination," said Sparks, "where I believe he infiltrated the Thuggee murder cult, a much more immanent and verifiable band of terrorists. Not easy work for an Englishman, their avowed enemy, but by this point he had mastered languages and the art of disguise. The Thugs are particularly adept at garroting. The double-weighted scarf you so admired on the night of our escape in Cambridge is one of their *spécialités de la maison*."

"You've learned a good number of these techniques yourself."

Sparks shrugged. "As a consequence of tracking Alexander's movements over the years, a rather extensive body of . . . profane knowledge has come into my possession. Does that trouble you, Doctor?"

"On the contrary. I shall sleep much more soundly."

"Good man," said Sparks, almost allowing himself a smile.

Doyle had that feeling once again of being in a cage with a dangerous animal. God forbid his skills should ever be turned against me, he thought. "And so during these years in the East, Alexander's passion for the occult grew more obsessive."

"Precisely," said Sparks. "While I was in my teens absorbing the principles of geometry and the conjugation of intransitive French verbs, Alexander was scaling the Himalayas, penetrating the legendary yogic schools of northern India and Kathmandu."

"I've read of these places. Surely, if they exist and their morality is as advanced as are their reported powers of mind, they would have refused a man like Alexander entrance."

"No doubt some of them did. No doubt there are others directed toward those who wish to tread the—what was Blavatsky's term for it?"

"The Left-Handed Path."

"The word *sinister* derives from the Latin for left-handed, did you know that?"

"It must have slipped my mind."

"For all we know, Alexander may have been carried by a legion of chattering, cloven-hoofed demons across the threshold of the Dark Brotherhood's Advanced Conservatory of Thirty-third–Degree Mayhem. As painstakingly as I've attempted to trace his itinerary, the full extent of his matriculations during these years remains at best elusive."

"During your travels to the Far East," Doyle said, stitching another part of Sparks's patchwork quilt past into place.

"The very reason I left university before graduation, having absorbed the better part of what they had to offer. Following in Alexander's admittedly sketchy footsteps has endowed me with a fuller scholarship in the . . . practical workings of the world."

Doyle decided to leave that assertion where it lay. "When did Alexander return to Britain?"

"Difficult to say. His trail died in Nepal. I came home and for many years believed he'd vanished into the mysteries that consumed him. My best estimate: Alexander returned to England twelve years ago, not long after I actively began my career."

"How did you know he'd returned?"

Sparks formed a spire with his fingers, pressed them to his chin, and stared intently into the fire. "I had for many years been aware of—call it a directing intelligence behind the activities of London's criminal community. This web of connective tendrils suggested a shadowy hand manipulating pieces on a game board, a lurking presence felt more than seen. But the faint signals I have been able to verify point consistently to a conspiracy of purpose behind the random and brutal practices that comprise the majority of the underworld's labors."

"Have you no idea what that purpose might be?"

"None whatsoever. As you know, I have recruited a number of these denizens—rehabilitating them in the process, one hopes. Many can speak to rumors of an overlord sitting at the hub of the city's wheel of vice—gambling, slavery, smuggling, prostitution—the fruits of these crimes flowing always toward the center."

"You believe that this overlord is Alexander."

Sparks paused. "I'm not completely certain such a figure even exists. No single one of my acquaintances can confirm anyone has ever had direct experience of such an individual. But if so, no other man on this earth would be more capable of it than my brother. And in the doing, no other man would be more dangerous."

"Then surely that's been the status quo in London for some time—predating Alexander's tenure, certainly. Crime has always been a regrettably consistent element of the human experience."

"I cannot dispute that: What is your point?"

"Something more than the routine conducting of illicit enterprise is at work here, Jack. Something beyond the scope of their ordinary reach."

"You're referring to the Dark Brotherhood," said Sparks.

"Presumably an organization separate from this criminal organization, with its own distinct and self-interested objectives."

"Indeed."

"And you're quite certain Alexander has sworn his allegiance to the Brotherhood?"

"Alexander's only allegiance is to himself," said Sparks. "If he's aligned himself with them, it is solely for the purpose of furthering his own ambitions. The moment their paths diverge, he will not hesitate in severing the bond."

"But even so, a partnership between two such groups, no matter how provisional—"

"Represents a greater threat to the general well-being of our country than any war or pestilence imaginable. No point in sheltering ourselves from that unpleasant truth."

Doyle let that sink in for a moment. "When was the last time you saw your brother, Jack?"

"Outside the window at Topping."

"No, I mean face-to-face."

"Not since that last Easter, at school. Twenty-five years ago."

Doyle leaned in. "And when did you first realize Alexander was this mastermind you've described?"

"Yesterday. When I saw that great house burning."

They looked at each other.

"So at last you understand the game we are playing," said Sparks.

Doyle nodded. Now it was his turn to stare deeply into the fire and wonder if the New Year the crowds outside had ushered in would be his last.

❉   ❉   ❉

Larry stood sentinel outside their doors as Doyle sought some small renewal in sleep. He woke from a fitful dream that fled before him to find their luggage packed by the door, and Sparks at the table in the sitting room, poring over a map of London. It was half past five, dawn hardly a rumor in the sky outside. It took Doyle, wiping the grit from his eyes, the entire pot of coffee and tray of cakes Larry brought in to strip the rust from his muscles and brain. Both cried out for a day of rest, but as Doyle suspected, there would be no such luxury for some time to come.

"There are a dozen publishers on Russell Street within hailing dis-

Bodger Nuggins

tance of the museum," said Sparks energetically. "Did you by any chance submit your manuscript to the firm of Rathborne and Sons?"

"Rathborne? Lady Nicholson's maiden name—yes, yes I believe I did," said Doyle. "By God, do you suppose—"

Doyle was distracted by a small, boxy contraption he had never seen the like of before weighing down a corner of the map. As he idly reached to examine it, Sparks snatched the box away, dropped it into his pocket, and began vigorously rolling up the map.

"Then that's where we will begin," said Sparks. "In the meantime, Larry will move us to other lodgings. I'm afraid you may not find our subsequent housing as congenial as the Melwyn, but it's prudent we spend no more than one night in a single place."

"I could do with a shave first," he said ruefully, watching Larry carry their bags out of the room.

"Plenty of time for that later. Come along, Doyle, the race is to the swift," said Sparks, and he was out the door as well. Doyle grabbed the last cake from the platter and hurried after him.

Halfway down the backstairs, they encountered Barry running up to meet them—at least Doyle's blistered eyes thought it was Barry: Yes, there was the scar.

"Found a bloke you should have a bash at," said Barry, with uncharacteristic urgency.

"Be more specific," said Sparks, continuing down.

"Aussie bloke. Boxer. Claims he had the acquaintance of Mr. Lansdown Dilks. After he was hanged."

"Excellent," said Sparks as they exited the hotel. "Doyle, go with Barry. Turn the screws: Find out if the man can enlighten us regarding the estimable Mr. Dilks. We'll meet at noon, Hatchard's Bookshop, Picadilly. Good luck to you!" Sparks jumped aboard a small hansom with Larry at the reins, gave a single sharp wave, a salute really, and they pulled away.

This wasn't how the game was supposed to be played, grumbled Doyle, left to his own devices at six in the morning before a proper breakfast. Doyle looked at Barry, who seemed entirely unfazed by Sparks's sudden departure.

"This way," said Barry, with a tip of the hat, and he started walking.

Doyle stuffed the rest of the cake in his mouth and set off after him. The first light of day peeked over the eastern horizon.

❂   ❂   ❂

THE LIST OF 7

Barry led Doyle briskly through the maze of Covent Garden, where in the stalls of the vegetable and flower sellers the commerce of the New Year was off to a bustling beginning. Yawning flower girls smoked cheap cigarettes and leaned against each other to ward off the chill, awaiting turns to fill their peddler's trays. Costermongers combatively picked over the marketed yields of the farmers' winter gardens. Doyle's digestive juices were whipped to a boil by the marriage of aromas that souped the morning air: Arabian coffee beans, fresh breads leaving the oven, grilled sausages and hams, hot French pastries. His gastronomic longings lurched toward despair when he realized he'd left his purse and all his money in the bag that Larry had transported by now to God-knows-where. Appeals to Barry to pause for a restorative snack—at Barry's expense—fell on deaf ears. By the repeated tipping of his hat, bobbing up and down as regularly as a mechanical dandy in a Dresden clock tower, Doyle deduced that Barry was passingly familiar with more than a few of the merchants' wives and an unusually high percentage of the female shop attendants. Where there's smoke, thought Doyle: Barry's gay-blade reputation must be authentic after all.

Their trail took them to a gymnasium in a Soho side street, a squat, filthy brick of a building, its walls a palimpsest of posters trumpeting the forgotten but once epic collisions of yesterday's fistic gladiators. A soot-obscured homily traced the arch of the Greek Revival entryway, extolling the virtue of exercise to the development of a sound moral character.

Inside the gym, on the far side of the squared circle, a boisterous knot of wrestlers, bare-fisted boxers, and physique enthusiasts knuckled around a cutthroat game of dice. Well-wrinkled cash and cheapjack gin bottles defined the area they'd set aside for the bones to settle after hitting the musty wall—a most unsavory scene that had seen more than one dawn pass by unnoticed. Barry instructed Doyle to wait some distance from the bunch—he was only too happy to comply— while he waded in to separate the object of their quest from the pack. He returned a minute later with a flat-faced hulking mass of hardened flesh, whose bulging bare arms were adorned with tattoos of mermaids and pirates engaged in a succession of suggestive *pas de deux*. The man's nose spread out horizontally to the width of his gaping mouth, the only useful organ for breathing he had left. His eyebrows were an omelet of scar tissue and scraggly hair, his eyes set as deep as pissholes in the snow. A well-traveled trail of tobacco juice trickled down his chin. The man's haircut was distressingly similar enough to the one

Bodger Nuggins

Doyle now sported to suggest that Barry must be the man's barber, if not his confidant.

"I'd like to introduce you to Mr. Bodger Nuggins, former light-heavyweight champion of Her Majesty's colony of New South Wales and Oceania," said Barry, bringing the two men together.

Doyle accepted the behemoth's two-handed handshake; it was flaccid, and the man's palm was as soft and moist as a skittish soubrette's. The stink of gin wafted off him in clouds.

"Arthur Conan—" began Doyle.

Barry cleared his throat with emphatic vehemence, followed by a vigorous shaking of the head just behind and out of Bodger's field of sight.

"Maxwell Tree," corrected Doyle with the first name that leapt to mind.

"Bodger Nuggins, former light-heavyweight champion of New South Wales and Oceania," said the boxer redundantly, still holding Doyle's hand in both of his and moving it semicircularly. "Call me Bodger."

"Thank you, Bodger."

Bodger's eyes were slightly askew, the one on the right cheating in as if it secretly desired a better look at the incredible nose plateau prominent to the south.

"That's what folks who knows the Bodger calls him. Calls him Bodger. Rhymes with Dodger," Bodger elaborated cooperatively.

"Yes. It does at that," said Doyle, trying gently to liberate his hand.

"Cedric," said Bodger mysteriously.

"Cedric who?"

"That's me Christian name. Me muther named me Cedric."

"After . . . ?" offered Doyle, trying to help him to his anecdote's destination in the hopes of effecting a release from Bodger's determined grasp.

"After I was borned," said Bodger, simian brow creased with the profundity of a Mandarin court astrologer.

"Tell the gent'l'man wot you told me, Bodger," prompted Barry, and then whispered to Doyle: "He's a coupl'a sheep short in the top paddock."

Doyle nodded. Bodger's facial contortions redoubled. His eyebrows rode out the effort like a mechanical wave machine in a stormy melodrama.

"Wot you told me about Mr. Lansdown Dilks," Barry added.

"Ow, right! Bugger!" *Thwap!* Bodger punched himself in the nose. Judging by its pancaked state, it had to be a habitual response, whether an aid to jog the memory or stern corrective to the stubborn gears of what remained of his mind it was difficult to say. "Lansdown Dilks! Balls! Bodger Nugs, wot a muffer!" And he punched himself a second time.

"Here, here—perfectly all right, go easy now, Bodger," said Doyle. If the man was indeed a former champion, he didn't want a knockout self-administered before beginning his interrogation.

"Right," said Bodger, finding a sudden forgiveness for himself.

"Did you know a Mr. Lansdown Dilks?" asked Doyle.

"Ahh. There's a story goes with this," Bodger said, intimating that an imperishable drama loomed just around the corner. "Let's see. . . ."

Being somewhat more familiar with his narrative technique, Barry slipped a pound note into Bodger's mitt.

"Right," said Bodger, his pump primed. "I come from Queensland, see. Down under. Brisbane, to be exactical. Across the deep and briny."

"Yes," said Doyle. "I do follow you: You're from Australia."

Bodger snapped his fingers, pointed at Doyle, and winked broadly, as if he'd just discovered they were brothers in the same secret lodge. "Eggzac'ly!"

"We understand each other. Do go on, Bodger."

"Right. Fisticuffs, that's my nut, see. Bloodsport. A man wants to strut his stuff among men, let 'im do it wit' his hands as naked as a newborn babe, that's what I say. Done all right by Bodger Nuggins, hadn't it? Champeen of New South Wales and Oceania, light heavyweight."

By way of demonstrating his credentials, as boxers are compulsively wont to do, Bodger threw a punch at Doyle's midsection, pulling it an inch away from sending him to his knees in search of oxygen.

"Mind you," Bodger went on, "this Marquis of Queensberry ponce, he'd like to put dresses on us bare knucklers, wouldn't he, have us dance about and slap each other with lit'le tea gloves." Unable to resist an additional compulsion to editorialize, Bodger contemptuously hawked a plug of tired tobacco to the floor. "The old ponce wants to watch lit'le girlies fight, why don't he go to St. Edna's Academy for Women and Ponces?"

"I'm sure I don't know," said Doyle. "Regarding Mr. Lansdown Dilks—"

"I'm gettin' 'ere," said Bodger, flexing his muscles ominously. "So the Bodger takes his leave from his old Homestead to have a go in the fight game on this side of the puddle. England. By boat it was. Uh . . ."

Bodger Nuggins

"The pursuit of your boxing career brought you to London," said Doyle.

"Promised the Bodger a bash at the heavyweight title, these blokes did, but first they wants Bodgkins to fight this other bouff head. You know, like a . . ." He went blank. Frozen as if he'd spilled sand in his gears.

"A tune-up fight," said Barry, after a respectful silence.

"Right," said Bodger, thwacking himself in the face again and jolting his mental machinery free from its rut. "Like a tune-up fight. Some drongo. Want to see what Bodger's made of 'fore they puts their precious title on the line. So the Bodger says to them, wot's fair is fair. Never let it be said Champeen Nuggins is a piker: Old Bodger puts on a show, he does, when some right gents lays out a few spon-duliacks to catch my action."

"So you had this tune-up fight," said Doyle.

Bodger nodded and squiffed out another squirt of hot juice. "First thing, they tells me the tune-up's not to take place in your stadium, your gamin' hall, or even in your ring, as such. What they do is, see, they takes me to this warehouse like, down by the ribber."

"This was not a legally sanctioned bout," said Doyle, feeling more and more like an interpreter for some idiot prince.

"Not the full quid, no," said Bodger, seeming to comprehend. "But truff be known, we bare knucklers are not unfamiliar wit' the procedure."

"So I take it that once you reached the wharf, these gentlemen introduced you to your opponent," said Doyle patiently.

"Some ponce," snarled Bodger. "Soft. Face like a stunned mullet. Like he's never tussled wit' the gloves off in his life. So we're off: The ponce won't mangle much, but 'e won't lie down neither. No technical know-how. Bodger blinds him with science. Sixty-five rounds we go: His face is a mask of claret. Ask me, his corner should'a skied the towel long about fifty. But it's not my fate they should take the advice of Bodger, was it?"

"Apparently not, no."

"And now we comes to round sixty-sixth. That's why to this day sixty-six is the Bodger's unlucky number."

Bodger took Doyle by his lapels and pulled him closer as his death-less tale built to its thrilling climax. If I hadn't already shaved my mustache, thought Doyle, Bodger's breath would have torched it right off.

"We comes out and touches fives, good sportsmen that we were.

173

Then Bodger greets him with a wicked-fair left hook to the liver. The drongo doubles down. Then the Bodger straightens his starch with a Bodger special: an uppercut to the nozz, a cracklin' good judy settin' him up for the bone-crushin', death-deliverin' grand finale Bodgerific combination to the point of his pozzy that sends the wowser airborne. And by the time his head hits the ground, the spirit of man has fled his poncey body."

"He was dead," said Doyle, as agreeably as possible.

"Dead as a duck in a thunderstorm," said Bodger, still holding Doyle close enough to count his back teeth.

"How unfortunate."

"Not for the ponce; he's gone to his reward, 'adn't he? After all that muckabout, it's Bodger who'll have the hard rain fall. In comes the coppers. Manslaughter, they says. Bare knuckles and all, no Marquis of Queens-berry, they says. Trial by jury. Fifteen years' hard labor. Hello, Newgate Prison; bye-bye Bodger."

Bodger released Doyle and sent a stream of variegated brown glop ten feet into the air, rattling over the edge of a spittoon in the corner.

"Where I take it," said Doyle, rearranging his clothes, "you at long last make the acquaintance of Mr. Lansdown Dilks."

"Mr. Lansdown Dilks. A hard moke in his physicaliosity, not all that dif'ernt than the Nugger man hisself."

"Somewhat Bodgeresque, you might say," said Doyle.

"A most Bodgerlike top dog indeed," confirmed Bodger. "All very fine and large to 'ave one such feller in a given coop-up. 'Sonly nature's way. Put two such specimens in the same yard, and wot you's got there is one rumbustrious ruck-us."

"So you quarreled, the two of you, is that what you're saying, Bodger?" said Doyle, with another stab at translation.

"Most violent and frequently," said Bodger, cracking his knuckles: They reported like a rifle volley. "And neither one of these two smug pups ever able to best the better of the other. The first time, Bodgie's not ashamed to say, that the Nuggins ever met his match on either side of the ropes."

"And so you served your time together until the execution of Dilks's sentence."

Bodger's eyebrows knit together again. "Execution."

"Last February. When Dilks passed on."

Bodger's mystification deepened. "Passed on."

"Died. Gone west. Slipped the cable. Hung by the neck," said Doyle, finally losing his patience. "And flights of angels sing him to his rest. Do you mean to say this represents some sort of news to you, Bodger?"

Bodger Nuggins

"Not half. Dilksie looked in the pink last time the Bodger clapped eyes on him."

"And when was that, pray?"

"When we gots off the train together—"

"Surely you're mistaken," said Doyle.

"If Bodger means off the train, that's what he'd say, idn't it?" said Bodger, giving vent to no small irritation. "Off the train is what the Bodger means, and off the train is wots 'e's sayin'."

Doyle and Barry exchanged a quizzical look. Barry shrugged: This was fresh embroidery on the story for him as well. "Off the train where?"

"Up north. Yorkshire, like."

"When was this?"

"So happens the Bodger remembers the exactical date, seeing as how it was 'is own birt'day: March the fourth."

"March the fourth of *last* year?" Doyle was growing more confused with every word the man uttered.

"Say, wot are you, a ponce?"

"Bodger, forgive my thickness," said Doyle. "Are you telling me that you and Dilks took a train to Yorkshire a month after he swung and years before your sentence was due to expire, on March the fourth of last year?"

"Right. Lansdown and me and the others wot signed on."

"Signed on how?"

"Wit' the bloke wot come round the prison."

"Newgate Prison?"

"You catch on fast, don'tcha mate?"

"Please, I'm doing my best to understand: What man was this?"

"Don' know his name. Din't give it, did he?"

"Can you describe him?"

Bodger rolled his eyes skyward. "Beard. Glasses. Looked like a ponce."

"All right, Bodger, what did this gentleman who came around give you to understand you were signing on to do?"

"I can tell you this: He didn't tell us nuffin' 'bout what went on in that bleedin' biscuit factory. No, sir. That's why I run off like I did. And don't think they're not after me for it neither—"

The air was shattered by a piercing chorus of police whistles.

"Coppers!"

The alarm went up, and the men in the dice game scattered. Before Doyle could react, Bodger turned tail and sprinted for the dressing room, the front doors burst open and a squadron of bobbies, batons

175

raised, rushed into the gym. Another phalanx burst through the back
exit, and the battle was joined, a half-dozen of them occupied solely
with Bodger, whose prowess did not by its demonstration seem in the
least bit overstated. Barry took Doyle's arm, holding him in place.

"It'll go better for us if we don't run, guv," he shouted over the din.

"But Bodger was just about to tell us—"

"No worries; chances are ripe we'll be sharing a cell soon enough."

"But we're not here to play dice."

"Try telling the grasshoppers that. Rum go, but there it is."

Two policeman were moving toward them. Barry put his hands on
top of his cap and advised Doyle to do the same. Doyle instead began
walking lively toward the officers.

"Now see here," asserted Doyle, "I'm a doctor!"

"And I'm queen of the May," said the bobby.

The first blow caught Doyle along the side of the head.

❈   ❈   ❈

Barry's concerned face was the first sight that greeted Doyle when
he opened his eyes.

"Feelin' a bit wonky, guv?" asked Barry.

"Where are we?"

"The clink. Gaol. Pentonville, I fink."

Doyle tried to sit up, and his head spun like a multicolored pinwheel.

"Easy on, guv," said Barry. "Quite the cue ball you're cultivatin'
there."

Doyle raised a hand to the blood-pounding site on his forehead and
found a swollen goose egg residing there. "What happened?"

"You missed the ride in the Black Maria. Bein' hauled into lockup
was nuffink special. Been ten minutes additional since I set you on
this bench."

As his vision stabilized, Doyle perceived they were in a large common holding cell, shared by a milling mix of roughnecks and repro-
bates, many of whom he recognized from the gymnasium dice game.
The room was filthy and reeked to high heaven, a quality traceable to
the common latrine adorning one wall. Roaches the size of thumbs
scuttled fearlessly around the margins and over the boots of men who
seemed all too accustomed to their company.

"Ever been between the bars before, guv?"

"Never."

Barry regarded him sympathetically. "Not much to recommend it."

Doyle searched the faces roaming the cell. "Where's Bodger?"

"Bodger Nuggins is not among our number," said Barry.

"Was he in the Black Maria?"

"I would have to answer in the negative."

"Did you see him escape the gym?"

"No."

Doyle gingerly probed his throbbing head. "What have they charged us with?"

"Charged us? Nuffink'."

"They can't very well hold us here if they don't charge us with a crime."

"This *is* your first time, idn't it?" asked Barry with a subtle smile.

"But this is all a dreadful mistake. Tell them we demand to see a barrister," said Doyle, with somewhat hollow conviction. "We have our rights, after all."

"Well . . . suppose there's a first time for everything," Barry replied, trying to make a good show of mulling it over.

Doyle studied him: The irony in Barry's musing quickly communicated the utter futility of pursuing what Doyle had assumed to be the ordinary channels. Instead, Doyle searched his pockets and fished out his physician's prescription notepad; the sight of the *Rx* gave him a jolt, as if he'd uncovered a relic of some long-forgotten civilization.

"Barry, can you secure me something to write with?"

Barry nodded and sidled over into the flow of convicts. He returned minutes later with a scrounged nub of a pencil. Doyle took it and scrawled out a hasty message.

"Now we're going to need some money," said Doyle.

"How much?"

"How much can you manage?"

Barry sighed heavily. "Stand over here, please, guv."

Doyle stood and shielded Barry from the rest of the room as he turned to the wall, unbuttoned a hidden flap on the inside of his waistcoat, and pulled out a bulging roll of five-pound notes. "Will this do?"

"Just one, I think, will be more than sufficient," said Doyle, trying to conceal his amazement.

Barry peeled one note off and replaced the rest. Doyle took the note from him and tore it neatly in half.

"Cor . . . wot'zat then?" gasped Barry.

"Do you know an officer here you can trust?"

"There's a contradiction in terms—"

"Let me rephrase that: Do you know one who can be relied upon to do a job for money?"

Barry looked out at the guards patrolling the corridor. "Could do."

Doyle folded the written note around half the bill and handed it to him. "Half now, the rest when we get word the message's been received."

"Give it a go," said Barry, sneaking a look at the note as he moved toward the bars. He couldn't help but notice the note was addressed to Inspector Claude Leboux.

✿　✿　✿

Two hours later, Doyle was summarily escorted without explanation to a small room at Pentonville set aside for the questioning of suspects. Minutes afterward, Leboux appeared alone, his mustaches fairly bristling with anger. He closed the door and stared at Doyle.

"Hello, Claude."

"Corralled at a dice game, Arthur? I don't recall gambling as a vice you were given to indulge."

"I wasn't there to gamble, Claude. This is a clear case of being in the wrong place at the wrong time."

Leboux sat opposite to Doyle, folded his arms, splayed out his feet, and toyed with one waxed end of his mustache while he waited for the next line of questions to coalesce in his mind. Trying to heed Sparks's repeated advice about mistrusting the police, Doyle weighed how much he needed to divulge in order to secure his release, without drawing down the unwelcome attention of Leboux's superiors.

"You look like a valet," Leboux finally said.

"There have been repeated attempts on my life by the identical parties who tried the other day. This is by way of avoiding detection."

"Why haven't you come to me?"

"I've been out of the city since you last saw me," said Doyle, thankful to employ some small grain of truth. "Leaving London seemed the safest course."

"Was it?"

"No, as it happens. These assailants have pursued me relentlessly."

"When did you return, Arthur?"

"Last night."

"Have you been to your flat?"

Petrovitch, thought Doyle; he knows about Petrovitch. "I haven't, Claude. I wasn't at all sure it would be safe." Doyle waited, summoning the bland countenance he employed in the presence of patients who had ventured beyond hope of recovery but weren't up to receiving the news.

"Your building has burned down," Leboux finally said.

"My flat?"

"A total loss, I'm afraid."

Doyle shook his head. Fire again. Not hard to reason who's responsible for that, thought Doyle. My flat gone. It wasn't the thought of losing his possessions that troubled him so—he'd considered those lost already. Now not only all evidence of Petrovitch's murder but the outrage they had visited to his rooms as well was gone forever. A hot coil of anger went red inside him.

"Claude, I want to ask you something," said Doyle. "In your capacity as inspector."

"All right."

"Are you at all familiar with the name . . . Alexander Sparks?"

Leboux looked up at the ceiling and squinted. After a moment, he shook his head slightly and took out a notepad and pencil. "Let's have it again." Doyle spelled it for him.

"That's the man who's after me. The one you're looking for. The man responsible for these crimes and perhaps a great many others as well."

"And what leads you to believe this is the man?"

"I've spied him pursuing me now on three different occasions."

"What's his appearance?"

"I've never seen his face. He's given to wearing black. And a cape, a black cape."

"Black cape . . . what places is he known to frequent?"

"No one seems to know."

"Acquaintances?"

Doyle shrugged.

"Other recent offenses?"

"Sorry."

Leboux's cheeks filled with color. "Do you happen to know his hat size?"

Doyle leaned forward and lowered his voice. "You'll have to forgive my vagueness, Claude. He's an elusive figure, but there's a better than even chance this man is nothing less than criminal mastermind of the entire London underworld."

Leboux shut his notebook and shifted uncomfortably in his seat. "Arthur," Leboux said, measuring his words like a printer. "You're a doctor. Well on your way to becoming a pillar of our community. I say this to you as a friend: You are not on the straight and narrow to reaching that post by running around England dressed like a butler going on about plots to murder you in the night by mysterious kingpins of crime."

"You don't believe me. You don't believe I've been under attack at all."

"I believe that you believe that you have been—"

"What about what I found on the floorboards at Thirteen Cheshire Street?"

"Yes. I had that substance analyzed by our chemist—"

"You can't tell me that wasn't blood, Claude."

"That it is. It does appear that you did in fact witness a murder."

"Just as I told you—"

"The murder of a large hog."

There was silence. Leboux leaned forward. "It was pig's blood, Arthur."

"Pig's blood? That's not possible."

"Perhaps someone got carried away carving the Sunday roast," said Leboux. "A bit on the rare side for pork, if you ask me."

What did this mean? Doyle raised a hand to his throbbing head.

"You could do with a nice slab of rare meat about now for that knot on your bean," said Leboux.

"Forgive me, Claude, I'm a trifle confused. It's been a very trying few days."

"I don't doubt that."

Leboux folded his arms and gave him a look that was more parts police inspector than trusted friend. Feeling the leverage of Leboux's scrutiny, Doyle was prompted out onto an even less sturdy part of the limb to which he was so precariously clinging.

"John Sparks," he said, almost a whisper.

"Excuse me?"

"John Sparks."

"Any relation to the other gentleman?"

"Brother."

"What about John Sparks, Arthur?"

"Does the name ring a bell?"

Leboux paused. "Perhaps."

"He tells me he's in the service of the Queen," whispered Doyle.

That brought Leboux to a momentary halt. "What am I to do with this piece of information?"

"Perhaps you could verify it."

"What else can you tell me about John Sparks, Arthur?" Leboux asked quietly, as close as he had come to an open appeal for Doyle's cooperation.

Doyle hesitated. "That's all I know."

They looked at each other. Doyle could feel his bond with Leboux stretch to its breaking point; for a long moment there was no telling whether it would hold. Finally, Leboux flipped open his notebook, wrote down Sparks's name, closed the book, and rose.

"My strong advice to you is stay in London," said Leboux.

"Am I free to go then?"

"Yes. I need to know how to reach you."

"Leave word at St. Bartholomew's Hospital. I'll make a point of checking there on a daily basis."

"See that you do." Leboux stopped to offer a more considered opinion. "I don't think gambling is at the heart of your difficulty, Arthur; I don't think you're particularly well. If I were you, I would seek out the opinion of a doctor. Perhaps even the services of an alienist."

Fine, thought Doyle, he doesn't think I'm a criminal, he just thinks I'm mad.

"Your concern is not unappreciated," said Doyle humbly, trying not to offend.

Leboux opened the door and hesitated, without looking back. "Do you need a place to stay?"

"I'll manage. Thank you for asking."

Leboux nodded and started out.

"One more name, Claude," said Doyle. "A Mr. Bodger Nuggins."

"Bodger Nuggins?"

"He's a prizefighter. He was at the dice game but apparently wasn't apprehended along with—"

"What about Bodger Nuggins?"

"I have it on good authority the man's an escaped convict from Newgate."

"Not anymore he isn't," said Leboux.

"Sorry? I don't follow."

"We pulled Mr. Bodger Nuggins from the Thames about an hour ago."

"Drowned?"

"His throat was slashed. Like he'd been attacked by an animal."

CHAPTER 13

Ancient Artifacts

I T WAS A long walk from Pentonville Prison to the center of London for a man with no coins in his pocket or food in his belly. He hadn't judged it prudent to press Leboux for Barry's release; he was still inside Pentonville and might be for some time. Prison held no surprises for Barry, and fewer now for Doyle. He had already missed his noon rendezvous with Sparks at Hatchard's Bookshop, and he dared not hire a hansom without the surety he could pay for its services at journey's end. Now that hope was gone. The road was muddy and slow going, passing wheels routinely baptizing him with spume. From their sheltered perches, the carriage trade stared down at him with suspicion, disdain, or, worse yet, looked through him as if he were a pane of glass. Doyle experienced a surge of kinship for the tramp's disenfranchisement from the propriety and narrow-mindedness of genteel city life. Riding high in their private coaches from one privileged location to the next, an endless roundelay of social engagements and leisurely luncheons and shopping and smug preoccupation with their beastly children, these upright citizens seemed a species of life as foreign to him as the electric eel. Doyle was stunned to discover he had more innate sympathy for Barry the East End burglar than for these bourgeoisie parading past him on the street. But weren't these prosperous gentlefolk the highest purpose of a civilized society, a permanent, expanding middle class able to enjoy the products of society's labors in safety and freedom? Weren't they the audience he himself aspired so strenuously to entertain, deepening their appreciation of the human condition by exposure to his craft? How close-minded they were! How effortlessly led to accept the values of school, church, or institution. The thought of exerting himself to touch the hearts of these unfeeling brutes in their hermetic carriages suddenly felt empty and profitless as their supercilious pursuit of a happy, care-free life.

Industrialized society demands a terrible tribute from its parishioners, thought Doyle. Did any of us realize how few of our ideas or feelings were truly, originally, our own? No, or how could we go on day after day, enacting the same lifeless rituals, repeating the same deadening actions, if we acknowledged their lack of meaning? So much of our ability to survive is predicated on the conscious limiting of our mind and senses. We're wearing blinders like the swaybacked dray pulling that beer wagon, peering out at the world through a spyglass, peripheral vision denied, excluded, and our choice in the matter removed because we've been taught from birth that such narrowing is compulsory. Because to remove the lens from our eye is to be confronted with the pain and anguish and sorrow we've shunted so diligently away from view. But the misery around us remains regardless, constant, immutable, a legless beggar by the side of the road. Suffering must be the inevitable tariff exacted from spirit for residing in human form. No wonder tragedy wields the only hammer stout enough to crack the resilient bubble of complacency we construct around our petty lives, shrouding our gaze from the furies that patrol the darker corridors of the night. War, famine, mass disaster. That's what it takes to wake us from this sleep. Terror and the sudden severing from everything familiar turns the trick quite neatly, too, I can attest to that, thought Doyle. The scales have surely been ripped from my eyes.

Was such a loss so catastrophic? Doyle turned the question over more thoroughly than a roasting game bird. He might be hungry now, but he knew full well starvation was not to be his fate; there would be another meal somewhere soon along the way, and hunger would only make it taste the sweeter. He had lost his home and possessions, but there was another home to be made, other possessions to replace what had been taken. He had his wits, his strength, his relative youth, good boots, the clothes on his back, and the courage of his convictions. He had adversity, and an imposing adversary, against which to measure his own worth, and in Jack Sparks a comrade-in-arms to stand beside and face this sea of troubles with together. What more did he require?

If one could only remain as aware as I am in this moment, thought Doyle; had he fortuitously stumbled onto the secret of peace of mind? Here it was then: The circumstances of a life must not dictate our terms of living it; that decision resides only in one's *reaction* to circumstance. And those reactions must be susceptible to our control. The mind, it all began in the mind! How blindingly simple! It bolstered him with a feeling of freedom as expansive as he could ever recall. His step quickened as his spirits soared. The open road ahead was an invitation to discovery, not disaster. He would embrace his hardships, forge ahead and brave the dangers in his path with equanimity and fortitude. Damn the Dark Brotherhood! Let this degenerate Alexander Sparks do his worst! He would consign them all to the same damnation they sought to visit on the earth!

A speeding wagon hit a deep puddle, and a heavy shower soaked Doyle through to the skin. Mud glopped from his forehead in clots. Water ran down his back and into his boots. A sudden gust of wind froze his bones to the marrow. It started to rain, sheets of the stuff, stinging like frozen bees. He sneezed. His newfound resolve fled before him like a flock of starlings.

"I'm in hell!" he shouted miserably.

A cab pulled up beside him. Larry sat in the driver's seat. Sparks threw open the passenger door.

"Come along, Doyle, you'll catch your death out here," he said.

Salvation!

✾ ✾ ✾

Larry poured a kettle of steaming hot water into the basin where Doyle was soaking his feet. He sat wrapped in a blanket, shivering wildly, a hot plaster planted on his forehead. Larry replaced the kettle on top of the coal fire, on the screen of which Doyle's clothes lay drying in their dingy Holborn hotel room whose meager trappings rendered the memory of the Hotel Melwyn on par with the Savoy.

"Not a first-rate idea, Doyle, seeking out Inspector Leboux. For the *second* time," said Sparks, stretched out on the room's only sofa, idly forming a cat's cradle from a length of yarn.

"I was in prison. In possession of what I believed to be information vital to our cause. We had a noon appointment. I saw it as my foremost obligation to obtain the quickest possible release," said Doyle testily, fighting off the ague, in a completely foul humor.

"We would have gotten you out soon enough."

"Gotten me out how?—achoo!"

"Bless you. They know we're back in London now," said Sparks, weaving around the yarn, ignoring Doyle's question. "A considerable disadvantage. We'll be forced to move much more rapidly than I'd hoped we'd have to."

"And just how do they know we're back in London? I trust Leboux implicitly, and I daresay I know him a good sight better than I know you."

"Doyle, you hurt my feelings, you really do," said Sparks, holding out the cat's cradle to solicit the use of Doyle's hands.

Doyle reluctantly thrust his hands out, and Sparks loomed it expertly around his fingers. "How could they possibly know, Jack?"

"You spent two hours in a cell chockablock full with an honor roll of London lowlife and made a grand show of buying your way out. Alexander would have every dirty ear in town listening for the approach of our step. Do you imagine some word of your performance hasn't filtered back up the vine?"

Doyle sniffled and snorted, dearly wishing he had the use of his hands back to stem the flow of effluent from his nose.

"What about Barry?" asked Doyle, conceding the point.

"Don't you worry none 'bout Barry, guv," said Larry, sitting in the corner, happily dipping Scottish shortbread biscuits in his tea. "Many's the worse scrape he's shimmied out of before. The toffs ain't dreamed up the ark-e-tecture of a cell that can hold the likes of Brother B for long."

"Doesn't talk much, your brother," said Doyle, for the moment wishing Larry shared the trait.

"Barry's of a mind it's better to be silent and presumed a fool than to open your mouth and remove doubt altogether," said Larry cheerfully.

Sparks whistled "Rule Britannia" as he plaited another variation on the yarn between their fingers.

"At least we found Bodger Nuggins," said Doyle defensively. "And we got a fair amount out of him, too. At least give me credit for that."

"Hmm. Not a moment too soon, I'd say."

"You can't very well hold me responsible for his death."

"No, I reckon we have another party to thank for that. Pity. Just before Bodger might have revealed to us what purpose was behind the shipping of those convicts to Yorkshire—"

Doyle sneezed mightily, nearly kicking the yarn off his fingers.

"Bless you," said Larry and Sparks jointly.

"Thank you. Jack, when I last laid eyes on Nuggins, he was all but very firmly in the hands of the police. An hour later he's found face-down in the river. Are you suggesting the police had something to do with this?"

"Why do you suppose I persist in warning you against speaking to them?" said Sparks patiently.

"Which implies, fantastically, that in addition to his alleged criminal empire, your brother holds some sway over Scotland Yard."

"Policemen are no more immune to the influence of his magnetism than the moon is to the earth."

"So what would you have me believe? Lansdown Dilks, the police, escaped convicts, General Drummond, Lady Nicholson and her brother, her husband's land, your brother, the gray hoods, the Dark Brotherhood: It all points toward a great indefinable hooking-up some-where, does it?"

"I daresay that's never been very much in question," said Sparks, deep in contemplation of his increasingly complicated string work.

"And the pig's blood from Cheshire Street—may I ask what that suggests to you?"

"Something very odd indeed. Show Dr. Doyle the picture, Larry."

"As you say, sir."

Larry produced a photograph from the pocket of his coat that he held up for Doyle to peruse. It depicted a woman leaving the rear of a building down a flight of stairs toward a black coach in the lower left-hand corner of the frame. A tall, strong-featured woman with raven hair, near thirty, Doyle estimated, not attractive in a conventional way, but handsome, commanding. Although her face was slightly blurred by movement, her attitude was unmistakably surreptitious and covert.

"Do you recognize this woman, Doyle?"

Doyle studied the photo closely. "She looks somewhat like Lady Nicholson, a good deal like her, actually, but this woman is . . . stronger somehow, physically larger as well. This is not the same woman."

"Very discerning," said Sparks.

"Where did you obtain this?"

"Why, we took it ourselves, this morning."

"How is that possible?"

"All you need's one good eye and one flexible digit," said Larry, holding up the box Doyle had seen Sparks pocket at the hotel that morning.

"A camera. How ingenious," said Doyle, anxious to examine it although his fingers were thoroughly enmeshed with yarn.

"Yes," said Sparks, making a last maneuver with the string. "Extremely useful. Seeing as how we happened to be concealed outside the rear of the Russell Street publishing house owned by Lady Nicholson's family at the time."

"But who is this woman?"

"That remains to be seen."

The teakettle started to boil. Sparks extracted himself from the string to retrieve it, leaving Doyle with a rigid net of webbing snarled around both hands. The only thing in the room more twisted was the tangle of his unmitigated perplexity.

"But what does this mean?" Doyle asked.

"It means you must lead us to the most accomplished medium in London, Doyle, and you must do it straightaway. How are you feeling?"

"Wretched."

"Physician, heal thyself!" said Sparks, adding the boiling water to Doyle's basin.

✿　✿　✿

Wrapped in blankets, sweating out the grippe that had seized hold of him, Doyle slept hard as the afternoon waned. Feverish and disoriented, he awoke to find Sparks gone off and Larry sitting attentively bedside with a sketchpad and a piece of charcoal. He was under instruction from Sparks to obtain from Doyle a description of the female psychic who had presided over Cheshire Street's murderous congregation and to reproduce her likeness. They toiled for an hour—Larry sketching, Doyle adding and subtracting—and in the end arrived at a satisfying facsimile of the poxy, pug-ugly clairvoyant.

"Now there's a face could scare the life right out of a dead man," pronounced Larry, as they inspected the finished portrait.

"I don't think I could ever forget it," said Doyle.

"Come on then, Doc, up and at 'em," said Larry, pocketing the picture. "Let's see if we can find this handsome filly somewhere among the living."

Doyle roused himself from his sickbed, dressed in fresh, dry clothes and an enveloping greatcoat Larry had secured for him—God knows how or where. As the sun paid its final respects, they set out from the hotel in search of the mysterious medium.

"I'll follow your feather, guv," said Larry, taking the driver's seat atop their hansom. "You're the one's acquainted with the local fish and fowl."

"How do you propose we go about this?"

"Travel about, flash the crystal-gazers wot are familiar to yourself our pretty picture and sniff out what leads as may present themselves to us."

"There are a great number of mediums in London, Larry. This could take a considerable amount of time," grumbled Doyle, bundling up in the back, muscles aching, dearly wishing he were back beneath the covers.

"Detective work ain't all oysters and beer. The expenditure of shoe leather while keepin' an alert mind, that's the truth of it."

"What a business."

"Better 'an a kick in the head with a frozen boot. Your desired address please, sir?" asked Larry, in a parody of hack etiquette.

Doyle gave him the number of a knowledgeable psychic who would provide as adequate a starting place as any. Larry tipped his hat, snapped the whip, and they drove off into the misty evening.

Mediums tended to be night-dwellers, eschewing the restorative warmth of the sun for candles and moonlight, melancholy creatures more possessed by their uncommon talents than in possession of them. Although Doyle had on occasion encountered the odd solid citizen, no more troubled by the unaccountable presence of his or her eerie abilities than by a double-jointed knee, mediums were for the most part vague and insubstantial souls, one foot planted uneasily on either side of the Great Divide. Their gift, such as it was, seemed to deprive them of an even more precious ability: feeling at home in the world of the living. Most subsisted in relative poverty, unable in even the most rudimentary ways to engage with society's cogs and wheels. Although their aberrant sensitivity to other realms rendered them frightening, even leprous to many, actual practitioners were no more to be feared than the sails of a windmill, at the mercy of a capricious wind they neither comprehended nor controlled. In his experience of the type Doyle had consistently found them merely pitiable and sad.

Until meeting the duenna of Cheshire Street, that is. There had been something queasy and complicit in the woman's elicitation of that *basso profundo* spirit. Even if much of the proceedings that followed were sophisticated variations on tried-and-true theatrical mechanics, the stone-cold presence of evil in that room when the guide revealed itself had been undeniable. She had not simply allowed this baleful spirit to move through her; the thing had been invited. The woman was obviously equipped with some *force majeure extraordinaire,* the antithesis of the divine.

The first few objects of inquiry they visited during their rounds did not fail to disappoint. No, didn't recognize the woman, hadn't seen that face before, hadn't heard of any such new rival practitioner—despite its ethereal trappings, mediumship was nothing if not a fiercely competitive business—bringing her services onto the local marketplace. Keep an eye out, though. Do what they could. Upon closer questioning, they did, each of them, however, report a recent, disturbing increase in nightmares and waking visions—indistinct, flashing glimpses that inspired a blinding terror, then vanished before memory could capture a lasting impression. Each of the first five mediums described remarkably similar experiences they were deeply reluctant to discuss, leaving Doyle to suspect they remembered more than they were willing to divulge.

The apartment of Mr. Spivey Quince was their sixth stop of the evening. Doyle had never quite made up his mind as to whether Spivey was more con man or clairvoyant. A recluse and masterful hypochondriac—his seeking out of Doyle's medical acumen had served as their introduction—he nevertheless maintained a razor-keen awareness of the world at large by voracious digestion of a dozen daily newspapers. Contrary to most of his brethren, who required the mediation of a spouse or dependent to tend to the daily servicing of life's barest necessities, Spivey was aggrandizingly self-sufficient. He resided in a splendid Mayfair building, a constant stream of errand boys delivering the finest food, clothing, and goods—Spivey kept accounts with every smart tailor in town and had worked his way through the menus of all the best restaurants without ever setting foot in a single one of them—and although he never left his house, Quince had nonetheless managed to make himself a veritable font of information on every aspect of the London social scene.

Since he never advertised his skills, and by all appearances had no regular clientele clamoring for his services, Spivey's method of maintaining himself in such high style had remained for many years a much-conjectured-about mystery, until one day Doyle spotted one of Spivey's boys leaving a well-known tout's office the day after the Epsom Derby with a knapsack full of hard cash. On his next consultative visit to Spivey's flat—tending to the latest in a series of ever-more-imaginative phantom disorders—Doyle noticed that among the floor-to-ceiling stacks of newspapers that Quince kept neatly rimmed around his living room stood two piles exclusively devoted to back issues of the *Racing Form*. The source of Spivey's secret fortune came clear. Whether a quotidian genius for handicapping was responsible or the ponies were the principal direction in which he had chosen to exercise a genuine psychic gift was the fulcrum upon which Doyle's uncertainty about Spivey's native character continued to perpetually seesaw.

Doyle asked Larry to stay with the cab, knowing Spivey would be thrown sufficiently off stride by Doyle's surprise appearance that he was unlikely to admit to his house any stranger unequipped with a written and sealed bill of health. Quince answered the bell himself— he kept no household staff; penuriousness was another cornerstone of his wealth—in his customary monogrammed red silk pajamas, matching robe, and amber-tasseled brothel creepers. Although his closets were bursting with a plenitude of fashionable styles, Doyle had never known Spivey to appear in any ensemble other than this boudoir outfit he was currently sporting.

"Hallo, what's this—why, Dr. Doyle," said the slight Quince as he opened the door a crack. "Heavens, I don't remember sending for you—"

"You didn't, Spivey," said Doyle.

"Thank God. I thought perhaps for a moment I was suffering the effects of a dread delusional fever, you know, something tropical, Amazonian, treatable with massive doses of quinine. Is something wrong? Am I ill?"

"No, you appear to be fine, Spivey—"

A rebuttal of tubercular proportion burst from the depths of Quince's chest. "There, you see? I could feel it coming on all day. You have arrived not a moment too soon," Quince said upon recovering. He took a cautionary look outside at the spreading fog. "It's the change in weather; I'm simply not myself. A London Particular like this so soon after such an unseasonable warming trend could spell the death of me—come in, come in—I hope you've brought your complete pharmacopoeia, God knows what you'll eventually diagnose me with."

Doyle entered, and knowing Spivey's reluctance for making contact with anything foreign, took off his hat and coat and hung them on the rack.

"I don't have my bag at the moment, Spivey. This is more a social than a medical call," explained Doyle, trying to harness every symptom of his own nagging affliction down to undetectable proportions; one whiff of contagion in the air would send Spivey racing for quarantine.

Ancient Artifacts

"You see, I haven't been sleeping well recently, and I always feel more susceptible when I'm not getting my rest," Quince said, ignoring Doyle's opener as they moved down the hall.

"Any disturbing dreams?"

"Terrible. Giving me fits. Can't seem to remember them, though. I'm just about to drift off when something jolts me awake. No doubt my general lassitude contributes to this feeling of imminent dis-ease."

Quince led Doyle into the living room/newspaper morgue. Although the room was grand and spacious, the furnishings were handed down, threadbare, antimacassars serving yeoman duty on every shiny arm and back. Except for the towering newsprint monoliths obscuring the walls, the room was fastidiously clean. Neat rows of patent medicines lined the surface of the table beside which Quince took a seat. He racked out another spasmodic cough and patted down the rebellious thatch of ginger hair on his head that threatened to sprout in every direction. His color was good, his posture strong and correct. In every observable way, Spivey Quince seemed the very picture of robust and hearty health.

"Haven't you even brought your stethoscope?" said Quince anxiously. "I feel something loose rattling around in my chest with every cough. Perhaps I've dislodged a rib, or God forbid a blood clot might be forming. One can't be too careful about these things. Not in January."

"I wouldn't worry about it—"

Quince elaborately hawked up something unsavory into a handkerchief, which he then examined like a parson poring over Scripture. "What do you make of this, then?" he said, offering the handkerchief to Doyle.

"Eat more oranges," said Doyle after a moment of feigned sagacity. Afraid that any further hesitation would plunge him into prognostic purgatory, he unveiled the medium's portrait from his coat. "What do you make of this?"

Quince would not touch the picture—he seldom touched anything if he could avoid it, not without gloves on, and at the moment he was absent them—but he studied it alertly. Doyle chose not to reveal who the woman was or why he was seeking her; if Spivey had the second sight, let him use this opportunity to authenticate it.

"You wish me to read it for you," said Spivey.

"If at all possible, yes."

Spivey continued to stare at the picture. His eyes grew drowsy. "Not right," said Spivey after a while, almost a whisper. "Not right."

"What's not right, Spivey?"

191

THE LIST OF 7

A caul of nervous energy had settled over Spivey's countenance; skin taut, he trembled with pulsing energy. His eyes went as wide as an owl's, and they midged about as if his sight had been inverted. Doyle recognized the signs of entrance to a waking trance; he was seeing internally now.

Slipped into it as quick as a pair of his pajamas, thought Doyle. Perhaps Spivey was the real item after all.

"Can you still hear me?" asked Doyle after an appropriate interval. Spivey nodded slowly.

"What do you see, Spivey?"

"Daylight . . . a clearing . . . there's a boy."

Better than I could've hoped for, thought Doyle. "Can you describe him?"

Spivey's eyes squinted blindly. "No hair."

No hair? Doesn't sound right. "Sure he's not blond?"

"No hair. Bright clothes. Blue. Near horses."

The ponies. Apparently, Spivey wasn't inclined to clairvoy anything other than the track when he went under. Maybe the "boy" was a jockey in his multicolored silks. "Is he . . . at the races?"

"No. Curved road outside. Men in red."

Doyle thought for a moment. "Buckingham Palace?"

"Tall building. Grass. Iron gate."

He's describing the Royal Mews, thought Doyle. "What is the boy doing there, Spivey?"

No answer.

"What is the significance of this boy?"

"The sight. He sees."

Fine. That and thruppence will buy me a biscuit. "That's very helpful about the boy, Spivey. Can you by any chance divine something about the woman herself?"

Spivey frowned. "A biscuit?"

"A biscuit?" He plucked that right out of my head fair enough, didn't he? thought Doyle with a start.

"Biscuit tin."

Something nagging about a biscuit tin. Yes, it came back to him: the séance, in the corner of that vision of the boy—a cylinder with the letters CUI. Of course, that's what it was, a biscuit tin. But where was Spivey reading this, wondered Doyle, out of thin air or from my imperfect memory?

"You don't happen to know what brand of biscuit that was, do you, Spivey?"

"Mother's Own."

Here was help uncounted on. Mother's Own Biscuits. He could hardly wait to tell Sparks how he'd single-handedly cracked the case open like a soft-shelled peanut.

"Anything there besides the biscuit tin, Spivey?"

Spivey shook his head. "Can't see. Something in the way."

"What's in the way?"

Quince was having difficulty "seeing." "Shadow. Great shadow."

Curious. Not the first person to use that same phrase—Spivey suddenly reached forward and grabbed the drawing from Doyle's hand. As he took hold of it, his body jerked and shuddered as if the paper were electrified. Doyle half expected to see smoke pouring from Spivey's ears: He was loath to touch the man for fear this dangerous energy would be conducted back to him.

"The passage! Close the passage!" Spivey shrieked alarmingly. "Block his way! The throne! The throne!"

That's enough, thought Doyle, and he seized hold of the drawing— odd, he did feel something like an insistent buzz pulsing through the page—but Spivey's grip on it was fierce; as Doyle tried to pull it away, the paper ripped to pieces. That seemed to break the current; Spivey relaxed his grip, the shards of the drawing fell between them, and Quince slumped back in his chair. His eyes cleared slowly. His entire body shivered, and his forehead beaded with sweat.

"What's happened?" asked Spivey.

"You don't remember?"

Spivey shook his head. Doyle told him.

"Something came at me off that woman's image," said Spivey, staring down at his quivering hands. "Something that's made me feel quite ill."

"You don't look particularly well at the moment," said Doyle. For once.

"I'm all at twos and eights. Good heavens. Good heavens. Can you provide me with something? My nerves are in a frightful jangle."

Feeling liable for inciting Spivey to this hysteria, Doyle surveyed the array of medicines on the table and concocted a compound that might soothe his discomfort. Spivey accepted the recommended dosage docilely.

"Why I prefer to stay indoors, you see," said Spivey gently, trying to catch his breath and control the shaking that beset him. "Never know what I'll encounter in the street. Like a wild river. Dangerous currents. Rocks and eddies. I couldn't survive unprotected in those waters. My mind couldn't take the strain, I'm afraid."

That seemed true enough. Doyle felt a wave of sympathy for the

man: *He's as helpless to control himself as a tuning fork. Any adjacent vibration might set him off. What a predicament. Who's to
say I wouldn't care to leave my rooms in that case either?* thought
Doyle.

"My father wanted me to be a doctor," said Spivey, his voice fluted
with exertion. "He was one, too, you see. Surgeon. The same life he'd
planned for me. I was a boy, he'd take me round to hospital with him.
First time he led me into the wards I . . ."

"It's all right," said Doyle.

Spivey's eyes misted with tears. "How could I explain to him my
horror? I discovered I could see the patients' illness on them. I could
see . . . these people . . . covered with . . . blossoms of waste . . . flowering
on them . . . weeds consuming a landscape, I could see it . . . inching
its way across them, their disease . . . eating them alive. I fainted.
Couldn't tell him why. I begged him never to take me back to that
place. What if a like illness should trespass onto me? That was the
rub. What if I was forced to watch that excrescence slowly make a
meal of my own flesh, before my own eyes? I'd go mad. I'd sooner
end my own life."

"I understand, Spivey."

Shades of Andrew Jackson Davis, the Appalachian mystic, thought
Doyle. Spivey had the gift, all right, and it had proved too much for
him, poor bastard. *Never again will I regard this particular hypochondriac's complaints too lightly.* He made elaborate apologies for
his intrusion and started toward the door.

"Please—could I trouble you to take this with you, Doctor?" Spivey
asked, eyes closed, gesturing weakly toward the shredded picture on
the floor. "If you don't mind. I don't wish to have it in my house."

"Certainly, Spivey. No trouble at all."

Doyle gathered up and pocketed the tatters. He left the depleted
Spivey Quince reclining in his chaise, left hand resting on his heart,
the right, palm out, touching lightly to his forehead.

✿   ✿   ✿

"A bald boy in bright colors hangin' round the Royal Mews. Hope
you didn't lay out too many readies fer that priceless pearl. And me
luvely drawin' torn to bits in the bargain."

"I've known Quince for three years, Larry," said Doyle. "Something
tells me this may be worth looking into."

"Mother's Own Biscuits indeed. You know what his problem is: He's hungry. He needs to get out more. He's got biscuits on the brain pan. What time've you got, guv?"

"A quarter to ten."

"Right. Mr. Sparks wanted us to run by his flat at ten sharp."

This was the first Doyle had heard mention of a London residence. "Where is his flat?"

"As it happens, sir? Montague Street, adjacent to Russell."

Larry whipped the horse and drove the hansom due east on Oxford to an address on Montague, directly across from the British Museum: number 26, a whitewashed, well-kept, but otherwise nondescript Georgian town house. The carriage was stabled in the rear, they entered, and Doyle followed Larry up a narrow flight of stairs.

"Come in, Larry, and bring Dr. Doyle with you," Sparks shouted through the door before they'd even knocked.

They entered. Sparks was nowhere to be seen, the room's only human presence a ruddy-cheeked, middle-aged, roly-poly Presbyterian clergyman. He was seated on a high stool, conducting an experiment at a long chemistry bench covered with a mystifying array of apparatus.

"Charcoal dust on your fingers; you've something interesting to tell me," said Sparks's voice out of the minister's mouth.

If one wasn't aware of his genius for disguise, thought Doyle, the only possible explanation would be demonic possession. He replayed for Sparks his visit to Spivey Quince.

"Eminently worth investigating," said Sparks.

Doyle squelched a prideful impulse to shame Larry with a look and glanced around the room. Shades were drawn—Doyle doubted they were ever opened, so close and musky was the air—and every inch of available wall lined with bulging bookshelves. A stack of index cabinets filled one corner. Above them a bull's-eye target of thatched straw with the letters VR spelled out in bullet holes. Victoria Regina. A strange way for Sparks to demonstrate devotion, but a sort of tribute nonetheless. The largest map of London Doyle had ever seen, studded with legions of red- and blue-headed pins, consumed the wall behind the chemistry bench.

"What do the pins signify?" asked Doyle.

"Evil," said Sparks. "Patterns. Criminals are generally thickheaded and inclined to ritualize their lives. The higher the intelligence, the less predictable the behavior."

"The devil's chessboard," said Larry. "That's what we calls it."

A tall glass-front highboy standing in the opposite corner caught Doyle's eye. It displayed a diverse collection of antique or exotic weaponry, from primitive Stone Age daggers to flintlock muskets to a cluster of octagonal silver stars.

"See anything in there that you'd prefer to your revolver?" asked Sparks.

"I prefer the predictable," said Doyle. "What are these little silver gewgaws?"

"*Shinzaku*. Japanese throwing stars. Absolutely deadly. Kill within seconds."

Doyle opened the cabinet and picked out one of the gadgets: expertly crafted from high-tensile steel, edges serrated like fishhooks that were thin and viciously sharp. It sat as lightly in the hand as an oyster cracker.

"I must say, Jack, wicked as it feels to the touch, it doesn't look all that dangerous," said Doyle.

"Of course you have to dip them in poison first."

"Ahh."

"Care to try a few? Terribly easy to conceal. You just have to be careful not to prick yourself with them."

"Thanks just the same," said Doyle, gingerly replacing the star.

"I've collected these lovelies around the world. If man could apply half the ingenuity he's exhibited in the creation of weapons to more sensible ends, there's no limit to what he might yet accomplish."

"May be 'ope for the rotter yet," said Larry, sitting on a corner of the bench, rolling a cigarette.

"What's in the filing cabinets?" asked Doyle.

"It's plain to see my secrets aren't safe for a moment with you in the room," said Sparks, with a wink at Larry.

"That's the Brain," said Larry.

"The Brain?"

"Inside that cabinet is a painstakingly detailed compendium of every known criminal in London," said Sparks.

"Their criminal records?"

"And a great deal more. Age, date, and place of birth, family history, schooling and service records; recognized methods of operation, known confederates, cell mates, bed mates, and habitats; physical description, aliases, arrests, convictions, and time served," said Sparks, without interrupting his chemistry experiment. "You will not find a more encyclopedic assemblage of information useful to the tracking and apprehension of felons in the Scotland Yard or, I daresay, any other police department the world over."

"Surely the police must have something similar?"

Ancient Artifacts

"They haven't thought of it yet. Fighting crime is both an art and a science. They still treat it like a factory job. Go on, have a look."

Doyle randomly pulled open one of twelve drawers; it was lined with rows of alphabetically arranged index cards. Picking a card from the drawer, Doyle was surprised to see it was covered with a hand-written scrawl of what appeared to be incomprehensible gibberish.

"But how can you read this?" asked Doyle.

"Information as sensitive as this by rights has to be rendered in code. Wouldn't want this particular body of knowledge falling into the wrong hands, would we?"

Doyle studied the card from every angle. The method of encrypting went far beyond the limits of any code he'd ever attempted to decipher.

"I take it the encoding is of your own invention," said Doyle.

"A random amalgam of mathematical formula, Urdu, Sanskrit, and an obscure variation of the Finno-Ugric root language."

"So this is all really quite useless to anyone but yourself."

"That is the point, Doyle. It's not a lending library."

"What does this say?" asked Doyle, holding up the card for Sparks to see.

"Jimmy Malone. Born Dublin, 1855. No education. Fifth son of five; father a miner, mother a char. Wanted in Ireland for assault and highway robbery. Served local apprenticeship with brothers in a roving gang, the Rosties and Fins, County Cork. Emigrated to Britain 1876. First arrest London; assault, January 1878. Served two years, six months Newgate. Came out a hardened criminal, began work as a free-lance stickup. Favors the spiked cudgel. Suspect in at least one unsolved murder. Last-known residence: East End, Adler Street off Greenfield Road. Five-eight, twelve stone, green eyes, thinning sandy hair, favors a wispy goatee. Vices: gambling, drinking, and prostitutes—in other words, the lot. Also known as Jimmy Muldoon or Jimmy the Hook—"

"I get the idea," said Doyle, carefully replacing the card in the file.

"That Jimmy," chuckled Larry, shaking his head. "What a silly prawn."

"Ever worry you'll wake up one day and find you've forgotten the key to translating all this?"

"Should anything untoward happen to me, the decoding formula is in a safe-deposit at Lloyd's of London, along with instructions to deliver the archives to the police," said Sparks, pouring a beaker of smoking substance into a larger container. "Not that they'll ever make good use of it."

"Are you at all concerned someone might break in here and steal it nonetheless?"

"Open that door," said Sparks, hands full, nodding toward the opposite door.

"What do you mean?"

"Just open it."

"This one here?"

"That's right," said Sparks. "Give it a go."

Doyle shrugged, grabbed the knob, and pulled. In the instant before he slammed the door shut, Doyle was overwhelmed by an impression of a pair of crazed, red-rimmed eyes, a slathering tongue, and huge canine teeth leaping for his throat.

"Good Christ!" said Doyle, his back pressed against the door, trying to hold back whatever beast from hell lurked on the other side. To add to his aggravation, Larry and Sparks were having a good laugh at his expense.

"If you could see your face," said Larry, holding his sides and whooping with delight.

"What the devil was that?" demanded Doyle.

"The answer to your question," said Sparks. He put two fingers in his mouth and gave two piercing whistles. "You can open the door now."

"I don't think."

"Go on, man, I've given the signal, I assure you, he's perfectly harmless."

Doyle hesitantly moved away from the door, cracked it open, and concealed himself behind it as a colossal mass of dappled black-and-white canine muscle squeezed through the gap. The dog had a head as big as a melon, floppy ears, and a long, solid snout. Around its neck was a studded leather collar. It paused in the doorway and looked to Sparks for instruction.

"Good boy, Zeus," said Sparks. "Say hello to Dr. Doyle."

Zeus obediently sniffed Doyle out in his hiding place around the corner of the door, sat down before him, his head well above the level of Doyle's waist, looked up at him with impossibly alert and intelligent eyes, and offered a hand in greeting.

"Go on, Doc," urged Larry, "he'll get testy if you refuse the hand of friendship."

Doyle took and shook the dog's extended paw. Thus satisfied, Zeus lowered his paw and looked back at Sparks.

"Now that you've been properly introduced, why don't you give Doyle a kiss, Zeus."

Ancient Artifacts

"That really won't be necessary, Jack—"

But Zeus had already reared up on his hind legs, perfectly balanced, and looked Doyle straight in the eye. He leaned forward with his paws on Doyle's shoulders and pinned him gently to the wall. Then, tail wagging, out came his tongue for an affectionate lashing of Doyle's cheeks and ears.

"Good boykins, Zeus," said Doyle uncertainly. "There's a good bowser-boy. Good doggie. Good doggiekins."

"Wouldn't talk to him like that, Doc," cautioned Larry. "Complete sentences, proper grammar; otherwise he'll fink you're patronizin' him."

"Can't have that, can we?" said Doyle. "That's quite enough now, Zeus."

With uncanny comprehension, Zeus lowered himself, resumed his place at Doyle's feet, and looked back at Sparks.

"As you can imagine, with Zeus in constant attendance, any concern one might have about the inviolability of the flat is completely unfounded," said Sparks, ending his experiment with a flourish. He poured the resulting contents down a funnel into three vials and set them to cool in a rack.

He was a handsome and impressive animal for all that, thought Doyle, reaching down to give Zeus a scratch behind the ears.

"Remarkable creature, the dog," said Sparks. "No other animal on earth so willingly gives up his freedom to serve man, a devotion unapproached by the hypocritical custodians of our so-called human faiths."

"Helps if you feed them," said Doyle.

"We feed our vicars and our bishops, too. I've never known one to give his life to save another."

Doyle nodded. Looking around, he was struck by the room's lack of amenities. There wasn't even another place to sit besides the stool at the bench. "Is this your home, Jack?"

Sparks wiped his hands on a towel and began to peel off the applied features of his false identity, setting a brace of white eyebrows down on the table. "I do on occasion sleep here and, as you've surmised, use it as a base of operations. The considered answer is, I regard myself a citizen of the world; consequently I'm at home wherever I find myself, therefore I have no home, per se. I have had none since my brother reduced the one place I ever called home to ashes. Is that a satisfactory answer?"

"Quite."

"Good." Sparks removed the cleric's collar, unfastened his plain coat, and extracted from underneath it the stitched padding that had shaped his ample stomach. "If you're at all curious about where this company of characters issue forth, follow me."

Doyle stepped after Sparks as he moved into the room where Zeus had been quartered. The walls in this cramped chamber were lined with racks supporting an array of costumes imaginative enough to keep the Follies in business for a year. A makeup table ringed with lights sported every conceivable paint pot and brush of the cosmetic arts. A jury of featureless wooden heads wearing a rainbow of wigs and facial hair presided over one corner. There were stacks of hatboxes, drawers of cataloged accessories, wallets with platoons of forged identities, and an armory of padding to form any desired body shape. A sewing machine, bolts of fabric, and a tailor's dummy—bearing a half-completed brass-buttoned tunic of an officer in the Royal Fusiliers—suggested this vast wardrobe originated from strictly local labor. Sparks could enter this room and emerge as virtually any other man, or woman, for that matter, in the city of London.

"You've made all this yourself?" asked Doyle.

"Not all my seasons in the theatrical trade were spent in wanton dissipation," said Sparks, hanging up his parson's jacket. "Excuse me a moment, would you, Doyle, while I become myself again."

Doyle walked back to the other room, where Larry was feeding Zeus a pocketful of soup bones, which he crunched and cracked delightedly.

"Amazing," said Doyle.

"Be honored if I was you, guv. First time I've ever known his nibs to bring an outsider here. Strictly off-limits, it is, and for good reason."

"Forgive my ignorance, Larry, but is Jack well known in London?"

Larry took a thoughtful pull off his cigarette. "To answer, there's three sorts of folk wot fall under different classifizations. There's folks wot never heard of Jack and never had no call to—your majority of Londontowners, decent sorts going 'bout their business who don't know nowt about that hidden underbelly called the world of crime. Second lot's a most fortunate few who's experienced firsthand the benefit of Mr. Jack working on their behalf—a limited number, seeing as how his efforts been spent in secret gov'ment service but has on occasion been known to spill over into the so-called private sector. Then there's a third category of your garden-variety crook, bandit, twister, and scoundrel, who by virtue of their vice has the greatest familiarity with Mr. S—and his name tolls in their hearts the bells of doom. This bunch is far more numerous and career-minded than the

Ancient Artifacts

other two categories would like to believe. Also the type to which you, in your life as a respectable physician, to your credit, would be the least familiar. So I can well understand your asking."

Larry gave the last of the bones to Zeus and scruffed him under the chin.

"Happens to be the category to which brother Barry and I once accounted ourselves, and not so long ago. Nothing to be particular proud of, but there it is."

"How did you come to meet Jack, Larry? If I may ask."

"Yes, you may, sir. And may I take this opportunity to say it's one of the great pleasures of the work we do to find myself in the acquaintanceship of such a fine, upstanding gentlemen as yourself."

Doyle tried to wave off the compliment.

"I mean it serious true, sir. The only chance I might otherwise had of meeting you face-to-face would've been by your unexpectedly arrivin' home in the midst of a misguided attempt on my part to burgle you, or my seekin' emergency medical for injury taken during the commission of a similar crime. We was sorry lads, Barry and I, and no blame to attach to none but ourselves for it. Our Dad was a good, hardworkin' railroad man who provided for us best he could. Even with him alone as he was, his worst was a damn sight better than most from what I've seen. It was the strain of a twin birth, see. Our Mum was of such a delicate nature, so he told us—here, I got a picture of her."

Larry took a cameo from his vest and opened the clasp. A photograph of a young woman rested inside: close, blurry, her hair in a fashion twenty years out of date. Attractive in an unremarkable shopgirl way, but even the shabby, faded quality of the picture couldn't obscure the same light dancing in the eyes that so distinguished her two sons.

"She's very pretty," said Doyle.

"Her name was Louisa. Louisa May. That was their honeymoon: a day and two nights in Brighton. Dad had that picture taken on the pier." Larry closed and repocketed the locket. "Louisa May was seventeen. Along Barry and I come to spoil the party later that same year."

"You can't blame yourself for that."

"You wonder about such things. All I can muster up is that Barry and me, we had some unstoppable reason to be born into this life together that was not to be denied. Destiny, I'm tempted to call it. Cost us our Mum, but life is hard and sorrowful and filled with trouble, and your own is no exception. If our old Dad took it hard on us for

201

losin' her, we never knowed it. But wot with him on the rails and his poor relations hard-pressed to manage their own, let alone such a pair a devils as us, it weren't long 'fore we came to mischief. School couldn't hold us. A pair of whizzy boys, pickpockets, that's how it started. How many thousand times have I asked myself, Larry, wot was it led you and Brother B to a life of such criminal destitution? After years of deliberation, I think it was shop windows."

"Shop windows?"

"Used to be you'd go right by a place of business and never know what they had to offer without venturing inside. Nowadays walk past any decent establishment, the stuff's all laid right out for your perusal, and the best of it, too. A tease, that's wot it is. Lookin' in those windows, seeing all this booty and not being able to *have*, that's what pushed us over the edge. By the time we turned ten, the lure of loot by pilfery captured our imaginations. Dedication to craft's wot we practiced from that day on; there's few limits to what a couple eager country boys with a bit of know-how and a burning desire to make good in the city can set their minds to. That is, till we met the Master hisself."

"How did that happen, Larry?"

Finished grinding the bones, Zeus circled twice and curled up under the chemist's bench. With a mighty yawn, he settled his head down on a foreleg and watched Larry alertly for signs that he might produce additional delicacies.

"It was late one night, near three. Barry's turn at the pub—not long after his unfortunate set-to with the fishmonger; we'd grown beards to cover the scar—I'd hit a house in Kensington for a healthy haul of collectibles, and we're back at our flat feelin' more than a bit eager— we'd been through some lean weeks waitin' for Barry's scarifica- tion to settle—when the door flies open and standing there like the wrath of God was the Man, a stranger to our eyes, and a pistol in either hand that spelled serious business. The game was up. A few baubles ain't worth dying for: Don't get hurt for the loot, that was our motto. So this gent first-off confiscates our ill-gotten gains, as expected, but then gives out the confoundedest confabulation we'd ever heard: Forsake this petty life of crime, he says to us. Come work for me in the service of the Crown, or else. Or else what? we wants to know. Or else our fortunes will turn sharply downward and future events go badly for us, with a decided lack of details as to how this might transpire. We've a lunatic in our midst, that's what Barry and me are thinkin'—and our thoughts are ofttimes as loud to each other as speakers in the House of Commons. So we posthaste agree to this malarkey, let him take the loot and be done with the mucker, and the man blows out of there like June rain. A thief steals from a thief. No tears shed. Hazards of the trade. Plenty of other flats in London, so we flies ourselves out of that coop and sets up across town by the very next afternoon.

"Four days pass, and we can't help notice we're not gettin' any richer, so we pull another job. Barry hits a silversmith—he's always been partial to silver; useful with the ladies—and he's no sooner through the door of our new crib when this selfsame avenger crashes in and seizes the bag right out of Barry's mitts. This is our second chance, he spells it out for us; put your lawless ways behind you and follow me, or the end is near. He don't even wait for an answer, just takes the swag and scoots. Now Barry and me got our monkeys up; we're spooked: How'd this bloke pick us out of all the crooks in town; if he's so hard up for boodle, why don't he rob his own houses; exactly what's he mean the 'end' is near; and how on earth do we stop this moke from hittin' us where we live again?

"So it's desperate measures for desperate times. We lay lower than dirt. Move our base around like fireflies in a bottle: four times in a week. Not a word to nobody. Watch our tail religiously for the slightest sign of this troublesome shade, and all we draw are blanks. Three weeks go by, and we've got stomachs to feed. Safe as houses by now, we figure. Maybe the bloke's spied one of us in the pub and followed us home, that's how he's capered us, so for luck we go out on the stoush together this time, and there'll be no more unpleasant surprises. We picks our target more careful than a bleeder shaves. An antique store down Portobello, far off the beaten path. In we go down the air shaft easy as pie, ready to grab and stuff.

"And there's the selfsame bloke sittin' in a chair, cool as iced tea, pistol in hand. Cornered bang to rights. Not only that, this time he's brought a copper; he's behind us ready to make application with his nightstick and hear our confessions. This is your final opportunity, the man says as a how-do-you-do. And he knows our names and our latest address and everywhere else we been up to the minute.

"It's the second time in me life the hand of Destiny reached down and smacked me in the north and south. This is the end, Larry, I says to myself. Third time's the charm, I says to Brother B, who's by nature a bit more pigmy-minded than yours truly. Turns out he's had a sudden rush of brains to the head. Stranger, we says, you is too much for us; we will do our best to answer the call. The gent proves good as his word; he gives the high sign, the copper takes his leave without so much as a good-night kiss from his stick. The Stranger says follow me, boys, and so we marched out of the antique store on Portobello Road with Mr. John Sparks six years ago, our brilliant criminal careers at an end."

"He threatened you with arrest?"

"He did better than threaten: He *convinced* us. 'Course, it wasn't till months later we find out the 'copper' was one of his Regulars in costume."

"His Regulars?"

"That's what he calls us, those of us in his employ," said Larry modestly.

"How many of you are there?"

"More than a few, never enough, and as many as necessary, depending on your point of view."

"All former criminals like yourself?"

"There's a few recruits from the civilian side. You're in good company, if that's the worry."

"Did he tell you right off he was working for the Queen?"

"He told us a great many things—"

"Yes, but regarding the Queen, specifically?"

"Now it won't do any good your outthinkin' the chief, I can tell you straight away," chided Larry. "Transmogrification, that's the ten-pound word for what he does. And you has to give yourself over to it."

"What work is that?"

"Transmogrifying: You know what that means, don't you?"

"The transformation of souls."

"That's the ticket. And I'm here to give witness. Gave me appreciation of the finer things that in my thickheaded way I was sorely lacking. I goes to plays regular now and sits in the stalls like a genuine swell. I listens to music. Taught me how to read proper, too. No more penny dreadfuls for yours truly, I enjoys lit-ter-a-ture. There's this French feller, Balzac, I'm partial to; writes about life in a real sort of way. Common folk and their predicaments."

"I'm partial to Balzac myself."

"Well, one day we should have a proper chat about him, and I do look forward to it. That's what the guv'nor does, see; provokes you to think. Has a way of askin' questions that takes you up the next rung of the ladder. Hard work. Surprisin' how few folks ever develops the habit. This is where you want it, right here." Larry tapped himself on the side of the head. "So what do I owe Mr. S, you ask? Only my life. Only my life."

Larry stopped to roll a cigarette, using the distraction to veil some deeper vein of emotion. Just then Sparks emerged from the inner room, dressed again in his customary black. Zeus immediately scrambled from under the bench to shake his hand.

"Gentlemen, let's be off," Sparks said, cuffing Zeus affectionately. "The hour is late, and we've a full night of burglary and stealth ahead of us."

"I'll fetch me tools," Larry said eagerly, as he skipped to the door.

"All for the cause, Doyle," said Sparks, seeing the hesitancy on his face. "Sorry, Zeus, old man, we shan't be taking you with us tonight."

Sparks pocketed a handful of vials from a rack on the bench and straightaway left the flat. Doyle bit his tongue and followed. Zeus dealt with his disappointment admirably and resumed his solitary vigil.

❊   ❊   ❊

Except for the occasional after-theater cab, Montague Street was deserted by that time of night, and a fleecy mass of fog made subterfuge all the easier. The imperial facade of the British Museum presided over the street like a tomb of the ancients. As they made their way to Russell Street, Doyle glanced back at the windows of Sparks's apartment and was surprised to see a light burning and the silhouette of a man framed in the sill.

"Tailor's dummy," said Sparks, noticing his interest. "Took a sniper's bullet intended for me once; never complained. There's a soldier for you."

Ducking through a cobbled alley, they arrived at the rear of the building Doyle recognized as the one seen earlier in the photograph of the woman. They blended into the shadows; then, with a nod from Sparks, Larry skipped silently across the alley and up the steps to the back door.

"Larry always appreciates a chance to polish his cracksmanship," said Sparks quietly. "Barry's no slouch, and he's a damn sight better scaling a wall, but Larry's touch with a lock is second to none."

"So this is breaking and entering, plain and simple," said Doyle, a touch of fustian unease creeping into his tone.

"You're not going to blow the whistle on us, are you, Doyle?"

"How can we be sure this is the right establishment?"

"Our friend the Presbyterian minister made the rounds of Russell Street today, peddling his deathless monograph on advanced cattle-breeding techniques in the Outer Hebrides."

"I had no idea I was earlier in the company of such an esteemed author."

"As it happens, I did have such a monograph in my files, dashed off on holiday there a few years back. I don't know about you; hard for me to sit quiet on holiday. All I think about is work."

"Hm. I do like a bit of fishing."

"Casting or fly?"

"Fly. Trout mainly."

"Gives the fish a sporting chance. In any case, imagine my surprise this afternoon when one of the Russell Street firms made an offer to purchase my pamphlet right on the spot."

"You sold your monograph?" asked Doyle, feeling the sour drip of authorial envy.

"Snapped it right up. I tell you, there's no accounting for people's taste. I hadn't even gone so far as to invent a name for the man: a monograph-bearing Presbyterian is usually more than sufficient to ward off even the most inquiring mind. Had them make the check out to charity. Poor chap: four hours old and already denied his proper royalties." Sparks looked across the street, where Larry was giving them a wave. "Ah, I see Larry has completed the preliminaries. Here we go, Doyle."

Sparks led the way across the alley. Larry held the door as they slipped inside, then followed and closed up behind them. Sparks lit a candle, throwing reflections off a building directory on the corridor wall.

"Rathborne and Sons, Limited," read Sparks. "There's a service door round the corner that I think you'll find preferable, Larry."

Down and left around the hallway they moved to the entrance, where Sparks held the candle aloft as Larry went back to work.

"Let me get this monograph business straight: They paid you on the spot right then and there for it?" said Doyle, unable to let go of his fixation.

"Not a princely sum, but enough to keep Zeus in soup bones for a stretch."

Larry eased open the door to the offices.

"Thank you for those kind words, Larry, why don't you keep an eye on the hall while we have a look inside?"

Ancient Artifacts

Larry tipped his cap. Not a peep from him since they'd left the flat, observed Doyle, whereas Barry went positively jabberwocky in a tight spot: How odd, their patterns of speech are directly reversible.

By the dim light of the candle, they explored the offices of Rathborne and Sons. Subdued reception area. Rows of clerks' desks: sheaves of invoices, contracts, bills of lading. It seemed a neat and orderly concern, handsomely accoutred, run with a minimum of fuss, but other than that, utterly unremarkable.

"So this is the last house to which you submitted your manuscript, and you don't recall receiving it back from them," said Sparks.

"Yes. So Lady Nicholson's father and brother must be involved somehow."

"One brother we know of. The late George B. Other than that, nothing's available on the Rathborne family in public record. I've found no reference to a Rathborne the Elder whatsoever."

"That's odd."

"Perhaps not. This firm is six years old. Hardly an enduring tradition passed down for generations."

"You're suggesting there is no Rathborne the Elder?"

"You do run a fast track, Doyle. I wanted to have a look back here," said Sparks, leading him toward the rear. "Our friend the clergyman was rather firmly denied access to any of the senior executives."

They moved to a row of closed doors. Finding one with CHAIRMAN emblazoned on the smoked-glass window panel locked, Sparks handed the candle to Doyle, took a small set of twin picks from his pocket, and worked them into the keyhole.

"No interest in cattle-breeding?"

"From what I could gather during my visit, they didn't seem terribly interested in books generally."

"Whatever do you mean, Jack?"

"I fingered a catalog of their published works. Singularly unimpressive; works on the occult seem to be the *spécialité de la maison,* a trickle of legal publishing—hardly enough volume of trade to support such a well-appointed concern as this—and no fiction whatsoever," said Sparks, manipulating the picks like a pair of chopsticks. A click was heard inside, and the door popped open. Sparks pushed it open the rest of the way.

"I now recall it was their interest in the occult that prompted me to send my manuscript here originally. In my amateurish eagerness, I didn't take the time to discover if they had an ongoing interest in fiction."

THE LIST OF 7

"I didn't wish to put it so indelicately," said Sparks as he took back the candle and entered the office.

"Quite all right; any author worth his salt needs to inure himself to criticism. So, if they have no interest in fiction here, the question is why wasn't the book simply returned to me straight off?"

"I suspect your title—'The Dark Brotherhood'—must have caught someone's eye."

"*Ipso facto,* Rathborne and Sons must be the intersection from where my work fell into, as you put it, the wrong hands."

"Just so," said Sparks.

He crossed to and rifled through the drawers of the massive executive desk that anchored the spare furnishings of the sober, oak-paneled office.

"And if I interpret your observations correctly," said Doyle, "your feeling is that Rathborne and Sons is in its primary purpose not a publishing company at all, but a front for some far more sinister concern."

"Sinister. Or Left-Handed," said Sparks, producing a correspondence with masted letterhead from a desk drawer. "Have a look at this, Doyle."

The letter itself was of no apparent concern, a routine memorandum regarding contractual dealings with a bookbinder. But the list of company directors on the masthead was something else again:

Rathborne and Sons Publishing, Ltd.
Directors
Sir John Chandros
Brigadier General Marcus Drummond
Maximilian Graves
Sir Nigel Gull
Lady Caroline Nicholson
The Hon. Bishop Caius Catullus Pillphrock
Professor Arminius Vamberg

"Good heavens," said Doyle.

"Let us put our minds to work. This room bears no stamp of personality at all: no pictures, no personal effects. At the very least, executives tend to display their distinguishing marks of achievement: diplomas, honorary titles. This office is for show, along with everything else we've seen. And as far as we can determine, there has been no Rathborne Senior."

"Which explains the presence on the board of Lady Nicholson."

"Unusual enough to find a woman in a position of such responsibility, although times are changing. Without knowing exactly what the nature of that position is, it's safe to assume that she is the true power behind Rathborne and Sons."

"Or was."

"I shall have more to say about that very soon." Sparks directed their attention back to the list. "What distressed you about these other names?"

"One in particular. Until his recent retirement, Sir Nigel Gull used to be one of two physicians exclusive to the royal family."

"I believe his primary responsibility was tending to young Prince Albert."

"That's a full-time job," said Doyle scornfully. The Queen's grandson was a notorious roué, a reputed simpleton, and a dependable source of minor scandal.

"Most unsettling. And I can tell you this: Gull's orderly retirement—he's a man of about sixty now—was merely public perception. There was a strong scent of impropriety surrounding his final days in service, the details of which shall now require my fullest attentions. Who else do you recognize on this list?"

"The name of John Chandros is familiar, but I can't quite place it."

"Former member of Parliament, from a northern district, Newcastle-on-Tyne. Land developer. Steel plants. Enormously wealthy."

"Wasn't Chandros involved in the prison-reform movement?"

"And chaired the prison commission for two terms. His name also surfaced in my investigation of the Nicholson-Drummond transaction; he owns a sizable freehold of land adjacent to the property sold by Nicholson to General Drummond."

"No coincidence there, I'd say."

"There is no such thing as coincidence: We now have a twofold connection from Chandros to Drummond to Rathborne Nicholson. How Gull fits into this mesh we have yet to discover."

"What of the others?"

"I am acquainted with the name of Bishop Pillphrock. Church of England. His diocese is North York, near the port of Whitby. Vamberg and Graves are unknown to me. What is the common thread?" asked Sparks searchingly. "Wealthy, powerful, prominent citizens. Four with ties to Yorkshire, where those convicts were allegedly sent. Chandros on the penal commission. All united through a false business front..."

"Isn't it possible, Jack, that this company is nothing other than what it appears: a small, albeit well-capitalized, firm of modest ambitions, with a board of experts to advise them on various areas in which they wish to publish—Drummond for military works, Gull for medical text, Chandros political perspective, Pillphrock the theological, and so on?"

Sparks nodded thoughtfully. "With due consideration given to the other variables, I'd say there's a ten percent chance of that. If not, there is every reason to believe that what we have in our possession here is nothing less than a list of the Dark Brotherhood's innermost council. Seven names: Seven is a profane as well as sacred number."

"Strikes me as a bit of a leap of faith," said Doyle, as a thin line of white under the blotter on the desk caught his eye. He lifted the blotter and pulled out a creased square of slick paper, unfolding it to reveal a poster advertising a theatrical troupe's appearances in London. The play dates listed were for a run of one week in late October of the previous year.

"The Revenger's Tragedy," read Doyle. "I'm not familiar with it."

"Court melodrama, late Elizabethan, attributed to Cyril Tourneur. Adapted from Seneca. Grim piece of business: plot-heavy, lots of onstage violence. Deservedly obscure. I don't recall this production."

"Seems they came and went fairly quickly," said Doyle. "The Manchester Players."

"I don't know them, but there are dozens of companies touring around Britain at any one time. More to the point, what was this doing here?"

Doyle refolded the poster and lifted the blotter to slide it back into its hiding place. As he did so, a fountain pen rolled off the blotter and fell to the floor. Sparks pushed the chair away, knelt with the candle to retrieve the pen, and noticed a set of matched diagonal scratches at floor level on either side of the desk.

"Hold this for me, would you, Doyle?"

Doyle took the candle. Sparks inspected the edges of the desk where it rested ponderously on the varnished wood. He took a small vial of liquid from his pocket, uncorked it, and poured its contents out onto the floor. Mercury.

"What is it, Jack?"

"There's a seam here in the flooring where there shouldn't be one."

The quicksilver beaded up on the wood, and then, in a single rush, vanished down in between the floorboards. Sparks leaned in and ran his hands around and under the desk.

"What are you looking for?"

"I've found a hook. I'm going to give it a pull. I shouldn't stand just there for the moment, Doyle."

Ancient Artifacts

Doyle stepped away from the desk. Sparks pulled the hook; the flooring at the hidden seam lifted up and slid neatly back under the desk, diagonally scratching its facing on either side and leaving a hole two foot square directly under where the president's chair had been resting.

"Uneasy sits the head that wears the crown," paraphrased Sparks.

Leaning over to have a look, Doyle saw a bolted steel ladder descending straight down a masoned shaft too deep by the light of his candle to spy the end of. The air wafting from below was fresh and smelled of water.

"I daresay your garden-variety publishing company would have little use for such an exit as this," said Sparks excitedly.

"None I can immediately think of."

Sparks clapped his hands. "By God, we've found them out! The Brotherhood quartered less than half a mile from my flat. Sometimes the best place to hide is in plain sight."

Sparks gave one quiet bird whistle, and moments later Larry appeared in the doorway.

"Tunnel, Larry. Have a look, eh?" asked Sparks.

"Straightaway, sir."

Larry stripped off his jacket, took out his own candle, cadged a light from Doyle's, and nimbly scampered one-handed down onto the ladder.

"Perhaps you'd better take this as well," said Doyle, extending his service revolver to him.

"Thanks just the same, guv," said Larry, lifting aside his vest to display a brace of holstered knives. "I'm a blade man myself."

Larry began his descent. Doyle and Sparks watched the warm glow from his candle quickly diminish to a thin, shimmering halo.

"How is it, Larry?" asked Sparks down the shaft, his voice husky and low.

"There's an end to it just ahead." Larry's voice echoed metallically back up to them, along with his footfalls on the ladder. "The ladder stops here. Open space beneath. Can't tell how big. Somethin's down there . . . I can see . . . wait a moment . . . good 'eavens . . ."

The light from the candle disappeared. Then silence. They waited.

"What is it, Larry?" asked Sparks.

No answer from below. Doyle looked to Sparks, who appeared equally concerned. "Larry? Are you there, lad?"

Still no reply. Sparks gave out the whistle with which he'd summoned Larry into the room. Again nothing. Sparks took off his jacket.

"I shall have to go after him, Doyle. Coming with me?"

THE LIST OF 7

"I don't know that I'm properly equipped—" said Doyle evasively.

"Fine, then if I disappear as well, you will have to come after me alone."

Doyle took off his coat. "Will you go first, or shall I?"

"Me first, with your revolver, you following with the candle."

"Right," said Doyle, handing over the revolver, his heart beating wildly. He was not overly fond of heights or tight places, and the shaft below served up a generous helping of both. And if whatever was down there had already gotten the better of the ever-capable Larry— *that's quite enough of that line of thinking, Doyle; one rung at a time, Jack in the lead, hold the candle and your peace.* Sparks went down. Doyle steadied himself on the edge of the trap, then lowered himself in until he found purchase on the ladder with one foot and then the other.

"Mind my hands as you go," said Sparks, a few rungs below. "And don't speak unless you absolutely must."

Breathe, Doyle, don't forget to breathe. He quickly realized that, much as he'd like to keep eyes forward, he was going to have to look down continually, if only to keep from crushing Jack's hands. Fortunately, the supply of candlelight was so meager that the sheer dizzying depth of the shaft beneath him lived only in the mind, not the eye. Unfortunately, in the absence of the visual, his mind perversely manufactured images far more terrifying than any hazard that was likely to be waiting below.

The descent was laborious. The first thirty feet took nearly ten minutes but seemed endlessly longer. In order to obtain the vaguest idea of what lay ahead, Sparks was obliged to stay within a few rungs of Doyle and their source of light. One-handed as he was, Doyle refused to take the next step down until his free arm was securely entwined in and around the ladder. A steady drizzle of hot wax spilled onto his candle hand. Both palms were slippery with sweat.

What if I should drop it? thought Doyle. What if a gust of wind comes up; how would I ever relight the damn thing?

"Stop there," said Sparks finally.

"Where are we?"

Glancing up the shaft no longer gave any indication of where the door above was in relation to their position, a limbo precisely defined by the limit of the candlelight.

"Hand me the candle, please, Doyle."

Doyle carefully transferred the light down to Sparks's outstretched hand, grateful that for the moment he was now able to hug the ladder

212

with both arms. Sparks hung down by one hand, leaned over, and held the candle as low as he could carry it.

"The ladder ends here, as Larry said," said Sparks. "There's a drop-off."

"How far?"

"I can't make out. This is where he called us from: I hear water moving somewhere below."

"What should we do?"

Just then they heard the scrape of wood on wood from far above and a sound like the sealing of a tomb. The silence that followed was deafening.

"I say, Jack. . . ."

"Ssshhh!"

They listened. Doyle kept quiet as long as he could bear.

"I think someone's closed the trapdoor," he whispered.

"Do you hear anyone above you on the ladder?" Sparks whispered back.

Doyle slowly turned to look up the shaft. "I . . . don't believe I do."

"It's possible that the trap closed automatically. That it has some sort of mechanical timing device."

"Yes, well, *anything's* possible, isn't it?

"Do you prefer to believe someone's just imprisoned us in this vertical hell?"

"No harm in considering the full range of possibilities, Jack." Doyle's heart hammered like operatic timpani. He struggled to keep it from bleeding into his voice. "What do you suggest we do?"

"I don't recommend climbing. Even if we find a way to open the trap from this side, if someone is waiting for us—"

"With you all the way on that one."

Sparks paused and peered down into the Stygian darkness below. "You will have to lower me by hand."

"Is that our only alternative?"

"Unless you prefer that I lower you. Need I point out you're a good deal more stout than I—"

"Point well taken."

"Can you get your braces off? We're going to need some sort of reinforcement."

"I don't really fancy my trousers falling down in the middle of this—"

"Without belaboring the point, your buttons are near enough to bursting that I don't honestly see it as a problem—"

"Right, you will have them," said Doyle, irritation getting the momentary better of fear.

Maneuvering one hand at a time, Doyle peeled the braces off his shoulders, unbuttoned them from his waist, and handed them to Sparks. He looped both ends through the tops of his own braces, which he still wore, and handed them back to Doyle.

"Ever done any mountain climbing?" asked Sparks.

"No."

"Then there's no point in my describing what we're about to do in mountaineering terms. I shall hang down by hand from the last rung as you wrap the braces twice around the bottom of the ladder. Hold the ends tightly in your hands; give me any additional slack if I ask you for it."

"What if they won't hold?"

"We'll find that out soon enough, won't we?"

"What are you doing to do with the candle?"

"For the moment, I shall hold it in my mouth. Quickly now, Doyle."

Sparks bit down on the candle and lowered himself, hanging off the bottom rung with both hands. Doyle crabbed cautiously down to the ladder's final station, quickly wrapped the braces twice around the steel as instructed, and grabbed hold of the reins.

"All set, Jack."

Sparks nodded, let go of the ladder with one hand, and took the candle from his mouth.

"Here I go then," said Sparks.

He let go with his other hand and fell away. The force of his weight hit the braces hard and nearly pried Doyle loose from the ladder, but the braces held. Sparks bounced and swung gently below in the open air, holding the candle out into the darkness.

"It's an entirely new shaft," said Sparks. "Runs horizontally. Much wider. Ours empties out into its middle. Water trickling down the center."

"Sewer tunnel?" said Doyle, straining to hold him.

"Doesn't smell like it, does it?"

"Thankfully, no. Any sign of Larry?"

"Not as yet."

"How far to the ground?"

"Another twenty feet or so."

"What do you suppose Larry was reacting to?"

"Must have been the large Egyptian statue standing directly below me," said Sparks.

Ancient Artifacts

"Large Egyptian statue?"

"I can't quite make out who it is from this angle. Looks jackal-headed—"

"Did you say large Egyptian statue?"

"Yes. Possibly Anubis or Tuamutef—funereal deities, similar purpose, concerned with weighing a man's soul as he passes to the other side—"

Doyle's muscles were shaking violently with exertion. "Could we forgo the mythology lesson long enough to decide if you're heading up or down? I don't know that I can hold on much longer."

"Sorry. If you let me down slowly, Doyle, I think I can grab hold of the statue, let go the braces, and climb down the rest of the way."

"Fine."

Doyle lowered Sparks until he could reach down with one foot and steady himself against the statue's shoulder. He unsnapped his own braces, and both pairs flew into the air. Doyle reached out, caught them, and slumped back against the wall in relief, the knots in his arms relaxing into merely agonizing spasms.

"I believe it's definitely Tuamutef," said Sparks, sliding down the figure's body to the ground. "Quite rare outside of Egypt. Remarkable. I can't actually recall ever seeing one this size before."

"How interesting for you. What do you suggest I do now, Jack?"

"Tie off the braces and lower yourself down. You really shouldn't miss this, Doyle."

"I wouldn't dream of it."

Doyle collected himself, tied the braces as securely around the ladder as his knowledge of seafaring knots would allow, and let himself ever-so-gently down into the arms of dog-faced Tuamutef.

"Tuamutef assisted Anubis in the preparation of bodies for mummification and burial," said Sparks, walking around with the candle, inspecting the statue at its base as Doyle attempted a difficult, chafing passage down Tuamutef's bumpy torso. "His particular province was the stomach, specifically the removal and preservation of the viscera for the journey into the underworld."

"This, I can say with some assurance, is as far into the underworld as I ever hope to go," said Doyle, finally touching down beside him.

"The viscera were packed in airtight jars with a compound of herbs and spices that delayed decomposition, so you could take them out and stick the organs right back into place once you reached the other side," said Sparks, preoccupied to the point of obliviousness.

"Fascinating, truly, but, Jack, if you don't mind my asking, if someone has in fact sealed us in down here with evil intent—one of many
possibilities, I realize, but one we really ought to consider—don't you
think it would be a good idea—a really first-rate idea, in fact—for us
to quickly find our way out of here?"

"Right."

Sparks looked off in both directions. Doyle couldn't help but notice
that their candle was growing perilously small. Behind the statue, he
spotted what appeared to be a blackened torch set in a bracket on the
wall and quickly retrieved it.

"This appears to be an old Roman conduit—can't seem to shake
off those persistent old buggers, can we? London's lousy with them.
This one has been rather extensively refurbished. Aside from the parties responsible for the construction of the shaft we just descended,
a fairly recent addition, it's likely no one else is even aware this tunnel's
down here. And if the used torch you've just handed me is any indication, it has been used by those parties sometime within the last few
days."

Sparks ignited the torch from the candle, filling the chamber with
twenty times the previous supply of light. A huge, pulsating shadow
of Tuamutef was thrown menacingly onto the opposite wall.

"Which way should we go?"

"The tunnel runs north to south." He pointed south, where the
walls curved gently away around a turn, just as a muffled scuffling
issued faintly from that direction.

"What was that?" asked Doyle.

They listened. The scuffle repeated, slowly and rhythmically. It
seemed to be moving toward them.

"Footsteps?" said Doyle.

"The person is injured. Dragging one foot behind."

"Larry?"

"No, they're not wearing shoes." Sparks turned back to the north
and examined the bricks on either side of the water. "If we follow the
wax drippings in this direction, which Larry has thoughtfully provided
for us, we will much more quickly discover his whereabouts."

Maintaining the same sluggish pace, the footsteps behind them drew
closer to the nearest turn.

"Then who do you suppose that is?" asked Doyle, lowering his voice.

"I never ask questions I don't really wish to know the answer to.
Let's move on."

They sloshed through the shallow water and made for the north.

"As to what Tuamutef is doing here a hundred feet below the offices of Rathborne and Sons..." Sparks mused as they walked.

"You mentioned the removal of the viscera. Similar to what was done to the body of that streetwalker Leboux showed to me, isn't it?"

"The thought had occurred to me. It suggests the Dark Brotherhood is paying obeisance to an ancient Egyptian deity."

"You mean as a sacrificial offering of some kind?"

"These people are dedicated pagans—that opens their field of worship to the collective pantheon—and with his years in Egypt, Alexander is surely up to snuff on his Tuamutef," said Sparks. "Something has just struck me about one of the seven names on our list."

"Which?"

"Maximilian Graves—what does that bring to your mind?"

Doyle ran it back and forth. "I'm sure I don't know."

"An alias, a play on words. Do you see it? Makes-a-million graves. Precisely the sort of diseased jest Alexander used to play with obsessively in his letters. Beware the inveterate punster, Doyle, it's a sure sign of brewing mental disturbance."

"You think Alexander's responsible for Tuamutef being there?"

"Yes. In which case he's responsible for that woman's murder."

"But if it was a ritual of some kind, why were her organs left at the scene? Surely they would have returned them here, to their shrine."

"Perhaps the ritual was interrupted before completion, that's not a worry—the thing is, I'm puzzled by what the statue itself is doing here."

"Convenience—pop down the ladder with a bowl of guts for the old boy whenever the mood strikes—"

"No, Doyle," said Sparks somewhat impatiently, "we're in complete agreement on the *reason* for the statue being here; I'm trying to work out how it physically arrived."

A light flickered around the curve of the tunnel ahead. Sparks stopped and gave out with another low whistle. A moment later, the whistle was returned.

"Larry," said Doyle.

"Step lively, Doyle. We're still being followed."

Trotting on a hundred yards around the bend to where the tunnel terminated abruptly, they found Larry working by the light of his candle on the padlock of an immense double doorway set into the dead-end wall.

"Sorry for the inconvenience, guv," said Larry as they approached.

"Are you all right?" asked Doyle.

THE LIST OF 7

"Never better. The drop down was a bit more steep than I'd bargained for, I can tell you, knocked the Jenny Lind right out of me when I hit bottom. By the time I got my bellows and candle goin' again and caught an eyeful of that bloody dog-man, I thought silence might be the advisable course of action."

"The trap was closed after us," said Sparks, inspecting the doors.

"Figured this for a setup job," said Larry, lining his center bit up on the padlock. "Got in a mite too easy, didn't we?"

"Why didn't you say something?" said Doyle.

"Not my place, is it?"

Sparks knocked on the iron door and got back a booming, hollow echo.

"Listen to that. Hardly sounds like the end of the passageway, does it?"

"We gots a right rusty padlock to get through before we find out," said Larry, pounding on his center bit. "Bloody stubborn."

"I say, Larry," said Doyle, "you didn't happen to venture down that tunnel the other way before coming up here, did you?"

"No, sir—come on, give!"

"I only ask, you see, because we heard what sounded like someone walking toward us from that direction."

"I wouldn't know about that—bloody bastard!" Larry hammered away again at the lock.

"Hold up for just a moment, Larry," requested Sparks.

Larry paused. The echo of his last blow faded, and issuing out of the quiet that descended they heard the same relentless step-drag approaching from the south. Only now there were multiple variations on that familiar rhythm: three, four, five footfalls, possibly more— whether there were actually others present or it was simply some acoustic peculiarity of the tunnel was impossible to determine.

"Proceed, Larry," said Sparks, moving back toward the curve.

"Anything I can help you with, Larry?" asked Doyle.

"One-man job, idn't it?" said Larry irritably.

Sparks used the light to scan the walls. Lifting a second torch from the clutch of another iron sconce, he set it aflame and handed it to Doyle.

"Do you think it's gray hoods?" said Doyle quietly.

"They're a good deal swifter afoot than whatever we're hearing at the moment, wouldn't you agree?"

"Yes."

"And if someone did close that door with the intention of trapping us here, it's not unreasonable to assume they must be confident something was going to stand rather forcefully in the way of our escaping."

The footsteps grew close enough to hear intermittent splashing, and not promisingly, the pace of the steps seemed to be quickening.

"More than one now," said Doyle.

"More like ten."

Doyle and Sparks moved back away from the turn.

"Come along now, Larry," said Sparks. "Speed is of the essence."

"Got it!" said Larry, as he pierced the lock with a final blow and ripped it off the clasp. "Give a hand, gents."

All three men grabbed one side of the double doors and heaved. The neglected hinges protested mightily but began to resentfully yield. Doyle looked behind them as they labored; he saw the outline of a column of tall black shapes emerging from the darkness fifty feet behind them.

"Pull, damn it! Pull!" exhorted Sparks.

With Sparks's and Doyle's ability to apply useful leverage hampered by the torches in their hands, the gap grew to an inadequate six inches. They dropped the torches and put their whole backs into the effort, but the door stubbornly gave up only fractions of an inch at a time. Larry squeezed through the crack and pushed back on the door toward them. Hinges wailed like a wounded ox; the breach widened another inch. Doyle chanced another hurried glance backward; the tall shapes formed a picket line of angular, indistinct, but decidedly human silhouettes, lumbering and weaving toward their position at the doors. There were considerably more than ten of them. The three men were apparently visible to their pursuers now, for a collective sound came out of the pack, a hideous, breathy, burbling snarl. Redoubling their assault on the door with the inspired strength of angels, they secured another precious two inches of space.

"Go, Doyle, go!" said Sparks.

Doyle turned sideways, shoved himself through to the other side, put his shoulder to the door, and pushed back with all his might, as Larry stuck out a hand and pulled Sparks through.

"The torches!" said Sparks.

Doyle reached back into the gap. As he took hold of the torch, a blackened, fingery mass of exposed sinew, tendon, and bone, dripping seared and tattered rags, clamped a viselike grip on his wrist; Doyle bellowed in pain and surprise. In one swift move, Larry drew a knife from its holster and swiped the attacking arm: The blade sliced cleanly through its tissues as through wax paper; an appalling howl clawed the air as the severed limb fell away from the hand. Doyle shook the hand frantically off his wrist as Sparks took hold of his collar and yanked Doyle back through the opening, the torch still clutched in his hand.

"Pull, pull it shut!" Sparks shouted. "Help us, Doyle!"

Doyle scrambled to his feet and joined them as they grabbed a handle fixed to the inside of the door and pulled for their lives, the memory of their ancestors and their progeny to come. The hinges moved more cooperatively back toward them, and the gap quickly closed, but not before they saw a squalid, feverish windmill of fetid arms and hands foul the air they'd just been breathing. Frantic, frustrated squeals worthy of a saint's last temptation tormented their ears, and a smell of a hundred desecrated sepulchers made a mockery of innocence before the void was sealed. They quickly lifted and slid a thick steel bar designed for such a purpose through the twin handles of the doors, securing their position, at least for the moment; the pounding and pummeling and scratching of nails on the other side of the iron doors that followed made speech, if not thought, impossible. At a signal from Sparks, pointing the torch in the direction he wanted them to go, the three men moved quickly and gratefully away from the doors.

They ran headlong, without a thought to direction or distance. As their senses returned from the brink, and the torchlight revealed their surroundings, they realized this was no continuation of the tunnel; they were greeted by dimly lit vistas of a vaulted, train-station-sized chamber, where boxes and crates of every imaginable size, shape, and function were stacked like building blocks, forming a jagged-toothed skyline. They stopped to catch their breath and still the awful beating of their hearts. The hammering on the doors behind them continued, but at enough remove to allow them the luxury of brief respite.

"Jesus Christ!" said Larry. "Spectacles, testicles, wallet, and watch, wot the bloody hell!"

"It was going to crush the bones of my wrist or pull the arm right off my shoulder," said Doyle, testing the area for trauma.

"The devil's own punchbowl is what that was," said Larry. "That was old Horns and Hoofs himself nearly put the pinch on us. Up your uncle, Nick!"

"Easy," cautioned Sparks.

Knife still in hand, Larry would not be stilled, angrily semaphoring an eloquent series of obscenities back in the direction of their attackers.

"Feather and flip you, daisy boots! Back to hell where yer mother waits patiently! I'll carve you like a Christmas pudding, you mingy pross! I'll sort you out large, Sinbad the Sailor your skidgy hide, 'n' have your guts for garters! You twig me, yobbos? A handful a' fives for you!' "

The pounding on the door stopped abruptly. Larry took a couple of deep breaths, then slumped exhaustedly down onto a crate. "Lord, I need a drink," he said, his head in his hands. "I'm whacked to the wide."

They regained themselves in the shelter of a cove of crates. Time slowly resumed its normal curve, and Doyle's attention was drawn to the sea of curiosities surrounding them. He joined Sparks, who was standing on top of the tallest box surveying their position, holding the torch high.

"Good Christ . . . "

The room stretched out in every direction as far as the eye could see. The landscape was populated by small principalities of statuary: kings, queens, artists, scholars, scientists, foot soldiers and generals on horseback, heroes and villains of antiquity and folklore captured in their defining moments of triumph or infamy, parliaments of demigods and goddesses, their white marble skins aglow with a milky, luminescent sheen.

"What is this place?" asked Doyle.

"I believe we are in a subbasement of the British Museum," said Sparks.

"So there's a way out then, up above," said Doyle, encouraged.

"We'll have to find a door first."

"Jack, what in God's name were those—"

"Not now, Doyle," said Sparks, leaping lightly down off the box. "Up and on, Larry, we're not clear of this yet."

Larry roused himself to his feet, and they set off trailing after Sparks.

"You all right, guv?" Larry asked Doyle.

"Nothing a few stiff yards of scotch wouldn't set right," said Doyle.

His stoicism seemed to put the starch back in Larry's step. "Second the motion. Thought for a minute you was goin' to chuck the sponge."

"If you hadn't been so quick with that lock, we'd have all turned up our toes by now."

"Easy as winking. Should've had it off before trouble turned the corner."

"No worry," said Doyle. "Worse things happen at sea."

They hustled to catch up to Sparks, who led them by torchlight willy-nilly through the immense storeroom. There were no paths to follow, no aisles or columns through which to plot a course. The cavern's wonders seemed to have been scattered recklessly, without benefit of any discernible design. Each turn through the dreamworld delivered them to a cargo of new wonders: a colony of urns as big as boxcars, others as delicate as acorns; ponderous sarcophagi of silver and lead inlaid with precious stones, baroque coronation carriages of alabaster and gold leaf, catafalques of ebony, ivory, and shining steel, headless mannequins in ceremonial costume from Africa, Asia, and the subcontinent; immense tapestries illustrating wars of lost and legendary kingdoms; a comprehensive zoography of savage animals taxidermed to passive domesticity—bears from every corner of the earth, great cats, ravenous wolves, rhinoceroses, elephants and ostriches, crocodiles and emus, and a spate of stranger, night-dwelling species undreamt-of or never seen before; a gallery of epic paintings in gilded frames assaying every imaginable scene, battles, seductions, royal births and deaths, bucolic Arcadias and nightmarish holocausts. At one juncture, they wandered through a ghostly fleet of skeletal ships, stripped to the ribs, awaiting resurrection. Gigantic cannons, engines of war, battering rams, catapults, and siege machines. A cityscape of uprooted walls, huts, houses, transplanted tombs, and reconstructed temples. Great stone heads. Flying machines. Feathered serpents. Instruments of music or torture. In its breathtaking totality, the chamber's contents added up to nothing less than an exhaustive anthropology of the known and unknown worlds, all of it shrouded in a thick dust of contumely and neglect.

"Have you ever seen the like?" said Doyle in amazement.

"No. I've heard rumors of the existence of such a storeroom for many years," said Sparks, as they stopped again in a clearing, not a foot closer to finding an exit.

"Like civilization's graveyard," said Larry.

"The spoils of the expansion of British Empire," said Doyle.

"Lord have mercy on the white man. Looks like we brung back every last stick we could carry and then some," said Larry.

"That's exactly what we've done; plundered the world's countinghouses and looted its tombs, and what booty we don't display upstairs in pride of conquest we covet from view down here in shame," said Sparks.

"Just as every other dominant culture in history has done in its ascendancy," said Doyle.

"I daresay the world above's a poorer place for it," said Larry, sadness magnified by his intimate acquaintanceship with unlawful greed.

Ancient Artifacts

"Let it be no cause for worry," said Sparks. "Another conquering civilization will come along soon enough to relieve us of our burden."

"It looks as if no one's been down here in years," said Doyle, wiping a black thumbprint's worth of dust off the toe of a warlike Athena.

"Someone has: long enough to steal that statue of Tuamutef, at the very least," said Sparks, laying that mystery to rest. "If not a great deal more."

"How's that, Jack?"

"Although the arrangement of these items seems willfully haphazard to the eye, there is still a loose, categorical method to it. And there were significant pieces missing from nearly every valuable collection we encountered. Here's an example, do you see?"

Sparks drew their attention to a quintet of Hellenic statues depicting a series of animated and sensuous nymphs. "Calliope, Clio, Erato, Euterpe, and I believe this sprightly lass is Terpsichore," said Sparks.

"The Nine Muses," said Doyle.

"I had an uncle played the calliope," said Larry.

"And only five of them left in attendance. You can clearly see here by these marks on the floor that the four missing ladies—help me, Doyle: Polyhymnia, Melpomene—"

"Thalia and Urania."

"Thank you—you can see by these marks that the other four previously resided here alongside their sisters."

"You think the others were stolen?"

"I do. I've noticed similar patterns of selective larceny throughout. As you've observed, Doyle, the curators of this circus are largely absentee. The members of the Brotherhood inserted that shaft into the tunnel in order to gain access to this room; they could siphon a steady stream of treasures out of this trove from now until doomsday and not so much as a teaspoon would be missed."

"But to what purpose?"

"One of two reasons: to keep for themselves or sell off. You could hardly begin to put a price on what's in here."

"Is that the Brotherhood's purpose then? Cornering the market on antiquities?" asked Doyle.

"To assemble an elite circle of movers and shakers like the heavyweights on that list to run a fencing operation, no matter how ambitious, strikes me as a tiny bit prosy, wouldn't you say, Larry?"

"Like the great chefs of Europe gettin' together to bake hot cross buns."

"Quite. I suspect the reasons behind these thefts are twofold: the acquisition of specific and sacred items they believe necessary as their bridge to the mystic plane—i.e., our friend Tuamutef—and the profitable illicit sale of those items they don't require to finance the rest of their efforts."

"But as you pointed out, they are all enormously wealthy," said Doyle.

"And I'll acquaint you with the first ironclad rule of the enormously wealthy: Never spend one's own money."

"Amen to that," said Larry, the memory if not the light of larceny shining in his eyes.

"Pardon me, Larry. That principle is undoubtedly a good deal less class-conscious than I just stated."

"No offense taken," said Larry. " 'Fink I'll have a peepers." He lit his candle off the torch and wandered off around the next cluster of boxes.

"We can put a stop to their wanton thievery, that much is certain," said Doyle.

"Sealing that tunnel will put an end to the robberies, though I fear the worst has already been done and the trail gone cold: Witness the ruined condition of that padlock on the iron doors."

Doyle nodded, conceding the point.

"Whether or not we can successfully bring charges to bear against the firm of Rathborne and Sons for these crimes is a good deal less certain. It may not in fact be in our best interest."

"How so, Jack?"

"Without a shred of physical evidence to support the accusation, an assault on the venerated, unsullied names of the Brotherhood through the plodding course of the courts will only vouchsafe their acquittal and drive them deeper to ground, while heaping untold ridicule upon ourselves. If we're to pursue them to the heart of their purpose, it's best we keep our efforts from public view until the moment we can strike decisively."

A low whistle came from Larry on the other side of the bend. "Have a muggins at this, then."

Sparks and Doyle traced the light of Larry's candle and joined him, climbing up onto a barrier of crates that seemed to be a shield for the sight that greeted them. Sparks held high the torch, and they looked down at a solid square block of identical mummies' coffins, at least twenty in number, set shoulder to shoulder like cots in a crowded flophouse. The lids had been removed and stashed in a heap to one side. Two of the boxes still held their occupants: rangy, blackened, and withered corpses sheathed in rotting bandages. The rest were empty.

"Good Christ," said Doyle, as they moved forward to examine the lids.

"Weapons, defensive actions," said Sparks, studying the pictographs. "These were warriors' graves. Coffins of similar size and design, identical hieroglyphs: These bodies were the royal household guard, entombed en masse. When Pharaoh died, it was custom to kill and bury his garrison alongside, an escort to the Land of the Ancients."

"There's service above and beyond the call," said Larry.

They looked at each other.

"Makes you wonder, doesn't it?" said Sparks with a strange grin.

"What should we do?" asked Doyle.

Before he could answer, the room was electrified with the expressive screech of rusty iron hinges from far across the chamber.

"For the moment," said Sparks, instantly on the alert, "I strongly suggest that we run."

Run they did, as far and as fast from the iron doors as their legs and limited light would carry them. The storeroom's fabulous inventory was reduced to an ill-defined blur. Moving along the wall, they searched for an exit and finally found one in the farthest corner— double oaken doors, exceptionally stout. Larry lit his candle and examined the locks.

"Dead bolts," said Larry, sizing up his opposition. "No access to 'em."

Throwing their collective weight against the doors did not cause so much as a quiver in the wood.

"Chains on the other side for good measure," said Larry. "Guess they don't want tourists wandering in unannounced."

"Blasted museum," said Doyle.

"Shall I have a skivvy for another way?" asked Larry.

"No time," said Sparks, casting a sharp eye around. "Larry, we need loose metal, rocks, steel, scrap iron, whatever you can find, a whole mass of it—"

"On it," said Larry, as he moved off.

"We passed some cannon a while ago, Doyle, can you remember where that was?"

"I remember seeing them. Back a ways, I think."

"Then look for them as if our lives depended on it. Because they do."

Heading back into the open room, they tried as best they could to retrace their steps through the motley collection. The passage looked frustratingly unfamiliar. Another cry of rusty hinges found its way across the vasty chamber, but as yet there was no other sign of their attackers.

"Jack, provided we find one, what do you propose to do with a cannon?"

"That depends on which of our needs arises with more urgency."

"Our needs?"

"Much as I hate the defacing of government property, we shall have to blast our way out through those doors or turn and defend ourselves. Whichever comes first."

Doyle kept his opinion about his preferred alternative to himself. Each new protest from the hinges pounded a spike of fear deeper into his mind.

Their search seemed to last an eternity but took no more than five minutes, by which time the hinges had ceased their soundings. Save for the echoes of the two men's footsteps, the room grew ominously silent. They did find cannon, masses of cannon, cannonades of cannon. The difficulty now was in choosing one to suit their purpose: Sparks quickly settled on a Turkish sixteen-pounder attached to a caisson. They lifted either side of the hitch and muled it behind them, negotiating through the storeroom as rapidly as their haphazard path and the gun's ungainly weight would allow.

"How do we know it works?" asked Doyle as they ran.

"We don't."

Doyle would have given the shirt off his back for enough grease to silence the caisson's squeaky wheels, for behind them in the direction of the iron doors they heard boxes and crates toppling over, crashing; their pursuers were in the room, ignoring the aisles and taking the shortest route to their quarry. Sparks stopped and looked around.

"Is this the way we came?" he asked.

"I was following you. I thought you knew."

"Right. Grab a couple of those sabers while they're handy, will you, Doyle?" said Sparks, pointing to an overflowing cache of weapons nearby.

"Do you really think we'll need them?"

"I don't know. Would you rather find yourself at a point where you regret not having them?"

Doyle took two of the long, curved blades, and they resumed hauling the cannon. Please God, let him know which way we're going, prayed Doyle, and not into the arms or claws of whatever it is that's behind

Ancient Artifacts

us—if they are behind and not in front of us—please God, let them be far behind us and more hopelessly lost in this labyrinth than we are. There, that statue of Hercules slaying a lion—one of the Twelve Labors, he had to muck out a stables as well: What a time to think about that!—at any rate we definitely passed Hercules on our way to the cannons—

"We're going the right way!" announced Doyle.

Larry was waiting for them near the double doors beside a heap of collected debris: bricks, broken lances, fragments of metal.

" 'Fraid I had to vandalize a touch, pulling odd bits off this and that," Larry said, with a slightly stricken conscience.

"You're absolved," said Sparks. "Give us a hand."

They maneuvered the cannon into position: point-blank at the oaken doors ten feet away.

"Doyle, find something to anchor the base," said Sparks, "or the recoil will neutralize the thrust. Larry, front-load the muzzle, pack it in tight, heaviest and sharpest items last, we'll only have one shot at this."

They fell to following orders. Sparks took one of the vials from his chemistry bench out of his vest, set it gently on the ground, pulled the shirt from his pants, and began tearing a strip off the hem. Doyle returned to the clearing moments later, dragging a rusty chain and anchor.

"Will this do?" he asked.

"Splendid, old boy."

They wrapped its chain securely around the cannon as Larry tamped the payload into the barrel with a Venetian barge pole.

"Ready here," said Larry.

"How do we set it off?" asked Doyle.

"Thought I'd use this nitroglycerin," said Sparks, as he uncorked the vial and lowered it gingerly into the cannon's breach.

"You've been carrying nitroglycerin around in your pocket this entire time?" asked Doyle, retroactively alarmed.

"Perfectly harmless; detonation requires ignition or a direct blow—"

"My God, Jack! What if you'd fallen in the tunnel?"

"Our worries would be well over by now, wouldn't they?" said Sparks, stuffing the strip of linen into the fuse hole.

Boxes crashed only a hundred yards behind them.

"Here they come," said Larry, unsheathing his knives.

"Stand back," said Sparks.

Larry and Doyle took cover to the rear. Sparks set the torch to the fuse and joined them. They sank down behind some crates, closed their eyes, covered their ears, and waited for the explosion as the fabric burned down into the hole. Nothing.

"Will it go?" asked Doyle.

"Hasn't yet, has it?" said Sparks.

More boxes fell, moving relentlessly closer.

"Better hurry, then," said Larry.

Sparks moved carefully forward to inspect the cannon. Doyle took a firmer grip on the scimitar, looking down at it for the first time; he felt as if he were caught in a dream holding a prop from the *Pirates of Penzance*. Sparks peered down into the fuse hole, then quickly sprinted back toward their hiding place.

"Still burning—" He dove for safety.

The cannon exploded magnificently in a hail of sparks and a great burst of white smoke. The men rose immediately and ran forward; the caisson had crumbled, and the little cannon pitched cockeyed to the floor, half-cracked, but it had bravely held the charge and effectively delivered its freight. The double doors hung off their hinges, splintered to matchsticks and not a moment too soon; they could hear that blighted, festering gurgle as the creatures on their tail closed in.

"Let's get the hell out of here," said Sparks.

They ran to the doors, kicked the vestigial wreckage out of their way, and climbed over the chains that had secured its other side, where a flight of stairs led up and away to freedom.

"Go on ahead," said Sparks, stopping on a landing at the foot of the stairs to tear another strip from his shirt.

"Whatever are you doing, Jack?"

"I don't particularly fancy this bunch chasing us down the streets of Bloomsbury, do you?"

Shadowy black shapes moved toward them through the dispersing clouds of smoke.

"Go on, I'll catch up to you," said Sparks, uncorking a second vial of explosive and pouring it out onto the floor.

"He says go, we should go, guv," said Larry, tugging on Doyle's sleeve.

The first shapes were nearly at the doors.

"My revolver, please, Jack," said Doyle, standing his ground.

Sparks looked at Doyle as if he'd gone insane, then pulled the gun from his belt and tossed it to him. Doyle calmly aimed and emptied all six chambers at the advancing figures, eliciting some memorably inhuman howls and knocking the leaders of the pack a few feet back from the opening, allowing Sparks just enough time to finish pouring the nitro and lay out the long shirt strip from the puddle back toward the stairs.

"Run!" shouted Sparks.

Larry yanked Doyle up the steps as Sparks lit the fabric with the torch and sprinted after them. As they made the turn at the landing, Doyle looked back and caught a glimpse of the lead creature as it lurched into view at the foot of the stairs: tall and impossibly wasted, gaunt, spidery limbs waving spasmodically, hair and teeth in a decayed face held together by rotted linen, pinprick red eyes lit with venomous intensity. That's what Doyle thought he saw in the split second before the entire basement disappeared with a disequilibrating boom: The explosion obliterated sight and sound. Walls crumbled, smoke shot everywhere, obscuring everything. The stairs beneath their feet undulated like piano keys.

Pushed by the momentum of the blast, the three men threw themselves through the nearest door. Their torch extinguished by the rush of air, they lay in darkness on the cool marble floor, stunned, ears ringing, trying to recapture their wind; it was as if they'd been struck massive blows to the head and solar plexus. Time passed. They stirred, tentatively at first, a low moan escaping from each, but with the tintinnabulary ringing in their ears, they were unable to hear themselves.

"All in one piece?" asked Sparks finally.

He had to ask twice more before the question registered. They blinked repeatedly and looked at each other like amnesiacs, testing their extremities, amazed to find them still in working order. Although nothing felt broken, Doyle couldn't find a part of his body that didn't feel pummeled. The monster came rushing back into the eye of his mind as if he were adjusting a refocusable lens. He realized he still gripped the purloined sword: His fingers felt as if they'd grown into the handle; he had to use his free hand to pry them off. The men slowly helped each other to their feet, and it was just as well they couldn't clearly hear the painful groans the effort cost them.

Doyle looked back warily at the double doors. "Think that's done for them, then?"

"Bloody well better," said Larry, trying to coax a kink out of his back. "I couldn't fend off an evil baby armed with a rattle 'bout now."

"That was the last of the nitro, anyway," said Sparks.

"Is that what you were doing at your flat, Jack, cooking nitroglycerin?"

Sparks nodded.

"I'm glad I'm not your neighbor."

"That last lot was a bit too vigorous on the volatile side, I'm afraid."

"If it put paid to those bleedin' rag-heads, you'll hear no complaint from me," said Larry.

They felt around in the darkness until they found their torch. With some small trouble facilitating the use of his fingers, Larry dug out a match and struck it on the floor. The torch flared and revealed their location; an empty marble antechamber, more reminiscent of the museum's public rooms than the strange place from which they'd come. Behind them hazy motes of smoke issued from under the still-swinging doors.

"Let's find a proper exit," said Sparks.

They turned and were about to take their tottering leave when the doors behind them swung open. They wheeled stiffly, steeling themselves for combat. But what crawled through the door to confront them was not an angry host of the undead, or even a single intact opponent; dragging the crushed head and half a torso of one of the creatures doggedly forward was a single, clutching, mutilated arm. A line of ashen sludge trailed behind the seeping wreckage. The face worked its loose and shattered jaw, as if trying to summon some thousand-year-old curse. The thing in its surviving form was more loathsome than formidable, but the eyes were still powered by the same malevolent fire.

"Jesus," said Doyle, backing away.

"Persistent bastards, ain't they?" said Larry.

Sparks took Doyle's saber, strode forward, and with one decisive stroke beheaded the ruined monstrosity. The creature froze; the light faded from its eyes, arm and torso collapsed as the head rolled harmlessly away. Larry ran forward and booted the head through the open door like a football.

"He scores!" shouted Larry. "Wickam over Leicester, one to zed in extra time! Wickam takes the Cup!"

Doyle knelt down to inspect the wreckage; what little had been left behind was already sifting into a quintessence of dust. Nothing about the decrepit leavings suggested any life force had animated those dry and dusty cells in the millennia since their original tenant had slipped its mortal coil.

"What do you see, Doyle?" asked Sparks, kneeling beside him.

"The remains are completely inert. Whatever energy or spirit that directed this thing is gone."

"What sort of energy?"

Doyle shook his head. "I'm sure I don't know. Something alive but not living. Puts me in mind of the gray hoods."

"Energy isolated from spirit. A form of will without mind."

"Black magic then, is it?" asked an oddly chipper Larry.

"Words we could put to it, I suppose," said Doyle. "For categorization, if not understanding."

"No disrespect, guv, but wot you want to understand an unholy creepin' terror like that lot for? Be glad we got the better of it and move on, that's how I look at it."

"We should move on in any case," said Sparks, rising. "The explosion should have awakened the soundest sleeping guard in the empire."

With Sparks leading the way, they left the antechamber by way of a corridor that held the greatest promise of an exit.

"Wouldn't want to be the watchman happens across this mess on my go-rounds," said Larry. "Put me right off my kip."

"I could do for that scotch about now, Larry," said Doyle.

"Pleasure, sir. Get ourselves home first. Never had to break *out* of a museum before," said Larry, begging the question of how many times he'd been required to break into one.

"I'm quite sure you're up to the task," said Doyle.

CHAPTER 14

Little Boy Blue

Lᴀʀʀʏ ᴡᴀs ɪɴᴅᴇᴇᴅ up to the task. One judiciously broken window later, they were back on the street and quickly across it to the safety of Sparks's apartment, where they administered themselves a full measure of vintage single-malt from a beaker on Sparks's bench and settled in for what little remained of the night. Doyle assessed their injuries and pronounced them relatively intact, if not a great deal the worse for wear, and fit to travel, which Sparks stated as their task for the following day. Without even the energy left to inquire as to where tomorrow might carry them, Doyle fell swiftly into a thick and leaden sleep.

The next evening's newspapers would be dominated by ripsnorting accounts of an audacious criminal attempt to grave-rob the British Museum's priceless Egyptian reserves. In their eagerness to gain access to the treasures, the looters had apparently blown themselves up along with their targeted plunder, a rare collection of Third Empire mummies. Just why the mummies themselves had been lifted by the thieves—and likewise destroyed in the explosion, one of the bodies having been quite incredibly hurtled up a flight of stairs and through a door by the blast—and not their priceless gold-leafed coffins, was

Little Boy Blue

the sort of minor journalistic inconsistency to a sensational headline-grabber that didn't seem to tax the tabloids' credulity in the slightest. Along with breathlessly overstated descriptions of the carnage inflicted on museum property, there were the predictable cries of outrage from members of Parliament and other oft-quoted pillars of culture, deploring the desecration of such a conspicuously public institution, with blame obliquely laid at the feet of a far-too-liberal immigration policy, followed by the usual stern nostrums for correcting the social faults that were so clearly at the root of such hooliganism: no respect for God, country, and Queen, et cetera, et cetera. The facts suffered their habitual neglect. No word of the connecting Roman viaduct or a statue of Tuamutef in evidence, nor a whisper regarding a vertical tunnel leading directly to the office of the president of the publishing firm of Rathborne and Sons, Limited.

But long before those papers even hit the streets, while the streets were still awash with police inspectors and hand-wringing Egyptologists and a host of rubbernecking civilians, before Doyle had roused himself from his deathlike slumber, John Sparks had been out the door since dawn and returned from his morning's work to rouse the others and set them on their way. Bidding the noble Zeus farewell, the three men slipped down the back staircase before noon, climbed aboard their hansom, and slipped through a gaping hole in the investigative net that had been so hastily thrown over the blocks circumferencing the British Museum.

Sparks's morning had been highly productive, he informed Doyle and Larry. Breakfast in the company of a former theatrical colleague—now a leading producer-manager of the London stage—had yielded the current whereabouts of the Manchester Players, the troupe advertised in the poster they'd found on the president's desk at Rathborne and Sons.

"On tour in the northeast of England; Scarborough tonight, finishing up a three-day stint," he said, "then north for an engagement in Whitby."

Whitby. York again. Wasn't that the parish where the Hon. Bishop Pillphrock, one of the names on the List, tended his flock? Doyle inquired.

Not only that, Sparks told them, but through an acquaintance at the mercantile exchange he had discovered Whitby was also the winter residence of Sir John Chandros, one of Pillphrock's prominent companions on the List of Seven. Doyle was beginning to take Sparks's admonition about the nonexistence of coincidence to heart.

For his final revelation, Sparks handed Doyle a slender, cloth-bound volume he had unearthed at Hatchard's Bookshop: *My Life Among the Himalayan Masters* by Professor Arminius Vamberg.

Vamberg. Yet another name from the List!

"Look at the publisher," said Sparks.

Doyle opened to the frontispiece: Rathborne and Sons, Limited. He quickly scanned the enclosed author's biography wherein Vamberg was described as a native Austrian who had collected an alphabet's worth of advanced degrees from the elite among Europe's ivory towers before a ferocious wanderlust carried him from the islands of the Caribbean to the Tibetan Highlands, with stopovers on the Dark Continent and the Australian outback.

"No picture of him," said Doyle.

"I'll wager he has a beard," said Sparks cryptically.

"A beard?"

"The man who obtained Bodger Nuggins's release from Newgate was described to you as having a beard."

"What makes you think that man was Vamberg?"

Sparks smiled. "Simply a hunch. One can't know everything with absolute certainty."

"Does the book give us any clues to the man?"

"Although the title would give the reader to believe he's about to embark on a highly personal journey of discovery, there's almost nothing to be gleaned from it regarding the author's personality. The tone is benign, academic, and investigatory. He makes no attempts to proselytize, persuade, or otherwise make insupportable claims for the powers of the spirit world."

"Bet he don't make a nickel from that piece a' dreadful," said Larry.

"How do you mean?" asked Doyle.

"No ghosts and goblins, no hairy mountain-dwelling fiend swoopin' down on its victim like a night wind? Hardly sell two copies in the open market; folks want a little blood with their gruel, don't they?"

"It seems Professor Arminius Vamberg is precisely what he presents himself to be," said Sparks. "A sober, serious scientist laboring in the academically unsanctioned field of the metaphysical."

"No wonder we've never heard of him," said Doyle.

"Study it at your leisure, Doctor. We've a long train ride ahead of us."

"To Whitby, I assume."

"But of course," said Sparks.

As they snaked through the crowded noontime streets, Doyle was jolted by the memory of his promise to Leboux, the promise he'd made—was it only yesterday? It felt like months ago—not to take leave of London again without leaving word. Sparks's putative ability to throw his weight around within the confines of government aside, Doyle's sense of obligation to his old friend was strong and binding. He asked Sparks if they might quickly stop by St. Bartholomew's Hospital on the way; he wished to secure some of the few personal effects he kept there and, since they were heading into the possibility of more and greater danger, replenish his stock of medical supplies as well. Returning Sparks's subtly questioning gaze with impassive stolidity, Doyle felt reasonably confident he hadn't betrayed his true intention. Sparks's response gave him no reason to believe otherwise.

"St. Bartholomew's Hospital, Larry," Sparks instructed.

"Might we afterward drive by the Royal Mews to look for that boy Spivey Quince described?" asked Doyle.

"I had already planned on doing so," said Sparks. His look was closed and inaccessible again.

Maybe he's seen through my request, thought Doyle, growing flustered. Maybe he doesn't trust me. Such a hard man to decipher! Well, in truth, what business is it of his if I want to let Leboux know where I am? Am I to rely on John Sparks to inform my family and sort out my loose ends should anything happen to me? The police are good for something: dependable in their plodding, predictable sort of way, if nothing else.

The remainder of the trip passed in an uncomfortable silence. Reaching the hospital, Sparks joined Doyle as he left the carriage and entered along with him. Can't very well ask him not to come, thought Doyle, how would that look? He said nothing. Sparks sat on a bench outside the physician's quarters to wait while he requisitioned the supplies he needed and checked his locker. There were in fact precious few things of any use inside, but at this point, he realized with an odd mixture of regret and elation, they constituted the sum of his worldly possessions: a silver brush and comb set, a razor and shaving mug, and a crucifix his father had given him on the occasion of his confirmation. He put the brush, comb, and razor into his bag. He considered putting the crucifix round his neck but settled for dropping it in a vest pocket.

After receiving the additional medical supplies from the disbursement office, Doyle walked back to the door and peered out the porthole window. Sparks was no longer on the bench. Doyle quickly walked to the reception desk, grabbed a pen, and was about to hastily scribble a note to Leboux when the nurse on duty noticed him.

"Oh, Dr. Doyle, I've a message here for you," she said, moving to the pigeonholed wall behind her.

"A message?"

"Came this morning. Policeman delivered it." She handed him an envelope.

"Thank you," said Doyle. He opened it.

ARTHUR,

Mr. John Sparks is an escaped lunatic from the asylum at Bedlam. Violent and extremely dangerous. Contact me immediately.

LEBOUX

"*Billet doux* from some secret paramour?" said Sparks.

"What?" Doyle looked up, startled. Sparks was beside him, leaning on the desk.

"The letter, old boy—is it from a lover?"

"An old acquaintance wants me for a game of racquets," said Doyle, folding it and returning it to the nurse as casually as nature would allow. "Please let the gentleman know I shall be unavailable to play for the next week or so, but will be back in touch immediately at that time."

"Very good, Doctor," said the nurse, carrying the note safely out of harm's way.

"Shall we go, then?" Doyle said.

He picked up his bag and started out. Sparks fell into step beside him.

"Find everything you needed?" asked Sparks.

"Yes."

Good God. Good God. I can't run, thought Doyle, and I can't seem to hide anything from him, not even my thoughts. I've seen only too well what he's capable of; he's the last man on earth I'd want opposing me—is it all lies, everything he's told me? Could any one man be as pernicious and cunning as that? Yes, if he's mad, who better? But wait, Doyle, what if it's not true? What if Leboux's got it wrong? After all you've been through together—he's saved your life how many times now?—shouldn't you give him at least the benefit of that small doubt?

"You all right, Doyle?" asked Sparks evenly.

"Hmm. Couldn't say there's not a lot on my mind, could I?"

"Certainly not."

"Guess I've as much right to my own brooding silences from time to time as anyone else."

"I shan't dispute you."

"I mean, I'm the one who's had his life fairly well taken apart—"

Little Boy Blue

A cry from the door of the ward they were passing interrupted, an extended scream, high-pitched and agonized. A child's voice. Doyle turned and looked inside.

The beds had been pushed to one side, and a mechanical carousel, children in hospital smocks seated on its six wooden horses, filled one side of the spacious L-shaped room. Three stocky tumblers in red Russian blouses were coming down off one another's shoulders. A shambling red-nosed clown had just left off playing a hurdy-gurdy organ and was crowding in behind a quartet of nurses attempting to calm the child whose ululating outburst had stilled the room: a small boy, dressed in a bright satin Harlequin outfit of many vibrant colors, predominantly violets and blues. About ten years old. His head was as pale and bald as a hen's egg; the skin edging the back of his neck was warped and strangely puckered.

Spivey's vision! Men in red, horses, a boy in bright blue—a bone-chilling wallop jumped Doyle's spine, his skin tingled with goose bumps. Sparks brushed past him into the room, then Doyle quickly advanced around him to close in on the child.

"Blaglawd!" Doyle thought he heard the boy wail. The child's eyes had rolled back into his head. His arms thrashed about as his entire body jerked in fitful spasms.

"What's happened?" asked Doyle of the senior nurse.

"We're having a show for the children—" she said sturdily, trying along with the others to grab hold of the boy's flailing limbs. "He came with them; he's one of the performers."

The white-faced clown pushed forward. "What's wrong wid 'im?" asked the clown, with more irritation than concern.

"Blaglawd! Blag lawd!" shouted the child.

"What's a matt'r wid 'im then?" asked the man in a flat Midlands accent. Doyle could smell rum and peppermint on his breath.

"Stand clear, please," the nurse instructed him.

As the nurses struggled to hold the boy steady, Doyle checked his pulse and looked into his eyes; his heart was racing, his pupils widely dilated. A thin, clear froth bubbled freely from the corners of his mouth.

"Black Lord! Black Lord!" His words were becoming clearer.

"Wot's 'e talkin' 'bout then?" the clown crowded in again to ask.

"What's the boy's name?" Doyle asked of the man.

"Joey—"

"Is he your son?"

" 'E's my apprentice," the clown replied defensively. "I'm Big Roger; 'e's Litt'l Roger."

Beneath the clown white, the man's face was oily and cratered with vivid pocks. Viewed closely, the wide red artificial smile painted over his mouth only accentuated a tight-lipped sneer that was clearly his customary mien.

"Has he ever gone off like this before?" asked Doyle.

"No, never—ow!" the man cried painfully.

Sparks had clamped a pincer grip on the back of the clown's neck.

"You'd best answer the doctor truthfully," said Sparks.

"Once! Once 'bout six weeks ago. We was down Battersea, outside the train station durin' a matinee: Right in the mid'le, 'e goes like this 'ere—"

"Black Lord! Black Lord!" the little boy cried.

"Hold him steady," Doyle said to the nurses.

With a culminating yell, the boy pulled his hands free from the nurses and clawed wildly at his head; his fingers dug into the skin and ripped it clear away from the bone. The other children who'd been gathered in a fearful knot around them screamed and ran about, hysteria spreading like a transmittable airborne germ.

"Stop him!"

There was hair beneath the boy's faltering skin, a full head of sandy hair. The boy was wearing a bald pate, Doyle realized as the shock wore off, a guise identical to his elder partner's. As the uncomprehending nurses fell back in horror, Sparks stepped forward, took firm hold on the boy, and carried him away from the crowd and behind a stand of bedside screens.

"Quickly, Doyle," said Sparks, sitting the boy on a bed.

Doyle kneeled down and moved closer to the child. "Joey, listen to me, listen to my voice: Can you hear me?"

The boy's face remained blank and inexpressive, but he spoke not another word; Doyle's voice seemed to penetrate the thick haze surrounding him. He allowed Doyle to take his hands without resistance.

"Can you hear me, Joey?"

Sparks pulled the screens around the bed to shield them and stood guard behind Doyle and the boy, but in the caterwauling din that had resulted, the source of its instigation had almost been forgotten.

"Joey, you can hear me, can't you?" said Doyle.

Joey's eyes flickered shallowly behind their half-closed lids, only the whites visible. The boy slowly nodded.

"Tell me what you see, Joey."

The boy licked his cracked, parched lips; blood seeped from serrated, self-inflicted wounds. "Black Lord..."

"Yes, Joey. Tell me."

Little Boy Blue

His small, round face assumed a quiet dignity. The boy's voice was high and bell-like, but it now possessed a mellifluous maturity that belied its innocent frame. "Black Lord...looks for passage. Passage to this side."

Passage. Spivey Quince in his trance said something about passage.

"To which side, Joey?"

"Physical."

"Where is he now?"

Joey paused, his eyes darting around, seeing. Then he slowly shook his head. "Not here."

"Passage how, Joey?"

"Rebirth."

"Rebirth into physical life," said Doyle.

Joey nodded weakly. Doyle caught Sparks's eye, glancing back at them over his shoulder; he was listening.

"They try to help It," said Joey.

"Who does?"

"The Seven."

The Seven. Good Christ. "Who are the Seven?"

"They serve...have served It before."

"What do they want?"

"To prepare the way. They are on this side."

"Who are they, Joey? Who are the Seven?"

There was a pause before Joey shook his head again.

"What does It want?"

"It seeks the throne. It will be King...King a thousand years."

Quince went on about crowns or thrones as well, when he took hold of the medium's picture.

"What is It, Joey? What is this thing?" asked Doyle, trying to will more energy into the boy, feeling him going limp in his arms.

Joey's face grew paler. He seemed to reach down to a deeper level of responsiveness. Froth foamed from his lips, a bright salmon shade of pink. His chest heaved with effort; his voice lowered considerably.

"It has many names. It has always been. It waits outside. Souls nourish It....It feeds on their destruction. But It will not ever be satisfied...not even the Great War will satisfy Its..."

The boy inhaled, and his eyes opened, clear and conscious. He looked up at Doyle, fully awake for the first time, with a pitiable awareness of his own frailty.

"Joey?"

Joey shook his head with a beatific air of acceptance; then, looking past Doyle, he feebly raised a hand and pointed directly at Sparks.

"He is an *arhanta*," said Joey.

Sparks was watching the boy raptly, a dark edge of dread shading his lowered eyes. There was a sharp barking sound, and Doyle turned back to Joey. He'd heard an explosive cough as the boy's insides fatally hemorrhaged; a flood of hot pink fluid was cascading down from his chin and onto the satin blouse. The boy's weight increased suddenly, settling and collapsing down into Doyle's hands; he could feel that life had entirely fled from Joey's small body. Doyle gently lowered him to rest on the bed.

"Is he dead?" asked Sparks.

Doyle nodded.

"We must go. Quickly," said Sparks. "There'll be too many questions."

Sparks took Doyle by the arm, his fingers digging deep, directing him back into and through the chaotic scene around them toward the door. Nurses, doctors, and guards were still trying to mollify the children. Two bobbies appeared at the door through which Doyle and Sparks had entered. Doyle felt the grip on his arm tighten as Sparks steered Doyle away, and they headed for a door at the far end of the ward. Behind them, the acrobats were moving toward the screens where Joey's body was lying. Sparks and Doyle were about to clear the edge of the crowd when Big Roger the clown stepped directly into their path.

"Wot's 'appened wit' me boy, then, Mister? Got a right to know, 'aven't I? It's me wot paid for 'im, quite the investment that boy is—"

A cry of alarm sounded from behind the screen.

"He's dead! Joey's dead!"

Big Roger grabbed hold of Doyle. "'Ere, what'd you do with 'im, then?"

The bobbies moved through the crowd toward the acrobats, who had emerged and were looking around the ward.

"You killed 'im!" The clown's face twisted with sclerotic rage. "Wot about my readies! You killed my—"

Sparks reached out, and Big Roger was on the ground making muted, strangulated sounds while clutching at his neck, the blow struck with such blinding speed Doyle could not remember seeing it applied.

"Keep walking; don't run," said Sparks.

Doyle pulled up short and shook off Sparks's grip; they looked hard at each other. Doyle's ambivalence shot through his studied mask of passivity, and Sparks did not misinterpret it.

"There! Over there!"

Little Boy Blue

The acrobats had spotted them and were pointing frantically through the crowd. The bobbies headed in their direction.

"Doyle, this is no time—"

"I don't know."

"I can't allow you to stay here—"

"You're telling me I have no choice?"

"It's a longer conversation—"

"We need to have it."

"Not now. For God's sake, man."

Doyle wavered but would not be moved. The bobbies closed in.

"The boy, what he called me: Do you know what an *arhanta* is?" asked Sparks.

Doyle shook his head.

"It means savior."

The bobbies were only a few yards away.

"Here, then, stand clear, you two!" said one of them.

Doyle shoved a bed in their direction, breaking their stride, and then he broke for the door. Sparks flew after him, and they burst through the door into a hospital corridor. An alarm sounded, and the pursuit behind them intensified.

"Which way?" asked Sparks.

Doyle pointed to their left, and they ran, dodging a host of startled patients and doctors and medical paraphernalia. Using his intimate knowledge of the hospital, changing directions frequently—in and out of wards, up and down stairs—and finally through a ground-floor window, Doyle led them to the entrance where Larry waited. A half-dozen bobbies were just arriving via Black Maria; Sparks blew a silver whistle that he'd pulled from his pocket and authoritatively waved them toward the doors.

"Inside, hurry! They're getting away!" shouted Sparks.

The bobbies hustled toward the entrance and collided with the officers and guards who were just running out of the building. A smaller coach pulled in behind the Black Maria; Doyle saw Inspector Leboux step out onto the running board as it slowed.

"Doyle!" Leboux cried. There was a pistol in his hand.

In a rush and clatter of hooves, Larry brought their carriage racing through the half-moon drive directly between them and Leboux, showering the air with gravel. Sparks grabbed Doyle and leapt up onto the moving cab. Through the windows, Doyle could see Leboux aiming his pistol at them, trying to clear a shot. Sparks and Doyle hung on to the rails as Larry steered into the turn; momentum edged them up onto the two outside wheels, a fraction of an inch from toppling over, before the cab crashed back down onto all fours. Doyle and Sparks bounced hard but clung to the frame, arms looped around the bar of the open window.

"Don't stop!" Sparks yelled.

Larry cracked the whip and made straight for the hospital gates ahead. Behind them in the drive, Leboux's carriage and the Black Maria started after them. Hand-cranked siren wailing, a hospital cab was coming directly at them through the gates at a steady clip. There was barely room for two carriages to negotiate the opening when both were at a slow walk; a head-on collision seemed certain.

"Hang on!"

Sparks and Doyle flattened themselves against the outside of the cab as the two vehicles passed within inches. The wheels sparked as they engaged, but the hubs failed to lock. Doyle felt the side of the ambulance brush his shoulder as they rushed clear through the gate. But in the immediate aftermath of their near collision the ambulance driver was not so fortunate; trying to brake as he confronted the following police sent him into a disastrous skid; horses reared and the ambulance went over, blocking the drive and any immediate access to the gate. Leboux's cab stopped short of the wreck; bobbies poured from the Black Maria and rushed to the fallen horses, but it would be too late to effectively follow Larry. He drove Sparks and Doyle, still holding fast to the outer rails of the cab, around a corner out of sight of the hospital gates and into the covering flow of London traffic.

CHAPTER 15

Theatrical Types

To Doyle's surprise, they made for the north, a straight course out of London; it had been his assumption they would return to Battersea to reclaim the engine that had provided their deliverance from Topping. Larry maintained a pace rapid enough to outdistance any pursuit without calling any undue attention to them—it wouldn't be long before the telegraph wires were singing with news of their escape.

Doyle sat uneasily across from Sparks as they drove, Sparks staring moodily out the window, glancing only occasionally at Doyle, and then never meeting his eyes.

Whom do I believe? Doyle was forced to ask himself with such urgency that the logical vivisection of its separate issues proved impossible. There was only the question itself filling his mind, repeating like a church bell.

A lunatic from Bedlam. Was it possible? He was forced to admit that it was so. A man tormented by imagined persecutors. Living in a shadowy world of secret connections to high places—no less than the Queen, for God's sake—constructed by a diseased mind while trapped in the confines of a madman's cell. But Sparks had always seemed so lucid, so supremely rational. Although even lunatics were capable of sustained lucidity, or its flawless simulacrum, as Doyle knew full well; perhaps Sparks's sapient belief in the incredible tales he told was the most damning indictment of his madness. Could Jack actually be all the things he claimed he was? There were the supporting testimonies of Larry and Barry to take into account, but they were recruited criminals, quick to follow and easily influenced, perhaps even knowing accomplices in the charade. A charade to what end? What possible purpose? None occurred to him. If Sparks were truly mad, there might very well be no discernible reason to his actions; the man could be acting without a script, tailoring his stories as he went to suit the cut of the moment's fancy.

A darker question suddenly loomed behind these worrisome speculations; what if there was no Alexander Sparks? Was it possible this man was himself the criminal mastermind he had described his brother to be? He certainly possessed all the same attributed talents—and what other individual had he ever heard described who came closer to fitting the known profile of Alexander Sparks? What if this brooding puzzle of a man seated across from him embodied both brothers at once, fragmented selves residing in the troubled crucible of a single imagination, each believing the other as separate and autonomous, one stalking and killing at will, the other haunted by a memory of foul deeds committed in the eclipse of an obscuring derangement? Did that mean Jack was also the defiler and murderer of his parents? Painful to consider, but couldn't it have been the very commission of those vile acts that had somehow split his mind, shifting responsibility for the unthinkable to a phantom figure that he constantly pursued or felt constantly pursued by?

The cooler side of Doyle's mind rallied in protest; how then to explain the figure in black he'd encountered twice now, the man Jack had identified as his brother? There were the gray hoods and the séance, the destruction of his flat and the madness of Topping, all consistent with Sparks's story, however strange it sounded, all of it his own direct experience. The murders of Petrovitch and Bodger Nuggins, the visions of Spivey Quince and the doomed boy in blue, and the evidence he had seen all too clearly with his own eyes—and felt on his skin; he could still see the vivid welts on his wrist where the ghoul had grabbed him—in the basement of the British Museum. Even if John Sparks was as mad as a March hare, he was only one figure in a crowded, cockeyed landscape that had long since lost the shape and flavor of the everyday world.

Doyle parted the curtain, looked out the window, and tried to purchase a sense of where they were; there was Coram's Fields to the left, that put them on Grey's Inn Road, yes, the carriage was heading due north out of London, toward Islington.

Should he share these wayward thoughts with Sparks? Or was there a more skulduggerous way to test the fidelity of his character? After all, wasn't it just as likely that Leboux's information was at fault? If only he'd had a chance to speak with him, hear firsthand the source of this news about Sparks and more details. That opportunity might now be lost for good; after Doyle had fled from the hospital in full view of his friend, Leboux's patience had surely reached its end. He was a fugitive from justice, plain and simple, and his choices had narrowed considerably: He could either attempt an escape from Sparks to throw himself on the uncertain mercies of the police—risking the untold consequences of Sparks's formidable wrath—or cast his lot with the man and his band of outsiders to whatever uncertain end lay in store.

"Anything in Blavatsky about the Seven or a Black Lord?" asked Sparks.

"What's that?" said a startled Doyle.

"I'm not as conversant as you are with her work: Is there any mention in her writings about the Seven or the Black Lord?" Still deep in thought, Sparks didn't so much as glance at him.

Doyle rummaged through his scattered recollections of Blavatsky. It seemed a hundred years since he had spent that last quiet evening in his rooms, leisurely pondering her text.

"I recall something about an entity—the Dweller on the Threshold," said Doyle, wishing he had the book in front of him. "It could nearly answer to the same description."

"What was the Dweller on the Threshold?"

"A being...an entity of high spiritual origin that, as part of its pilgrim's progress, consciously chose to come down into the world—"

"To live in human form, you mean."

"Yes, as all souls do, according to Blavatsky: a way of learning, matriculation."

"Why was this being different?"

"In its disembodied state, this one supposedly held a place of favor at the right hand of whatever word you wish to use for God. And when it entered the physical world, it fell—I'm trying to remember her wording; this wasn't it precisely—it succumbed to the temptations of material life."

"The ways of the flesh," said Sparks.

"Devoting itself to the accumulation of earthly power and the satisfaction of earthy appetites, turning its back on its exalted spiritual heritage. In this way was conscious evil born into the world."

"The Christians call it Lucifer."

"The boy in blue said it is known by many names."

"The myth of the fallen angel exists in every discovered culture. How did it come to be described as the Dweller on the Threshold?"

"At the end of each term of physical life—it has had more than a few apparently—Blavatsky claims this being, upon leaving the earthly plane, retires to a limbo at the door between worlds, collecting around it the lost, corrupted souls of persons who fell to its influence while alive and followed it blindly to their deaths—"

"Are they the Seven?"

"I don't recall a specific number, but they were spoken of collectively."

"So these twisted devotees are the first to return from this *purgatorium* to physical life," said Sparks, his mind leaping ahead, "where their purpose is to prepare the way—the 'passage'—for their Black Lord who 'dwells on the threshold' between the physical and mystic worlds, awaiting return to the earth."

Doyle nodded. "That does her account of it some small justice. I don't remember her alluding to the being and its acolytes as the Black Lord and Seven; they were simply referred together under the rubric of the Dark Brotherhood."

Sparks fell back into pensive silence. They were by now clattering through the farthest outskirts of London, onto dirt roads through pastoral land. Were they going to venture all the way to Whitby by horse and carriage? A rough two or three days' ride at the least.

"Many of the mediums you spoke with were having disturbing visions," said Sparks.

"Vague sorts. Impressions, feelings. Fleeting and ephemeral, at best."

"No specifics?"

"Only from Spivey Quince and of course the boy he foretold our seeing at the hospital."

"This boy was a genuine medium, in your estimation?"

"I'd say he was an extreme sensitive. Dangerous to speculate without knowing his underlying physical condition, but it seemed to me the impact of the vision that assailed him contributed in no small way to his death."

"As if the vision itself had turned and attacked."

"And the very weight of it had crushed him," said Doyle reluctantly.

Theatrical Types

"What does this suggest to you? That many experiencing these similar visions?"

Doyle thought for a moment. "Something stirring in the plane from which they draw their information. A powerful disturbance, like a storm at sea before it draws within sight of land."

"The equivalent of psychic barometers registering an otherwise invisible change in pressure."

Doyle shifted in his seat. "I admit I'm uncomfortable with the idea."

"In the East, dogs and cats grow restless before an earthquake strikes. We send canaries into mine shafts to detect the presence of deadly gas. Is it so hard to imagine human beings are capable of similarly subtle perceptions?"

"No," said Doyle patiently. "But it doesn't make me any more comfortable."

"The activation of an entity as formidable as the one described as this Dweller on the Threshold would generate quite a thunderhead on whatever plane it resided."

"If such a thing were true—"

"If the return of this being is indeed what the members of the Brotherhood—the Seven—are after, how would these black magicians prepare the Dweller's 'passage' for rebirth?"

"I'm sure I don't know—"

"The spilling of blood? Ritualized murders?"

"Perhaps," said Doyle, growing weary of the interrogation. "I'm not familiar with these things."

"But It would have to be born as a child first, wouldn't It?"

"Maybe they're shopping around for a nice couple in Cheswick to adopt the little nipper."

Sparks ignored the jibe. "A child with blond hair, seen in a vision? Taken from his father against his will, his mother an unwitting conspirator?"

"I'm sorry, Jack, but it's all a bit too much for me. I mean, Blavatsky gets away with this sort of thing, but the reader naturally assumes, or at least I did, that it's all metaphoric or at the very least archaic mythology—"

"Isn't that what you wrote about in your book? The ill use of a child?"

Doyle felt himself go pale; he'd almost forgotten his damned book.

"Is it, Doyle?"

"In part."

"And you wonder why they've come after you with such aggressiveness. What further confirmation do you require?"

THE LIST OF 7

The question hung in the air between them.

"Doyle . . . let me ask you," said Sparks, softening his tone. "Knowing what you do about its history, what do you suppose this Dweller would be on about once it got its feet back on terra firma?"

"Nothing too out of the ordinary, I imagine," said Doyle, refusing to commit himself emotionally to the answer he knew was correct. "World dominion, total enslavement of the human race, that sort of thing."

"With a good deal more sophisticated weaponry available to the bugger this time around. Our capacity for mass butchery has increased a hundredfold."

"I would have to agree with you," said Doyle, recalling the presence on the list of Drummond and his burgeoning munitions empire.

Satisfied with the impact he'd made, Sparks sat back in his seat. "Then we'd best put a stop to this business straightaway, hadn't we?"

"Hmm. Quite."

But first I need to know you're not one of them, thought Doyle. I need to ask you why I should believe you're who you say you are, and I can't, I can't just now, either ask or believe, because if you are mad, you may not know or recognize the difference, and by asking I endanger my own life.

"What is an *arhanta*?" asked Doyle.

"You've never encountered the term?"

Doyle shook his head.

"*Arhantas* are Adepts in the Tibetan Mystery schools. Possessing spiritual powers of the highest order, an elite warrior class. Perhaps the most extraordinary thing about them is the degree of sacrifice they are required to make."

"What sort of sacrifice?"

"An *arhanta* spends the body of his life developing certain arcane—you might call them psychic—abilities. At the height of his strength, after years of hard, thankless study, the *arhanta* is asked to entirely forsake the use and exercise of those powers and to undertake a life of silent, anonymous contemplation, far removed from the centers of worldly life. It is said there are twelve *arhantas* alive in physical life at any given time, and it is their radiant presence and selfless service alone that prevents mankind from self-destruction."

"They're not supposed to use these alleged powers to fight evil?"

"The teachings say that has never happened. It would be a violation of their sacred trust, with far more grievous consequences."

Doyle chewed on that thought with no little difficulty. "Why would

Theatrical Types

the boy call you one, then? On the face of it, you don't readily answer to the description."

"I have no idea," said Sparks. He seemed as genuinely conflicted and confused as Doyle.

They wrestled with these thorny contradictions awhile. Doyle was jostled out of his brown study by the carriage running over a rough patch as Larry led them off the road onto a cart path leading through a dense copse of woods. Emerging into a clearing on the far side, they were greeted by the heartwarming sight of the Sterling 4-2-2 they'd left in Battersea, waiting on north-running tracks. Smoke belched from its stack, the furnace stoked and ready to roll. Behind it trailed a full coal hopper and, even more encouragingly, a passenger car. Emerging from the cab with a welcome wave was none other than Brother Barry, late of Pentonville Prison. There was nothing of the sentimental reunion about this meeting, however; it was grim, fast business, and hardly a word was spoken. Effects were transferred to the train, horses set loose to run, and the carriage carefully concealed in the woods. Sparks and Doyle boarded the passenger car, and the brothers took to the engine. Within moments they were under way. The sun slid low on the horizon; they would make most of their northern run at night.

❁   ❁   ❁

Although customized, the passenger car was Spartanly appointed: four double seats facing each other, removable tables between them. Two bunked sleeping berths in a rear compartment. Planked wooden floors, oil lamps set in otherwise bare walls. A simple galley with a loaded icebox, stocked with provisions for the journey.

Sparks assembled one of the tables and sat down to pore over a packet of maps. Doyle took a seat across the car from him and utilized the silence to arrange his medical inventory and clean and reload his revolver. He obeyed an instinct to keep his pistol close at hand.

After an hour had passed, Barry joined them and laid out a peasant's supper of bread, apples, cheese, salted cabbage, and red wine. Sparks ate alone at the table, making notations and working with his maps. Doyle sat with Barry in the galley.

"How did you get out?" asked Doyle.

"Coppers let me go. 'Alf an hour after you went off."

"Why would they do that?"

"Tried to follow me, didn't they? Hoped I'd lead 'em straight to you."

"And you eluded them."

"Only in a trice."

Doyle nodded and took a bite of apple, trying not to appear over-anxious. "How did you know to meet us where you did?"

"Telegram. Waitin' for me at the train yard," said Barry, with a nod toward Sparks, indicating the telegram's sender.

That followed logically; Sparks must have sent the wire when he was out this morning, Doyle thought. He finished his wine and poured another cup. The hum and rattle of the tracks and the wine's warming properties applied an agreeably stabilizing remedy to his apprehensions.

"Barry, have you ever seen Alexander Sparks?" asked Doyle, keeping his voice low but not unduly confidential.

Barry cocked an eyebrow, glancing at him sideways. "Odd question."

"Why is it odd?"

"That's the maestro's middle name, idn't it?" said Barry, nodding towards Sparks. "Jonathan Alexander Sparks. That's my under-standing."

Confident their voices wouldn't carry over the racket of the train, Doyle casually turned his back to Sparks, placing himself directly between him and Barry. Doyle felt a trickle of cold sweat slide down his back.

"You mean to say," said Doyle, "that you've never heard Jack mention a brother by the name of Alexander?"

"Don't mean much if he 'adn't. Doesn't gab about hisself. Don't gab much to me in any case." Barry bit into a plug of chewing tobacco. "Larry's the talker. He could jaw the shine off a mirror and sell you the frame. Beggin' your pardon. I just remembered Larry's expectin' his supper."

Barry tipped his cap, wrapped the remainders of the meal in a bundle for Larry, and went back to the engine. Doyle stood alone in the galley, staring across the car at Sparks. His worst fears ran riot through his mind, trampling the shards of security to which he had been struggling to cling. When Sparks glanced up at him, Doyle responded with a false, overquick smile and raised his glass in anemic bonhomie, feeling every bit as exposed and remorseful as a red-handed pickpocket. Sparks turned back to his work without any notable reaction.

Doyle was stricken; what was he to do now? Hadn't his treacherous thoughts been writ as plain on his face as a sandwich-board advert? Every step he took seemed to be precisely the wrong one, ferrying him deeper into still and murky waters. He made a small, efficient dumb show of yawning and picking up his bag.

"Think I'll turn in," said Doyle.

"Fine," answered Sparks.

"Long day. Long, long day."

Sparks did not respond. Doyle's feet felt rooted to the floor.

"Berths in the back then," he said with a smile, pointing congenially toward the rear of the car. Why was he making these ridiculous and obvious statements?

"Right," said Sparks, without looking up.

"Rhythm of the train. Comforting. Ought to help us sleep, that. Rocking motion. Clickety-clack, clickety-clack." Doyle could scarcely believe the words were leaving his mouth; he was chattering like some demented nanny.

Sparks took a lingering look at him. "Are you feeling all right, old boy?"

Doyle's antic smile lit up like a fun house. "Me? Tip-top. Never better!"

Sparks winced slightly. "Better leave off the wine then."

"Right. Off to dreamland!" Doyle couldn't stop grinning to save his life.

Sparks nodded and went back to his studies. Doyle finally convinced his legs to move and walked back to the berths. "Off to dreamland"? What had gotten into him?

Doyle stood before the bunks debating which would be the safer to accommodate his doubts and fears for the night. This took some time. When Sparks glanced back at him again, Doyle smiled and waved, then climbed into the lower bunk and pulled the curtains shut, sequestering himself in the cubicle.

Staring at the bunk above, Doyle clutched his bag to his chest and held the revolver tightly in his hand. Scenarios of doom hovered in his mind like enraged hummingbirds. If he comes after me, thought Doyle, I won't go down without a fight. Maybe I should just fire a few preemptive bullets into the upper bunk while he's asleep, give the emergency-stop cord a rip, and slip away into the wilderness.

Doyle peered discreetly out the crack in the curtains; he could see Sparks's back, hunched over his work, reading, writing, looking through a magnifying glass. Even his posture suggested a hitherto unnoticed mania: cramped, nervy, and obsessive. How readily apparent the man's madness seemed to him; how could it have escaped his attention until now? Distractions, yes, there had been no shortage of them, not to mention that the man's unquestioned genius put up such an impenetrable screen it was nearly impossible to detect where invention ceased and true character began. But still Doyle chided himself; for all his observational acuity the signs of Sparks's instability had been there all along: the moody silences, the disguises, the veiled grandiosity—*arhanta* indeed!—his fixation with secrecy and global conspiracies, the folderol that passed for his criminal filing system— maybe those cards held nothing but random scribblings; lunatics typically create entire worlds animated by nothing but private, delusional significance. And there was no lingering question about the man's talent and capacity for violence. He would be spending the night in a space no larger than a good-sized steamer trunk with one of the most dangerous men alive.

Time passed in this fashion. Sleep was out of the question; rest itself was tenuous. Doyle hardly dared utter a sound or move a muscle; *Better let Sparks think I'm asleep, passive and unsuspecting.* His body was plagued by a painful oversensitivity: his mouth grew dry and cottony; his legs felt like stilts. Every blink of his eyes produced a clap as loud as castanets.

He heard stirring in the car. He longed to know what time it was, but reaching for his watch seemed far too complicated a procedure to initiate. Slowly shifting his weight, Doyle reached over and parted the curtains; Sparks was no longer at the table. He was out of sight altogether, but only half the car was visible from Doyle's limited vantage. There was a sound at the door to the engine, also out of view; the latch being thrown, the door was now locked. Sparks moved back into Doyle's range of vision, then out again. A repeated click of metal on metal. Closing the curtains on the car windows; those were the rings as they slid along the rods. Then Sparks moved from one wall fixture to the next, rolling down the wicks on the oil lamps; the room darkened. Door locked, curtains closed, lights drawn low. Either he's turning in, thought Doyle—but why would he lock the door against Barry and Larry? And on a moving train!—or he's setting the stage to make his fatal attack.

Doyle brought the revolver to the edge of the curtain and braced himself, but Sparks made no move to the rear; he was still walking around the cabin. Pacing restlessly. He clasped and unclasped his hands several times, ran his fingers through his hair, stopped and stood with a hand pressed hard to his forehead, then resumed pacing again. He's trying to decide whether to kill me or not, Doyle couldn't help thinking. Then, with one sweep of his arm, Sparks cleared the maps off the table, took a small leather case from the inner pocket of his jacket, set it down on the table, and opened it. Doyle saw a glint of light on metal; he strained to make out the case's contents, but Sparks still moved between him and the table, and the light in the room was too dim for details.

Sparks wheeled and looked suddenly back at the sleeping berths; Doyle resisted the impulse to snatch shut the curtains the fraction they were open. I'm in total darkness, Doyle said to himself, he can't possibly see me. Doyle didn't move, his hand frozen in air, lightly touching the curtains. Sparks looked long and hard and then turned back, apparently satisfied he wasn't observed. Sparks's hands moved to the objects on the table. Doyle heard the clink of metal on glass. What did he have in that packet?

Sparks took off his coat and began a complicated sequence of actions completely screened from Doyle's view. When Sparks turned back, in profile now, vividly outlined by the lamp on the wall behind him, Doyle saw a syringe in his hand. Sparks tested the plunger; the needle emitted a fine spray into the air.

Good God, thought Doyle, he means to kill me by way of lethal injection. Doyle's finger tightened on the trigger, ready to gun down Sparks where he stood. But Sparks did not turn toward the berths. He set down the syringe, unbuttoned the left sleeve of his shirt, and rolled it over his elbow. He fixed a length of slender twine around his bicep and pulled it taut with his teeth. Flexing and releasing his left arm, he tapped at a vein in the hollow of his forearm, swabbed the area with antiseptic, picked up the syringe from the table, and without hesitation squidged it into his arm. He paused, inhaled evenly once, twice, then pushed smoothly forward on the plunger, emptying its contents into his bloodstream. He extracted the empty needle, set it down, and released the rope from his arm. Sparks staggered slightly as the needle's message was swiftly delivered. He moaned once, softly, a lurid sound, full of hideous appetite gnawing on satisfaction. His body shook with illicit excitement as he surrendered to the seductive intruder.

A morphine derivative? thought Doyle, judging from the drug's visible effects. Maybe cocaine? He gladly embraced his analyzing as a welcome refuge from the horror of what he was watching.

Sparks closed his eyes and weaved unsteadily, the intoxication swimming toward its heady peak. The moment of his rapture seemed hideously extended. When it passed, Sparks meticulously gathered up the contents of the packet and relaced them. Doyle saw three small vials of liquid set alongside the needle before the case disappeared into Sparks's coat. The cleanup completed, Sparks slumped down into a chair and moaned again, involuntarily. This time the pure expression of sensual ecstasy was tempered by a tone of invidious guilt and abject self-disgust.

Despite his recent suspicions, Doyle was nearly overcome by a Hippocratic impulse to compassionately rush to his aid, but common sense froze him in his tracks. A secret enslavement to narcotics hardly decreased the chance that Sparks was out of his mind; it made the possibility that much more likely. There was no denying Sparks's shame in the behavior; the man kept it from his closest confederates. As great a hazard as he might pose to anyone else, it was clear Jack Sparks provided just as real a danger to himself.

Sparks rose to his feet again and moved from sight. More sounds. Clasps being thrown. A pizzicato plucking of strings. Sparks stepped back into view, holding a violin to his neck. He tested the bow across the bridge, turning the pegs, checking for tune. Then he leaned against the back of a chair and began to play. A black dissonant thrumming issued from the instrument, but there was a cold and brutal sense to it, not melody precisely, it bore no evidence of song, this order of notes could never have been set to paper; it seemed rather the direct expression of a terrible wound, sharp, torn and ragged, flushed with pain. Doyle knew this was the sound of Sparks's secret heart, and the burden it placed on the listener's mind was nearly as harsh as the one it sprang from and so eloquently described. Before long it reached an unresolvable impasse. There was no crescendo, no climax; it simply had to stop. Sparks lowered his head, slumped down onto the arm of the chair, and his arms hung limply at his sides. Doyle's breath shuddered in his chest; a sob wanted to escape.

Sparks slowly raised the violin again and began to play a second piece. This one possessed both coherent rhythm and harmony: a low, sweet threnody, laced with grief, a trickle from a dammed-up sea of unshed tears. It sent into the air a vibration of almost unbearable emotional resonance. Doyle could not see Sparks's face in the shadows, only the graceful belly of the instrument and the shape of the man's arm drawing the bow. He was grateful for the relative discretion of the sight. He knew that, however they had met their end and at whosoever's hand, he was listening to Sparks mourn for his dead.

The piece ended. Sparks did not move for many minutes; then, with considerable effort, he roused himself from the somnolent embrace of the narcotic, returned the instrument to its case, and walked slowly toward the back. His step was faltering and uncertain; thrown off balance by the movement of the car, he was more than once forced to support himself against the walls. He stopped in front of the berths. Doyle drew back from the curtain, but through the gap he could see Sparks's thighs swaying. Sparks lifted a foot onto Doyle's berth and hoisted himself, hesitating halfway up, trying to re-center his balance; Doyle could see the buckles shining dully on his boots. With a guttural grunt, Sparks pulled himself the remainder of the way and landed heavily on the thin ticking of the upper bunk. His body shifted once and did not move again. He was lying on his back. Doyle listened to the rhythm of Sparks's breathing as it flattened, growing shallow and strained.

Doyle lifted the pistol, his heart beating wildly. I could fire now, he thought. Put the gun to the mattress, empty the chambers, and kill him. He placed the barrel gently against the bed above and cocked the hammer. He worried about the sound, but there was no audible change in the respiration above; Sparks was, in every sense of the phrase, lost to the world. Doyle lost track of how long he lay there, pistol in hand, on the thin edge of that fateful decision. Something in him prevented his pulling the trigger. He couldn't name the reason. He knew it had to do with the music he'd heard, but he fell into sleep while trying to discover why.

❖   ❖   ❖

The gun was still in Doyle's hand when he woke, but the hammer had been eased to rest. Dirty gray light seeped through the curtains on the outer window. He reached over to part them and looked outside.

The train was still clipping along at a considerable pace. They had driven into the leading edge of a storm during the night. The sky was deeply overcast. A fresh mantle of snow frosted the flat, featureless land; more of the stuff gently fell in puffy clusters the size of dandelions.

Doyle rubbed the film from his eyes. He was hungry, sore, drained by the emotional exertions of the long night before. He looked at his watch: seven-thirty. He could smell shag tobacco and strong, brewing black tea, but it took the unexpected sound of laughter to rouse him from his bunk to the front of the car.

"Gin!" he heard Larry say.

"Blast you for a sod!" said Sparks.

More laughter. Larry and Sparks were playing cards at the table, a tea service laid out beside them. Sparks was smoking a long-stemmed pipe.

"How-do-you-do and look at this fine news," said Larry, picking over the cards as Sparks laid down his hand. "These stray members of the royal family you've clutched to your bosom will cost you a queen's ransom."

"Don't torment me, you devil—ah, Doyle!" said Sparks cheerfully. "We were just debating about whether to wake you; got a fresh pot here, care for a cuppa souchong?"

"Please," said Doyle, requiring no further invitation to join them and help himself immediately to the offered plate of biscuits and hard-boiled eggs.

Sparks poured the tea as Larry totaled up his cards and added the resulting figure to a long, snaking column on a well-traveled pad of paper.

"That's the game then, guv. More's the pity," said Larry. "My stars and stripes, you're in a pretty fix now, I can tell you, break out the violins."

"What's our running total then?"

"Roundin' off the figure—and I can gladly do you that small favor, can't I?—you look to owe me . . . five thousand, six hundred forty quid."

Doyle nearly choked on his tea. "Lord . . ."

"We've been at the same game for five years," explained Sparks. "The man's simply unbeatable."

"Tide's bound to turn your way eventual, guv," said Larry, reshuf-fling the cards with alarming adroitness. "Every dog has his day."

"That's what he'd like me to believe."

"Wot else is it but 'ope of eventual good fortune wot keeps bringing you back to the table? Man's gotta have 'ope to live."

"I'm convinced he cheats, Doyle," said Sparks. "I just haven't dis-covered his methods."

"I keep tellin' him there's no substitute for the favor of old Dame Luck," said Larry, with a theatrical wink at Doyle.

"They haven't found an adequate one for money yet, either," said Sparks good-naturedly, rising from the table.

"A man's got a right to lay somethin' aside for his idle retirin' years, don't he? He wants a bit of leisure and layin' about when the stems and pies give out, as we all knows they must in the end." Larry offered the deck for Doyle to cut and smiled cheesily. "Care for a game, guv?"

"Doyle, I'll not say a word regarding the decision you're about to make other than this: It's a good deal easier to resist the first step on the road to ruin than any of the thousand that inevitably follow."

"I'll decline, thanks all the same, Larry," said Doyle.

"Cheers, Doc," said Larry happily, fanning out a handful of aces before pocketing the cards. "It's plain to see you learned something in that fancy college besides where to find a man's ticker."

"I'm a firm believer that if one must entertain a vice, better not to take on more than one at a time," said Doyle, with a casual look at Sparks.

"And what might your one solitary vice be, Doyle?" asked Sparks jauntily, leaning against the galley, arms folded, puffing on his pipe.

"Belief in a man's innate goodness."

"Ho-ho!" said Larry. "That's not a vice so much as a guaranteed noose round yer neck."

"Naïveté, then," said Sparks.

"So might a more cynical mind call it," said Doyle evenly.

"And you might call it ..."

"Faith."

Sparks and Doyle looked at each other. Doyle saw a tightening around the corners of Sparks's eyes. Had he shamed some vulnerable place in him, or was it simply a reflex of remorse? Whatever the case, Sparks retreated from the openness of their exchange, the jocularity of the mood he'd built with Larry forfeiting its bright sheen.

"Long may it serve you well," said Sparks.

" 'In God We Trust,' " said Larry. "That's what they stamp on the money in America. There's the proper place for faith, you ask me."

Sparks started for the door to the engine. "I've squandered enough of my dwindling fortune in your direction for one sitting, Larry; time to earn your keep and shovel some coal—"

"Right with you, sir."

"You're more than welcome to join us, Doyle."

"A bit of exercise in the fresh air would do me well," said Doyle.

Doyle followed them out the door, traversed the agitated coupling, and climbed onto the tender. Sparks gave a wave to Barry, hand on the throttle, bundled up ahead of them in the engine cab. Each man grabbed a shovel and went to work pouring fuel into the scuttle. The cold and whipping wind sent up motes of coal that bit into their skin; driven snowflakes exploded on contact with their clothes, crystals melting in the woolen threads, dissolving into the black of the scattering dust.

"Where are we?" shouted Doyle.

"An hour from York," Sparks yelled back. "Three hours to Whitby, if the weather holds."

The cold inspired them to great exertions, the quicker to remove themselves from its glare. Soon the fire in the engine burned hotter than a sinner's conscience.

THE LIST OF 7

❀   ❀   ❀

Whitby began as a sixth-century fishing village, grown over the years to a minor port, a seaside resort in the short summer of Northumbria, but in the depths of winter a forbidding destination to any but those required to seek it out by either trade or custom. The river Esk had carved a deep rift between two summits as it made its way to the sea where it formed a natural, deep harbor, and in that narrow valley the village first found life. Over the years, the community sprawled to incorporate both hillsides. Some combination of mood and the harsh landscape had down the centuries created a fertile haven for stern religious feeling, ofttimes fervor. The crumbling Celtic abbey of St. Hilda dominated the high headland south of the village proper, as it had on that site since before England had known kings. The ruins of the ancient abbey cast a long shadow over its less austere successor, Goresthorpe Abbey, which shared the southern hill, halfway between its forerunner and the town. Its spire was the first landmark Doyle noticed as the train pulled into the station. The hour was not quite noon, but few people were about; those that were moved in halting submission to the bitter cold of the deepening storm and lowering sky. The town seemed mired in a gray and fog-bound hibernation. Barry saw to the disposition of the train, while Larry took charge of their bags, settling them at a nearby inn recommended by the stationmaster. Sparks immediately recruited Doyle for a visit to Bishop Pillphrock's abbey.

No carriages were available at the station, every shop and service battening down in anticipation of the storm's worsening, so they crossed the bridge and walked a mile to the southern slope. A dense sea fog rolled in from the harbor and together with the falling snow reduced visibility to zero. Bent against the wind, they ascended the steep and winding stairway up the hill, mufflers protecting their faces from the growing gale, which howled more fiercely the farther up they climbed.

Arriving at Goresthorpe Abbey, the more contemporary parish church, they found snow accumulating in blowing drifts and the doors to both church and rectory secured tight. No lights burned in the windows; no signs of life inside. Sparks raised the thick iron ring on the rectory's massive wooden door and slammed it three times against its plate, the sound quickly smothered by the rising blanket of snow. Sparks knocked again. Doyle, his mind benumbed by the cold, tried in vain to remember which day of the week this was: a day of rest for the clergy? Where else would they be?

"There's no one here," said a deep and resonant voice behind them.

They turned; a giant of a man stood before them, six-and-a-half feet tall if he was an inch, cloaked against the cold as they were, but he wore no hat; a leonine shock of red hair crowned his massive head, and his face was framed by a thick red beard encrusted with icicles.

"We're looking for the Bishop Pillphrock," said Sparks.

"You won't find him here, friends. The diocese is deserted," the stranger said, advancing. The musical lilt of Erin danced in his voice. His face was broad and welcoming; his great size suggested power but no menace. "They've all gone, at least three days now."

"Would they be at the other abbey then?" asked Doyle.

"You mean in the ruins?" said the man, turning in the direction of the ancient abbey and pointing with a silver-tipped walking stick of black zebra wood. "There's been no shelter within those walls for near to five hundred years."

"This is Bishop Pillphrock's diocese?" asked Sparks.

"That is my understanding. I don't know the man. I'm a stranger to Whitby myself, a condition I assume you share, or do I assume too much?"

"Not at all. But I must say you look familiar to me, sir," said Sparks. "Do we know one another?"

"Are you gentlemen up from London?"

"We are."

"Have you a passing familiarity with the theatrical scene there?"

"More than passing," said Sparks.

"Perhaps that explains it," said the man, extending his hand. "Abraham Stoker, manager to Henry Irving and his theatrical production company. Bram to my friends."

Henry Irving! My God, thought Doyle; how many times had he stood for hours to watch the legendary Irving on the stage? Lear, Othello, Benedick to Ellen Terry's Beatrice, the greatest actor of his generation and perhaps the age. Such was the magnitude of his fame that Doyle felt dumbstruck by proximity to someone even remotely connected to the man.

"Of course that's it then," said Sparks companionably. "I have seen you on many occasions, first nights and the like."

Sparks and Doyle completed their side of the introductions.

"And may I ask what brings you gentlemen to this hibernal corner of the earth on the deadest night of winter?" Some note of cautious reserve in Stoker's voice rendered the query as a good deal more than idle curiosity.

Sparks and Doyle looked at each other. "We might do well to ask you the selfsame question," said Sparks evenly.

There followed a short silence in which each sized up the other, during which whatever Stoker sought in Sparks he apparently found.

"I know a pub," he said, "where we might sit by the fire and more congenially satisfy each other's interest."

❖   ❖   ❖

Half an hour's trudge through the thickening tempest brought them to the Rose and Thistle, a post-and-beam establishment in the center of town overlooking the banks of the Esk. The snow now fell so rapidly it formed connective bowers between rocks in the channel below. Hot mugs of coffee laced with Irish whiskey warmed their hands as the three men shook off the cold in the embers of the dying afternoon. Idle chat about the couplings and customs of various well-known or otherwise notorious theatrical types—and what outrageously melodramatic personal lives they all seemed to lead, thought Doyle—had occupied their journey and the early minutes after their arrival at the public house. In the void of the first conversational lapse, with a marked change in tone toward the hushed, anxious, and mesmeric, Stoker, unsolicited, began his tale.

"As you well know, Mr. Sparks, the world of the theater is a terrifically small community—a stone doesn't enter that pond without the far end receiving immediate word of the ripples—and whereas most of the talk-of-the-town is as perishable as a bucket of prawns in the noonday sun—as there's always some sensational, up-to-the-minute chat coming along as grist for the rumor mills—it takes a good deal more than the usual fare to capture one's interest for the turn of a single evening, let alone shock one into a state of more or less sustained agitation. Theatrical types love their gossip, and it usually goes down easier with a generous dusting of salt."

Stoker had not spent his years around the stage in vain, his delivery practiced to wring maximum dramatic effect from every pause or inflection, but the result was so spontaneous and virtually laden with import to come that the listener was effortlessly persuaded to deliver himself into this storyteller's crafty hands. Doyle found himself aching to provoke the man forward with questions, but he took his cue from Sparks, held his peace, and sat forward on the edge of his chair in restive anticipation.

Theatrical Types

"A strange story began making the rounds of my little world about a month ago and reached my ears one night in the green room of the Lyceum Theatre not long after. Even allowing for the distortions and inevitable embellishments common to any well-traveled trifle, there was at its center such a persistent, original kernel of collusion and intrigue that it took absolute command of my attentions."

"What was it?" blurted Doyle.

Without looking at him, Sparks made a slight gesture toward Doyle, trying to gently dampen his eagerness.

"The word came down to me," resumed Stoker, "that a certain high-placed gentleman—he was not mentioned by name—through a series of obscure intermediaries, had retained certain members of a provincial theatrical company—actors, professionals, likewise unknown—to enact a newly scripted performance in a private London house. Not a play or a piece ever intended for the stage, mind you—an original creation. One time only, never to be repeated. Performed for an audience of one. No contractual arrangement, other than certain verbal agreements, were entered into. We might ask what motivated these actors to accept such an unorthodox assignment? A disproportionately large sum of money for this performance was guaranteed; half apparently disbursed to them ahead of time. The other half would be receivable upon completion.

"What was the purpose of this mysterious performance? It was never stated to them, but the implication echoed that, which I'm sure you will recall, of Hamlet's second-act importunity to the Player King: as in the Bard, this reenactment of a cold-blooded murder was intended to achieve some provocation in the sole member of its audience."

"Murder," said Doyle. He felt a squeamish tightening in his throat. A sidelong glance to Sparks saw him return a look of equal intensity.

"Who that person might have been or what his or her desired reaction was to be was never remarked upon. Even at that, the story was up to snuff as a bona fide nine-day wonder, but this dog has a tail that grew stranger still. During the performance, new and unanticipated characters made an impromptu entrance onto the scene, carrying these itinerant players far beyond the scope of what they had so carefully rehearsed. Something went terribly awry." Stoker leaned in closer to them, lowering his voice to a hush. "Actual blood was shed."

By some superhuman effort, Doyle did not say a word, although he was not at all certain he could keep his heart from leaping out of his throat.

"The players scattered," Stoker went on. "One of their number had fallen at the scene and was never recovered. Presumed dead." Stoker paused, looking back and forth between them.

Don't let it be her, thought Doyle. Dear God, if she's alive, my own life before hers.

"Needless to say, the survivors feared for their lives, not without reason. They sought protection in the shelter of the only safe haven they knew and rejoined their original company."

"The Manchester Players," said Sparks.

Stoker did not so much as bat an eye. "Yes. The unfortunate Manchester Players."

Stoker removed and unfolded a flier from his coat, trumpeting the Manchester Players' production of *The Revenger's Tragedy*, the same design as the one they had discovered on the desk in Rathborne and Sons. The dates advertised an engagement the previous week in the nearby city of Scarborough. A small strip pasted diagonally across the poster read CANCELED.

"Upon hearing this, I tracked the rumor to its source: A stage manager once in my employ heard it from an actor who had in turn left the Manchester troupe on family business while they were playing London last fall. Intrigued, I made some inquiries and learned their itinerary from a booking agent. This was December twenty-eighth; that same day the Manchester Players reached Nottingham, where they had a two-day engagement. That same afternoon they were rejoined by two of the actors who had participated in the ruse—"

"How many were in it altogether?" Damn the man's vanity and his orderly unfolding of information; Doyle felt fully justified in asking.

"Four," said Stoker. "Two men, two women."

"Which of these had fallen at the scene?"

"Doyle—" said Sparks.

"I must know: which one?"

"One of the men," said Stoker. He paused now, not petulantly, but in a way that demanded respect to both the gravity of the tale and faith in his expertise as its teller.

"Please, continue," said Doyle, his heart beating ever faster.

"On that night of December twenty-eighth, at their hotel in Nottingham, these same two members of the troupe disappeared. Although they had stated to their confreres that they feared for their lives—and indeed took all commonsensical precautions to ensure their safety; windows and door secured, lights left burning—when the morning arrived, these two were gone from their beds, without a trace, luggage left behind, without any visible signs of struggle. Considering the extremity of their state of mind, it seemed to others in the company

Theatrical Types

not altogether perplexing that the two had decided during the night to take flight. At least that is what was presumed until the discovery was made during the troupe's evening performance." Stoker took a long draught from his drink; he seemed to require it. "Are you familiar with *The Revenger's Tragedy*, Mr. Sparks?"

"I am," said Sparks.

"A broad meller and a bloody bit of Grand Guignol," said Stoker. "Not exactly an edifying spectacle; plays to the cheap seats, as we say in my business. There's a steady stream of gratuitous savagery throughout, but its denouement delivers a particularly vivid session with the guillotine, featuring a stage effect that can only be described as a severing bit of ultrarealism. That night, as the property master went about his backstage task of placing props in all the proper places, he checked the hooded basket that rests below the blade. Inside that basket were the wooden heads used to simulate the remains of the recently dispatched. Later that evening, during the performance's climactic scene, when the lid was lifted to display the contents of the basket...inside were the heads of these two missing actors."

"Good Lord. Good Lord," said Doyle. Chief among the commingling of feelings Doyle felt pulsing through him was a dizzying sensation of relief: Jack Sparks had been with him throughout the night of December 28—on the road, and onboard ship, between Cambridge and Topping. If these murders were the work of Alexander Sparks, and they bore the gruesome and unmistakably original stamp of his foul hand, then clearly his fears that the two brothers were one and the same man were groundless.

"The actor who made the discovery fainted onstage. The performance was, of course, suspended, and all the Manchester Players' following engagements were summarily canceled by wire that same night. The next morning I first learned of the killings and traveled immediately to Nottingham, arriving late on the afternoon of the twenty-ninth. But it seems that before any of the chores regarding the disposition of their business could be conducted—return of received receipts, packing and shipping of costumes, scenery, and the like—the rest of this traveling company of players had gone missing, simply vanished, just as the first two had disappeared—hotel bill unpaid, bags and personal effects left in their rooms. The local constabulary were only too happy to attribute their sudden departure to the still lingering perception of actors as opportunistic gypsies fleeing from creditors, and perhaps from their culpable involvement in as unsavory a pair of murders as that quiet Midlands community would ever hope to see."

"How many in the troupe altogether?" asked Sparks.

263

"Eighteen."

Sparks shook his head slowly. "I fear we will not see them again."

Stoker looked at him for a long moment before responding, "I share your concern, Mr. Sparks."

"This murdered couple, they were a man and a woman?" asked Doyle.

"Man and wife. And the woman six months pregnant," said Stoker, his repugnance at the atrocity surfacing for the first time from under the polish of his delivery.

The couple he'd seen at the séance, thought Doyle, the young couple seated beside him, the working-class man and his pregnant wife. So that meant the medium and the dark-skinned man were the genuine article, not for hire, they'd been on the inside of the job. Which meant the man killed at the scene was the actor hired to play the part of George B. Rathborne.

"Excuse me, Mr. Stoker," said Doyle urgently. "Is there a stage effect, a way of realistically simulating the cutting of someone's throat, with a knife or razor?"

"Not difficult at all," said Stoker. "The blade would have a hollow edge, and on it a slit to an interior cavity filled with fluid, triggered by a button which the holder would push as he drew it across the skin."

"The fluid would be . . ."

"Stage blood. A mix of dye and glycerin. Sometimes animal's blood."

Pig's blood on the floorboards of 13 Cheshire Street.

She's alive. She's alive, I know it, thought Doyle.

"There were four actors involved; you've accounted for three, what happened to the fourth, the second woman?"

Stoker nodded. "I knew this poor company had not left Nottingham of their own volition, if in fact they ever got out alive. Thus confronted with the most confounding mystery I have ever in my life encountered and in light of the profound disinterest of the police, I undertook to pursue what I could learn of their fate myself. I am a writer of fiction, you see, or so I aspire to be. My family obligations necessitate my work in theater management, but writing is the means whereby I derive my greatest personal satisfaction."

Doyle nodded, irritated at the intrusion of the man's self-interest but sympathetically aware of how his own good nature was often at odds with the impulse to mine the rough ore of his experience for gold.

"My first action was to obtain a roster of company names from the hotel in Nottingham, then track the schedule of the Manchester Players to the next few cities on their tour, on the chance they had made some plan to regroup down the road and one of them or more might surface there. That took me to Huddlesfield, then York on New Year's Eve, on to Scarborough, and finally here, to Whitby, two days ago. I checked with the theaters in each city, and the hotels they had reserved to lay over. I watched stations and piers for arrivals and departures, visited restaurants and pubs touring actors were known to frequent. I questioned tailors and cobblers; actors are in constant need of repairs to shoes and costumes while on the road. For all that, I had not had, in any of these cities, a single encouraging response. I was indeed on the verge of returning to London when yesterday afternoon I happened upon a laundress in Whitby who had the day before taken in a woman's black satin dress damaged with a peculiarly persistent red stain—"

Sparks stood bolt upright. Doyle looked at him; he was wearing the most curious expression he had ever seen on the man's face. Doyle turned to see what could have wrought such an effect in him.

She was standing in the doorway. She was looking for Stoker, and her face wore the small, concentrated satisfaction of having found him, when her eyes traveled to his companions. The impact of seeing, and a moment later recognizing, Doyle appeared to weaken her; splotches of color rushed to her cheeks, and she put out a hand to the wall for support. Doyle immediately rose to his feet and moved to her, but he had no sense, or later, memory, of movement. There was only her face, the pale, delicate oval that had so haunted his thoughts and dreams, the soft black curls that framed her forehead before cascading gently to her shoulders. The noble eyes and full rose-pink lips. The elegant, swanlike gracefulness of her white neck. Unmarked, unscarred.

As he reached her, Doyle held out his hands, and she unhesitatingly took both in greeting, stepping forward to him even as she seemed to retreat, full of surrender and fear and apology uncertain of its reception. Realizing the forgiving welcome of his look, she let her weight list gently back against the door; it was the slightest, but to Doyle the most stunning, yielding to the turbulence of her feelings. She looked at him and looked away repeatedly, unable to hold the fullness of his gaze for any length of time. Emotions played across her face with the clarity and speed of minnows in a shallow stream. She seemed temperamentally incapable of any intentional deception; her beauty provided only the most quicksilver transparency to her innermost looking glass. Feeling the warm, moist touch of her hands, Doyle realized with a jolt that they had never spoken a single word to one another. Tears came freely to his eyes. He searched through his mind, quite sure he hadn't the remotest idea of how to begin.

"Are you all right?" he finally asked.

She nodded, repeatedly, trying to find her voice. There were tears glistening in her eyes as well.

"I had no hope that you could have been alive," he said, letting go of her hands, trying to keep his emotions in check.

"I had none," she said finally, her voice a dusky contralto, "but that which you, sir, by your courage and kindness had given me."

"But you are alive," said Doyle. "Here. That's what matters."

She looked up at him and held his look and nodded again. Her eyes were large, bracketed by dark, shapely brows, slanted appealingly downward at the outer corners, their color a startling sea green.

"You don't know how often I've thought of your face," she said, reaching out a tentative hand to touch him, withdrawing before making contact.

"What is your name?"

"Eileen."

"We must straightaway remove ourselves from common view," Sparks's voice intruded sharply. He was suddenly standing beside Doyle. "We'll use Stoker's room. This way, please, Madam."

Sparks gestured to where Stoker was waiting by the stairs. Doyle was disturbed at the curtness with which he had addressed her and gave him a cold look, which Sparks refused to meet. Doyle followed Eileen across the room, where she accepted Stoker's offered arm before climbing the staircase. Sparks trailed them to the second floor. No one spoke until all had entered Stoker's slanted, low-ceilinged room, and the door was secured behind them.

"Please be seated, Madam," said Sparks, grabbing the back of a chair and slamming it down unceremoniously in the center of the room.

Eileen gave a pained and vulnerable glance back to Doyle even as she moved to the chair and settled herself.

"Here now, Jack, must you take that tone—" started Doyle.

"Be quiet!" commanded Sparks. Doyle was too dismayed to reply; he'd never before heard Sparks display such an imperious manner. "Or need I remind you, Doyle, that this woman, while in the employ of our enemies and through the effectiveness of her false office, made one of the principal contributions to your entrapment, betrayal, and near murder!"

"Most unwittingly, I assure—" protested Eileen.

"Thank you, Madam; when your self-defense is required, it will be most swiftly called upon," replied Sparks corrosively.

"Jack, see here—"

"Doyle, if you would be kind enough to contain your ill-informed, moonstruck affections long enough to allow me some small opportunity to arrive at the truth with this adventuress, it would be very much appreciated."

Stung by his unalloyed scorn, Eileen began to weep, quietly and helplessly, looking up at Doyle for assistance. Contrary to ameliorating his anger, her flood of feeling only served to stiffen Sparks's bellicosity.

"Tears, Madam, in this instance, are wasted. I assure you that as persuasive as you may have found them in the past—and as effortlessly as you can simulate them according to your well-practiced craft—you will find them here as bootless as rain to a river; I will not be moved. Treachery of this high order, whatever form it takes, however unwitting, deserves no presumption of innocence. I will have the truth from you, Madam, make no mistake, and any further attempt to manipulate the gentle nature of my companion to your advantage will avail you not at all!"

In the interests of discretion, Sparks had hardly raised his voice above the conversational, but the silence that lay in the room when he finished speaking rang out with the vehemence of his rancor. Stoker had backed up against the door, stunned and speechless. Doyle found it difficult to move, shamed both by his friend's explosive outburst and the nettle of unattractive truth that he knew nested in his harsh judgment. He was perhaps even more disturbed to see Eileen stop weeping almost instantly; she sat upright in her chair as stiff as a celluloid collar, entirely and eerily composed. Her eyes coolly regarded her interrogator without fright or anger, clear and steady and with enormous self-possession.

"What is your name, Madam?" asked Sparks less aggressively, apparently appeased by the greater authenticity of her current state.

"Eileen Temple." Her voice wavered not at all; there was pride in it, and a hint of no longer undeclared defiance.

"Mr. Stoker," said Sparks, without looking at him, "I take it that, upon your discovery at the local laundress's, you traced Miss Temple back to this address, whereupon you sought her out last night."

"Correct," said Stoker.

"Miss Temple, you have been an actress in the employ of the erstwhile Manchester Players for how long a period of time?"

"Two years."

"Last October, while playing an engagement in London, were you approached by someone in your company regarding the appearance you were eventually to make on Boxing Day at Thirteen Cheshire Street?"

"Sammy Fulgrave. He and his wife, Emma, were understudies with our company. She was with child; they were in fairly desperate need of money."

"So they introduced you to the man who had offered them this situation—a small, swarthy man, with a foreign accent—whereupon he extended the same offer to you."

The Dark Man at the séance, thought Doyle. The one he'd shot in the leg.

"That he did," said Eileen.

"What were the terms of that offer?"

"We were to receive one hundred pounds, fifty of which he paid to us immediately. His accent was Austrian, by the way."

"He then recruited the fourth and last actor with your assistance?"

"Dennis Cullen. He was to play my brother—"

"And was no doubt in equally exigent financial distress," said Sparks, unable to keep the edge of scorn from his voice. "What did this man require of you for his hundred pounds?"

"Our participation in a private performance for a wealthy friend of his who was interested in spiritualism. He said it was the intention of a well-meaning group of this man's friends to play a sort of joke on him."

"What sort of joke?"

"He told us that this man, their good friend, was a resolute disbeliever in the spirit world. He said they planned to invite the man to a séance, which he would be given every reason to believe was genuine, and then give him a proper fright, using all manner of elaborate stage effects. This was to take place in a private home, and in order to pull off the effect, they had decided that professional actors, people the man didn't know and whose behavior would appear credible, were required to play the parts."

"Nothing about this offer aroused your suspicions?"

"We discussed it among ourselves. To be honest, it sounded like fairly harmless fun. Nothing about the man's attitude suggested otherwise, and we, all of us, frankly needed the money."

She looked at Doyle and then away, somewhat ashamed, Doyle thought.

"What did he subsequently ask you to do?"

"Nothing for the moment. We were to return to London the day before Christmas for another meeting to organize the performance.

Theatrical Types

At that time, the man took us to Cheshire Street and showed us the room where the séance would be staged. He gave each of us our character's name, told us what sort of person they were supposed to be, and asked us to supply our own appropriate costumes. That's when we learned that Dennis and I were to play brother and sister."

"Had you ever before heard the name Lady Caroline Nicholson?"

"No."

"Have you ever seen this woman before?" Sparks asked, showing to her the photograph of the woman taken outside Rathborne and Sons.

"I have not," she said, after a moment's study. "Is this Lady Nicholson?"

"I believe it is," said Sparks. "You're younger than she. You wore makeup that night to make you appear older."

She nodded.

"I believe that you were singled out by someone who saw your London performance in October and sought you for this job because of your resemblance to Lady Nicholson. The others were relatively immaterial; you were the key to their plan."

"But why go to all this trouble?" asked Stoker.

"To protect against the eventuality that our friend Dr. Doyle had ever seen the real woman. I assure you the man responsible is capable of far more absolute thoroughness than this."

"But what in God's name was their intention?" pressed Stoker with evident frustration.

"Dr. Doyle's murder," he said.

Stoker leaned back. Eileen turned to look at Doyle again; he saw outrage register there, on his behalf. He was beginning to gain a measure of the woman's substantial fortitude.

"Did the man introduce you to the medium before the night of the séance?" asked Sparks.

"No. I suppose we all assumed it would be just another actor. He did say he would be playing a part as well. He was wearing makeup that night—you described him as swarthy; actually the man himself was quite pale."

"Our friend Professor Vamberg again, Doyle," said Sparks in an aside.

"Really?" said Doyle eagerly, almost pathetically grateful to hear a comradely word from Sparks. "You can't say we didn't get our licks in."

"No: When next we see him, the Professor should be walking with a pronounced limp."

Doyle felt a visceral, decidedly uncharitable surge of satisfaction as he recalled the gun going off in his hand and the man's wounded bellows.

"What did this man tell you to do on the night of the séance?"

"He wanted us to arrive in character, in case his friend happened to see any of us on the street. We met him a few blocks away; Dennis and I were picked up by carriage and delivered to the house by another man, who played the part of Tim, our driver."

"What was his name?"

"We didn't know him; he didn't speak to us. But just after we boarded the carriage, and the Professor, as you refer to him, was leaving for the séance, I overheard him call the driver Alexander."

Good Lord, that was him, thought Doyle, the driver he had spoken to outside 13 Cheshire, that was Alexander Sparks; he'd been as close to the man then as he was now to his brother. A shiver ratcheted through him. The man's immersion in his role had been consummate, undetectable.

"Miss Temple, the things we saw in the séance," Doyle asked, "did they demonstrate any of those tricks to you beforehand?"

Eileen nodded. "They had one of those devices—what do you call them?—a magic lantern, hidden behind the curtains. It projected an image into the air—"

"The picture of the little boy," said Doyle.

"With all the smoke, it appeared to be moving, and it was difficult to tell where it came from—and there were wires suspended from the ceiling, holding the trumpets and the head of that hideous beast—"

"You saw that before the séance?"

"No, but of course I just assumed," she said, looking for reassurance.

Unsure that he could provide any, Doyle only nodded.

"What specific directions were given to you regarding how to behave toward Dr. Doyle? Did they give you his name?" asked Sparks.

"No. I was told he was a doctor that my character had sent for, requesting help; my son had been kidnapped, I had turned reluctantly to this medium for guidance, but unsure about her intentions had written to the doctor asking him to meet us there." She looked at Doyle again. "But when he arrived, I don't know why, but I sensed immediately that something was terribly wrong, that the stories I'd been told were untrue—I could see it in your face. The others kept playing along—I don't know that they even noticed. I wanted to say something to you, to give you some sign, but once the thing began, it became so completely overwhelming ... "

"Did you believe what you were seeing was real?" asked Doyle.

Theatrical Types

"I had no way to judge: that is, I know what we're capable of onstage, but..." She shuddered involuntarily and crossed her arms around herself. "There was something so vile in the touch of that woman's hand. Something...unclean. And when that creature appeared in the mirror and began to speak in that dreadful voice...I felt as if I were losing my mind."

"So did I," said Doyle.

"And then came the attack," said Sparks.

"An attack was to be part of the entertainment; we had rehearsed it. We would fall at the hands of these intruders, you would have your reaction, then everyone would bounce to their feet, and have a good laugh at your expense. But when those men came into the room... they weren't the ones we'd seen before. I heard the blow that struck Dennis down, I saw the look in his eyes as he fell and..."

Her voice caught. She put a hand to her forehead, lowered her gaze, and with an immense show of will righted the keel of her emotions.

"...and I knew that he was dead and that they meant to kill you, Dr. Doyle; that had been their intention all along. In that moment, I found voice in my mind to pray; if they would take my life for the part that I had played in this, my life for yours. Then I felt the knife at my throat and the blood running down, and I had no reason to believe it wasn't mine, that they hadn't murdered me as well. I fell, I suppose I fainted, the next moments are unclear...."

She closed her eyes and took a deep breath; it hitched raggedly as she exhaled, fighting off tears again. She had told them the truth, thought Doyle; the greatest genius of the stage the world over could not have dissembled so effectively.

"I came around as Sammy and his wife were carrying me from the house—they hadn't been hurt, but we heard screams and moans behind us. Gunshots. Chaos. Such a terrible shock to realize I was still alive and everything I remembered had actually happened, that Dennis had been killed."

"The driver of the carriage, did you see him outside?" asked Sparks.

She shook her head. "The carriage was gone. We ran. We began to encounter people in the streets. Emma was screaming, Sammy tried desperately to quiet her, but she wouldn't be stilled, he couldn't comfort her; he insisted it would be safer for me if we parted, so we went our separate ways. He gave me his handkerchief to wipe the blood off my throat. I didn't see them again. Mr. Stoker told me what happened to them.... I tried to make myself presentable. I didn't dare return to the small hotel where we'd been staying. I walked until

271

morning, then took a room somewhere in Chelsea. I had the money we'd been given with me. I considered going to the police, but my part in it seemed impossible to explain, too deserving of blame; what could I have told them?"

Doyle shook his head, trying to grant her absolution. She took no solace from it, shaking her head self-reproachingly and looking away.

"All I could think of was getting back to the company. Get back and tell them what had happened, because I thought they would know what to do. I tried to remember where they were playing—I knew it was in the north, but I was so confused—then I remembered Whitby. I remembered Whitby because we'd played here once before, in the height of summer, and the sea and the sailing ships in the harbor had been so very beautiful, and I wanted to sit on a bench by the seawall and look out at the ships as I had that summer and not move and not think for the longest time, and maybe then I would begin to forget what had happened, maybe I could heal what had been done to my mind. . . ."

Tears were flowing down her cheeks, but she made no move to brush them away. Her voice remained even and strong. "The next day I took the train here. I had no other clothes to wear, but my cloak was full enough to cover the bloodstains on my dress. I spoke to no one. I completed the journey undisturbed, although I'm sure many remarks were made about the strange woman in the fancy evening dress, traveling without luggage or companion. I took a room here, like some haunted, heartbroken lover. I bought these poor clothes and sent my dress out to be cleaned. The blood had spoiled the satin, but I couldn't bear to part with it; it was my best dress, the only time I'd worn it before was New Year's Eve a year ago—I was so absurdly happy the night I wore that dress, I thought my life was just beginning and . . ." She paused again, before pulling back and saying, simply: " . . . and so I took a room here and slept and waited for the company to arrive."

She looked back at Stoker, indicating the next chapter of the story was his arrival, which brought the tale to its current pass. Even Sparks's rectitude seemed mollified by the plain harshness of her ordeal. Doyle offered her his handkerchief, which she accepted without a word.

Stoker was the first to gently advance the conversation. "Miss Temple, you should tell them what happened here the night before I found you."

She nodded and lowered the handkerchief. "I was awakened in the middle of the night. Gently. I don't know why, I didn't move, I just opened my eyes. I wasn't sure, I'm not sure now, if I wasn't dreaming.

Theatrical Types

A shape was standing in the shadows in the corner of my room. I looked at it for the longest time before I could be sure what I was seeing. A man. He didn't move. He looked . . . unnatural."

"Describe him for me," said Sparks.

"A pale face. Long. All in black. His eyes—it's hard to describe— his eyes burned. They absorbed light. They never blinked. I was so terrified I couldn't move. I could hardly breathe. I felt as if I were being watched by . . . something less than human. There was a hunger. Like an insect."

"He never touched you."

She shook her head. "I lay there for the longest time. I had no sense of time. I felt paralyzed. I would close my eyes and reopen them, and still he was there. With the first morning light coming in, I opened my eyes again, and he was gone. I got up from my bed. The door and windows to my room were locked, as they had been when I went to sleep. I hadn't truly been afraid until that moment . . . even though he never touched me, he never moved, I felt so . . . violated."

"Miss Temple spent last night in this room," said Stoker. "I sat up all night in that chair with this in my hand . . . " He picked up a double-barreled shotgun from behind the dresser. "No one came into this room."

Doyle looked at Sparks with alarm. "We shan't leave you alone again. Not for a moment."

Sparks didn't answer. He sat down on the bed and looked out the window. His shoulders slumped slightly.

"Am I mistaken in believing that the man in Miss Temple's room is the same man responsible for the crimes we've been discussing?" asked Stoker.

"No. You are not mistaken," said Sparks softly.

"What manner of man is it who can move through the night this way, move through doors and windows into rooms without a sound, who can strike down people in their sleep, carry them off, and never be seen?" Stoker moved closer to Sparks as he spoke, never raising his voice. "What manner of human being is this? Do you know?"

Sparks nodded. "I will tell you, Mr. Stoker. But first you must tell me what you were doing when you found us at Goresthorpe Abbey."

Towering over Sparks, Stoker folded his arms and thoughtfully stroked his generous whiskers.

"Fair enough," he said. Stoker leaned against the windowsill, and took a pipe and pouch from his pocket, busying himself with the small, precise rituals of smoking as he began to speak. "I spoke with a great many people in Whitby when I first arrived. Few had anything of substance to tell me. Then I met a man in a pub down by the bay. A whaler, a grizzled old dog, seventy if he's a day. Been round the world a dozen times. Now he sits and watches the harbor and drinks his stout from noon to closing, alone. The publican and his regulars regard the man as a sot and a harmless nutter. The sailor called me over to him soon after I came into that place. He was most agitated and very eager to tell me something he was sure no one else would credit—or rather something he had tried to tell repeatedly that no one else believed.

"He never slept much, he told me, some combination of alcohol and age, and so he spent many long nights walking by the shore and up the hill, toward the abbey, where his wife was laid to rest ten years since. She speaks to him sometimes, he said, he hears her voice on those late nights, whispering out of the wind in the trees above the graveyard. One night about three weeks ago as he made his way through the headstones, she called to him. He said her voice was stronger than he'd ever heard it.

" 'Look to the sea,' she said. 'Look to the harbor.' The graveyard runs along a ledge directly above the harbor. It was a blustery night, and the tide was high. He looked down and saw a ship running in with the waves, running fast in to shore, too fast, sails flapping, lines loose; it was looking to go directly aground. The old sailor picked his way as quickly as he could down to the beach where the ship was headed; if they hit the rocks there, it could mean disaster; he'd have to sound the alarm.

"When he got to Tate Hill Pier, a small cove out of sight from the seawall, he saw the ship had dropped anchor fifty yards off shore. She was a trim schooner, showing a lot of hull, lying light in the water. A skiff was coming from it toward the beach; he saw with surprise there were people waiting onshore with lanterns, waving them in. He moved closer to them but stayed hidden, deciding not to reveal himself. He saw the Bishop among their number."

"Bishop Pillphrock?" asked Sparks.

Stoker nodded. "The others he didn't recognize. The small boat made land, two men on board, one all in black. Their cargo was two crates, the size and shape of coffins, which were quickly unloaded. The man swore he saw a large black dog jump off the boat as well. The schooner did not wait for the return of the small boat; she had already pulled anchor, tacking against the wind for the open sea. The group onshore shouldered the crates, which did not appear to be heavy, and headed up the hill toward the abbey. They passed not ten feet from the old sailor's hiding place. He heard the Bishop say something about 'the arrival of our Lord'—he thought it was the Bishop who'd said this—and the man in black shouted at him in a harsh voice to be still. The sailor followed them and said he watched them carry the crates, not to Goresthorpe, but to the ruins of the ancient abbey farther up the hill. And he swears he watched that black dog run into the cemetery and disappear into thin air. Since then, he'd seen strange lights burning late at night in the ruins. What disturbed him most was that since that night his wife's voice had not spoken to him again."

"We must speak to this man," said Sparks.

"They found him the next morning in the graveyard. His throat had been ripped apart, as if he'd been attacked by an animal. The caretaker said that during the night he'd heard the baying of a wolf."

Sparks and Doyle looked at each other. Eileen wrapped her shawl tight around her shoulders and stared at the floor. She was shaking. The walls seemed suddenly both too small to contain what they were feeling and far too insubstantial to hold at bay the forces arrayed against them.

"What's that?" asked Sparks, pointing to a package on top of the dresser.

"That was my breakfast this morning," said Stoker. "A local product, apparently."

Sparks picked up the package of Mother's Own Biscuits.

"We'll tell you the rest of our side of the story now," said Sparks. And so they did.

CHAPTER 16

Devil Dodgers

SPARKS AND DOYLE spared no details from Stoker and Eileen, save Sparks his alleged government connection and Doyle his lingering reservations about Sparks himself—that note from Leboux still lay across his thoughts like an iron pike—and it was dark and evening before the telling was done. Snow continued to fall throughout the afternoon. Streets were already muffled with a fresh foot of it, and the storm showed no signs of abating. They sent down to the kitchen for a light supper of soup, cold mutton, and corn bread, which they shared in Stoker's room and from which they all took no small, restorative comfort. Eileen said little during the meal, never meeting Doyle's eye, withdrawing inside herself to some fortified place of sanctuary. Feeling a greater strength in numbers was called for, Sparks excused himself from their company to collect Barry and Larry from the inn near the station where they had registered earlier that long day. Eileen lay down on the bed to rest. Stoker took the occasion to draw Doyle out into the corridor for a private word, leaving the door slightly ajar so as to keep an eye on the room and more specifically the windows.

Devil Dodgers

"As one gentleman to another," began Stoker quietly, "it is my fervent hope that the situation here does not appear to be an indelicate one."

"How so?" asked Doyle.

"I am a most happily married man, Dr. Doyle. My wife and I have a young child. Miss Temple, as you cannot have failed to notice, spent last night in my room."

"You were standing guard over her life—"

"Even so. Miss Temple is an actress and, you cannot have failed to notice, an extremely attractive woman. If any word of this were to find its way to London . . . " Stoker shrugged in a way common to the private rooms of the most exclusive gentlemen's clubs.

"Given the circumstances, such a thing would be unthinkable," said Doyle with unexpressed amazement. Was there no end to their society's fanatic preoccupation with propriety?

"I shall depend on your discretion then," said Stoker, greatly relieved, offering his hand. "I'm going to fetch a brandy, may I bring you one?"

"Thank you, no," said Doyle. He wanted nothing to cloud his mind during the coming night.

"Miss Temple asked for one as a soporific before retiring last night. Perhaps I shall bring her one as well."

With a slight bow, Stoker took his leave. Doyle reentered the room. Eileen was sitting up awake on the bed, deftly rolling a cigarette from a pouch of shag tobacco. Doyle's eyes widened.

"Do you have a match?" she asked.

"Yes, I believe I do. Just a moment. Here we go," Doyle fumbled through his pockets, produced a match, and lit the cigarette for her. To steady the trembling—the result of nothing more complicated than being alone in the room with her—as he held the match near, she gripped his hand.

"Do you really think they'd attack us here with all these people about?" she asked, with a casualness and familiarity he'd not heard in her voice before.

"Oh, it is possible, yes, I would have to say, that it is, quite." Why did English suddenly seem something a great deal less than his native tongue?

"You ought to sit down. You look terribly tired." She crossed her legs and blew smoke into the air.

"Do I? Thank you, I am. I shall," said Doyle formally, and he looked busily around for a place to sit. He finally picked up the straight-backed chair from across the room, set it facing the windows, picked up the shotgun, sat down, and tried to appear purposeful.

"You look like you know how to shoot," she said after watching him for a moment, with the slightest trace of a smile.

"I sincerely hope I won't have occasion to demonstrate while you are in such, uh, proximity." He felt himself blushing. Blushing!

"And I have no doubt that if the occasion were to arise, I would be most suitably impressed."

Doyle nodded and smiled like a mechanical bird. It was hard to look at her. Was she toying with me? he asked himself. Is it because I'm behaving like such a filbert?

"Do you treat many women, Dr. Doyle?" she asked, that Gioconda smile surfacing again.

"What's that?"

"In your practice. Do you have many female patients?"

"Oh my, yes. That is, I have my share. I'd say a good half, at any rate. Half of the whole, that is." Half of eight, at its height, truth be told: all lost to him now. And not a one of them under the age of fifty with a swan's neck and skin like the petals of a rose and...

"Are you not married?" she asked.

"No. Are you?"

She laughed a little. It reminded him of tinkling crystal goblets at an impossibly glamorous dinner. "No, I'm not married."

Doyle nodded intently, looked down at the shotgun in his hands, and with great concentration rubbed an imaginary smudge off the barrel.

"I've never given you proper thanks," she said more soberly.

"None necessary," he said with a casually dismissing wave.

"Still. I owe you my life. You and Mr. Sparks."

"There's no reason for you to feel indebted in even the slightest way, Miss Temple. Given the chance, I would gladly do the same again and more," he said, feeling emboldened. This time he held her eyes until she looked away.

She needed somewhere to stub out her cigarette. There was no ashtray on the bedstand. Casting around, Doyle came up with the wrapper from the biscuits and held it for her on the table as she tapped out the smoke. Their fingers brushed together lightly with an electric tingle that he didn't believe he was imagining.

"I want to help you," she said in a low and husky voice. "In any way I can. You must convey that to Mr. Sparks. Because, you see, I feel a certain responsibility."

Devil Dodgers

"You acted out of need. Urgent financial need. You couldn't know what would happen. You had no way of knowing."

As she finished with the cigarette, she looked up, and their faces were only inches apart.

"Nevertheless," she said. "Will you convey that to him? Perhaps there is a way. I can be very resourceful."

"Of that I have no doubt whatsoever."

Her tongue flicked a tiny speck of tobacco off her lower lip. Their eyes met, and her look was far from discouraging. Doyle felt a sharp tug in his chest, as if caught in a strong gravitational field. *Beauty is the promise of happiness;* that phrase leapt to his mind from some long-forgotten source. He found himself leaning in to kiss her when multiple footsteps preceded the opening of the door. With a single sharp rap, Sparks entered the room. Doyle hastily pulled away and disposed of the biscuit wrapper. Larry and Barry took up stations on either side of the door.

"I've had a look at the other inn; we must move ourselves there at once," said Sparks. "It's a far less vulnerable structure. We will be able to protect ourselves for the night more efficiently there."

"I hope that you're not organizing this defense around any presumed incapacity of mine," said Eileen, rising energetically to her feet, "because I'm quite capable of defending myself as well as if not a good deal better than any man could ever do."

"Miss Temple, after the fate that's befallen your colleagues, surely you do comprehend that you are a target of considerable urgency and importance to our enemies," said Sparks, with measured reasonableness.

"What I comprehend is that you, sir, have no comprehension whatsoever of my ability to aid and abet you in this matter," said Eileen, not backing down an inch.

"This is not the time to—"

"And if you expect me to remain locked in a room like so much bait on a hook waiting for trouble to arrive while you men are free to come and go as you please, you, sir, are very much mistaken—"

"Miss Temple, please—"

"I will not be a party to it, nor will I honor your antiquated notions of what a woman is or is not capable of: I begin to suspect that you would be equally disapproving of giving women the vote—"

"What on God's green earth has that to do with moving to the other inn?" Sparks protested. Doyle could not remember seeing Sparks so

279

beleaguered. Barry and Larry were staring at their shoes, trying hard to keep the smiles off their faces.

"I have been an expert shot since the age of ten: A man raises his hand against me at his own peril—I've shot a man before; I would not hesitate to do it again—"

"Don't be a fool—"

In a single, swift move, Eileen seized the shotgun from Doyle's hand, drew back the hammers, dexterously swung the gun around to draw a bead on the hat rack in the corner, pulled the trigger, and blew Stoker's bowler hat to kingdom come. Larry and Barry dropped to the floor. Stoker chose that unfortunate moment to appear in the doorway toting two full snifters of brandy; Eileen spotted movement in the corner of her eye and whipped around to train the second barrel on him. Stoker's hands flew up, and the snifters fell to the ground.

"Lord, no!" cried Stoker.

"How emphatically do you wish me to demonstrate my point, Mr. Sparks?" she asked calmly.

"Your point," said Sparks, his face taut with rage, "is made."

Eileen lowered the gun. Other guests, curious about the loud report, appeared in the hallway.

"Everything's all right," said Doyle to them, taking Stoker by the arm and pulling him into the room. "Go on about your business. No trouble here."

"What in great heaven's name is going on?" said Stoker shakily as Doyle closed the door behind them. "Miss Temple, please, these are our friends."

Eileen broke down the barrels, slipped out the remaining live round, and handed the gun back to Doyle. "Mr. Stoker, I owe you a new hat."

Larry and Barry sat up on the floor and tried unsuccessfully to keep from laughing out loud. Doyle was unable to resist joining them.

"I'm sure there's been some terrible misunderstanding. Can't we discuss this reasonably?" said Stoker, retrieving the shredded corpse of his bowler.

"If a move to the other inn is no longer in order, Mr. Sparks, what is your alternate plan?" asked Eileen.

Sparks glowered at her, but she proudly stood her ground. When Doyle snorted, trying to stifle a laugh, Sparks shot him a venomous look.

"Sorry," said Doyle, turning the laugh into a cough. "Perhaps staying on here is not such a bad idea, Jack."

Devil Dodgers

"You will have your opportunity to contribute, Miss Temple," said Sparks, ignoring Doyle entirely. "Only with the understanding that I entirely absolve myself of further responsibility for your safety."

"Understood," she said, and thrust out a hand. Sparks stared at her hand for a moment as if it were a lobster claw and then shook it, once, hard.

"So what will we do then, Jack?" asked Doyle.

"The brothers have during the afternoon each made a most interesting discovery," said Sparks, moving away to the window.

Both men had by now climbed back to their feet, hats in hand. Barry, Doyle noticed, had a good deal of difficulty removing his eyes from Eileen.

"Train pulled into the station, three o'clock sharp," said Barry, turning on the charm. "Webb Compound and one passenger car. Special from Balmoral. Royal seal."

"Was there a royal on board?" asked Doyle, alarmed.

"Just the one: Prince Albert—"

"Young Eddy?" asked Stoker, aghast.

"Himself. He was met by carriage and driven off to the southeast."

"You'll recall that Sir Nigel Gull, former physician to the prince, is one of the List of Seven," Sparks reminded Stoker.

"What could he be doing here? Do they plan to kill him?" asked Stoker.

"There's the waste of a perfectly good bullet," said Eileen.

"And are you acquainted with the prince personally, Miss Temple?" asked Sparks.

"As a matter of fact, I am," she said, rolling another cigarette. "I spent an evening in Eddy's company last year after he saw me perform *Twelfth Night* in Bristol."

"One can't fault him his taste," said Barry gallantly.

"The man's got the mind of a Guernsey," said Eileen. "Put a pint in him, and he sprouts more arms than an octopus—"

"Thank you for that edifying report," said Sparks.

"Not at all," said Eileen, and held up the finished cigarette. Both Barry and Larry rushed forward with lit matches before Doyle could even get one out of his vest.

"Larry, would you care to share with us what you've found out today?" said Sparks, with a disapproving schoolmaster's tone.

"Right, sir," said Larry, blowing out his match as Barry had beaten him to Eileen. "Goresthorpe Abbey is mysteriously deserted, no one about these three days past, as Mr. Stoker has so astutely sussed out. So how do we finds the Right Honorable Bishop Pillphrock and where he's got to? A grocer and his goods; that's the life's blood of any household. I spent the afternoon chatting up the dollies in the local shops—mind you, I'm no Barry, but I get by—and following outward along the lines of supply, I learn the Bishop has repaired to a secluded slice a' heaven down the coast where, judging by the considerable volume of provisions purchased and delivered, he must be, as we speak, playing the country squire to a goodly number of guests."

"The Bishop's own estate?" asked Doyle.

"No, Sir John Chandros's," said Sparks.

"Correct, sir, and as it happens, sharing the grounds of this same estate is a factory that produces—"

"Mother's Own Biscuits," said Doyle.

"You're miles ahead of me, sir," said Larry modestly.

"What is the name of the estate?" asked Doyle.

"They call it Ravenscar," said Larry.

"And it's to the southeast, past the ancient ruins," said Doyle.

"Correct once again," said Larry.

"Where Prince Eddy was likely taken from the train station," added Sparks. "And adjacent to Ravenscar is the tract of land General Drummond purchased from Lord Nicholson."

"We must go there immediately, Jack," said Doyle.

"Tomorrow's business," said Sparks, looking out the window at the falling snow. "Tonight we pay a visit to the ruins of Whitby Abbey."

"You can't be serious—in this weather?" asked Stoker.

"Your attendance is not required, Mr. Stoker," said Sparks, picking up the shotgun. "However, I should like to borrow your gun."

Barry, all this while, had been taking the opportunity to size up Eileen as she smoked her cigarette, towering a good five inches above him.

"I've seen you someplace before, haven't I?" he said with a confident grin.

Eileen cocked an amused eyebrow at the little man. Perhaps Barry's reputation is not overstated after all, thought Doyle.

✿ ✿ ✿

Armed with lanterns, a shotgun, one pistol, and five sets of snowshoes procured from the inn, Sparks, Doyle, the brothers, and Eileen—Stoker having elected to exercise the better part of valor—set out in the dark for the ruins of Whitby Abbey. The bulk of the storm had passed, and the wind had expired; snow fell straight down and more gently now, to depths in excess of a foot and a half. Thick clouds obscured the moon. Smoke poured uniformly from the chimneys of the huddled houses they passed; curtains drawn, almost no light escaping to the ill-defined streets. The night was broken by nothing but the soft crunch of snowshoes on fresh powder and the vaporous columns of their breath. Navigation was problematic at best; the travelers felt sealed in a mute, hermetic sphere of white.

Slogging up the hill demanded patience and stamina. Sparks took the point, consulting a compass to maintain their bearings against the sheer cliffs to their left. Barry and Larry kept a rear guard with the other lanterns, while Doyle walked beside Eileen in the middle. She wore pants, boots, and a coat borrowed from Sparks's wardrobe. Her stride was long, steady, and brisk, and the climb seemed dismayingly less arduous to her than to Doyle himself, who welcomed each of Sparks's frequent pauses as an opportunity to reclaim his wind.

Half an hour passed before they reached the cold, dark contour of Goresthorpe Abbey; no change in its lack of occupancy was evident. A formation of curious rectangular shapes studded the snowfield before them. Doyle realized it was the heads of the cemetery's gravestones peering out of the drifts. Following the turn of the rectory grounds, they moved through a stand of trees and were soon confronted by the craggy black outline of the ancient ruins looming on the crown of the hill above. As devoid of life as its sister building below, the old sepulcher emanated a visceral menace considerably more threatening than life's mere absence.

"Nasty-looking piece of business," said Doyle quietly.

"All the better to strike fear in the hearts of poor, ignorant parishioners with, my dear," answered Eileen in kind.

Sparks waved them forward, and they attacked the final leg of the ascent. The slope was steeper here, and it more than once required the collective efforts of the group to pull each other up and over the sharpest inclines. With the last of these banks surmounted, they found themselves on a flat plane level with the ruins. Their lamps bled a pallid light on the crumbling walls, which were black and harrowed with age. Its doors and windows had long since been ravaged by time, and in many areas even the roof had fallen victim, but the overall impression imparted by what remained of the abbey was one of tremendous sturdiness and power. A slow circumambulation of the structure revealed both its impressive scope and its builders' fantastic indulgence of detail. Every ledge, cornice, and lintel was adorned with nightmarish Gothic statuary, embodying every imaginable species of night-dweller: kobold, incubus, basilisk, and hydra, lich, ogre, hippogriff, gremlin, and gargoyle. This fearsome menagerie had suffered far fewer insults from the passing centuries than the walls they swarmed over, each now patiently collecting a mantle of snow that did nothing to diminish their dread presence. Placed here to ward off demons, not to welcome them, remembered Doyle from his history books. Or so one hoped. He couldn't keep from regularly glancing over his shoulder to see if any of the creatures' dead eyes were tracking them.

Sparks brought them back around the ruins to their starting point, completing the loop of their footprints in the snow, trailing away in either direction into darkness.

"Shall we have a look inside?" asked Sparks.

No answer came, but when Sparks walked through the open doorway, no one lingered behind. Because of the remaining irregular ribs of roofing, snow had not gathered to the same depths inside. They removed their snowshoes, leaning them against a wall. Sparks led them into the next room, a grand, vaulted rectangular space with uniform rows of broken stone running across the floor. A raised deck at the far end of the nave identified the room's original function.

"This was the church," said Sparks.

Sparks moved forward toward the altar. Larry and Barry fanned out with their lanterns, and the room grew more evenly illuminated. Snow continued to fall through the open ceiling. The air felt as dense and ponderous as the glaze on a frozen lake.

"There used to be witches used this place for sport," said Larry.

"You mean nuns," corrected Barry.

"Nuns wot had lost their way is wot he said."

"Feller told us in some pub," said Barry to Doyle and Eileen—mostly Eileen.

"That's wot he said. Whole convents' worth, the lot of 'em, went chronic, over to the other side. Devil dodgers one day, consortin' with the Prince of Darkness the next. That's why people put the torch to the place."

"People from the village?" asked Doyle.

"That's right," said Larry. "Took matters in their own hands. Killed and tortured and otherwise beat the devil right out of them nuns, right here in this room, that's what we heard."

Devil Dodgers

"Tommyrot," said Eileen.

"That's the jimjams," agreed Barry. "The fella was wonky wit' gin."

"I'm not sayin' it's the virgin Gospel, I'm just sayin' it's what he—"

"Bring the lanterns!" shouted Sparks.

Barry and Larry scurried to the front of the cathedral, bearing the light. Doyle and Eileen quickly followed. Sparks was standing over a closed and weather-beaten crate lying in the altar area on a loose pile of dirt.

"What's that then?" asked Larry.

"It's a coffin, idn't it?" said Barry.

Doyle thought of Stoker's account of the old sailor's story and the night cargo he saw brought ashore from the ship.

"The nails securing the lid have been removed," said Sparks, kneeling down with one of the lanterns.

"Didn't the old man say they brought two coffins up here?" said Doyle.

"Yes," said Sparks, looking at the wood.

"So what's inside the bloody thing?" said Eileen.

"Only one way to find that out, isn't there, Miss Temple?" said Sparks, and he reached for the lid.

As Sparks's hand made contact with the wood, a chilling howl went up from just outside the building: the cry of a wolf, almost certainly, but the timbre lower, more guttural than any Doyle had ever heard. They froze as the sound echoed away.

"That was very close," whispered Doyle.

"Extremely," said Sparks.

Another animal answered back an identical howl from the other side of the abbey. Then a third sounded, at a greater distance.

"Wolves?" asked Barry.

"Doesn't sound like springer spaniels, does it?" said Eileen.

"Turn very slowly around and face the room," said Sparks.

"No need to turn slowly, guv," said Larry, already facing that way and pointing to the center of the cathedral crossing.

A dizzying welter of blue sparks was spinning in a loose circle around a still point two feet above the floor. As it continued to gyrate, the circumference of the circle expanded, first horizontally, then vertically, until it equaled the span of the broken stone pews. The air crackled with a noxious energy. Doyle felt the hairs on the back of his neck elevate.

"What the bloody hell—" muttered Eileen.

The blue sparks faded as a shape emerging out of them defined itself: five translucent, cowled figures kneeling in prayer, knees resting a foot off the floor, as if supported by a spectral prayer rail. Issuing from exactly where it was impossible to determine, but the room was suddenly alive with a chorus of soft, whispery voices. The words were obscure, but the harsh, fervent tone of the invisible chorale penetrated sharply the ear of the listener, a heavy, distressing blow to the conscious ordering of the mind.

"Latin," said Sparks, listening carefully.

"Is it a ghost?" Doyle heard himself ask.

"More than one, guv," said Larry, crossing himself.

"See, there's your nuns," said Barry, who seemed not the slightest bit discomfited by the sight.

Upon longer examination, the figures did project an aspect more feminine than monkish, and the high, insinuating voices that swirled around them did nothing to alter that perception.

Eileen grabbed Larry's lantern, stepped fearlessly down off the altar, and started directly toward the apparitions.

"Miss Temple—" protested Doyle.

"All right, ladies, that'll be quite enough of this prattle," she said in a strong, projected voice. "Vespers are done for the evening, now run along; back to whatever hell-place you came from with you."

"Barry," said Sparks, a command.

Barry immediately jumped down after her. Larry pulled his knives and moved to the right, while Sparks drew a bead with the shotgun.

"Be gone, stupid spirits, fly away, disperse, or you'll make us very angry—"

The ghostly voices suddenly stilled. Eileen stopped ten feet away from the penitent wraiths.

"That's better," she said approvingly. "Now the rest of you girls just trot on off as well. Go on."

The ghostly figures lowered their hands. Barry slowly moved after Eileen, only a few strides behind her now.

"Miss Temple," said Sparks, loud and clear, "move away from the center of the room, please."

"We run into ghosts in the theater all the time—" she said.

"Please do as I say, now."

She turned back to Sparks to argue. "There's nothing to worry about, they're perfectly harmless—"

Moving as one, the ghostly figures threw back their hoods, revealing hideously deformed and hairless heads that looked half human and half predatory bird. They let loose a shrill, paralyzing shriek and rose up above Eileen to a height of ten feet or more, preparing to strike. At that moment, two huge wolves sprinted into the nave from either side of the apse, growling ferociously, making straight for Eileen. Barry dove forward and tackled her to the floor as the wolves leapt to attack. Sparks fired the shotgun, both barrels, knocking the lead animal backward off its airborne course; it hit the ground with a hard thump and lay still, ruptured and bleeding. In the same instant, Larry let fly his knives; there was a loud yelp as the second animal came down on Barry, handles of the knives protruding from its neck and upper chest. The beast still had enough ebbing strength and instinct left to tear into Barry, the arm he'd raised to fend it off gripped in its ripping jaws. Barry reached around, pulled the knife from the wolf's side, and plunged it decisively into the back of its skull. The animal spasmed and fell back, dead before it landed.

"Stay down!" cried Sparks.

But Eileen jumped to her feet, grabbed a lantern, and hurled it at the phantom figures towering above her. The lamp exploded on contact; the images combusted, disintegrating into a shower of silvery sparks and red smoke.

"I hate nuns!" shouted Eileen.

Doyle heard a low, feral growl behind him and turned cautiously. A third wolf stood beside the crate, a few feet behind Sparks, his back completely exposed to the animal.

"Jack . . . " said Doyle.

"My gun's not loaded," said Sparks quietly, without moving. "Is yours?"

"I'll have to reach for it."

"Do that, would you?"

Doyle undid his coat and slid his hand delicately inside. With fiercely intelligent eyes, the wolf looked slowly back and forth from Doyle to Sparks. This was by far the biggest of the three brutes: six hands high, at least ten stone. As it inched forward, Doyle pulled out the pistol, but instead of attacking, the king wolf took two running strides and in a high arc leapt out one of the open windows behind the altar. Doyle got off one errant shot and rushed to follow it. Looking down, he saw the drop from the window was at least twenty feet to the cushion of drifts below. He held out a lantern, but the animal had already disappeared from view.

Eileen and Larry attended to Barry, whose lower left arm had borne the brunt of the wolf's attack. Blood ran freely down his hand as she guided his arm gingerly out of the sleeve.

"Not too bad, is it, old boy?" asked Larry.

"Coat took the worst of it," said Barry, testing his fingers, the movement of which was not impaired.

"Ghosts, can you fancy that?" said Eileen, with the calm neutrality of a practiced nurse.

"Seen worse," said Barry stoically.

"I hate nuns," said Eileen. "I've always hated nuns."

"These woolly sheep-eaters were real enough, weren't they, though? No hocus-pocus here," said Larry, leaning over to kick one of the corpses and then retrieve his knives from its hide.

"All right then, Barry?" asked Sparks, reloading the shotgun with shells from his pocket.

"Ugly as ever, sir," said Barry, with a toothy smile for his ministering angel as she examined the puncture wounds on his forearm.

Doyle's heart rate was just coming under control again when he glanced back out the windows.

"Have a look at this, Jack," he said.

Sparks joined him. In the distance to the south was a line of bright orange lights, moving in formation toward their position.

"Torches," said Doyle.

"Coming for something. Us. Maybe that," said Sparks, gesturing back at the crate. "Keep an eye on them."

Doyle estimated they were still a good mile away. Sparks moved to the crate and knelt down to examine the dirt on which it rested, rubbing it between his fingers, sniffing it. Sparks dislodged the lid. He made no sound, but when Doyle turned back, he saw a sick, stricken expression on Sparks's face.

"What is it, Jack?"

"Games," muttered Sparks darkly. "He's playing games."

Doyle moved to Sparks's side and looked into the crate. There was a corpse inside, little more than bones really, amid rotting burial clothes and matted clumps of scorched hair and flesh. A photograph in a gilded frame had been positioned between its skeletal hands in a travesty of covetous possession: a formal posed portrait of a man and woman, married and upper-class English by the form and style of them.

"What is this?" asked Doyle.

"My parents," said Sparks, nodding at the photograph. "Those are my parents."

"Good Christ."

"And this is my father's body."

The outrage that welled inside him rendered Doyle speechless. Any remaining doubts he harbored regarding the monstrousness of Alexander and Jack's relative innocence were finally and irrevocably removed.

"Soulless monster," spat Doyle finally.

Sparks took a series of deep breaths and clenched his fists, closing and opening them rhythmically, trying to bring his tumultuous emotions under control. Moving back to the window, Doyle saw that the lights were moving closer, at least six torches, and moving against the snow beneath them he could make out dark shapes. A formidable number of them. A quarter-mile away and closing fast.

As Eileen finished dressing a strip of shirt cloth around Barry's wounds, Larry joined Doyle at the window.

"What should we do?" asked Doyle.

"The odds don't favor a fight here, guv. Not against those numbers. No cover or high ground. Too many doors. Too hard to defend."

"Tell him," said Doyle, gesturing toward Sparks.

"He knows," said Larry. "Give him a minute."

"A minute's all we've got."

Larry winked at him. "Minute's all we need."

Larry picked up the shotgun and gave a short whistle, Barry jumped to his feet, kissed Eileen on the cheek, and the brothers quickly moved out of the cathedral toward the trackers. Doyle could differentiate individuals in the group now; there were at the least two dozen in the pack. Eileen stepped back onto the altar. To prevent her from disturbing Sparks, Doyle gestured for her to join him at the window.

"Are we just going to stand here and wait for them?" asked Eileen.

"No," said Doyle, steadying his pistol on the window, taking aim on a lead torch-bearer. Before he could squeeze off a shot, he heard the rolling crack of the shotgun from off to the left; there were shouts, and two figures in the group went down. The man with the torch stopped to look in that direction; Doyle fired, the figure fell, and its torch was extinguished in the snow.

"Here! Over here, you rotters!"

More taunting shouts followed. Doyle saw Barry wave their lanterns, trying to draw the party away from the abbey.

"Come on then! Get a wiggle on, we 'aven't got all night!"

Six attackers ran after Barry; the rest continued toward the ruins.

Doyle emptied his pistol at the advancing column, felling another of them. As he reloaded, he heard the shotgun boom again and saw one of the men headed for the brothers fall silently.

The rasp of the cover coming off the coffin pulled his attention back to the room. Sparks emptied the oil from his lantern into the crate, then set it aflame by crashing the lantern on top of it. The crate ignited like dry tinder. Sparks stepped back, intoned something Doyle couldn't hear, and watched the fire consume the box, committing his father to final rest.

"We really should go, Jack," said Doyle, waiting a decent interval as he reloaded his pistol.

Sparks turned away from the flames and picked up the lid to the crate by its handles. "This way," he said, heading toward the end of the nave they'd entered.

"What does he want with that?" asked Eileen, pointing at the lid.

"I'm sure I couldn't say," said Doyle, as they caught up to Sparks and ran into the antechamber where they'd stacked the snowshoes.

"We'll need those," snapped Sparks, pointing at the shoes.

As Eileen bent to retrieve them, three gray hoods came in through the front entrance. One raised a spiked cudgel to strike at Sparks.

"Jack!"

Sparks whirled, lowered the lid, and drove it into the chests of the three hoods, his legs pistoning mightily, pushing them back and pinning them against the wall. Doyle stepped forward and methodically fired two shots into each of the hoods as they squirmed behind the wood.

"Behind you!" shouted Eileen.

Two more hoods rushed in at them from the cathedral. Doyle spun around and pulled the trigger, but the pistol was empty. The three dispatched hoods slumped to the ground as Sparks let go of the coffin lid and turned to face this new assault. Eileen swung a snowshoe up by the tail and cracked the trailing one hard across the face, knocking it off its feet. A blow from the onrushing hood's club clipped Sparks on the arm; he dipped, caught the hood's momentum with a shoulder, straightened up, and flipped the creature against the wall. Eileen whacked the downed hood a second time as it tried to find its footing; Doyle turned the pistol in his hand and whipped the handle across the back of the hood until it lay still. Sparks drove a boot down into the neck of the second attacker, and it snapped like a hollow branch.

Bright light and the rush of many footsteps entered the cathedral. Sparks picked up the lid and ran out the door.

Devil Dodgers

"Hurry!" he said.

Doyle and Eileen gathered the snowshoes, and they scrambled after Sparks. He dropped the lid so it hung over the lip of the hill that sloped steeply away from the ruins and anchored it with his foot.

"You first, Doyle. Grab the handles and hold on," said Sparks.

The main band of pursuers burst out of the abbey behind them toward their position, a black-cloaked figure in the lead. Doyle pocketed his gun and jumped aboard. Sparks grabbed Eileen around the waist, pushed her down on the middle of the lid, and followed her onto it, using his weight to tip them over the edge. They slid forward and rapidly accelerated down the incline as the pack reached the lip: Two hoods hurled themselves after the makeshift sled, one raked a hand across Sparks's back, nearly dislodging him before they pulled away from the tumbling bodies. The sled gained speed as they plummeted down the embankment in the dark; every bump and hillock sent them flying into the air, only to be rocked heavily as they hit the snow again.

"Can you steer?" shouted Sparks.

"I don't think so!" answered Doyle. It was all he could do to hang on. The sheer cliffs falling to the sea somewhere on the right and their unknown proximity to them hurtled into his mind.

"Can you see?" asked Eileen.

"A little!"

The next thing he saw was two figures standing ahead of them waist-deep in the snow, frantically waving their arms. In the split second before the sled reached them, Doyle thought they might be Barry and Larry, but then he saw the hoods and the weapons in their hands. Doyle leaned all his weight to his right, and the lid veered slightly in that direction, enough to crash into the hoods, bowl them like ninepins, and scatter them down the hill. The collision knocked the wind out of Doyle, changed their direction, and shaved an edge off their velocity. He gasped for breath, trying to figure out where they were when he felt a sensation of skidding, looked to his right, and just ahead saw the white expanse of the snow pack end abruptly in sheer blackness.

"The cliffs!" cried Sparks.

Doyle threw all his weight to the left. Sparks stuck out his right foot as a runner to push them away from the brink, and a moment later that foot was suspended out over thin air. They screamed as the sled rocketed along the edge of the cliff for twenty yards, scraping stone, whipping through saplings that had grown up over the lip, before

291

Doyle's crude course correction inched them away from the precipice and back onto solid snow. He could see the shape of the new abbey ahead on their left, but Doyle had barely a moment to register relief, idly wondering what those gray shapes coming out of the snow straight in front of them were when he realized they were headed directly into the cemetery.

"Headstones!" Doyle shouted.

Doyle guided them through the first group of markers, then the next, but as they moved to the middle of the yard, the concentration of stones grew denser and the stones themselves larger and more grandiose. There was no way to brake, and a massive mausoleum dead ahead suddenly gave no opportunity to maneuver. Doyle yanked on the handles, turning them sideways; they went into a skid, hit a bump, flew skyward, and the coffin lid splintered beneath them. Doyle hit the snow, clutching the broken handles in his hands. Eileen and Sparks were thrown high into the air, landing out of Doyle's sight.

Doyle lay still a moment, trying to gather his wits. He was unable to loosen his grip on the handles—his knuckles locked and frozen around them—but he could move everything else, having touched down in a drift without suffering any disabling injury.

"Jack?" he asked tentatively.. He first thought the sound that came back to him was sobbing. Was it Eileen? "Are you all right?"

He realized Eileen was laughing. She emerged from a nearby snow-bank, covered head to toe in white, overcome with infectious laughter. Then he heard Sparks laughing, captivated by the same relieving impulse, before he appeared from behind the mausoleum that had precipitated their crash. The sight and sound of each other's laughter seemed to redouble their own. Jack bent over, hanging on to the edge of the monument. Eileen fell back into the snow and guffawed. The recent terror had been so completely overwhelming that for the moment there seemed no more sensible a response. Doyle felt the giggles come over him as well, and he gave into them.

"I thought we were dead," said Doyle.

"I thought we were dead four separate times," managed Eileen.

Doyle's entire body began to shake. They staggered toward a meeting point, put their arms across each other's shoulders, and let the healing laughter run its course. It was all they could do to breathe. As the laughter was cresting, Doyle revealed the handles stuck in his hands, which set off another round of hilarity.

"*JONATHAN SPARKS!*"

Devil Dodgers

The words rolled down the slopes from the ruins high above. The voice was harshly sibilant, but at the same time lush and orotund; it could cut glass and never leave a splinter. No anger in its tone, only insinuating derision that bespoke no disappointment at their escape but rather suggested satisfaction, that this was its desired outcome.

"Is it him?" asked Doyle.

Sparks nodded, looking toward the hilltop.

"*LISTEN!*"

Silence thicker than a church bell.

Then a bloodcurdling scream twisted and built to a hideous crescendo before fading away into exhausted, piteous bleating.

"Oh God. The brothers," said Eileen.

Another scream, more tortured than before. Was it the same voice?

"Bastard!" Doyle raged, surging forward. "*BASTARD!*"

Sparks put a restraining hand on Doyle's shoulder. His jaw was tight, but his voice stayed measured and calm. "That's what he wants from us."

The scream cut off abruptly. The ensuing quiet was even more unsettling.

"We must go," said Sparks. "They may still come after us."

"You can't leave them—" protested Eileen.

"They're soldiers," said Sparks, gathering up his snowshoes.

"He's killing them—"

"We don't know that it's them. Even if it is, what would you have us do? Throw our own lives away? Sentimental lunacy."

"Still, Jack, they're so loyal to you—" said Doyle, trying to soften the argument.

"They know the risks." Sparks wanted no more discussion. He walked away.

"You've got your brother's blood in you, Jack Sparks," said Eileen to Sparks's back.

Sparks stopped, tensed, but didn't turn, then continued on.

Eileen wiped the tears from her eyes.

"He's right, you know," said Doyle gently.

"So am I," she said, watching Sparks go.

They slipped into the snowshoes and trudged out of the graveyard after him. The trip back to the inn was passed in silence.

✦　✦　✦

293

A note had been pinned to Stoker's door. Sparks tore it down and briefly scanned it.

"Stoker's hired a carriage and started back to London," he said to the others. "He says he has his family to consider."

"Can't blame him for that," said Doyle.

"He's bequeathed us the use of his room." Sparks pocketed the note and opened the door. Eileen entered. Doyle looked at his watch: half past two in the morning.

"Excuse us a moment, Miss Temple," said Sparks, detaining Doyle in the hallway and closing the door. "Stay with her. If I'm not back by dawn, try and make your way to London."

"Where are you—"

"They've probably done their worst for tonight, but keep your pistol loaded and at hand," said Sparks, walking away down the corridor.

"Jack, what are you going to do?"

Sparks gave a wave without looking back as he moved quickly downstairs. Doyle looked at the door and cracked it open. Eileen lay on top of the bedclothes, her back to him. He was about to close the door. . . .

"Don't go," she said without moving.

"You should rest."

"Not much chance of that."

"Rest is what you need—"

"Stop being a doctor, for heaven's sake." She turned to face him. "I don't particularly wish to spend my last night on earth alone, do you?"

"What makes you think this is—"

"Come in here and close the door, would you? How plain do I have to make myself?"

Doyle acquiesced but remained across the room, standing rigidly near the door. She gave him a wry look, shook her head slightly, sat up on the bed, and caught a glimpse of herself in the mirror on the vanity. Her hair was tangled in disarray, fair complexion burned by the wind.

"Frightful," she said.

"Not so bad as all that," offered Doyle, instantly regretting it.

Another sardonic look from her consolidated his remorse. She moved to a chair by the mirror and dispassionately surveyed herself.

"I suppose a hairbrush is too providential to hope for," she said.

"As a matter of fact, it's one of the few possessions I have remaining to me," said Doyle. From his bag, which he'd left at the foot of the armoire, he produced his brush-and-comb set.

"You really should smile, Doctor," she said, her eyes brightening. " 'Rich gifts wax poor when givers prove unkind.' "

"I don't mean to be unkind . . . Ophelia," he added, recognizing the passage.

Eileen took off the mannish jacket, unpinned her hair, and let the soft black mass of it cascade down the back of her blouse. She shook it out and ran the brush down its lustrous length in long, sensuous strokes: an effect, to Doyle's eyes, of breathtaking intimacy, a balm to his battered spirits. It was the first time since they'd heard the screams on the hill that the brothers had been out of his thoughts for even a moment.

"Did you ever see me onstage, Doctor?" she asked.

"I never had the pleasure," said Doyle. "My name is Arthur."

She gave the slightest nod, acknowledging the new increment of familiarity. "There were good reasons why our guardians of decency wouldn't allow women to perform in public for so many hundreds of years."

"What reasons would those be?"

"Some would tell you it's dangerous to see a woman on the stage."

"Dangerous in what way?"

She shrugged slightly. "Perhaps it's too easy to believe the actress is exactly who she appears to be playing on any particular night."

"But that is the desired effect, after all. To persuade us of the character's veracity."

"It should be, yes."

"Then how does that represent a danger? And for whom?"

"For someone who encounters the woman off the stage and finds it difficult to distinguish the actress from the role she was playing." She looked at him in the mirror, out from under the wave of a curl. "Didn't your mother ever warn you about actresses, Arthur?"

"She must have felt there were more obvious dangers lurking about." Doyle held her eyes steadily. "I have seen you onstage, haven't I?"

"Yes, you have. After a fashion."

A long pause followed. "Miss Temple—"

"Eileen."

"Eileen," said Doyle. "Are you attempting to seduce me?"

"Am I?" She stopped brushing. Her forehead crinkled. She seemed as unsure of the answer as was he. "Is that your impression, really?"

"Yes. I would have to say that it is." Doyle felt surprisingly and utterly calm.

A poised thought flew over the plane of her face like the shadow of a flock of doves. She carefully laid the brush down on the table and turned to face him. "What if I were?"

"Well," said Doyle, "I would have to say that if this does prove to be the last evening of our lives, and I, for whatever reason, remained resistant to your charms, it would surely be the most senseless regret that would soon enough accompany me to the grave."

They looked at each other without pretense.

"Then perhaps you should lock the door, Arthur," she said simply, all aspect of performance gone from her voice.

He did exactly as she requested.

CHAPTER 17

Mother's Own

D OYLE LEFT THE bedroom before first light. Eileen was sleeping restfully. He gently lifted her arm from where it lay lightly across his shoulder and kissed the sweet nape of her neck before rising. She made a small murmuring as he dressed, but it must have been a response to a dream. She did not stir again.

He was astonished by the absence within him of shame. That conditioned Catholic response to pleasure of any variety—let alone carnal—had never quite been rooted out. Perhaps this time would prove the exception; it had been what she wanted, he told himself, and lest he forget, what he had wanted as well. He had often seen surgeons similarly moved when among the dead and dying by the need to reaffirm the life coursing inside them. What did this mean with regard to his continued relations with her? He hadn't a clue. Having satisfied the physical insistence of the moment, with almost equal urgency he required some small distance to assess the repercussions to his emotions.

Doyle quietly locked the door and pocketed the key. He looked at his watch: nearly five. He would allow Sparks until nine at the very least to return, well past dawn, perhaps longer, directly countermanding his orders. He walked downstairs to see if a cup of tea could be found.

No one was in the kitchen, and he heard nobody moving below. The inn carried the expectant repose that settled the air just before dawn. Timbers groaned expressively. Looking out a window, he noticed that the clouds had lifted; when it came, the morning would be bright, clear, and cold.

She had been sweet and yielding and, yes, experienced, undoubtedly more so than he was, a powerfully tempting avenue for bad feeling from which he turned resolutely away. What had moved him most, what moved him now, was how real in that hour she had seemed, how tangible, reachable: how *close*. No artifice or barrier between him and a direct experience of who she was. She had wept at one point, silently, wiping away the tears but asking him with her touch and movement not to stop or pay attention. He had complied. What was he feeling now? That knowledge danced away, just out of his grasp. Why did his emotions always lag so infuriatingly far behind his ability to reason?

Doyle felt slightly light-headed. He opened the door and stepped into the walled courtyard behind the public room. Snow covered the bricks that surrounded a gnarled, bare oak. The cold nipped through his shirt, but it felt clean and bracing. He breathed in the air deeply, greedily, trying to fill his lungs beyond their capacity.

"Fresh air is such a tonic," said a voice behind him. A voice he had heard quite recently.

Alexander Sparks stood in the shelter of the oak. Wrapped in his black cloak, motionless, hands out of sight, only his face visible in the wan light spilling from the windows. Long and narrow, facial structure similar to his brother's—the resemblance ended in the flesh. He looked nothing like the man Doyle had met outside 13 Cheshire, and yet he knew immediately they were one and the same. Skin lay taut over the bone, shiny and white as parchment, as if a relentless internal heat had seared away all excess, all comfort, everything but necessity. His eyes were pale and evenly set under dark slices of brow, with long black lashes of surprising delicacy. Lank brown hair hung straight to his shoulders, swept back off a high, smooth forehead that receded into the folds of the cloak. Only his mouth belied the geometric austerity of the arrangement; the lips were full, rosebud, red, and moist. As he spoke, a serpentine tongue flicked out from behind the small, neat lines of his teeth, the only visible concession to insatiable appetites that lit the man's interior as starkly as a candle in a jack-o'-lantern. His presence in the courtyard felt magnetic and riveting but somehow weightless; he didn't seem to occupy space so much as hover inside it. Doyle was reminded how much power was generated by absolute stillness.

"Do you favor this time of the night, Doctor?"

Alexander's voice was conveyed by a deceptive frequency that split itself into twin modulations; a second tone attached to the surface of his round, rich baritone, riding under the belly of the words, a buzzing or ringing below the conscious threshold that unpleasantly slithered in the ear of the listener like a thief.

"Not especially."

Doyle lowered his hands and gently touched his pockets.

"I believe you've left your gun in the room. With Miss Temple," said Alexander. He smiled in a way that might usually be described as kind.

Doyle flexed his hands. The adrenaline kicking into his bloodstream rapidly elevated his heart rate. He felt under a microscope and tried to suppress his alarm to undetectable levels. Wary the man might possess untold mesmeric abilities, he blinked often and avoided his gaze for any extended time.

"I must confess that meeting you in this way is quite strange, Dr. Doyle. I do feel as if I know you already," said Alexander, with no small modicum of charm. "Do you share that impression?"

"We have met before."

"However unknowingly." Alexander nodded slightly, the first movement he had made.

Doyle glanced casually around the yard. His only avenue of escape lay through the open door behind him, but that would expose his back for the time it would take to climb the stairs.

"What do you want?" asked Doyle.

"I felt it time for us to effect a more formal introduction. I fear, Doctor, that my young brother, John, may have imparted to you some severe and perfidious misperceptions regarding myself."

I don't want to hear this, thought Doyle instinctively, I mustn't listen. He did not respond with either word or gesture.

"I thought there would be decided value in our making an effort to know one another as, perhaps, a belated corrective to the more delusional of John's spurious inventions."

"Do I have a choice?"

"One always has a choice, Doctor," he said, smiling incandescently. The effect reminded Doyle of acid dripping slowly onto dark, polished wood.

Doyle paused as long as he felt able. "I should like to get my coat. I'm very cold."

"Of course."

Doyle waited. Alexander made no move.

"Now?" asked Doyle.

"We shan't get far if you freeze to death."

"It's in my room."

"How perfectly reasonable."

"So I'll go get it then."

"I will wait for you," said Alexander.

Doyle nodded and edged back into the building. Alexander watched without moving. Doyle turned, then walked through the public rooms and back up the stairs.

What is he about? wondered Doyle. How supremely confident, or heedlessly arrogant, the man was. *Relentlessly pursuing me for days on end, then allowing me to walk away when I'm dead-bang within striking distance.* He knew perfectly well that whatever sensibility the man evinced was nothing but a skillful and treacherous simulation. But what was his purpose?

Doyle silently slid in the key and opened the door. The curtains and windows were locked as before. Nothing appeared to have been touched. But Eileen was gone.

So that was it then; he kept me there long enough for them to take her. Doyle went for his coat. The pistol was not in the pocket where he'd left it, nor in any of the others. His bag was still on the floor. He opened it, rifling through the medical supplies for a handful of medicinal vials and two syringes. He inserted the needles into the tubes, filled both syringes with the liquid, ripped a small tear in the fabric of his coat alongside the inner breast pocket, and deposited the extra vials inside. The syringes he slipped one apiece into the sides of his boots.

Wary he had aroused suspicion by taking too long, Doyle hurried down the stairs. Alexander waited near the open front door, as composed and motionless as before.

"Where is she?" asked Doyle.

Alexander nodded to the outside.

"If you've harmed her—"

"Please. No threats." He sounded amused; a smile nearly congealed on his wet mouth. "She's quite safe."

"Let me see her."

"By all means."

Alexander raised a long, thin hand, gesturing out the door. A large black coach and four stood in the drive, if not the same menacing carriage Doyle had seen before, then an extremely reasonable facsimile. The horses snorted gutturally, stamping their feet. Doyle walked to the carriage. The driver, bundled on his perch, never turned to him. Curtains obscured the windows.

"She's inside."

Doyle started. Alexander stood directly behind him; he had not seen or heard the man move from inside the inn. Doyle opened the door and stepped into the coach. Feeble light spilled in from lanterns mounted on the chassis. Eileen lay on the rear-facing seat against the wall, unconscious, wearing her borrowed hat and clothes. Doyle checked her pulse and breathing; both were steady but faint. He detected the scent of a disabling chemical around her mouth and nose: ether, perhaps, or some more potent compound.

The coach door closed. Doyle turned to find Alexander sitting across from them. With a loud *thunk,* the handles moved down, locking mechanically. The carriage lurched forward. Doyle held Eileen in his arms. Alexander smiled compassionately.

"If you aren't offended by the compliment, Doctor, you do make a most attractive couple," he said pleasantly.

Loathsome as the thought was that this man had knowledge of their recent intimacy, Doyle held his tongue. He cradled Eileen closer to him and felt the tender warmth of her neck against his hand.

"Where are we going?"

Alexander did not answer.

"Ravenscar?"

Alexander displayed that raw bone of a smile. His face appeared skeletal in the dusky light, all trace of personality pared away, stripped to its naked essence.

"There's something you must know about my brother, Doctor. Our parents perished tragically in a fire when Jonathan was little more than a boy. Such a precocious and happy child, as you can imagine, he suffered dreadfully. I had already reached the age of emancipation, but Jonathan was made a ward of the court and regrettably placed in the care of a family friend, a physician of radically progressive ideas but indiscriminate methodology. After months with no noticeable improvement, this doctor undertook to treat Jonathan's hysterical disposition with a series of narcotic injections. These treatments initially succeeded in suppressing his disease; it was not too long before his spirits appeared to rise to, if not exceed, the levels he had enjoyed before the difficulties.

"Most unfortunately, the doctor declined to suspend the treatments; he continued these injections for many months. Consequently, he delivered to young Jonathan a lifelong craving for this drug from which he has not to this day been able to acquit himself. This has led him, often in times of emotional complexity, to periodic bouts of overindulgence, and these in turn to episodes of acute dementia that have required his being confined to hospitals specializing in the treatment of the mentally disturbed."

"Such as Bedlam," said Doyle.

"Sadly, yes," said Alexander, with a world-weary shake of the head. "I have attempted as best I could to care for my brother throughout his terrible ordeal. But as so often happens when one raises the hand of loving consolation to someone in this pitiably reduced state, so commanding is the drug's attraction that one tangled in its web comes to perceive the giver of aid as an enemy sworn to sever them from that substance which they believe provides them with their only succor. As a doctor, you would be well acquainted with this phenomenon."

Doyle had with his own eyes all too recently seen Sparks feeding that hunger, and he did know what pernicious effects these addictions wrought in the mind. Alexander recounted the story with such lubricious sincerity that Doyle was momentarily at a loss how much to credit. Nothing the man raised necessarily put paid to what Jack had said about him, and Doyle had not yet confronted him with any of Jack's accusations. It was nearly impossible not to consider, if only for a moment, Alexander's offered alternative as a disturbingly plausible scenario. On the other hand, if he owned only a fraction of the power Jack had attributed to him, this sort of routine dissembling would be as effortless to him as multiplication tables for a mathematical prodigy. If he's lying, thought Doyle, what is his purpose?

"Why was your brother confined to Bedlam?" asked Doyle neutrally.

"Assault on a police officer. He was attempting a forced entry to Buckingham Palace. One of John's more persistent delusions involves an imagined relationship to Queen Victoria."

"What sort of relationship?"

"He often claims to be working under the direct and secret orders of Her Majesty, investigating an assortment of conspiracies involving threats to the continuity of accession to the throne, most of which he is convinced I am responsible for. Consequently, he follows after me wherever I go, trying to interfere with my day-to-day affairs. This has been going on for years. More often than not, it plays out harmlessly. On this occasion, that was regrettably not the case."

"Why would he do these things?"

"As you know, with any mental aberration it is difficult to say with certainty. An acquaintance of mine, an alienist in Vienna whom I have consulted on the matter, speculates that Jonathan is driven by a compulsion to relive the devastating loss of our parents—wherein the Queen becomes a surrogate for his mother, you see—and that by 'saving' the Queen's life from imagined danger, he will somehow resurrect her."

"I see."

"What has he said to you about this matter, Doctor?" Alexander asked blandly.

He wants to know what I know, realized Doyle. That's what this charade is about. He wants to know how far the damage has spread.

"Jonathan was very close to your mother, wasn't he?" asked Doyle.

"A very deep attachment, yes," said Alexander.

Doyle was careful to betray nothing with his eyes. "And were you close to her as well?"

Alexander smiled, showing the milky-white line of his perfect teeth. "Every boy is close to his mother."

The carriage slowed as it started up a long and gradual grade. Eileen shifted slightly in Doyle's arms.

"And your father, Mr. Sparks?"

"What of him?" Alexander was still smiling.

"What was your relationship to him?"

"I believe it is John's relationships we are scrutinizing here." The smile remained, but Doyle detected an almost imperceptible strain to keep it in place.

"I don't disagree," said Doyle, subtly maintaining the offensive. "And as familiar as you seem to be with the rudiments of psychology, you must know that one of its principal areas of investigation is relationships within the family." Alexander did not visibly react. "For instance, how would you characterize Jonathan's relationship to you?"

Alexander's smile seemed frozen in place now. "We were . . . remote. I spent the better part of his childhood away at school."

"Did he have any contact with you during that time? Any visits? Correspondence?"

Alexander shifted ever so slightly in his seat.

"Nothing out of the ordinary."

"So you did write to him?"

"On occasion."

"And of course you saw him whenever you returned home."

Alexander hesitated. "Of course."

He's uncomfortable speaking about any of it, realized Doyle, but he doesn't want to evidence alarm that might raise my suspicion. He doesn't know what I know. The thought hit Doyle hard: He's underestimated me.

"Were there any difficulties in your relationship with Jonathan?"

"Difficulties of what sort?"

"Rivalries."

Alexander smiled. "Goodness no."

"Young boys ofttimes band together against figures of authority; were there any incidents of that sort your parents might have objected to?"

"Why do you ask?"

"I'm attempting to determine if Jonathan had formed any unresolved hostilities to your parents," said Doyle, manufacturing as fast as he could speak. "In other words, are there any reasons to suspect that this fatal fire might have been something more than an accident?"

The suggestion seemed to pacify his resistance. "How interesting. To be honest with you, Doctor, I have often wondered the very same thing."

"Hmm. Yes. Can you recall if Jonathan had any totems or small items of particular importance to him?" said Doyle, now consciously adopting the inflated airs and labored deductions of a pompous academician. "These commonplace objects—sometimes called fetishes— often provide clues to the underlying causes of derangement—"

"What sort of items?"

"They could be almost anything: rocks, baubles, trinkets, or necklaces. Even locks of hair."

A flash of uncertainty passed behind Alexander's eyes. Had he seen through the bluff? Doyle waited him out, innocently, the concerned physician, offering only a fussily furrowed brow of cooperative exploration.

"I can recall no such items," said Alexander. He parted the curtains to glance outside.

Doyle nodded contemplatively. "Did he ever exhibit any tendencies of violence toward other, particularly younger, children?"

"No," said Alexander, turning back to him, a tinge of annoyance creeping into his voice.

"Any violence toward women in general, particularly as he grew into adolescence?"

"None that I am aware of."

"When do you feel Jonathan's hostility became directed at you?"

"I've said nothing about any hostility toward me."

"I see; you deny that there was any—"

"I didn't say—"

"So there was hostility between you—"

"He was a very disturbed child—"

"Perhaps he was jealous of your relationship with your mother—"

"Perhaps so—"

"Perhaps he coveted his mother's affections solely for himself—"

"Oh yes, I know that he did—"

"And perhaps he was jealous of your father's relations with her as well—"

"Of *course* he was—" Alexander's voice whelmed with conviction.

"So much so that he felt compelled to eliminate all his rivals for her attention—"

"That's right—"

"And there was finally only one way to accomplish that, wasn't there?"

"Yes—"

"That's why you set the fire—"

"Yes!"

Doyle stopped. Alexander caught himself almost before the word had left his mouth. A reptilian coldness instantly sculpted his face into a mask of brutal contempt.

"So you *do* believe that Jonathan killed your parents," said Doyle, boldly attempting to maintain the guilelessness of his inquisition.

"Yes," said Alexander flatly. His upper lip curled in an involuntary sneer, his nostrils flared, and the lids of his eyes drooped ominously low. He appeared bestial. This is what he looks like, thought Doyle; this is his real face.

"I see," said Doyle, nodding again. "This is all so very interesting, Mr. Sparks. I shall be sure to give your analysis the most serious consideration."

"Will you now?" Alexander's voice was harsh and raspy, that ominous underlying tone moving closer to the surface.

"Indeed," said Doyle, swallowing his fear. "If what you say is true, and I have little reason to doubt that it is, your brother may be more than a danger to just himself. In all honesty, I must tell you I believe he almost certainly poses just as great a danger to you."

Doyle gave a self-satisfied smile, leaned back in the seat, and pretended to ponder the intangibles. Please God let him think me a harmless pedant, thought Doyle. He dared not look at Alexander again, but he could feel the heat of the man's eyes boring in on him. Had he gone too far? Too early to determine. The man had not leapt for his throat, although Doyle had given him adequate provocation. The fact remained that Alexander had for the moment been outwitted; if anything was more likely to prod him into a murderous rage, it would be difficult to name. And if his thickheaded performance had held up under scrutiny, Doyle had not even given the man the satisfaction of knowing he'd been *consciously* outwitted, in which case Alexander's wrath would more likely be directed inward, toward himself. Pride. That was Lucifer's failing, too. Every man has a weakness, simply human nature, but even if he had succeeded in stumbling onto that of Alexander Sparks, Doyle now had no doubt he was in the company of a man every bit as dangerous as Jack had described. He and Eileen were still alive only because of their enemy's uncertainty in how much Jack had told them and whomever else they might have told in turn.

Granted, there were untold questions to be answered on the subject of Jack Sparks, but at the least Alexander's inadvertent confession to the deaths of their parents exonerated Jack in those unnatural crimes once and for all. The anguished music he had heard Jack making was born of sorrow, not guilt. And if Alexander was responsible, as Jack had asserted, the rest of his account became that much easier to credit.

Doyle parted the curtains. The road they traversed ran high on a bluff, paralleling the treeless, windswept shore. The eastern sky lightened over the distant sea. Dawn was only minutes away.

Eileen moved again; her respiration deepened. The drug was wearing off. Was there any way to remove her from harm? Doyle was forced to admit that whatever could be done now he would in all likelihood have to do alone: The brothers' fate was in grave doubt; for all he knew, Jack may have been lost as well. But mourning was an unaffordable indulgence. The weight of responsibility for the life in his arms provided a surge of stamina and resolution. Doyle glanced at Alexander and felt the pressure of the syringes in his boot. Not yet, he thought. Not with Eileen so close.

The carriage slowed to a walk as the wheels encountered paved stone. Moments later they clattered through a horseshoed arch, flanked by twin granite statues of immense birds of prey.

"Ravenscar," said Alexander. His face had once again assumed its mask of polite formality.

Doyle nodded. He heard the gates shut behind them as the carriage came to a stop. The change in motion brought Eileen out of her languor. She saw Doyle's face, found herself in his arms, made a small sound of contentment, and moved closer to him. He held her tight and stroked her hair. At the sound of the door, Doyle looked up and saw that Alexander Sparks was gone.

A liveried servant opened the door on their side of the carriage, and in it appeared a broad, ruddy, smiling face adorned with two conical tufts of fleecy white hair floating on either side of a shiny pate.

Thick spectacles magnified the man's hazy blue eyes to the size of robin's eggs.

"Is it Dr. Doyle then?"

"Yes?"

"A-hoot, you've come to Ravenscar, and a pleasure it is to welcome you to us," said the man, in an agreeably reedy Scots Highland brogue.

Reacting to the intrusion of another voice, Eileen tried to rouse herself. Doyle leaned forward and shook the man's energetically offered hand.

"Bishop Pillphrock," surmised Doyle, spying the man's collar and frock.

"A-hoot, the very same, Doctor, and how-do."

"Miss Eileen Temple," said Doyle, holding her shoulders, balancing her upright.

"Well, yes, and am I most pleased to meet you, Miss Temple," said the Bishop with an expansive show of bad teeth, covering her hand with both of his dainty little mitts.

Eileen experienced no little difficulty focusing her eyes, but as social instincts engaged, she carried the moment.

"*Enchantée*," she said, with a heart-stopping smile.

"Charmed, I'm sure! A-hoot, please, come in, come in," said the Bishop, backing away from the door and gesturing graciously. "We've hot baths awaiting to repair the effects of the journey, warm beds for rest if you desire, hearty breakfasts to fortify your spirits. This way."

Doyle helped Eileen from the carriage. She leaned heavily against him, unsteady on her feet. Doyle assessed their position: a circular cobblestoned courtyard surrounded by high, thick walls. Early dawn washed everything in a dense gloom of iron gray. The gate through which they had passed was hewn from marbleized black wood, banded with steel. Two rows of formally attired servants, many holding lanterns, formed a gauntlet to the entrance of the house before them, more properly a medieval fortress: wings, flying buttresses, massive round towers topped with banners disappearing in the haze. In the scrimy light, Doyle could see cannon lining the battlements.

"A warm welcome. A very warm welcome indeed. Right this way with you, Doctor, Miss Temple," said the Bishop with a beatific smile. He started ahead of them, short and swag-bellied, with a splayfooted bounce characteristic of a much younger man. Doyle supported Eileen with one hand in hers, the other around her waist, as they followed.

As they passed between them, Doyle studied the footmen on either side. All men of impressive size and solidity. Faces cold and hard, impassive. Faces that might have been concealed behind hoods while hunting them down through the snow only hours before.

"Where are we, Arthur?" whispered Eileen.

"A very bad place," said Doyle.

"What are we doing here?"

"That's not altogether clear."

"Well then . . . if I can't say that I'm happy to be here, I am so very glad that you're with me."

He held her closer. A few men peeled off to follow them through the vast double doors to which the Bishop led them. The interior expounded on the grand themes established by the castle's facade. A welter of heraldic oriflammes enlivened the walls and ceiling. This expansive central hall was crowded with suits of armor, posed in warlike postures. A long, narrow table of burnished wood consumed the length of the room's middle. At its far end a fireplace as wide and as deep as Doyle's old bedroom burned a load of timber the size of a whaling boat.

"I'm afraid it's a wee trice early for our guests to be up and about," said the Bishop, leading them to an epic stone staircase, "but I can assure you they are most anxious to make your acquaintance."

"The gentleman we shared the carriage with . . ." said Doyle.

"Yes," said the Bishop brightly.

"Mr. Graves? Mr. Maximilian Graves?"

"Yes?" The Bishop smiled helpfully as they started up the stairs.

"Your colleague. On the board of Rathborne and Sons."

"Yes, yes. Rathborne and Sons, yes."

"So that was the gentleman?"

"Who did he say he was?"

"He didn't."

"Ah. Yes," said the Bishop with another grin.

Doyle couldn't tell if the man was being deliberately obscure or was simply an idiot.

"No, I'm attempting to determine," persisted Doyle, "if that was in fact Mr. Maximilian Graves."

"Oh, I wouldn't wish to speak for Mr. Graves."

"So that *was* Mr. Graves."

"Is that what he told you?"

Eileen and Doyle looked at each other, wide-eyed; the Bishop's moronic cheerfulness was cutting through even her foggy state.

"He said his name was Alexander Sparks."

"Well then," said the Bishop, "he would be in a position to know, wouldn't he? A-hoot, and here we are."

Mother's Own

A brawny servant standing outside a door in the hall opened it as they approached, and the Bishop extravagantly waved them inside. The room's furnishings and appointments were opulent, vivid contrast to the Spartan militarism throughout what they'd seen of the rest of the house. Plush Persian carpets lay underfoot. Gossamer canopies draped twin beds. Chairs and plump divans exuded overstuffed pulchritude. Tapestries covered the walls but couldn't conceal their curves, suggesting the room sat snugly in one of Ravenscar's many towers. A single narrow window faced northwest, the sky growing light with the dawn.

"The bath is through here," said the Bishop. He opened an adjoining door to reveal a black-and-white-tiled chamber, where servants poured buckets of steaming hot water into an elevated brass tub.

"Please don't hesitate to rest and refresh yourselves before joining us. Our guests here are all royalty to us. And if you require anything else, anything at all," said the Bishop, taking hold of a velvet rope suspended from the ceiling, "one ring will quickly bring someone running."

Doyle and Eileen thanked him, and the Bishop backed out of the room on a steady stream of gracious inanities. The door closed solidly. Doyle held a finger to his lips, moved to the door, and tried the handle. Locked. He opened the clasp to peer through the door's peephole and was greeted by the stony eyes of the servant stationed outside. Doyle shut the trap and moved to the window as Eileen plopped down on one of the chaises and tried to pull off her boots.

"I wholeheartedly approve of the bath," she said, still reeling a little.

The window looked directly down on the courtyard. Traffic in and out of the heavy gates through which they'd entered ran regular and heavy, covered wagons primarily, but a fair number of men on foot—patrols armed with rifles, as were the numerous sentinels parading the ramparts.

"If they mean to kill us," said Eileen, fumbling woozily with the buttons of her shirt, "they must want clean, well-rested corpses."

Doyle looked farther left as the first morning sunlight flooded the flat plain that lay to the west—the leading edge of the North Yorkshire moors, if Doyle had his geography in order. Somewhere therein sat the property General Marcus McCauley Drummond extorted from Lord Nicholson. Not much innate value aside from the peat bogs. Perhaps its worth had to do with its proximity to Ravenscar, reasoned Doyle. As the mist lifted, in the distance he could dimly make out shapes jutting from the fresh snow on the moors: low, man-made structures, perhaps storage sheds for the peat.

"I'm going first, Arthur, if you have no objection," said Eileen, peeling off the shirt, trousers falling around her ankles as she hobbled to the bath.

"Yes. Fine," said Doyle, almost but not quite engrossed enough to be distracted by her flesh before she disappeared. Moments later, he heard a healthy splash, followed in short order by an exclamation, a giggle, and then a contented sigh.

Resuming his survey, Doyle saw that the sprawl of Ravenscar proper filled the southern reaches of what was visible from the window. Outside the walls in that direction stood a high, rambling structure, serviced by a rail spur running to the west. Figures moved in and out of its cavernous doors. Boxcars waited in the switching yard. Black smoke poured from two towering stacks that rose from the building's core. Beneath the chimneys, an ornate and sentimentally rendered scene of a mother standing in a kitchen, handing a biscuit to a little boy, covered a large expanse of wall. Lettering above it inscribed: MOTHER'S OWN.

"Arthur?" He could hear the slip and burble of languidly moving water.

"Yes, Eileen."

"Could you come in here a moment, please?"

"Yes, Eileen."

Doyle removed his coat, took the vials of medicine concealed in the lining and the syringes from his boots, and stuffed them beneath the cushions of a davenport. Then he moved to the bath.

Arms folded across her breasts, eyes closed, Eileen lay back against the angled wall of the tub, which simulated the form of a brass dragon down to its four taloned claws. Her skin looked like alabaster. There was a fine glisten of moisture on her upper lip. Her hair was loosely piled on top of her head, but a few delicious strands dangled delicately down to the waterline. Doyle was instantly thrown into a reverie: the enduring fascination of a woman's hair. How did they know just exactly what to do with it in every conceivable situation? How did they move it around their heads in such graceful, effortless defiance of gravity?

"I'm in a kind of heaven," she said dreamily.

"Are you?"

"I assume I was given a drug of some kind."

"Yes, dear."

"It's difficult for me to think very clearly." She was taking great care to enunciate clearly. "My physical responses to things seem to be a bit . . . overwhelming."

"Which we can attribute to the drug as well, I think."

"So this feeling is going to go away soon."

"Yes."

"Hmm. Pity. I'm sorry, I'm not being very much help to you."

"You're safe. That's all that matters."

She rested an inviting hand on the edge of the tub. He took it, watching the water run off their entwined fingers.

"Mr. Jack Sparks did not come back?" she asked.

"No."

"That's very troubling."

"Yes."

"We're in quite a serious muggins, you and I."

"Yes, dear, I'm afraid we are."

"Then after I've had a few more minutes to soak," she said softly, "I would like you to take me to bed. Would that be all right with you, Arthur?"

"Yes, dear. Yes, it would."

She smiled and held his hand. He sat on the edge of the tub and waited.

✦　✦　✦

Familiarity breeds a few feelings other than contempt, thought Doyle as he lay on the enveloping feather bed and by measured steps gave in to the round, full weight of his fatigue. Passion, for one. Whether as a result of the drug in her system or need inspired by the precariousness of their position, the urgency and abandon with which she had submitted herself to him fell significantly further outside his limited experience than their lovemaking of the night before. She lay curled in his arms now, smooth and soft, sound asleep, her jet hair an exotic stain fanning the milky linen. To his surprise, he had no difficulty reconciling these more tender feelings with the urgent, animalistic coupling they had shared only minutes before. No single act in his life had ever seemed more genuine. As he fell asleep, he remembered thinking he had never been as grateful to his mother for anything more than her failure to warn him against actresses.

Doyle woke with a start, his dreams fleeing like burglars. The light in the room was low, a shade of burnt orange, filtering at a sharp, perpendicular angle through the window. Someone's been in here while we slept, his instincts informed him. He sat up. His clothes gone from the floor where he had hastily discarded them, nowhere to be seen. Laid out on the opposite bed were a set of gentleman's evening wear and a woman's black velvet dress. Eileen lay asleep beside him. A sharp pang in his gut told him he was gnawingly, ravenously hungry.

Doyle found his watch lying neatly on the pocket of the dinner jacket and snapped it open: four o'clock. The day was almost gone! He pulled on the trousers, a perfect fit, and slipped the braces over his shoulders as he padded to the window. The sun was fast approaching the western horizon. Activity in the courtyard continued, armed patrols on the walls still in force. Work had apparently ceased at the adjacent factory, the stacks quiescent. But a thin line of smoke issued from one of the smaller buildings farther out on the moors.

Feeling under the cushions of the sofa, Doyle determined the vials and syringes were in place where he'd stashed them, then he moved into the bath to attend to the body's necessities. A pitcher of hot water, a shaving mug, and razor sat beside a ceramic basin before the mirror, along with a shaker of astringent bay rum.

Freshly abluted, five minutes later Doyle reentered the bedroom. Eileen slumped on the edge of the bed, a sheet draped around her, the heel of a hand pressed to her forehead.

"Did you kick me in the head or just beat me with a truncheon?"

"You'll feel better once you're up and moving. They've left clothes for us, formal wear: Apparently, we're dressing for dinner."

"Food." The idea struck her as revelatory and seemed to ameliorate her discomfort. She looked up at him, to share the incredible thought. "Food."

"Not without its appeal," said Doyle, kissing her before moving to the other bed.

"I don't think I've eaten in months."

"Take your time. I'm going to have a look about," said Doyle, as he quickly donned the rest of the clothes.

"I have vague memories of food," said Eileen, as she traipsed to the bath, trailing the sheet, "but I can't seem to recall ever having tasted any before."

Doyle knotted the bow tie, checked it in the mirror, plumped the handkerchief in his breast pocket, and moved to the door. The handle was unlocked.

Sedate chamber music wafted from somewhere in the house below. Two men rose from chairs in the hallway as Doyle exited the bedroom. Both appeared in their early fifties and were similarly attired in evening wear. Each held a drink; the shorter of the two, a dapper, fastidious man with thinning hair and a trim black beard, smoked a blunt cigar. The taller one bore the broad shoulders and upright carriage of a military man, his white hair trimmed to a rough bristle, a full, white walrus mustache cutting across the length of his square, uncompromising face. He hung back a step as the shorter man moved immediately to Doyle with an extended hand.

"We were just discussing something—perhaps you can settle the question for us, Doctor," said the shorter man gregariously, in a flat, nearly American accent, beaming a gap-toothed smile. "My friend Drummond here insists that if the proper circulatory equipment were to be made available, a man's head could indefinitely be kept alive and functioning after separation from the body."

"Depends entirely upon which latitude the separation were to be effected," said Drummond, his upper-class voice as stiff with reserve as his spine. His eyes, drawn slightly too far apart for symmetry in the broad box of his face, stared perpetually down his nose.

"Whereas I continue to maintain that the body provides far too many essential elements that the brain requires in order to carry on," said the shorter man, as casually as if they were discussing the delivery of mail. "And leaving the issue of maintenance aside, it's my decided opinion that the trauma of cleaving head from torso to begin with proves far too injurious for any portion of the brain to survive."

"I will go one step further, John," said the General. "I submit that if the cut were made at a sufficiently low intersection, it would be possible for the head to retain the power of speech."

"You see, we disagree there as well: Where would the wind come from, Marcus?" argued Sir John Chandros, the owner of Ravenscar. "Even with the neck in all its unfettered glory, there's no bellows to move the air through the vocal cords. Come on, man! What expertise can you offer us, Doctor? From a purely medical perspective?"

"I'm afraid I've never given the matter much thought," said Doyle.

"But it is a most provocative subject, don't you agree?" asked Chandros, who apparently felt no further introductions necessary.

"A heady matter indeed," said Doyle.

Chandros laughed genuinely. "Yes. Heady. Very good. Heady: Do you like that, Marcus?"

Drummond snorted, Doyle assumed disapprovingly.

"Marcus has been in violent need of a good, solid belly laugh for the last thirty years," said Chandros. "And he needs it still."

Drummond snorted again, seeming to confirm the opinion.

"For an accredited cynic and somewhat notorious man of the world, my friend the General manages to retain a remarkable naïveté." Chandros took Doyle's arm in his before he could respond and directed him down the corridor. "However, Doctor, apropos our prior discussion, regardless of its particular unlikelihood, I strongly believe that as a race of people we are on the verge of such a vast sea change of scientific discovery that it will transform forever life as we have known it."

Another snort from Drummond: There were apparently shadings and nuances to the man's use of the exclamation that would require months to interpret.

"Drummond will warn you that I am an inveterate disciple of the future. Guilty as charged. I happen to believe that if man is in need of hope, he need look no further for it than tomorrow. Yes, I've been to America, spent many years there: New York, Boston, Chicago, there's a city for you, powerful, tough, raw as the wind. Done a lot of business with them—they understand business, the Americans, second nature to them—and perhaps they've infected me with their optimism, but I still say if a man with the right idea meets a man with the right money, together they can change the world. Change it, hell: transform it. God gave man dominion over the earth; it's high time we took the bit between our teeth and pulled the plow with which the Lord provided us. Tried politics. Not for me. Too damn dependent on consensus to get anything done. Committees didn't build the Great Pyramids; Pharaoh did. My point is: The business of living is a business. Let me give you an example."

As they passed a banister looking down on the entrance hall, Doyle saw the long table was set for dinner. Well-attired guests mingled before the fire. With the baleful shadow of General Drummond trailing them, Chandros took Doyle past the overlook and through a door, out onto a high balcony. A vast panorama opened to the west, where the sun balanced perfectly on the lip of the horizon.

"What's man's greatest obstacle in life?" asked Chandros, puffing away on his cigar. "Himself. That's the rub. His own damn animal nature. Perpetually at war with the higher power inside. Can't surrender. There's a genius living cheek by jowl in the same bag of bones with this lower man, and let me tell you, sir, that lower man is nothing but a troglodyte, a half-wit chucklehead without the common sense to live. Worse still, this dumb clot thinks he's the long-lost son of a god; it's only a matter of time before the world puts him back on the throne where he belongs. In the meantime, he works like a dull ox and he drinks and he gambles and he whores and he pisses his life away and he dies crying out for this god that deserted him to save his pathetic, penny-ante soul. Let me ask you this: What everloving deity in its right mind would waste a moment's precious thought on a worth-less wretch like that?"

"I'm sure I don't know," said Doyle, recoiling at the man's frigid assurance.

"I will tell you: no deity worth a tinker's dam." He folded his arms, leaned against the wall, and looked out over the land. "Now the Christians have had a good run. No question about it. One dead Jew with some neat tricks up his sleeve, promoted like hair tonic by a few fanatical followers, and one converted emperor later they've got themselves a Holy Empire to shame any in history. Going on two thousand years. How did they manage it? The secret of their success was sim-plicity: Concentrate your power. Wrap it in mystery. Hide it inside the biggest building in town. Lay down a few commandments to keep the peasants in line, get a regulatory grip on birth, death, and marriage, throw in the fear of damnation, some smoke, a little music—there's your first commandment: Put on a good show—and customers will come crawling on their knees for the stale crumbs of that Feast of Saints. Now that . . . that was a business."

Drummond snorted again. Doyle wasn't certain if it was meant as affirmation or rebuttal.

Chandros puffed and chomped his cigar. His dazzling blue eyes sparkled with inspirational zeal. "So: How do you change man from a dim-witted, randy farm animal to a domesticated, productive tool ready to roll up his sleeves and pitch in for the greater good? There's the puzzle anybody that aspires to rule has to crack, be it religion, government, business, what have you. And here was the plain genius of the Christians' solution: Convince your constituents of one big lie. We hold the key to the gates of heaven. You want to make the trip, brother, you'll have to do it through our auspices. Sure, advertising how dodgy the Other Place is helped close the deal: Fear puts those poor ignorant sods down on their knees lighting candles like there's no tomorrow. And let's be straight, Old Nick's always been their real matinee idol—the man you love to hate, he'll scare you so bad you piss in your union suit, but you still can't take your eyes off him. He's the one puts the ladies in a lather, not that simpering, doe-eyed Mes-siah. Throw the Devil in to spice up the soup, and you've got yourself a flawless formula for religious hegemony. Worked like a Swiss watch. Nothing came close.

"But the march of progress—and you know it moves independently of our measly concerns; there's mystery for you—the march of progress demands that those in power change right along with the times. We're at the big table now, boys, playing with a whole new deck of cards: heavy industry, mass production, international economies, weaponry like you never dreamed of. Pious homilies and weak cheese pulpit-pleading to the customer's spiritual virtue just don't cut the mustard anymore. The Christians, as they are fond of saying in Kentucky, are just about shit out of luck. Excuse my French."

As the sun sank below the horizon, its dying rays lit Chandros and the sandstone wall behind him with a fiery orange luster.

"Look down there, Doctor," said Chandros, pointing toward an enclosure near the outer walls. "What do you see?"

A number of men in identical gray-striped pants and jackets of rough, nubbed material were filing into the compound through a gate leading toward the biscuit factory. The hair on their heads was cropped close to the skull. Armed guards supervised their movement, barking instructions, as the men fell into formation, their voices responding with cadenced chants that faintly reached the balcony.

"Workers. Factory workers," said Doyle.

Chandros shook his head, leaned in, and tapped Doyle on the chest for emphasis. "The *answer*," he said. "The men you are looking at were until recently the lowest, most degraded form of human filth imaginable. Convicts: mean, vicious, blockheaded incorrigibles. Recruited for those very qualities, the worst of the lot from the lowest prisons and penal colonies of the nation and the world. Brought here—and believe me the prisons are only too glad to be rid of them—to take part in a program that will prove our deliverance from blind enslavement to man's essential nature. Look at them."

The group's movements in the yard were well drilled, disciplined but unenthusiastic, if not sluggish, although none seemed to be performing under any sort of duress.

"Not so long ago those men could barely share common living space with other human beings for an hour without committing senseless acts of violence. The problem of crime. The problem of intolerance. The problem of brutality. Do you see? They all spring from the same fountainhead. Here and now, for the first time, they are completely rehabilitated, well provided for, and willing to give an honest day's work."

And so Bodger Nuggins was released from Newgate, thought Doyle. The intention seemed admirable enough—not all that different in conception, if not in scale, from what Jack Sparks tried to accomplish with men in the London underworld. But what was their method?

"How?" asked Doyle. "How is it done?"

316

Mother's Own

"Direct intervention," said Chandros.

"What does that mean?"

"One of our colleagues has been studying this problem for many years. He has come to the conclusion that the fundamental aspects of personality begin in the brain. The brain is a physical organ, like the lungs or the liver, and it can be refashioned in ways we are only beginning to understand. You're a doctor. We believe that this low level of humanity—should we call it that? Why not?—is nothing more than a medical problem, a disease, like cholera or meningitis. It is a purely physical defect, and should be treated accordingly."

"Treated in what way?"

"I'm not familiar with the precise medical terms; the Professor will be happy to give you the particulars—"

"Treated surgically?"

"I am interested in results, Doctor. You see before you the more than encouraging results we have begun to realize with this program, and not just with those factory workers: The entire household staff at Ravenscar is comprised of our successful efforts—our graduates, if you will. Let me assure you of this: Give a man a second chance at life, and he will be as grateful as a hound at your feet."

A second chance at life. Doyle felt his head spinning. The gray hoods. The ghouls at the museum. Automatons deprived of a will of their own. Doyle nodded agreeably to Chandros, turned away, and gripped the rail, trying not to betray his profound revulsion.

That's what they wanted the land for, Doyle realized—isolation to do this ungodly work. Bodger Nuggins caught wind of what lay in store and escaped, and they tracked him down and killed him. Something told Doyle he might have been one of the lucky ones. Whatever horrors had been committed on those sorry men below, the real monsters were here beside him on the balcony.

The last of the sunlight faded swiftly. The convicts in the enclosure were being marched off to another part of the compound. Doyle looked down at the central courtyard, his eye caught by a single wagon pulling in to what looked like a service entrance. As the driver dismounted and two servants moved forward to unload the delivery, a body clinging to the undercarriage rolled out from beneath the wagon and slipped into the shadows. None of the sentries or servants noticed the intruder make his move. Doyle couldn't make out the face from this distance, but something unmistakably familiar registered about the way the figure moved.

Jack.

A deep bell rang somewhere inside the house.

"Ah. Dinner will be served shortly," said Chandros. "Why don't you see if that charming companion of yours is ready to join us, Doctor?"

"Yes. Good," said Doyle.

"We'll see you at table then."

Doyle nodded. He heard the door open behind him; Chandros and Drummond moved inside. Doyle scanned the courtyard for another glimpse of the intruder but saw no trace of him. He waited a few moments, then followed the others inside.

Doyle stepped quickly to his room, where the formidable servant was once again stationed at the door. As he entered, Doyle caught the blank, reflectionless plane of the man's eyes. They were as cold and lifeless as those of a fish on a platter. The door closed silently behind him.

CHAPTER 18

Dinner Is Served

Seated before a vanity, Eileen used the mirror to apply the lightest blush to her lips. She wore her hair in an elaborate chignon. A choker studded with what appeared to be diamonds encircled her neck. The form-hugging, off-the-shoulder black velvet dress their hosts had provided elevated her innate glamour to a classical level.

"Fitting they give me a dress in the bargain," she said, "seeing as how they ruined mine. Fasten me in the back, would you, Arthur?"

Doyle bent to attend to the disjointed hook and eye. She wore a subtle, entrancing perfume. He kissed her shoulder once, softly.

"They left makeup and jewelry as well." She touched the diamond earrings she was wearing. "These are not paste. What on earth are they up to?"

"Why don't we go find out?" said Doyle, moving to the davenport and, out of her sight, retrieving the syringes. He slipped them into his breast pocket, making certain they didn't create a giveaway bulge in the line.

"Who else is going to be there?"

"More than they bargained for," said Doyle, lowering his voice. "Jack's somewhere inside."

She looked at him. "Good. We won't give up without a fight."

"I'll try and keep you as far from harm's way—"

"Arthur, the bastards killed eighteen of my friends—"

"I won't let them hurt you—"

"Among them my fiancé. He was sitting beside me at the séance that night, playing my brother."

Doyle collected himself. "Dennis."

"Yes. Dennis."

"I had no idea. I'm so terribly sorry."

Eileen nodded and turned away. Moments later she picked up a small black purse and presented herself. "Do I look all right? Lie if you must."

"Stunning. God's truth."

She smiled brightly, illuminating the room. He offered his arm, she took it, and they exited to the hall. The servant stood aside as they made for the stairs. Music from below was accompanied by the buzz of conversation.

"I've a four-inch hat pin in my hair," she whispered. "Tell me when, and I won't hesitate to use it."

"Don't be shy about applying it where it does the most damage."

"Have I ever struck you as shy, Arthur?"

"No, dear," he said.

Eileen wrapped her arm securely around Doyle's, and they started down the grand staircase. The sight below was rare and sumptuous; lit by enormous candelabras, the table was set with fine silver and crystal. A string quartet played in the corner. Eight chairs occupied, guests dressed as if for a royal occasion. Sir John Chandros sat at the head of the table, the seat of honor empty to his right. As he spied Doyle and Eileen descending, conversation died, and attention shifted toward the stairs.

"Smile, darling," whispered Doyle.

" 'Half a league, half a league, half a league onward, all in the valley of Death rode the six hundred. . . . ' " murmured Eileen under her breath. "Oh, my Lord . . . "

"What is it?"

"Look what the cat dragged in," she said, smiling and nodding toward the end of the table opposite to Chandros.

At the prompting of the silver-haired gent to his right, a man in his early twenties rose to greet them; of medium height, portly and pale, pinched features distorted by a dissolute bloat. A wispy mustache laden with wax and a goatish goatee intended a rakish flair that failed to convince, suggesting instead overreaching immaturity. Bedecked with ribbons, medals, and a sash, a constellation of new stains blotted his immaculately starched white dickey. As Doyle and Eileen reached the bottom of the stairs, Bishop Pillphrock, in High Anglican surplice, steered them straight toward the young man, who waited as patiently as a well-trained ape.

"May I present His Royal Highness Prince Albert Victor Edward, the Duke of Clarence," said the Bishop, with extreme unction. "Dr. Arthur Conan Doyle."

"How do you do?" said the Duke blankly. Nothing registered in his eyes, set near together with the oafish glaze of a guinea pig.

"Your Highness," said Doyle.

"Miss Eileen Temple," said the Bishop.

"How do you do?" He displayed no spark of recognition. The man must be ill, thought Doyle; Eileen was not easily forgotten, even at a glance, and the Duke had once spent an entire evening in vigorous pursuit of her.

"Your Highness," said Eileen.

"The weather today has been unseasonably mild," said the Duke, with the spontaneous animation of a windup toy.

"An unusually clear day for this time of year," said Doyle, inundated by the sour wine saturating the Prince's breath.

"We are all truly blessed by such a day as this," added the Bishop, flashing an oily grin. "One can only attribute our great good fortune to the company of His Highness."

"The company of His Highness produces numerous fortunes," said Eileen graciously. "I know that at least one of his gifts, passed from father to son, has been repeatedly bestowed to women throughout England."

The Bishop appeared thunderstruck by Eileen's comment—a none-too-veiled reference to the unmarried Duke's renowned promiscuity and rumored venereal heritage. Prince Eddy wrinkled his brow slightly; confusion seemed almost too complicated a mental state for him to reach.

The eldest son of the eldest son of the Queen herself, second in line to the throne, thought Doyle; if there was ever a more convincing argument against the continued intermarriage of royal European bloodlines—

The throne.

The words of Spivey Quince and the boy in blue came rushing back—

The throne. Opening the passage.

We've been trying to interpret the warnings metaphorically. . . .

"It seeks the throne. It will be King."

"His Highness has been so generous with the distribution of his bounty, it must be difficult to remember exactly where he's deposited it," added Eileen, smiling pleasantly, vivid spots of color highlighting her cheeks.

Bishop Pillphrock had gone as pale as a ghost, mouth yawning open, momentarily devoid of his abundant social lubricant. The Prince blinked many times and worked his lips silently. He looked like a broken toy.

"On hot afternoons," said the Prince timidly, "I'm very fond of strawberry ice cream."

The oddness of the non sequitur stilled even Eileen. A solitary tear escaped the Prince's bleary light eyes and ran into his splotchy whiskers.

"All I want," said the Prince in a wee voice that must have been familiar in the royal nursery, "is some peace and quiet and a little fun."

The silver-haired man to the Prince's right asserted himself, taking the Prince by the arm. "And so you shall have it. Your Highness has been sorely tried by his day's demanding schedule," said the man, easing the Duke back into his chair, "and is in need of nourishment to replenish his spirits."

"More wine," said the Prince, eyes downcast, sullenly sinking into himself.

"More wine!" barked the Bishop. "Thank you, Sir Nigel. His Highness's welfare is of course foremost in all our minds."

"So I would've thought," said Sir Nigel Gull, the silver-haired man, erstwhile physician to the prince. As he took his seat, Gull shot a withering glare at Eileen. A woman-hater, concluded Doyle instantly, remembering that the prolific rumors of the Prince's debauchery were not exclusively limited to the fairer sex.

"Please, be seated, won't you?" said the Bishop, regaining his form. "Miss Temple, if you would be so kind; our host has requested you for his right hand."

The Bishop held out her chair as Eileen sat to the right of Chandros, directly across from Alexander Sparks. The upright hulk of General Marcus McCauley Drummond stood on Sparks's left.

Dinner Is Served

"And here for you, please, Dr. Doyle." Pillphrock indicated a chair two spots to Eileen's right. "Welcome, all, welcome, welcome."

Pillphrock rang the serving bell and settled his girth between Eileen and Doyle, who took his seat directly across from the only other female at the table, a darkly handsome woman whom he recognized as Lady Caroline Nicholson. Black hair bonneted a strong face, her features hawkish and unforgiving, more sensual than the photo had been able to convey. Her black eyes glittered with a predatory heat. She smiled cryptically.

The man to Doyle's immediate right had difficulty retaking his seat, wincing in pain. His right leg extended out as stiff as a board, the bulge of a poultice ballooning the pants leg around his knee. Slight, clean-shaven, pale, and pockmarked. Even with the spectacles he wore and the absence of makeup, Doyle recognized him as the Dark Man from the séance, the man he had shot in that leg. Professor Arminius Vamberg.

So they were accounted for, all seven, and the grandson of Queen Victoria in the bargain. Doyle looked up and met the willful, steady eyes of Alexander Sparks. The implied complicity of his smile was unnerving, as if he could gaze unimpeded into the private mind of anyone he scrutinized. Seeing no purpose in openly challenging him, Doyle looked away.

Sharing the same dull eyes and attentively vacant expression, a squadron of servants carried in a soup course, which, a ravenous Doyle was disappointed to see, proved to be a thin consommé.

"I made the discovery during my years in the Caribbean," offered Professor Vamberg unsolicited, in the harshly accented rasp that vividly recalled the night at 13 Cheshire.

"What's that?" asked Doyle.

"Have you spent any length of time in primitive cultures, Doctor?"

"Not if you exclude the French," said Doyle, trying to check his hunger from prompting him to pick up his bowl and drink.

The Professor smiled politely. "The signal difference, I find, is that, lacking the polished veneer of what we Europeans arrogantly pronounce 'civilized,' less developed societies maintain a direct relationship to the natural world. As a consequence, they enjoy a more straightforward experience of that part of nature which remains unseen to us: the spirit world, specifically the world of the *devas,* or elementals, who inform and inhabit the physical world which we presumptively assume to be the limit of existence. Our colleagues in the medical profession dismiss these peoples as foolish, primitive, superstitious, at the

mercy of irrational fancies and terrors. Contrarily, after years of examination, I'm inclined to consider them wise and knowing, attuned
with the world they live in to a degree undreamt of by ourselves."

Doyle nodded attentively, glancing at Chandros, deep in a one-sided
conversation with Eileen, who seemed as equally preoccupied as Doyle
with her soup.

"I myself was quite unconvinced of their existence for the longest
time," said the Bishop, between noisy slurps. "As you can well
imagine—public school, Church of England, already a vicar—"

"Unaware of whose existence?" asked Doyle.

"Why, the elementals, of course," beamed the Bishop. He had
managed to splatter droplets of broth all over his spectacles. "Until I
met Professor Vamberg—then the scales fell from my eyes like autumn
leaves!"

"They are known by different names in different cultures," said
Vamberg, clearly irritated by the Bishop's cheery intrusion. "You are
of Irish descent, are you not, Doctor?"

Doyle nodded. His soup was gone; he was tempted to ask Vamberg,
who hadn't so much as wet his spoon, if he wouldn't mind giving his
over.

"In Ireland you know them as leprechauns: the little people. Here,
in Britain, they're called brownies or elves, with many regional variations: 'knockers' in Cornwall, the pixies of Scotland, the trows of
Shetland and Orcadia. The Germans, of course, know them as kobolds
or goblins—"

"I'm familiar with the mythology," said Doyle, annoyed by the man's
condescending pedantry.

"Ah, but you see, it is a great deal more than mere mythology,
Doctor," said Vamberg, waving his spoon for emphasis.

In came the next course; thank God, thought Doyle. It's not enough
to perish by way of starvation, they have to bore me to death
simultaneously.

"Roast partridge on a bed of cabbage," announced the Bishop.

Partridge? There must be some mistake, thought Doyle. This was
a single wing, and it was easily the size of a turkey's. And that cabbage
leaf covered the entire plate. They were in the north of England:
Where did one find produce like this in the depths of winter? Gift
horses, decided Doyle, tasting the first cut of the wing; the meat was
succulent and tender and, he had to admit, on first bite as flavorful
as anything he'd ever eaten.

"These figures of legend, so familiar to us from folktales and children's stories, are in actuality the unseen architects and builders of the natural world," continued Vamberg, as disinterested in the partridge as he had been in the soup. "Wood nymphs, water naiads, sprites of the air—there is a reason why these traditions persist in every culture, even in one as ostensibly advanced as our own—"

"What reason would that be?" said Doyle, unable to resist picking up the wing with his hands and tearing into it.

"Because they are real," said Vamberg. "I've seen them. Spoken to them. Danced with them."

Not recently you haven't, thought Doyle. "Really."

"Shy creatures, extremely reticent, but once contact is made— and I was able to do so initially with the help of Caribbean tribal priests—one quickly learns how extremely eager they are to cooperate with us."

"How terribly interesting," said Doyle, finishing off his partridge.

"Isn't it just?" piped in the Bishop, trickles of grease shining like tinsel around his mouth and chin.

"Cooperate how, exactly?" asked Doyle.

"Why in doing what they do best," said Vamberg. "Growing things."

"Growing things."

Vamberg picked the immense cabbage leaf off his plate. "What if I were to tell you that the cabbage seed that produced this leaf was planted in dry sand three weeks ago, deprived of all water or nutrients, and harvested this very morning?"

"I would say, Professor Vamberg, that you've spent too much time dancing around toadstools," said Doyle.

Vamberg smiled dryly and lifted the wing from his plate. "And if I were to tell you that when it was freshly dressed this afternoon, this bird was only two weeks old?"

Servants were clearing and laying in the next course, two of them rolling in a silver-hooded steam table.

"So these elementals, as you call them, presumably have nothing better to do than help you raise partridges the size of eagles?" asked Doyle.

"Trout with lemon!" said the Bishop.

The hood of the table was rolled back, revealing a single, intact fish on a garnish of lemon and parsley. Its coloring and markings identified it as brown trout, but the thing was the size of a sturgeon. The servants carved and served. Doyle caught Eileen's eye, hers filled more with wonder than the profound unease stirring inside him.

Vamberg smiled like Carroll's Cheshire cat. "Oh ye of little faith."

THE LIST OF 7

A plate of the trout landed in front of Doyle. As savory as it looked and smelled, he was rapidly losing his appetite; the idea of this mysteriously denatured meat made him queasy. Glancing around the table, he noticed Alexander Sparks also refrained from eating, instead staring intently across at Eileen. At the other end, a napkin tucked in his collar like a child's bib, His Highness the Duke of Clarence aggressively sucked up his fish in greedy, gluttonous mouthfuls, sloshing it down with sloppy gouts of wine, all the while making noisy drones of infantile contentment, completely oblivious to the company and his surroundings.

"Delicious!" pronounced the Bishop. A beautiful fair-haired altar boy stood at his side. The Bishop whispered in his ear and ran his stubby fingers possessively through the boy's locks.

"Another benefit unlooked for came from that encounter—this was on the island of Haiti, by the way—when the priests introduced me to an elixir of various herbs, roots, and organic extracts they said the elementals had revealed to them," said Vamberg. "The priests of Haiti have been using this compound judiciously for centuries: They discovered that when administered in the right amount, in conjunction with certain medical practices, this compound virtually strips a man or woman—any man or woman—of their conscious will."

"I'm sorry?" asked Doyle.

"Their will is no longer their own. It renders them docile, pliant, completely under the command of the priests, who then employ these people however they see fit, as field or household help. Even the most intractable subjects become obedient. Trustworthy. Well behaved."

Slaves. Mute and unreasoning as marionettes, servers were laying in a meat course: Doyle tried not to think what manner of hideously altered beast might have yielded these ripe morsels of flesh.

"That's how Haiti solved the servant problem," chimed in the Bishop with a broad wink. "How nice to speak freely in front of the help."

Vamberg sent the Bishop another venomous look before continuing. "The priests are a closed fraternity; this knowledge is guarded with their lives. I was one of few outsiders—the only European—who has ever been given access to this treasure. I've even improved the effect with a simple, surgical procedure, used in conjunction with the compound."

No wonder Bodger Nuggins ran, thought Doyle. Better dead face-down in the Thames than an ambulatory corpse like Lansdown Dilks, stored away in some root cellar like a sack of nightsoil—

"Marvelous!" said the Bishop.

Dinner Is Served

"It was years later, during my travels in the high country of Tibet, that I met a man with the vision to see how this procedure might one day be utilized in a broader, more socially useful fashion." Vamberg gave a nod to Alexander Sparks.

So that's how it began, with Sparks and Vamberg. The meeting of two dark minds, a seed brought back to English ground to reach its full flower of corruption—

A crash of crockery startled him. A servant on the far side of the table had dropped a plate. The man bent down, his movements addled and sluggish, and attempted to scrape up the fragments of china and the scattered food around it with his hands.

"Clumsy fool," muttered General Drummond.

A jolt ran through Doyle; the back of the man's neck had been recently and roughly shaved, and a vivid, suppurating triangular scar ran across its length. Crude blue thread stitched the flaps of the wound loosely together. Another servant went to the damaged man, straightening the poor wretch to his feet.

Doyle's heart sank.

It was Barry.

His eyes were dead, light and life entirely gone from them.

"Here, here," said Alexander. "What's your name, clumsy boy?"

Barry shuffled slowly around and stared at him uncomprehendingly, a thin line of drool forming in the corner of his mouth.

Alexander sprang to his feet and cuffed Barry harshly across the ear. He accepted the blow as passively as an exhausted pack animal. Doyle gripped the arms of his chair to keep from leaping up at Sparks.

"Speak when you're spoken to, boy."

Some dim whisper of cognition surfaced in the well of his broken mind. Barry nodded. The weak noise that emerged from his mouth could hardly be understood for a word.

"Since you've demonstrated you're no use doing your job, perhaps you can entertain us, you stupid cow," said Alexander. "Dance for us now, give us a jig, come on then."

Alexander clapped his hands, encouraging the others at the table to join in, establishing a steady rhythm. The quartet at Alexander's prompting began to fiddle an Irish jig. Alexander slapped Barry again, spinning him around, then prodded him with the end of a cane.

"Dance, boy. Do as you're told."

Doyle could see the music seeping through to what was left of Barry. He tried to shuffle his feet, but the result was pathetic, the slightest movement costly and excruciatingly painful. His arms swung limply at his sides. A spreading stain appeared in the crotch of his pants.

The company of seven and their royal guest found the exhibition endlessly entertaining. Prince Eddy seemed on the verge of jumping to his feet and joining in. The Bishop laughed so hard he held his sides and doubled over in his chair, face red with exertion.

Doyle looked to his left. Eileen was pale, fighting her emotions; there were tears in her eyes. He gestured to her: Show them nothing.

Unable to sustain the effort, Barry slumped to his knees against a chair, gasping for breath, a dry rattle in his chest. A thin line of milky red fluid ran from his wound and around his neck. Alexander threw his head back and laughed, then waved dismissively. The music stopped. Two servants lifted Barry by the arms and guided him gently but firmly out of the room, as one would a doddering, incontinent pensioner.

"Delightful!" said the Bishop.

They put him here so we'd see, thought Doyle furiously. We'd see how they've decimated his mind and robbed him of his soul. This wasn't only Vamberg's drug at work; they had cut Barry, cut crudely into the back of his head and obliterated something essential to his humanity.

Doyle wanted to kill them for it.

Across the table, Alexander grinned viciously as he reclaimed his seat, looking slowly back and forth at Doyle and Eileen, showing his teeth. It was the most naked expression of feeling Doyle had seen the man display.

He likes to see fear, realized Doyle. He feeds off it.

"You were saying, Professor," said Alexander.

"Yes. Having made this providential association, my new friend and I continued our peregrinations around the world, but with renewed purpose," Vamberg went on, leaning close enough to Doyle that the first words gave him a start.

"Purpose."

"We pursued the acquaintance of elemental forces in other countries, other continents. To our amazement, we discovered they were more than willing to disclose their secrets to us—and among them, Doctor, are wonders to behold: life itself!—in trade for a service which only we, in turn, could provide for them."

Doyle nodded, not willing to speak, unable to trust he could keep from betraying his growing terror. Desecrating Barry in this grisly way, it was likely they had done the same to his brother. The inference that the same fate awaited himself and Eileen was unmistakable.

"These elementals of the earth had once been united under the governance of a unifying spirit," continued Vamberg. "A powerful entity, worshiped by primitive people of the world in a variety of guises throughout history. A being tragically, savagely misunderstood by our religiously intolerant Western forebears—I won't mention any names—"

The Bishop chortled agreeably.

"—who have systemically engaged in brutal, senseless persecution of this entity and its legions of worshipers. The ascendancy of Western man, with his paltry, self-centered concerns and small-minded monotheistic obsessions, finally succeeded in driving this being out of the physical plane altogether, into a twilight, purgatorial existence."

"The Devil," said Doyle.

"The Christian conception of him, yes. Here was their proposal: In exchange for the continued bestowal of their beneficent genius, the elementals asked our cooperation in returning this great spirit into the world, there to assume its rightful seat among them. This was the service they required of us—it seems only humans could provide such a service. And so, with the help of our assembled colleagues, for the greater glory of man and nature, this we have agreed to do."

The rest of the table grew quiet, watching Doyle carefully for his reaction. Insane, he thought. All of them. Beyond the pale.

"You're speaking of the Dweller on the Threshold," he said.

"Oh, he has many, many names," said the Bishop cheerfully.

Reaching in to grab the decanter of wine, Prince Eddy succeeded in knocking it over, flooding the tablecloth with a shocking stream of black-red claret. The Prince giggled girlishly. A dark look passed between Alexander and Dr. Gull, who responded by rising to his feet.

"His Highness extends his regrets," said Gull roundly, "but it has been a most exhausting day. He will take the remainder of his meal in chambers before retiring."

Prince Eddy gestured and grumbled an objection. Gull whispered in his ear and pulled the thoroughly sodden man to his feet. Balking petulantly at Gull's instructions, the Prince yanked his arm away; his elbow hit his chair, and it crashed to the floor. Gull's face turned beet red.

"Good evening, Your Highness," said Alexander Sparks. His voice cut through the silence like a scalpel. "Rest well."

The Prince's expression turned meek and docile. He nodded meekly to Alexander. Dr. Gull took the Duke firmly by the arm and led him toward the stairs. Gull whispered to him again, the Prince stopped, assembled his tatterdemalion dignity, and addressed the table.

"Thank you all . . . and good night," he said.

Similar felicitations were returned. Gull steered the Prince in a wide arc to the stairs. The Prince stumbled once, Gull righted him, and they began to climb, cautiously, one stair at a time. Prince Eddy looked as forlorn and toothless as a decrepit bear in a street circus.

As Doyle watched him go, something heavy dropped onto the table in front of him. His manuscript.

"Perhaps you can imagine my surprise, Dr. Doyle, when your . . . manuscript first crossed the transom of Rathborne and Sons." Lady Nicholson spoke now, her voice low and throaty, ripe with voluptuously suggestive pauses.

Perhaps I can, thought Doyle.

"When Professor Vamberg and Mr. Graves—that is, Mr. Sparks— introduced themselves to us—"

"Some eleven years ago now," said the Bishop.

The fussy cleric's elaborations appeared to go over no better with Lady Nicholson than they had with Vamberg.

"Thank you, Your Worship. Sir John, General Drummond, and myself had shared and studied occultic knowledge for many years: We are of like mind. From the moment the Professor and Mr. Sparks came to England, made themselves known to us, and we dedicated ourselves to our . . . joint interests . . . absolute secrecy has been our foremost consideration. So, yes, imagine our surprise when that . . . document . . . arrived on my desk. Written by a young, unknown, and unpublished physician—forgive me, a nobody—who, it seemed by the evidence available on the page, had been eavesdropping . . . over our shoulders for these many years."

But it was an accident, he wanted to tell them. I lifted half of that folderol straight out of Blavatsky, and the rest was blind, stupid luck. Doyle knew that was not what they wished to hear, and it would avail him not to offer it up.

"So we are . . ." Lady Nicholson purred, "and have been, for some time, most anxious to receive an . . . explanation for . . . this." She gestured languidly toward the book.

Doyle nodded slowly. He felt their eyes crawling over him like insects.

"I do understand, Lady Nicholson. To begin, may I just say how greatly I admire what the lot of you have accomplished," Doyle said, affecting the stuffy academician persona he'd worn in the coach with Alexander. "How grand and enterprising your work. Visionary indeed. Bravo all. Most impressive."

Dinner Is Served

"How did you come to know of . . . our work?" asked Lady Nicholson.

"I can see there's no use in pretending, I may as well confess," said Doyle casually, praying his powers of invention would not pick this moment to fail him. "The plain truth is . . . I've made a study of you."

"A study," said Lady Nicholson, cocking an eyebrow.

Veiled, discreet, and troubled looks passed back and forth among them.

"Oh yes," continued Doyle blithely. "Presumed and forsworn secrecy is one thing and all very well and good—heaven forbid it should be otherwise, given what you've been on about—and one would assume you'd have no difficulty whatsoever secreting the activities of seven such extraordinarily gifted individuals from the eyes and ears of such a modest admirer—a nobody, if you will. But an admirer in possession of such a profound desire to divine your purpose . . . well, that's quite another kettle of fish entirely."

There was a lengthy silence.

"How?" demanded Drummond.

Doyle managed a lighthearted chuckle. "One might as well ask you, respectfully, General Drummond, sir, to freely divulge your most cherished military secrets. No, no, my investigative methods are not a subject I intend to discuss. *Why*, however. Now there's a proper question. *Why?* And the answer to that, my lords and lady, is something I would be only too happy to share with you."

Doyle leaned back, took a sip of wine, and smiled brazenly. He caught Eileen's eye for the briefest moment, during which she silently inquired if he had gone mad, realized this was distinctly not the case, and indicated her improvisatory cooperation was available if needed or called upon. He covertly nodded his acknowledgment.

"Why, then?" asked Alexander Sparks. He glowered lupinely, but there was uncertainty in his face.

This is the second time I've confounded him, thought Doyle. For some reason, he can't see past this ludicrous, slapdash facade I've constructed: The man has a blind spot.

"Why, indeed, Mr. Sparks," said Doyle, leaning confidently forward. "Well. Here I sit among you. Granted, adjudged against this august company, I am a man of humble means and undeniably moderate accomplishments. I hold no place in the world to compare remotely with anyone's at this table. What I do share with you is a passionate sympathy for your objectives. I share with you a passionate desire to see your plans come to fruition. And I have nurtured a perhaps reckless aspiration that by creating an opportunity to meet you, face-to-face, I could persuade you to allow me to play some part, however insignificant, in the fulfillment of your plans, in which I so strongly and fervently believe."

Running through Doyle's head like an urgent telegraph: The longer they let me jabber—and the longer I spin out this web of weightless nonsense—the longer they'll let us live and the more time I'll afford Jack, if he's inside, to make his move.

"So that is why you wrote this . . . story?" asked Lady Nicholson, as if she found the word itself distasteful.

"That is precisely why I wrote my story, Madam, and exactly why I sent it to you as I did," said Doyle, opening his hands as if revealing cards in a poker game. "There it is. You've found me out."

More furtive looks exchanged. Doyle could see significant doubts persisting; Drummond, and to a lesser degree Chandros, seemed particularly unconverted.

"In addition to Rathborne and Sons, you submitted your manuscript to a number of other publishers," said Chandros reasonably.

"I did, Sir John, for one simple reason," said Doyle, assuming one would occur to him in the next instant. "One doesn't venture into a lion's den without creating a distraction. My method required subtlety. A straightforward approach to you I quite rightly felt would fall short, and I strongly suspected that you might well greet my efforts with no small disfavor, so I made those additional submissions, should you choose to investigate my intentions before responding, to lend yours an air of legitimacy. As it happened, I nearly lost my life in the bargain regardless, on more than a few occasions."

The table was silent. Doyle sensed he had a quorum leaning in his direction. He summoned his last reserves of sincerity to the fore.

"Please forgive me, but I must speak plainly; if you honestly thought I had no value to you I don't believe you would have gone to the trouble you did to test me with the séance. If, in your estimation, resolve and sacrifice and persistence count for anything—and I know they must or you would have killed me long before this—then I have faith you will, at the very least, allow me some nominal opportunity to prove myself to you and by so doing join you in whatsoever way you deem fit, to help bring your great plan to completion on this earth."

"What about my brother?" asked Alexander.

"Your brother?" Doyle had prepared himself for this riposte. "Your brother, Mr. Sparks, has abducted me against my will, twice, and come close to killing me more times than that. It has come to my understanding he is escaped from Bedlam; if his behavior is any indication, his internment there was not inappropriate."

"What does he want from you?"

"How does one decipher the ravings of a madman?" said Doyle dismissively. "One might as well try to solve the riddle of the Sphinx. Frankly, I'm just grateful to be rid of him."

A measured look passed between Sparks and Lady Nicholson; there's the axis of real power in this nest of snakes, noted Doyle.

"What do you know of . . . our plan?" asked Lady Nicholson, with a provisional, but therefore significant, measure of respect.

"My understanding is you are attempting to return this being which Professor Vamberg has spoken of—the being I refer to in my manuscript as the Dweller on the Threshold—to the physical plane."

And now Doyle chanced his most daring leap of the offensive.

"And you are currently preparing a second attempt because your first effort—involving the birth of your son, Lady Nicholson, the blond child whom I saw depicted at the séance—has sadly and tragically failed."

That sent a bolt rocketing through the woman and on through the rest in a tumbling ricochet. Eileen's eyes widened at this revelation. Doyle had gambled and come up aces. Prompted by an imperceptible signal from Sparks, Lady Nicholson extended their confidence in him another step.

"The physical vehicle was not strong enough," said the woman, without a trace of grief. "The boy was unable to . . . bear the weight."

The physical vehicle: Good Christ, she's speaking about her own flesh and blood with the regretful sentiment of a poorly played game of darts.

"We impute the father," added Bishop Pillphrock piously. "A weak man. A most weak and unserviceable man."

"It seems certain infirmities were . . . passed along," said Lady Nicholson.

"I have met Lord Nicholson. I would have to say that does not surprise me, not at all," said Doyle. "One can only trust that your next standard-bearer proves to be as physically advantageous as is his position in the world."

"And who would that be?" asked Chandros mildly.

"Why, Prince Eddy, of course," said Doyle, taking another not altogether wild stab in the dark.

Another look between Nicholson and Alexander. Another nerve struck.

So that was the reason for Nigel Gull's presence in their midst: a short leash around the neck of the Crown Prince. Doyle barely had time to let the shock course through him. They believed they were going to bring this crepuscular phantom—Dark Lord, Dweller on the Threshold, call the Devil what you will—back to the world as presumptive heir to the throne of England.

"We are not immune to the . . . persuasiveness and . . . ingenuity of your arguments, Doctor," said Lady Nicholson.

"Just as we are duly impressed with your perseverance," added Sparks. "The séance was indeed a test. We needed to determine what you were made of. And what you knew."

"But given the risks involved, as you yourself have suggested, it is altogether fitting and proper that we look for additional . . . proof of your . . . suitability," said Lady Nicholson.

Doyle nodded. They've taken the bait, now I'll set the hook. "Most reasonable indeed, Lady—"

Doyle was distracted by something landing on the table in front of him. Although he hadn't seen the man move, Doyle knew that Sparks had tossed the object toward him.

A straight razor, blade exposed, gleaming in the candlelight.

"We would like you to kill Miss Temple," said Sparks. "Here. Now."

Time stopped inside Doyle's mind.

"Kill Miss Temple," he repeated.

"Please," said Sparks.

You mustn't hesitate, Doyle. You mustn't blink. If Eileen is to have any chance at all . . .

Where was Jack?

Doyle looked around the table. Alexander grinned. Pillphrock tittered nervously. Lady Nicholson's breathing had grown rapid and shallow; the woman was aroused by what she thought she was about to witness.

They wanted him to reenact the killing at the séance; this time there was to be no simulation.

Doyle didn't dare turn to Eileen.

"Yes, all right," Doyle said calmly.

Doyle picked up the razor, rose from his chair, and grasped its back to move it out of his way. Taking a step toward Eileen, he saw that five stone-eyed servants had moved in behind the table.

Eileen turned to look at him. Doyle let her know with his eyes:
Now.

Doyle pivoted on the ball of his foot and used the momentum of his turn to slash the razor down at Vamberg. Vamberg's eyes lit up behind his spectacles. He let out a cry, raising his left arm to ward off the blow: The razor sliced through the man's jacket and across his arm and hand. Crimson spurted onto the table from a severed vessel, splattering the manuscript.

Reaching into his pocket, with one motion Doyle pulled out the syringes and spun round the other way. The first sight that registered—Chandros leaning over to clamp Eileen's left hand onto the arm of her chair, the Bishop turning in his seat to pin down her right. Eileen stood halfway, slipped the Bishop's grasp, and drove her right fist directly into the face of Chandros.

"Bastards!" she yelled.

As her hand made contact with his flesh, the man screamed violently, explosively, his hands flew to his face—to his right eye—and as her fist drew back, Doyle saw that Eileen had wedged the four-inch hat pin firmly between her fingers; she had driven it deeply into the man's eye socket. Blood streamed out between Chandros's spasming fingers.

Before the Bishop could grab hold, Doyle secured his grip on the first syringe and thrust it into Pillphrock's fleshy throat, dropped the razor, and pushed down hard with both hands on the plunger, emptying the drug into the man's carotid artery. The Bishop screamed; halfway out his mouth, the sound cut off, strangulated by paralysis. His eyes bulged, his face turned purple and sclerotic, as the drug—a massive overdose of digitalis—raced into his bloodstream, where it would within seconds stop his heart.

"Run!" shouted Doyle.

Stunned by the suddenness of the attack, servants only now moved toward them from both sides of the table. Drummond rose to his feet; Lady Nicholson pushed her chair back from the table.

Alexander Sparks was no longer beside her; Doyle had lost sight of him.

Eileen ran toward the stairs. Chandros's screams stopped, his hands fell from his ravaged eye, and gore slipped out of the cavity in thick red clots; the pin had penetrated into his brain. Although the message had not yet reached his extremities, Sir John Chandros was already dead. Pillphrock sat stock upright, hands at his throat, face turning black, mouth open in a silent, protesting bellow. Death was near at hand.

A moan from Vamberg—in shock, clutching his wounded arm—brought Doyle back to his left. He bent to retrieve the razor; Eileen's skirts moved by him at floor level as she rushed from the table.

As his hand touched the steel, Doyle felt hot liquid pour onto his cheek—blood, not his—then a pincer grip descended onto his neck. With a hoarse screech, Vamberg clawed at him with his wounded arm; nails raked Doyle's skin, drawing blood. Unable to raise his head against the pressure of Vamberg's surprisingly harsh grasp, Doyle fumbled the second syringe into position, jammed it hard into Vamberg's upper left thigh, and hit the plunger; half the hypodermic's contents emptied into the femoral artery before the man jerked violently away, and the needle broke off in his leg. Now the needle's function reversed; voluminous arcs of blood pumped out in the opposite direction.

Doyle pushed off for the stairs. A servant rushed at him; Doyle slashed with the razor, cutting the man and knocking him back.

"Eileen!"

A pack of servants turned a corner in the upstairs hallway and swarmed down the stairs toward her.

"There!" he shouted, pointing to a door off the landing.

Dust pocketed from a point of impact on the marble steps near her feet as a shot rang out; turning, Doyle saw Drummond advance toward the stairs, leading a charge of servants, revolver in hand. Doyle hurled the razor at him; Drummond deflected it with an arm.

"Consign you to hell!" shouted Drummond, raising the pistol again.

Falling from high above, a suit of armor crashed down onto the servants nearing Doyle. Drummond's second shot missed wide.

"Arthur!" shouted Eileen.

He turned; a servant stood over him, club raised to batter. Doyle heard a sharp whistle, and a silver star embedded itself in the man's forehead. The man fell away. Doyle looked up; a dark shape flew over the balustrade and sailed onto the servants advancing down the stairs. Driven into the steps by the impact, the attackers tumbled around Eileen as Doyle reached her on the landing. Dressed in servant garb, the figure who'd ridden them down jumped to his feet and began hurling assailants who hadn't been knocked senseless off the staircase.

"Go on," said Jack Sparks, gesturing to the door on the landing.

Sparks picked up a broadsword from the jumble of armor, and he used it to finish one of the men, swinging it wildly to prevent the others from advancing.

"Now, Doyle!"

Another bullet whistled past their ears. Drummond took aim again, struggling to line a clear shot through the knot of men working their way around the armor.

Eileen tried the door. "Locked!"

Doyle and Jack threw shoulders against the wood; the lock splintered

Dinner Is Served

on the second try. Doyle grabbed a torch from a sconce on the inside wall, took Eileen by the hand, and they rushed down a bare, narrow servants' passage. Sparks threw a vial onto the landing that produced a thick, noxious plume of smoke.

"Go, go, as fast as you can."

They ran. Sparks followed. They rounded a turn, hearing shouting and footsteps in the passage behind them as servants braved the smoke, driven on by Drummond's bellicose orders.

"Are you all right?" Doyle asked Eileen.

"I wish we'd killed them all," she said angrily.

"I saw you come off the wagon—" said Doyle back to Sparks.

"It took an hour to get this far into the house; they must have a hundred men inside."

"Did you see—"

"Yes: I reached the stairs before you attacked. I needed a distraction—"

"We understand, Jack—where are we?" said Eileen.

Good Christ, she's calmer than I am, thought an astonished Doyle.

They paused at an intersection. One fork of the passage led deeper into the house, the other sloped down and to the left.

"This way," said Sparks, leading them to the left.

"How do we get out?" asked Doyle.

"We'll find a way."

The passage walls grew rougher as they moved down, woodwork giving way to masonry and masonry to raw rock. Sounds of pursuit behind them grew encouragingly remote.

"They've killed Barry," said Doyle.

"Worse than that," said Eileen.

"I know."

"They must have Larry as well," said Doyle.

"No. He's alive."

"Where?"

"Safe."

They traveled nearly half a mile down. The temperature rose. Walls sweated moisture. Around another corner a heavy oaken door blocked the passageway. Sparks listened carefully, then reached down and lifted the latch. Open.

Carved out of the earth, the cave they entered stretched ahead indefinitely, as broad as it was long. The ceiling barely cleared their heads. Deep straw covered the floor. A wind draughted in from somewhere, guttering the flame, the torch blackening the rocks above with streaks of carbon. The air felt unusually warm, permeated with an unpleasant pungency, like a field of overripe fruit. Doyle knew he had encountered that smell before, but he couldn't place it.

Stepping forward they discovered shallow water underlying the straw, up to a foot of it in spots. As they sloshed cautiously ahead, the door behind them caught in the breeze and slammed shut, giving them a start.

"Did Larry come in with you?" asked Doyle.

"No. I found him at the train. Barry was taken at the abbey."

So those had been Barry's cries they'd heard raining down from the heights. Doyle hoped he hadn't suffered long. Who knew if he was suffering still.

They had passed halfway across the long chamber, their progress impeded by the curious combination of straw and water.

"Where did you go last night, Jack?" asked Doyle.

"A company of Royal Marines and two squadron of cavalry are on their way from the Middlesbrough. They'll arrive here before dawn."

Never had Doyle been more willing to take him at his word. "Why didn't you wait for them?"

"Eileen was with you," he said, without looking at them.

Doyle stepped on something soft and yielding; his foot slipped off before he could replant it, but he regained his balance before falling. He was left with a vague, unpleasant impression that whatever he'd stepped on had moved when he touched it.

"Jack, they've got Prince Eddy—"

"I understand—"

Something cracked sharply under Eileen's foot.

"What was that?" asked Doyle.

She shook her head; Doyle held the torch as Sparks cleared the straw under her feet.

"Oh God," she said.

Her foot had snapped the rib cage of a human skeleton lying half beneath the surface of the water, the bones bleached white, picked clean. A gruelly substance gleamed on the straw, trails of silver excretion circling around and away from the remains.

"We've seen this before—the stable at Topping," said Doyle.

"Don't move," said Sparks. He was looking over Doyle's shoulder.

An undulating shape humped toward them beneath the straw, a slow, rippling, ophidian movement. The distinctive smell suddenly grew more potent, stinging their eyes.

"Ammonia," said Doyle.

Dinner Is Served

Doyle looked to his left; another shape slithered toward them from that direction.

"There," said Eileen, pointing straight ahead to more movement in the straw.

"What are they?" asked Sparks.

"If they can grow cabbages as big as globes and trout the size of dolphin ... " said Doyle.

"I'm not sure we want to know the answer to that," said Eileen.

The straw on every side of them seemed alive, as active as sea foam. The shapes closed in from every direction, but a gap opened in front of them.

"Go. Straight ahead," said Sparks, readying the sword.

Doyle moved ahead, brandishing the torch. He felt something brush against his boot and stepped quickly to avoid it.

A black shape slithered out of the straw to their right to a height of five feet. Its limbless, cylindrical shape ended in a fluttering orifice rimmed with palpitating suckers that surrounded a set of three gnashing jaws, each equipped with symmetrical rows of sharp white teeth.

An identical shape lifted to their left, drawn by a rudimentary sense of smell. Another rose behind them. What they smelled was blood.

They were leeches.

Jack darted underneath the swaying head of the one to their right and ripped the sword down the length of its body. A sac punctured, spilling a fetid black fluid, and the creature tumbled back into the swampy water.

Doyle waved the torch, keeping the creatures to the front at bay. Their black wrinkled bodies recoiled instinctively from the fire, moisture sizzling on their glistening skin.

"Light the straw!" said Sparks.

Another monster reared up behind Sparks and struck; teeth ripped into his shoulder before Jack wheeled with the sword and severed the thing in two. The surviving halves scurried frantically away.

Doyle set the torch to the straw around them; the drier stuff on top ignited rapidly and spread across the room in a solid sheet of flame. The leeches nearest to them fell in its advance, combusting, bursting apart.

"This way!" yelled Doyle.

They chased the burning straw. Water sloshed as creatures fled from the heat, explosive plops filling the air as the fire consumed more of the loathsome worms. Sparks finished off the few survivors they encountered. The fire at this end of the room fizzled as it burned down to the soggy straw below. Holding the torch high, Doyle found a door in the wall ahead. Sparks lifted the heavy latch, and they were through the door.

They found themselves outside, near a cooperage, barrels stacked around them, limiting their vision. Horses' hooves, carriages, and angry voices could be heard nearby. A full moon burned high in the night sky above. Doyle extinguished the torch.

"I'm going to be sick," said Eileen quietly.

She moved off. Doyle went with her and held her gently as she voided the corrupt meal they'd been served. Sparks waited a discreet distance away. When the spasms had ended, she clung to Doyle and closed her eyes, shuddering against the cold air, nodding that she was all right in response to his entreaties. Refusing to speak about the nightmare they'd encountered was a way to deny its reality, Doyle supposed. He wondered how many other skeletons lay buried in that hellish breeding ground. Convenient way to dispense with disciplinary problems. Or drive one's enemies mad with fear—he thought of the lines of salt across the halls of Topping; they had indisputably done the job on Lord Nicholson.

Did these monsters give credit to Vamberg's ravings about dark spirits and relationships with elementals? Had some fundamental secrets of spirit and matter been revealed to them?

The thought broke off with the approach of Sparks.

"How many did you kill?" he asked quietly.

"Chandros. The Bishop. Probably Vamberg."

"Alexander?"

Doyle shook his head.

"Wait here," he said, patted Doyle on the shoulder, and crept out of sight.

"I killed him. That horrible man," said Eileen, her eyes still closed.

"Yes, you did."

"Good."

She lay quietly in his arms. Sparks returned minutes later with two servant's outfits and, even more welcome, warm woolen coats. They changed behind the barrels as Sparks kept vigil. Eileen stuffed her hair under a mobcap.

Through a gap in the barrels, they looked out at a grounds-eye view of the courtyard where Doyle had earlier seen Jack slip from under the wagon. Servants and convicts ran in every direction. Panicked horses reared as they were held at rein before wagons and carriages.

Dinner Is Served

Platoons of guards gathered and dispatched under the direction of officers.

"Evacuation," said Sparks quietly. "The soldiers will arrive in time to mop most of this lot up."

"They won't fight?" asked Doyle.

"Not without orders. And we've ruptured their chain of command."

"What about Drummond?"

"He won't make a stand unless Alexander is with him."

"Maybe he is."

"There's no cause on earth for which he'd sacrifice himself. He's miles from here by now."

"Where will he go?" asked Eileen.

Sparks shook his head.

"What about Prince Eddy?" asked Doyle.

"I would imagine Gull's already gotten him well away."

"To where?"

"Back to his train. Back to Balmoral. He's not much good to them now."

"He'll probably sleep through it," said Eileen.

"They wouldn't keep him a hostage?" asked Doyle.

"To what purpose? They'd be hunted down like dogs. He can't harm them as a witness. Why would they risk confiding in him? He was the guest of some distinguished citizens for a country weekend."

"If that's the case, we've beaten them, Jack. They've given up."

"Perhaps."

A more troubling question occurred to Doyle. "Why haven't they come after us?"

"They've got a few other wickets to mind, don't they?" said Eileen.

"They will," said Sparks quietly. "Not tonight, or the night after. But they will."

A long silence followed.

"How do we get out of here?" asked Doyle.

"Through that gate," said Sparks, pointing at an exit leading toward the factory.

"How do we manage it?"

"Simple, my dear Doyle. We'll walk."

Sparks stood and headed out from behind the barrels. Doyle and Eileen followed, heads down, blending into the milling mix of the courtyard. No one stopped or questioned them. It wasn't long before they cleared the open gates and left the walls of Ravenscar behind.

The path led directly to the biscuit factory. Jaundiced electric lights lit up entrances as figures scurried in and out its open doors. To the west behind the hulking structure lay the moors, what remained of the snowfall glowing faintly in the moonlight. Sparks stopped where the railroad tracks branched toward the factory loading dock.

"Let's have a look," he said.

They followed the tracks to a pair of huge double-hung doors through which the train line ran into the building. Closed boxcars crowded the sidings that flanked the main spur.

Inside the doors was no approximation of a biscuit factory. The air was sulfurous, choked with smoke, coal dust, floating cinders. Conveyors carried rough ore to crucibles suspended over howling, incendiary blast furnaces. Massive, lipped cauldrons poised over iron molds the size of houses. A concatenation of cables, belts, hooks, flywheels, pistons, linked in a dance of churning, perpetual motion, climbed impossibly high into the air under the sloping roof, an industrial Tower of Babel. Blossoms of flame spurted rhythmically out of twisted valves and malformed appurtenances. Smoke of various contaminated colors belched out of oscillating cavities and tubes. The army of shirtless workers moving about, blackened by the foul atmosphere, dwarfed by the monolithic machineries, seemed entirely superfluous; if they abandoned their stations, it seemed the host apparatus, with a frighteningly singular unity of purpose, would continue to grind on eternally.

What end product resulted from this manufacturing hell was far from certain. Hulking shapes on trolleys leading to the tracks outside suggested the silhouette of cannon, but of a size far greater than any they had ever seen. Engines of war of some kind, of a war not yet glimpsed or even guessed at. As they watched, a strenuous final effort was apparently under way in the despotic factory, hot steel flowing, boxcars frantically loaded by workers driven on by armed overseers.

No one spoke; they wouldn't have been heard over the tumult of the infernal works if they had. Sparks gestured. They stepped away from the doors, back to the relative quiet of the boxcars.

"What is it? What is it for?" Doyle asked, almost to himself.

"The future," said Sparks.

"Look there," said Eileen.

She pointed to a path tramped out of the snow, paralleling the tracks as they ran away from Ravenscar, where two armed figures bearing lanterns escorted a column of men. They were headed onto the moors. The wrists of the men being led were bound in irons connected by a long, unifying chain. Judging by the ungainliness of their shuffling gait, their ankles were similarly encumbered. Some wore the dirty gray suits of the convicts, others the familiar servants' garb.

Was there something even more familiar about one of those hobbled figures? thought Doyle.

"Where are they going?" he asked.

"We'll follow and see," said Sparks.

They set out along the spur. The track bed was elevated above the boggy ground on a levee of earth and cinder. Staying to the shelter of the opposite slope, they kept the light of the lanterns in sight maintaining pace with the column. Before long they saw a bright glow issuing from a shadowy structure set on a narrow rise a half-mile south of the tracks. Doyle identified it as one of the low buildings spotted from the window at Ravenscar. They heard what sounded like gunfire inside: single shots and occasional volleys. As the tracks drew even with it, the guards herded the column away from the rail line up a slight hill toward that dark building.

"What's in there?" said Doyle.

Jack peered down the tracks to the west. Looking for something.

"Let's find out," said Sparks.

Moon shadows led them down from the rails to the path below. The ground felt soft underfoot, covered with lichen and low shrubs, slick with melting snow. A hundred yards ahead, the column of men had just reached the building.

Keeping as low as the limited cover of the ground would allow, they crept up the hill and skirted the edge of the compound; two structures set on a level patch of land, roughly constructed of clay brick, adjoined by a narrow walled passage. Six stunted chimneys rose from the second building: Smoke and red heat chugged steadily from them, the origin of the glow they had seen in the distance.

A shifting wind sent the smoke in their direction; a fetid, malodorous stench swept over them, the overwhelming force of it driving them to their knees. Doyle fought off nausea. Sparks gave Eileen a handkerchief, and she gratefully covered her mouth and nose. Doyle and Jack exchanged a grim look, Sparks gestured for Eileen to hold her position, and the two men inched up the hillock to within twenty yards of the compound.

The row of men they had tracked stood idly outside the first building, behind a second shackled group herded around a single door. The armed guards who had guided the column stood off to one side. Two others flanked the doorway.

Doyle pointed to the figure he'd recognized in the middle of the group to the rear. Sparks nodded.

Rifle fire rang out from inside. Muffled echoes cracked sharply over the moors. The two guards at the door took the shots as a cue; one trained his rifle on the men nearest the door, the second took a key from his belt and unlocked their chains. Shackles removed, none of the men reacted to their freedom; they stood lifelessly, as before, eyes obediently downcast.

The steel door to the building opened from inside, and the first group of men were prodded inside. A row of riflemen lined an interior wall, reloading their weapons. Beyond them, carts laden with sprawling corpses were wheeled by men in gray down the passage to the second building.

To the ovens.

The door slammed shut. The second set of guards exchanged words with the two at the door—a transference of responsibility. The guards with the lanterns turned and headed down the path toward the tracks.

Sparks waited until the guards cleared sight of the building. The trailing man's neck was broken before he could make a sound. As the first guard turned, the butt of the second's rifle silenced him for good. Sparks and Doyle moved up the hill to the crematorium.

There was no stealth, no subterfuge. Sparks strode up to the guards at the door and cut them down before either man could lift his rifle.

Doyle retrieved the keys and removed the irons from the hands and feet of the second column of men. None moved. All bore the traumatic stamp of Vamberg's vile alteration. These were his failures. This was where they disposed of their waste.

Shots from inside. Doyle moved to the man they'd come for, took Barry by the hand, and led him away. He offered no resistance or recognition, following as docilely as a child. Sparks gestured Doyle to take him quickly down the path. He remained behind, near the door to the abattoir.

Doyle and Barry were out of sight of the door when he heard its hinges crack open, followed by a volley of shots and screams from within. Doyle stopped. Barry stared vacantly at the ground. Eileen moved up the path to join them; they turned toward the building and waited.

The shots ceased. Nothing moved. The sudden silence of the moors seemed as vast as the span of stars above.

Sparks appeared over the rise. He discarded the rifle as he drew near. His face and clothes were awash with blood, which looked black in the moonlight. Doyle had never seen such an expression on a human face: pity, horror, rage, like nothing so much as a god who had just destroyed a world of his own creation that had spun insanely out of control. Behind him, a column of flame shot up into the sky; Sparks had set fire to the buildings.

Sparks walked right by them, gathered Barry tenderly up in his arms, and carried him toward the railroad tracks. Eileen sobbed once, involuntarily. Doyle put an arm around her, and they followed.

As they neared the tracks, a curious sight appeared: an engine and two cars backing toward them down the tracks from the west.

"It's our train," said Doyle. "It's our train."

Hurrying to catch up to Jack as he climbed the embankment, from a distance they saw Larry leap from the cab and meet Sparks as he gently laid his burden down. Larry fell to his knees. The single, simple cry Larry gave out when he saw his fallen brother rent the still surface of the night like a spear.

Doyle and Eileen made their way up the slope. Larry knelt on the loose cinders, Barry in his arms, brushing an unruly cowlick of hair off his forehead.

"Oh law, oh law no, Barry, oh my boy, look what they've done, look what they've done to you . . . look what they done to him, Jack, oh my boy, my poor boy."

Sparks stood over them, eyes lowered, face hidden in shadow. Eileen turned away to bury her sobs in Doyle's shoulder.

Larry shifted, and a slice of moonlight fell across Barry's face. Doyle saw Barry's eyes go up to meet his brother's and focus there. They seemed to momentarily sustain the dimmest filament of life.

Barry moved his lips. A sound came out. He repeated it.

"Fin . . . fin . . . ish," Barry had said.

Then Barry drifted back down into the void that now possessed him.

Tears streaming from his eyes, Larry looked up at Jack, who gestured to himself. Larry slowly shook his head. Sparks nodded, understanding, gave a look to Doyle, and moved away. Doyle put both arms around Eileen and guided her farther down the tracks.

Doyle looked back over her shoulder. Larry bent down to kiss Barry's cheek. He whispered something to him and then slid his soft hands around his brother's neck. Doyle turned aside. Eileen trembled violently in his arms.

A short time passed. Doyle and Eileen looked at each other, but the intimacy of their shared distress felt insupportable. She looked away. Doyle sensed she had of necessity retreated to higher ground inside herself. He wondered intuitively if the resulting gap between them would ever again be breached.

Larry closed Barry's eyes. He cradled the body, rocking it slowly as if trying to soothe a child to sleep. Sparks stood over them, looking back toward Ravenscar. Dancing lights, lanterns, great numbers of them, moved along the tracks in their direction.

Doyle took Eileen on board the train. She collapsed onto one of the seats. Through the windows, Doyle watched Sparks crouch beside Larry and speak to him. Larry nodded, lifted up his brother's body, and carried it to the front of the train, out of sight.

Doyle heard shots, moved to the rear of the car and out onto the platform. The lanterns were a quarter-mile away. Bullets whistled through the air, pinging off the steel. Doyle steadied the rifle on the handrail and fired at the lights until he'd emptied its chambers.

The wheels of the engine engaged, and the train accelerated, pulling away from the pursuit. Before long, the lanterns faded to pinpricks of light that disappeared entirely into the darkness.

CHAPTER 19

V.R.

Eileen refused the brandy Doyle offered. She moved somnolently to the berth in the rear, turned her face to the wall, and lay silently, without moving; sleeping or not, it was difficult to tell.

Doyle did not spare himself a glass, draining it in two pulls. He caught a glimpse of his reflection in the mirror above the bar. The haggard, muddied, bloodstained visage staring back at him resembled no human being of whom he had memory. There are certain untoward advantages to shock, exhaustion, and grief, thought Doyle; a point is reached where one is no longer capable of feeling anything.

Opening the connecting door, Doyle climbed along the side of the tender, hand over hand along the guard line to the engine. Barry's body lay on the floor of the cab. Jack's cloak served as a shroud; a boot extended from under its cover, rocking casually with the motion of the train. Larry stood at the throttle, staring straight ahead at the rails.

"We're ten miles from the main spur," said Sparks over the roar of the engine. "The track's clear ahead."

"London?" asked Doyle.

Sparks nodded.

Doyle looked out at the desolate, downy moors, alien and unforgiving as the surface of the moon, lifeless as the body under the shroud. The cold bite of the air whipping through the open cab felt cathartic.

"I'll be inside," said Sparks.

Sparks climbed back to the passenger car. Doyle loaded coal into the fire from the scuttle, refilled it from the fuel car, then stood by in silence, ready to offer support only if called upon.

"You never heard him sing," said Larry after a while, without looking at him.

"No."

"That boy could sing like an angel. Had a voice like to . . . "

Doyle nodded, waiting patiently.

"He told me to go."

"What's that, Larry?"

"We drew 'em away from the ruins—that was the idea. Half those bastards went down 'fore they got near us. But a few doubled back behind. Had us pinched, dead to rights. He tells me to run. I says never, no sir. He says Jack needs least one of us can drive the train. I says it should be him. He says he's the oldest, and I has to do what he tells me."

"Was he the oldest?"

"By three minutes. He kept the gun, see. And I got off that hill. . . ." Larry wiped his eyes with his sleeve. "Took a mess of them buggers down with 'im, didn' he?"

"Yes, he did."

"We talked about it occasional, you know? Which of us would go first. He always said it would be him; Barry, see, he took chances. And he weren't afraid of the end, not at all. From what Mr. Sparks taught us, he always said maybe death was just the start of something. What do you think, guv?"

Larry looked at him for the first time.

"I think that it is very possibly just the start of something," said Doyle.

Larry nodded, then looked down at his brother's form beneath the flapping edge of Jack's cloak.

"Mr. Sparks says you killed the man wot did this to him."

Doyle nodded.

"Then, sir, I am . . . forever in your debt," said Larry, his voice breaking.

Doyle said nothing. He wasn't sure he could speak. Time passed. Larry wiped his eyes again.

V.R.

"If you don't mind," said Larry, apologetically, "I'd like to be alone with him now."

"Of course."

Doyle put out a hand. Larry shook it, once, without looking at him, then turned back to the throttle. Doyle worked his way back along the siding to the passenger car.

Sparks sat at a table, the decanter of brandy open, two glasses set out. Doyle took a seat across from him. Sparks filled the glasses. They drank. The warmth of the liquor spread through Doyle's belly, allotting some small distance from the horrors.

Doyle told Sparks how Alexander had appeared in the courtyard of the inn, how they had then come to Ravenscar, leading to the confrontation in the great hall. Sparks listened intently to his thorough account, asking questions only about Alexander, Doyle's impressions of him. When Doyle was done, they sat in silence for a while.

"Are they just all mad?" asked Doyle finally, his voice low. "To believe they'll bring this . . . being back to life."

Sparks thought for a while before answering. "What about those things in the basement of the museum? Can you offer an explanation?"

"Can you explain the life force?"

"One can have an opinion."

"But an explanation may be one mystery that's beyond us."

Sparks nodded. They drank.

"The story the old fisherman told Stoker, when he saw them come ashore from the schooner," said Sparks.

"They brought a coffin. Your father's remains."

"He said they brought two coffins. What was in the second?"

"We never found it."

"If this being they spoke of had in fact lived previously, presume for the moment they had some means of discovering the person it had been. Is it inconceivable Alexander and the Seven believed they required those remains in order to return it to life?"

"I suppose not."

"The reason for Alexander's sojourns in the East becomes the discovery of this person's identity and the acquisition of its body."

"That follows."

Sparks nodded his agreement. "Then that second coffin becomes the key to their entire enterprise. I imagine that wherever he might be, Alexander even now has it in his possession."

Doyle saw the silver insignia in Sparks's hand; he was turning it over, studying it, as if the riddle of his brother lived within like a scarab in amber.

349

"But what did they mean to do? Practically. How could such a plan have worked?" asked Doyle.

"To reason it out, it helps if one is able to simulate the thoughts of a madman," said Sparks, with a slight smile.

Doyle felt a blush of shame redden his cheek.

"A child was to be born to the Duke of Clarence, on the assumption they first found a woman to marry him who satisfied the royal prerequisites."

"No small task."

"No, but assuming so. A child, a son, who as a result of whatever ritual the Seven invoke, is no more than an empty vessel bearing the incarnate soul of this slouching beast. What follows logically?"

"Remove the obstacles remaining in the line of succession," said Doyle.

"Precisely. Since the boy requires some years to grow into his majority, they would be in no particular hurry that would arouse undue suspicion. The Queen's been on the throne nearly fifty years—they know she won't live forever."

"The Prince of Wales then."

"The boy's grandfather and next in line. But it's likely they leave him be for the time being; why remove the apparent heir from the scene and throw the regency into chaos? No, they can afford patience; Victoria passes on eventually—perhaps by the time our fair-haired boy reaches his adolescence—and Eddy, already a man of late middle age, takes the throne. Now who stands between the boy and the crown?"

"Only his father."

"And no one in their right mind will ever allow that misbegotten sot to assume the globe and scepter. Prince Eddy has to go, and not long after his son is born, I'd guess. His death given the appearance of natural causes. Wouldn't be difficult to arrange. Not with his medical profile."

Doyle agreed.

"Leaving his son the Crown Prince, half-orphaned, adored by all, to take his place in succession behind his grandfather the King. Then it's a fairly simple matter; shuffle King Bertie and any inconvenient heirs off their mortal coil and it's Bonny Prince So-and-so in the coronation coach on his way to Windsor."

"But it could take twenty years."

"Raising the child from infancy takes that long regardless. Meanwhile, our friends in the Seven consolidate their positions as peddlers

V.R.

of influence to the royal family. Before the accession, the young King is made carefully aware of the lineage of his left-handed path to power—initiated into the fold—and so begins his thousand-year reign at the head of the most powerful nation on earth."

Sparks sat back. Doyle was astonished at how the scenario could sound so practical and at the same time utterly insane.

"Why would they do it, Jack?"

"A king can wage war. They're in the business of building weapons. There's a pragmatic reason. Perhaps the only sort with which we should concern ourselves for the moment."

Doyle nodded, the coolness of this rationality as refreshing as spring water. "And the land. The convicts. Vamberg's drug."

"Man as rough clay. Playing at god," said Sparks with a shrug.

"There must be a more practical use."

Sparks paused. "Building a private militia."

"For their defense?"

"Or some more belligerent purpose."

"But the treatment didn't work. Not with any reliability," said Doyle, thinking of the ruined men being force-marched to their deaths.

"Man's a very difficult creature to enslave finally. Try as we might."

Doyle finished the brandy. He paused, treading lightly now.

"Jack. When we were last in London . . . the police told me you'd escaped from Bedlam."

"You gave them my name?"

Doyle nodded. "They said you were mad."

Sparks cocked his head at an angle and looked at him askew. Was there a trace of a smile?

"What did you tell them, Doyle?"

"Nothing more. I must admit there've been moments when it didn't seem altogether out of the question."

Sparks nodded calmly and poured himself another brandy.

"I was confined to Bedlam. For a period of weeks six months ago."

Doyle felt his eyes grow to the size of teacups.

"Against my will. So ordered by a prominent physician, a man I was investigating. Dr. Nigel Gull. In the course of my investigation, I posed as a patient of the doctor's. We became friendly. I was invited to the man's home one evening for dinner; I accepted as an opportunity to gather what I could about him from his place of residence. A lapse in concentration. A dozen men—police among them—waited for me as I stepped inside. I was subdued, strapped into a straitjacket, and taken to Bedlam Hospital."

351

"Good Christ."

"It's not difficult from our current vantage, is it, Doyle, to imagine who might have been directing the Doctor's actions?"

"No."

"I was kept alone in a cell, in pitch-darkness, the straitjacket never removed. I frequently felt someone observing me. Someone I knew. I realized then that Alexander was the man I had been hunting all along."

There was one additional burden Doyle longed to lay aside. "Jack, you'll forgive me. The night we traveled to Whitby. In this train car. I saw you self-administer an injection."

Sparks didn't move, but the words scalded him with shame. His cheeks drew in, rendering his long face more gaunt and wearied.

"That first night in Bedlam a hood was placed over my head. The jacket shackled to a wall. And the injections began. They continued around the clock, each applied before the previous one wore off."

"Vamberg's drug?"

Sparks shook his head. "Cocaine hydrochloride. Within a week, they had created in me a ... physical dependence."

"How did you escape?"

"Before long I lost all sense of time—an entire month passed before there was any change in my routine: My captors assumed by then I had similarly lost the power of cognition and muscular strength as well. They were mistaken. I had conditioned myself to resist the effects of the drug to a greater degree than my behavior led them to believe. On this particular day, the morning injection administered, I was taken from my cell and driven away. As we neared our destination, they removed the straitjacket. The three men escorting me did not live long enough to regret it. I jumped from the moving carriage. Nearly blinded by daylight, I was still able to complete my escape."

"What did they mean to do with you?"

"The carriage was riding through Kensington. Toward the palace. I believe that their intention, having created this craving in me, was to implicate me in the execution of some terrible crime."

Sparks drained his glass and stared at the corner.

"So as to what you witnessed on the night we rode to Whitby ... in spite of my best efforts in the intervening months, I have not altogether rid myself of this ... dependence."

"Is there anything I—"

"Having said just that much ... I must call upon you as a friend and a gentleman and insist that we never speak another word of this matter again."

V.R.

The muscles in Sparks's jaw clenched tight. His eyes went hard, his voice hoarse with emotion, withdrawn.

"Of course, Jack," said Doyle.

Sparks nodded, rose abruptly from the table, and moved out the door before Doyle could react. The weight of this new knowledge added to Doyle's oppressive weariness. He staggered to the rear of the car and looked in through the drawn curtains at Eileen in the lower berth. She hadn't moved from the position he had first seen her assume, her breathing slow and regular. As quietly as he could manage—holding at bay a befogged awareness that this decision carried more import than could possibly seem apparent—Doyle climbed to the upper berth. Sleep—a sonorous, black, unconscious deep—came and took him quickly.

✿　✿　✿

Doyle opened his eyes. No sensation of movement; the train was not moving. Daylight filtered into the berth. He looked at his watch—quarter past two in the afternoon—and parted the curtains, squinting against the brightness: a train yard, the one they had used before in Battersea, south of the city. He swung his feet over the side and climbed down. The lower berth was empty, as was the rest of the car. He exited.

The engine and tender were gone, uncoupled. The passenger car sat isolated on a remote siding. Doyle searched, but there was no sign of the engine anywhere in the yard. He ran to the stationmaster's office. An old, bewhiskered engineer stood at the window.

"The engine that pulled in that car," said Doyle, pointing. "Where did it go?"

"Left early this morning," said the man.

"There was a woman on board—"

"Didn't see no one leavin', sir."

"Someone must have."

"Don't mean they didn't; but I didn't, did I?"

"Whom can I ask?"

The old man told him. Doyle canvassed workers who'd been present when the train came in. They recalled the train arriving, but none saw anyone leave it on foot. Definitely not a woman; that they would have remembered.

Yes, you would have remembered her, said Doyle.

Doyle looked for a card to leave with them when he remembered his last few belongings had been lost at Ravenscar. But his pocket was

353

not empty. He found a thick roll of five-pound notes and Sparks's silver insignia. Placed there while he was asleep. He thumbed the notes; there was well over a year's salary. The most money he'd ever seen at once in his life.

Doyle walked back to the car and methodically searched for any sign or letter that might have been left behind but, as he suspected would be the case, found nothing. He retrieved his coat, stepped down from the platform, and left the yard.

The day was heavily overcast, not overly cold as the wind was down. Doyle stopped at a pub to sate his gnawing hunger with a shepherd's pie. He thought of Barry. He bought a cigar at the register, left the pub, and waited to light the smoke until he began to cross the Lambeth bridge. Stopping halfway, he looked down at the churning, impersonal gray water of the Thames and tried to decide where he should go.

Resume his old life? If his patients, such as they were, would have him. The generous stake he'd been left was more than sufficient to set him up in another apartment and replace his possessions.

No. No, not yet.

The police? Out of the question. Only one idea made any solid sense. He crossed the rest of the way, turned right through Tower Gardens, past Parliament, and north along Victoria Embankment. The rush of traffic, the blur of commerce, felt as insubstantial as apparitions. Eventually, he reached Cleopatra's Needle. How much time had passed since he'd stood here with Jack and heard the story of his brother? Less than two weeks. It felt like a decade.

He turned left away from the river and made for the Strand. He bought a leather satchel, a pair of sturdy shoes, socks, shirts, braces, a pair of trousers, articles of underwear, and a shaving kit from the first men's outfitters he encountered. From a tailor down the street, he ordered an expensive bespoke suit of clothes. Alterations would take a day or so, if the gentleman didn't mind. The gentleman was in no particular hurry, he replied.

He packed the clothes in the satchel and hired a room at the Hotel Melwyn. He paid in advance for five days and nights, requesting a suite by the stairs on the second floor. He signed the register as "Milo Smalley, Esquire." The clerk, whom he did not recognize from his previous stay, took no particular notice.

Doyle bathed, shaved, returned to his room, and dressed in his new clothes. The police would still be interested, if not seeking him actively, but that concern troubled him not at all. He walked out into the evening. He bought two books from a stall near the hotel: *The Adventures of Huckleberry Finn* and a translation from Sanskrit of the

Bhagavad-Gita. He dined alone at the Gaiety Restaurant, spoke to no one, returned to the hotel, and read Twain until sleep overtook him.

The next day he walked up Drury Lane to Montague Street. Sparks's apartment was closed tight, no signs of life, not even the sound of a dog. No neighbors were available to query. On the way back, Doyle bought a bowler and umbrella from a haberdasher on Jermyn Street. He picked up his new suit at the tailor later that afternoon.

No sooner had Doyle finished changing into his gray worsted suit— the finest he had ever owned—when there came a knock at the door. A hall-boy conveyed a message: a carriage waited for the gentleman downstairs. Doyle tipped the boy and asked him to tell the driver the gentleman would be there shortly.

Doyle put on the bowler and overcoat, picked up his umbrella— there was a threat of rain—and went down to the carriage entrance. The driver was not known to him, but waiting inside the hansom was Inspector Claude Leboux.

"Claude."

"Arthur," Leboux said, with a curt nod.

Doyle took a seat across from him. Leboux signaled the driver, and they drove away. Leboux was loath to meet Doyle's eye; he appeared simultaneously angered and chastened but was clearly in no mood for confrontation.

"Been keeping well?" asked Doyle.

"Been better."

The ride took twenty minutes, during which Leboux twice consulted his watch. Doyle heard gates open outside as they slowed, then the echo of hoofbeats as they entered a porte cochere. The carriage stopped; Leboux preceded Doyle out of the cab and ushered him through an open, waiting door, where they were greeted by a solid, dignified man of early middle age, alert, intelligent, but weighed by deeply private responsibility. The man struck a note of recognition in Doyle, but he was unable to track its source. The man nodded to Leboux, both thanks and dismissal, and led Doyle away.

They walked through a dimly lit antechamber, down a narrow, wain-scoted corridor, and into a comfortable sitting room. Nothing could be learned about its owner from the room; furnishings were exquisite but neutral and impersonal. The man waved a hand at a davenport, inviting him to sit.

"Wait here, please," he said. They were the first words he had spoken.

Doyle nodded, removed his hat, and took a seat. The man left the room.

He heard her footsteps first, a slow, stately rhythm of heel to parquet, then her voice, imperious, golden, asking something of her companion, the man who had escorted Doyle. Doyle heard his name mentioned.

The door opened. Doyle rose as she entered. There was a shock at seeing her in the flesh at such close distance. She was smaller than he'd imagined, not much more than five feet tall, but she projected a stout presence that flowed across the room, closing the distance between them. The familiar face—plain, doughty, as familiar to any English boy as that of his own mother—was nowhere near as stern and adamantine as he had so often seen it depicted. The gray bun of her hair, her simple, matronly black woolen dress, the white linen collar and mantilla, were all talismans as intimate to him as the backs of his own hands. She smiled at the sight of him, an animation never hinted at in pictures, and her smile was dazzling, a diamond in a field of posies.

"Dr. Doyle, I hope this has not proved an inconvenience," said Queen Victoria.

"No, Your Majesty," he said, surprised at the sound of his own voice. He bowed, hoping to offer some semblance of the proper protocol.

"It is very good of you to come," she said, and took a seat, quite informally. "Please."

She extended a hand, indicating the chair to her right, and Doyle sat there. He remembered reading somewhere that she had grown nearly deaf in her left ear. She turned to the man who had served as Doyle's guide. "Thank you, Ponsonby."

Henry Ponsonby, the Queen's private secretary—that's how I know him, from the newspapers, thought Doyle—nodded and left the room. The Queen turned back to Doyle, and he felt the intensity of will in her pale gray eyes turn their full attention to him. They sparkled with warmth at present, but woe be to whosoever feels their wrath, he thought.

"It seems you and I have a very good friend in common," said the Queen.

"Do we?"

"A very good friend indeed."

She's speaking of Jack, he realized. "Yes. Yes, we do."

She nodded knowingly. "We've had a visit from our friend recently. He has told me how you proved such a very great help to him in a matter of no small importance to myself and to my family."

"I hope he hasn't overstated—"

"Our friend is not generally given to inaccuracies of any kind. I would say he has a great fondness for precision. Would you not agree?"

V.R.

"I would. Most certainly."

"Then I would have no reason not to take him at his word, would I?"

"No, ma'am—Your Majesty."

"Nor you any reason to disavow the free expression of my most heartfelt gratitude."

"None whatsoever, Your Majesty. Thank you. Thank you so much."

"Thank *you*, Dr. Doyle."

She nodded. Doyle bowed his head in return.

"I'm given to understand that as a result of your generous assistance, you have experienced some difficulty with our London police."

"Sadly, yes—"

"Let me assure you that you may consider this a cause for no further concern."

"I am . . . most deeply appreciative."

She nodded again and was silent for a moment, regarding him with what seemed to be a benign fondness, if not coquetry.

"Are you a married man, Doctor?"

"No, Your Majesty."

"Really? A vigorous, handsome young man such as yourself. And a doctor? Why, I can't imagine."

"I can only say that the appropriate . . . situation has not presented itself to me."

"Mark my word," she said, leaning forward and raising a royal finger. "Someone will come along. The married state is not often what we expect it to be, but we soon discover it is most definitely what we require."

Doyle nodded politely, trying to take the words to heart. She leaned back, moving immediately to the next item on her agenda.

"How do you find my grandson's health? I mean the Duke of Clarence."

Having been so effortlessly disarmed, Doyle was set back by the directness of the question. "Without having had a chance to thoroughly examine him, I—"

"Your opinion only, Doctor, please."

Doyle hesitated, choosing his words carefully. "I would respectfully advise Your Majesty that the Duke should hereafter remain under close if not constant supervision."

The Queen nodded, digesting the full implication of his statement before moving on. "Now. We will demand of you, Doctor, your oath never to speak on any of what you have heard or witnessed, to any living soul, as long as you may live."

"I do so swear, my most solemn oath."

"And nary a word about our mutual friend and his friendship to us. On both these points, I am afraid, we must absolutely insist."

"Yes. Upon my life."

She looked at him, found satisfaction in the sincerity of his answer, and relaxed her scrutiny. Doyle sensed the audience was at an end.

"I find you a most impressive gentleman for your years, Dr. Doyle."

"Your Majesty is too kind."

She rose to her feet. Doyle preceded her, extending a hand, which she accepted, instantly fearing that he'd committed some dreadful faux pas. If so, the reassuring squeeze she gave before letting go set his mind at rest.

"You bear closer examination. We shall have our eye on you. And if we find just occasion to call upon you again, be fair warned we will not hesitate to do so."

"I only hope I shall not disappoint."

"Of that, young man, I have precious little doubt."

Queen Victoria smiled once more—the unexpected radiance dazzling again—and turned to go. For the moment, the weight of the world truly appeared to rest on those improbable shoulders. She hadn't taken two steps before Ponsonby, telepathically, it seemed, appeared in the doorway.

"If I may be bold enough to ask . . . " said Doyle.

The Queen stopped and looked at him.

"Did our mutual friend give Your Majesty any indication of where he might be going?"

He wasn't certain at first if the question—or the interruption itself— had violated some invisible line of propriety.

"With regard to the movements of our mutual friend," said the Queen in measured tones, "we have found it advisable . . . never to inquire." Victoria raised a sly eyebrow: Courtesy of Jack, a moment of unprecedented intimacy passed between them. Doyle smiled and bowed slightly as she passed from the room, Ponsonby falling in alongside like a tug escorting a clipper.

I'm a man who's been for a ride on a comet, thought Doyle: I know I'm back on terra firma now, but, for better or worse, it will somehow never look or feel the same again.

Ponsonby returned moments later, and they retraced their steps through the private corridors of Buckingham Palace back to the waiting carriage. The secretary opened the door for Doyle, waited for him to take his seat, and handed him a small, rectangular package.

"Her Majesty's compliments," said Ponsonby.

V.R.

Doyle thanked him. Ponsonby nodded, then closed the door, and Doyle rode back to his hotel alone. He waited to open the package until he was again inside his room.

It was a fountain pen. A sleek black fountain pen. It lay as delicately balanced in his hand as a feather.

CHAPTER 20

Brothers

HE WAS TO stay on at the Melwyn for another three days. He spent the mornings strolling leisurely from shop to shop, in search of replacements for the most necessary of his lost possessions. Which forced him to consider a most welcome question: What does one actually need?

After taking a long lunch alone, Doyle each day returned to the privacy of his room and wrote through the afternoon, letters to Eileen; all the many things he'd wished he'd said to her and hoped he would still one day have an opportunity to say.

Returning from lunch on his last day in London, he found a letter waiting for him at the desk. The envelope was shockingly familiar, identical to the one he had received at his apartment not so long and worlds ago: a vellum cream. The words inside were written in the same feminine hand, not printed this time, composed in a flawless, flowing script, unmistakably the same hand nonetheless.

DEAREST ARTHUR,
By the time you receive this, I will have left England.
I hope you can one day find it in your heart to forgive

me for not seeing you before I left and again, now, before I go. My heart, my very soul, had been so soon broken when we met, and the circumstances were thereafter so extreme, a moment never came that provided me with either the time or luxury to grieve. That time has come now.

I never spoke of him to you at any length and I shan't now except to say I was in love with him. We were to be married in the spring. I very much doubt if I will ever love a man as much again. Perhaps time will change that in me but it's far too soon to know.

I know that none of us who lived through those days and nights together shall ever see life with the same blind and blinkered eyes with which most around us look out at the world. Perhaps we have seen too much. I only know that your kindness, your decency, your tenderness to me and your courage are a beacon that will guide me through whatever remains of this dark passage.

Please know, dear man, that you will be forever in my thoughts, that you have my love always, wherever the tide may carry you. Be strong, my darling Arthur, I know in my heart, know truly and believe that the light you possess will burn to the great benefit of this world long after our poor footprints have been washed from the sand.

I love you.

YOUR EILEEN

He read it three times. He tried to find comfort in the words. He knew, objectively, that it was offered there. Perhaps he would discover it on some distant sunlit morning. But not today. He replaced the letter in its envelope and set it gently between the pages of a book.

Where I will find it—he thought with startling prescience—quite by accident, many years from now. And thanks to the dependable erosions of time, I will be unable to remember with any reliable precision the soft, exquisite pain of this terrible moment.

Doyle packed his things—two satchels now, beginning again from scratch—and took a train that afternoon to Bristol.

✿   ✿   ✿

THE LIST OF 7

Two months passed in this fashion: traveling by rail to a new town, somewhere in Britain. Taking a room, anonymously. Gleaning what he could about the environs and its history from libraries and circumspect conversations in public houses until his curiosity about the area was satisfied. Then, moving on, at random, without any pattern or plan, each new destination chosen on the morning of departure. He was assured the police no longer sought him; this was his way of avoiding any other interested parties whose intentions were not so reliable.

He read what newspapers he could find as he went, scouring the pages for signs. One day in northern Scotland, he came across an obituary in a two-week-old London paper: Sir Nigel Gull, erstwhile physician to the royal family. The body found in the study of his country home. A presumed suicide.

It was time.

Now late March when he returned to London, he once again took rooms at the Hotel Melwyn and settled into the same routine he had observed before, certain his life could not move forward until he had some word from Jack, equally certain it would not be long in coming.

Late one night after the passing of a thunderstorm, while he was watching the receding lightning spider across the sky from his window, there came a knock at Doyle's door.

Larry stood outside. The dog, Zeus, was with him. Both wet and sodden. Doyle let them in, and gave him towels. Larry removed his coat and took a seat by the fire, accepting Doyle's offer of a brandy. Zeus lay at his feet. Larry stared into the flames and finished the drink in a few draughts. He seemed smaller than Doyle remembered, his face harder and more careworn. Doyle waited for him to speak.

"We left you at the station like that. Didn't like it. Guv'nor said you'd had enough. Done more than enough, too. No reason to trouble you anymore, he said. He's the boss, wasn't he?"

"I don't blame you for that, Larry."

Larry nodded, grateful for the absolution. "First thing was, see, we had to give me brother a proper burial. Took him home. Put him in the ground besides our Mum. That was good."

"Yes."

"Then Mr. Sparks, he has some business in London. I goes down to Brighton like he asks me, and there I waited. Weeks go by. A month. Mastered every game on the boardwalk, I did. Then here he comes one night wit' news. The movements of a particular schooner. One wot left the port a' Whitby in the first week of the new year. Sailed for Bremen, that was its destination. That's where we're goin' now, he tells me.

"We catch the next packet 'cross the Channel. Make our way to the German harbor of Bremen. Inquiries are made in that city; Jack speaks the language, no surprise there."

"No."

"We're looking for a couple, a man and woman wot boarded in Whitby and disembarked from this schooner. Seems they brung a coffin in the cargo hold. Body of a relative, the captain's told, brought back to be laid to rest in native soil. This couple left Bremen by train, to the south. Here the trail goes cold. Every station, every bleedin' whistle-stop 'tween Bremen and Munich. Saw more of Prussia than the Prussians. No soap. By this time, I'm right keen to get back to a native soil of my own, but the guv'nor, he's got one more notion—"

"Salzburg."

"That's right, sir, where the brothers as you know went to school. Austria: That's where we're off to now, and we goes over that old town wit' a louse comb. Comes across a driver remembers pickin' up a couple wot answers to our description. Took 'em to a town two hours north. Called Braunau. Braunau am Inn.

"Seems this couple took a house there on the spot, paid cash money for it. Lucky for us there's a nosy parker livin' next door, an old woman's got nothing better to do than peep out her lace curtains all hours of the day and night.

"Yes, she seen 'em arrive, all right. And they did unload a large wooden crate from the wagon. The only baggage they brought wit' 'em, too, save wot she seen 'em carryin' by hand, and that impressed her mind. Kept strange hours, this couple, lights burnin' all hours of the night. Stayed two months and never spoke a whisper to her—not very neighborly, was they?"

"Were they there when you arrived?"

Larry shook his head. "Gone a week, she says. We goes into this house ourselves. To say it's a right shambles doesn't quite cover it: It was as if somebody'd held a furnace to the place, melted it halfway down, then let it cool. Everything soft, the walls like aspic . . . I can't imagine how they was still standin'."

Doyle knew these effects only too well: Blavatsky had described it as something breaking through from the other side. "Did they leave anything behind?"

"That coffin. What was left of it. Scorched, split to toothpicks. Empty. Sitting on a pile of dirt, like wot we seen at Whitby Abbey."

"No remains inside?"

"No sir."

Doyle didn't like the look on Larry's face: Something worse was coming.

"What happened then, Larry?"

"We endeavored to pick up their trail again, fresh as it was, only a week past. Led us southwest to a little town in Switzerland, 'tween Zurich and Basel. A resort area, this is, people goes to take the waters, and there's a waterfall folks like to see. Reichenbach Falls. Five cascades. Over two hundred feet high."

Larry asked for more brandy. Zeus watched attentively as Doyle poured and waited while Larry drank it down.

"We arrive. Check the hotel hard by the falls. Yes, the couple in question's been there two days now. We look to their room. Signs of life but no one about. Jack asks me to wait by the door while he goes round the other side. Little time goes by. I get a bad feelin' up the back a' me neck, so I runs out of there. There's a path leadin' up the mountain where one goes to look down at the falls, and there I can see Jack runnin' up that path. Fast as I can move, I'm on that path myself.

"I hasn't caught sight of him again when ahead of me I hear pistol shots, and I runs and I turns a corner and up there on the next switchback cutting 'cross the face of the mountain, not fifty feet from me, there's Jack and he's wrestling with a man in black and I know right off it's Alexander. Not sure who's fired those shots, but neither looks hit. I never seen two men go at each other so fierce and bad. Matched strength for strength, blow for blow, both battered and bleeding, neither one askin' or givin' quarter. I'm shamed to say I was paralyzed by the sight, I couldn't budge from that spot.

"And as I watched, I saw Jack begin to take a slight advantage, a margin so slim you couldn't measure but the tide turnin' ever so slightly in his favor. Alexander takes a step back, trying to pivot on his rear foot near the rim, and the ground gives out beneath him, a shower of rocks and dirt go down and he loses his balance and for an eternal moment he hangs on the edge of that cliff. And then he goes.

"Just as he's about to disappear into that black gorge, he reaches out and he grabs our Jack by the boot, and Jack staggers, digs in, and holds back, but the sheer weight of the man pulls Jack over the edge with him, and I watches them fall, sir, down, down that long way. Down till the mist of the falls swallows them up entire."

Tears were flowing down his face. Doyle couldn't move.

"Did they . . . did they find the bodies?"

Brothers

"I don't know, sir, because in that next moment a shot hits the ground at my feet, and I looks up and see that hellcat on the path above me drawing another bead—"

"Lady Nicholson?"

"Yes, sir. And so I ran, and I don't think I stopped running till I got to the station and boarded the next train. So you see, I don't know, sir, if they found the bodies. But it was a terrible long fall, sir, and I seen those rocks two hundred feet below, and I'm very much afraid that Mr. Jack Sparks has been taken from us long before his time, long before the good a man such as he could do 'as been done by half."

Larry buried his face in his hands and wept bitterly. Doyle inhaled, his chest catching and his eyes blind, and he put a hand on the poor man's shoulders, and tears sprang to his eyes because Jack was gone and because now in so short a time they had both lost their only brother. And there the two men remained, before the fire, deep into the longest of London nights.

❊   ❊   ❊

In the weeks that passed after hearing of the events at Reichenbach Falls, Doyle began again to crave the numbing comfort of prosaic daily routine. He sought employment and accepted an obscure medical post in the provincial harbor town of Southsea, Portsmouth, there beginning life anew, burying his grief and confusion in the welter of details and routine surrounding the maintenance of the health of this untroubled seaside community. The striking ordinariness of his patient's complaints proved a tonic for him. Gradually, in increments so small they passed unnoticed by his conscious mind, the overwhelming sense of terror and wonder that had swept him so nearly to the edge of madness fell slowly and quietly away.

Standing outside a small thatched cottage one morning, where he had just treated a child for colic, looking out at the lush green fields and crystalline ocean below as the sun broke through a spectacular thunderhead, he realized with a jolt he had not thought of Jack or Eileen or that unspeakable night on the moors in over a day.

You're on the mend, Doyle, he diagnosed.

Late that summer Tom Hawkins, a young farmhand from the village, strong and vital, enormously well liked, contracted cerebral meningitis. Responding to the most serious challenge of his medical career, Doyle moved the young man into his own house to care for him more thoroughly. The man's sister, Louise, a soft-spoken, comely woman in her early twenties, resolutely devoted to her brother, moved in with him as well. Their mutual dedication to Tom and his enormous dignity in confronting the end they soon realized was inevitable quickly brought Doyle and Louise closer than either had ever been to another. When Tom died in their arms three weeks later, his last act was to gently take Louise's hand and join it with Doyle's. Later that summer, Doyle and Louise were married. The following spring their first child was born, a daughter, Mary Louise.

With an unsurpassed sense of contentment and security informing his personal life, Doyle found himself able for the first time to consider with some perspective the time he had spent in Jack's company. He knew that none of the royals or government officers whom Jack had served could ever publicly acknowledge his contributions, but then he had never looked for or expected personal reward.

After puzzling it through, and after many long discussions with his beloved Louise, Doyle realized at last that what disturbed him most deeply, what haunted his waking hours, was the thought that this vivid, valiant, and extraordinary man, who had selflessly given his life for Queen and country, could vanish from the earth without so much as a moment's acknowledgment. This was a profound injustice. Although he had personally sworn his service and secrecy in this matter to the Queen—and she was to call on him again, repeatedly, in years to come—Doyle in the end devised a way to honor his sworn oath to her, while paying tribute to the memory of the late Jonathan Sparks.

That night, with his wife and child lying safely in their beds, he reached for the pen that the Queen had given him and sat down to write a story about their mysterious friend.

Epilogue

"THERE, THE RIVER goes deep there, at the base of the rocks. Current below is deep. Fast. The bodies, they are not always found."

Doyle stands on the boardwalk at the rim overlooking Reichenbach Falls, as his hired Swiss guide, a broad-faced genial young man, points down at the cataract below.

"People jump, from there, you see," the guide explains. "Women most frequent. Broken hearts. So many, over the years." The man shook his head in an earnest simulation of despond.

"I understand," says Doyle.

"Very sad place."

"Yes. Very sad."

A bright April morning in 1890. Publishing success about to transform his life forever, Dr. Doyle, Louise, and three-year-old daughter Mary Louise are enjoying their first excursion abroad.

"Has anyone ever survived?" asks Doyle.

The guide's brow knits tightly. "One woman. Yes. She comes out, seven kilometers south down the river. Does not remember her name."

Doyle nods, letting his gaze drift across the turbid water.

Farther down the boardwalk, strolling with her mother, little Mary

Louise is captivated by the sight of an infant in its passing perambulator.

"Mummy, look at the baby," she says, leaning over the edge to peer down at the child.

The parents, an unremarkable lower-middle-class couple, are taking a first vacation since the birth of their son the year before. The father, Alois, is a customs official, the mother, Klara, a simple country girl from Bavaria.

"Look at the eyes, Mummy," says Mary. "Doesn't it have the most beautiful eyes?"

The baby's eyes are indeed beautiful. Inviting. Transfixing.

"Yes, he does, dear. *Die Augen ist ... sehr schön,*" says Louise to the young parents, in her schoolgirl German.

"Thank you," says Klara politely.

"*Wo kommen Sie heraus?*" asks Louise.

"We come from Austria," answers Alois, uncomfortable with any foreigner, let alone an English gentlewoman.

Doyle, with the guard at the rail forty feet away, fails to notice their conversation.

"Braunau," adds Klara. "Braunau am Inn."

"We must go," says Alois, and with a brusque nod to Louise he takes Klara by the arm, turning her back the other way.

"*Auf wiedersehen,*" says Louise.

"*Auf wiedersehen,*" says Klara, with a sweet smile for Mary.

"Say good-bye now, Mary," says Louise.

"Bye-bye."

Mary spies her father and runs to tell him all about the baby with the extraordinary eyes, but by the time she reaches him, the thought has fled from her mind, like the mist rising from the falls below.

As Klara turns the pram around she leans down to straighten her son's bedding. She smiles at him, and says softly:

"*Komm mit, Adolf.*"

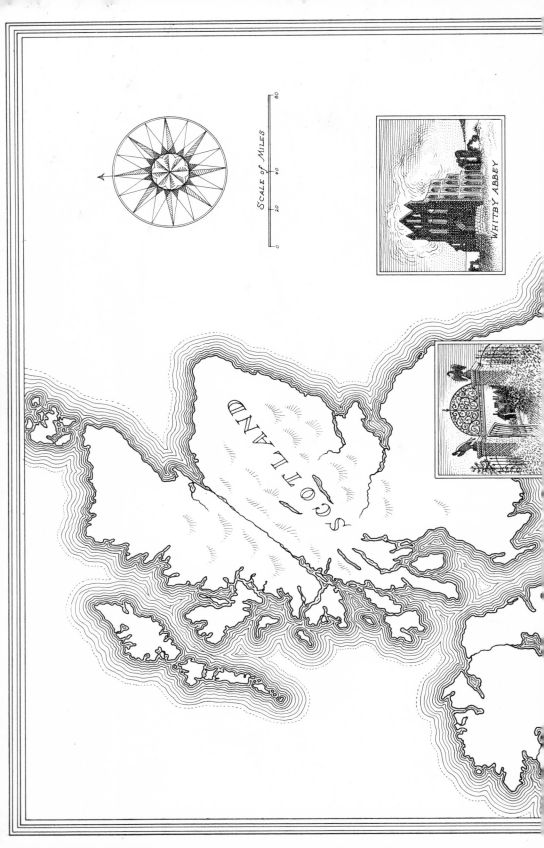

SCALE of MILES

SCOTLAND

WHITBY ABBEY